CAILEAN STEED is a writer, teacher and aspiring dog owner who lives in Helensburgh with their husband and son. They have also resided in Aberdeen and Dublin, and hope one day to live somewhere with less rain.

Cailean's work has been published by New Writing Scotland, Boudicca Press and Barren Magazine. *Home* is their first novel. Their mother would like them to write something more cheerful.

HOME

CAILEAN STEED

RAVEN BOOKS

LONDON · OXFORD · NEW YORK · NEW DELHI · SYDNEY

RAVEN BOOKS
Bloomsbury Publishing Plc
50 Bedford Square, London, WC1B 3DP, UK
29 Earlsfort Terrace, Dublin 2, Ireland

BLOOMSBURY, RAVEN BOOKS and the Raven Books logo are
trademarks of Bloomsbury Publishing Plc

First published in Great Britain 2023
This edition first published in 2023

A catalogue record for this book is available from the British Library

ISBN: HB: 978-1-5266-4166-3; TPB: 978-1-5266-4165-6; PB: 978-1-5266-4168-7;
eBook: 978-1-5266-4170-0; ePDF: 978-1-5266-4169-4

2 4 6 8 10 9 7 5 3 1

Typeset by Integra Software Services Pvt. Ltd.
Printed and bound in Great Britain by CPI Group (UK) Ltd, Croydon CR0 4YY

To find out more about our authors and books visit www.bloomsbury.com
and sign up for our newsletters

For Dave and Oisín

No man chooses evil because it is evil; he only mistakes it for happiness, the good he seeks.

– Mary Wollstonecraft

1

THEN

If you're looking from one of the windows of the schoolroom, beyond the Wall and the Gate, you can see a carpet of trees, and, further away, mountains. On a really nice day you can see the blue then white tops of the tallest peaks, but when it is rainy or cloudy it looks like the sky ends at our Wall.

You're not really supposed to look up at the sky, though. Not while you are working. I have already gotten into trouble for that today.

I'm keeping my eyes down now, carefully, looking only at the pebbles and gravel on the stones of the path behind the kitchen garden, watching them tumble and skitter back onto the earth as I sweep the path clean. The Daughters have to do this job every week.

I stop for a moment, and prop the broom against me so I can reach up and sort my hair. It has actually come loose from its pins, but it's only an excuse. I'm really doing it because if I don't do something other than sweeping for one second, I will scream. Or laugh, or shout, or any one of a hundred other things that get you in trouble.

There's a smack against the back of my legs. My knees crumple and the broom falls.

Angela hits the back of my knees with her broom again. 'You're supposed to be sweeping, Catherine,' she says. 'Not doing your hair. Vanity is a Transgression.' Her hair never seems to come loose from its pins. She never gets in trouble for looking up at the sky while she's supposed to be working. I bend to pick up my

1

broom, trying to ignore the smarting from my legs, but she kicks it away.

'I was,' I say. I try to pick the broom up again, but she plants her foot squarely on it.

'Was what?' she says.

Angela has spoken loud enough that the other Daughters dotted around the paths have looked up and are watching. Their teeth are out in grins. I look down at my feet.

'I was sweeping,' I say. One of the Sisters will be round to check on us soon. I have to be working when she does. I bend and pull at the broom, but Angela is still keeping her weight on it.

'Angela . . .' I say, and I pull again, harder. She lifts her foot at the exact right moment so that I fly backwards and fall hard on the ground, losing my grip on the broom so that it whacks me on the head. The laughter of the others is like a cheese grater over knuckles. They all hate me. They always have. Amy is the only person in the whole world who likes me, and she's not here right now.

I get to my feet. I won't cry in front of Angela.

She's not looking at me, anyway. She's looking at the other Daughters, and they're all still laughing.

I blunder down a side path, pushing past the other girls. I hate her. I hate her. She's a horrible, sly girl, but everyone loves her. The others, the Sisters – I've even seen some Brothers nodding approvingly as she passes the pews on the way to the female section of the Worship Hall. No one else seems to realise what a snake she is.

No. 'Snake' isn't quite enough. I need another word, a spitting word, a word I can use like the Sisters use their canes. But I can't think of it.

A breeze rushes past, cooling the skin on the back of my neck. I can't hear the others anymore. I've ended up right around the corner, further than we're supposed to go.

We had been working on the path that goes around the kitchen gardens, which are next to the Warriors' Training Grounds. The gardens are fenced in, so when you're in them it's hard to see the Grounds, which are also fenced in. There are gaps between the wooden slats, but you're rarely unsupervised enough, or Being Idle enough, to put your eye to them to try and see through.

But the path I'm on now has split off and led me around the corner of the Training Grounds, and here the wooden fence stops halfway along and the rest is only a wire fence like the one surrounding the chicken coop. I can see right through.

There's a huge field with neatly cut grass, and in the centre is a building with a roof but no walls, just evenly spaced pillars. There is a large space under the roof, like one big room that you can see right through. It's filled with Warriors.

They're too far away to notice me on the boundary here, but I press myself against the wooden section of the fence anyway and peep around the corner.

There's maybe twenty Warriors in the building with no walls, and they all have long sticks in their hands. The sticks look almost like the broom I'm holding, except without the bristles on the end. They're all moving together, as though they're one person. They look like water flowing over rocks. Their front foot slides forward, then the sticks swing around, then they spin, then the sticks slash down and thrust out . . .

This is it. This is what I've wanted to see for so long. This is what the boys are doing while the Daughters sweep and clean and cook.

My whole body aches with wanting. I want to be like that, part of that group, moving strongly and surely. Wearing clothes that let you jump and kick and spin.

There's a rhythmic thumping sound, and I pull back just in time as a group of boys run past, their feet all hitting the ground at the exact same moment. They sound like a thunderstorm beating on the roof of the dormitories.

I push myself back into the fence. My tunic is brown, not too different from the shade of the wood, but different enough to be noticed, if they look at the right angle.

There is a loud thump, and the fence judders and jumps behind me. I spring away. There is a boy pushing himself up on the other side, his white T-shirt flashing through the gaps.

'Fuck's sake, Caleb!'

3

'You know what Elder Thomas says happens to little bitches who come last!' another voice yells. There is laughter, and the boy jogs off after the group. The second voice – Caleb – floats back to me. 'You get slammed!'

The sound of the feet slapping the ground retreats, and I catch my breath. I've never heard boys so close before. I've never really heard them at all – being part of the chanting in the Worship Hall doesn't count, because you can't really hear individual voices then.

Boys' voices are loud, and they even seem to have words that girls don't have. Fuck. Bitch.

When the sound of their feet has totally gone, I peek through the wire again. The boys in the open-sided building are still doing their movements, and I can see the group of running boys round the far corner of the field.

It must feel amazing to run.

I catch the sound of voices again. Deeper this time. Men's voices.

If I try to sneak off, they will definitely see me. But if I stay still, they might see me anyway through the gaps in the fence.

I turn so I'm standing sideways against a wooden slat. Even if they look directly at the fence, they shouldn't see me. Oh Father, please don't let them see me.

'Not a bad pack, these ones.'

'Mm. Acceptable.'

'We're having some issues with Benjamin, the one at the back there. Just weak stock. But the rest are sound.'

The voices move past me, and I see glimpses of the men as they go, following the route the running boys took. One with a white shirt and grey trousers – an Elder – and one dressed all in black.

I press a hand against my mouth. The Hand of God. The man in black is the Hand of God.

The Elder keeps talking. 'We're quite proud of Caleb, actually. Future squad leader, certainly. Father's Guard, even. Unless you have other plans for him?'

'No. Not as yet. None of them are promising enough.'

The voices fade as they move away. I let myself relax.

Promising enough for what? Does the Hand of God personally train one of the boys?

'There she is!'

A claw in my hair, and my head is dragged back painfully. Angela's voice again, joyful: 'I found her! She's here!'

I reach out to slap at her, but she has a grip on me at arm's length. 'Let go!'

'She's here! I knew she'd sneaked off!' More excited voices, twittering and laughing, coming from the far end of the path, where it comes around the corner from the kitchen gardens.

My head screams where she's pulling at my hair. Hatred boils inside and comes up and out of my throat.

'Get off me! Get off me, you . . . you little bitch!'

There is a shocked silence. Angela's fingers pull away, strands of my hair ripping out with them. I clamp a hand to my scalp and turn to see not just Angela and the other Daughters, but the tall, brown-clothed figure of a Sister as well.

I want so very badly to be a boy. I'd be on the other side of the fence, running at the head of the pack, far away from all the eyes on me. If I could just be a boy, right now, I would leave my girl's body lying here on the ground, empty and hollow, and I'd never think about it ever again.

I open my mouth, but there's no use trying to explain. Nothing I could say would matter.

The Sister steps forward. It is Sister Morningbright, who takes us for Scripture once a week. She has never liked me. There are red slashes of colour high on her cheeks. 'You,' she says, and her voice is low but fills the air. 'You have a filthy mouth, Catherine. Do you know what happens to girls with filthy mouths?'

She advances, and I can't help backing away, but she's bigger and faster than me, and she catches me easily. Her fingers fix on the back of my neck as she forces me down and gets heavily to her knees behind me.

I find my voice. 'Please . . . please, Sister . . .'

'What's going on here?' A man's voice.

'Ah – ah – my apologies. My apologies.' The pressure lifts from the back of my neck. Sister Morningbright flaps a hand at the girls. 'Kneel, Daughters!'

Angela and the others hurriedly drop to their knees, keeping their gaze on the ground. Everyone knows that you can't look the Hand of God in the eye.

'This area is for the use of men only, Sister.' It's the Elder speaking. The Hand of God hasn't said anything yet.

'Of course, Elder, my sincere apologies. This girl—' she gives me a shake like she's a dog and I'm a rat in her jaws '—sneaked away from her industry. The Daughters were sweeping the paths beside the kitchen gardens.'

Her voice is strange. It's gone all sort of high and fluttery. I would laugh if it wouldn't just make everything worse.

I look down at the ground. We're at the edge of the path, and dark earth looms beneath the gravel strip in front of the fence. Just beyond are two pairs of shiny black shoes. The Elder's, and the Hand of God's.

'Sneaked away, did she?' the Elder booms. 'Abandoning her industry? That's a Transgression, you know, girl. My, my. What would Father think?'

I do not know what Father would think. I suppose He would be angry, like everyone else.

'That's ten of the best, then, Sister.'

'Of course, Elder. To be administered directly. But she also used profanity.'

'Profanity? Well. Well, well. So very disappointing, Daughter. Very, very disappointing.'

There is a small sound, like the noise made by someone blowing air out through their nostrils in a short burst. Almost like a laugh. It came from in front of me, where the Hand of God is standing.

'I was intending to administer the appropriate Atonement, Elder, if you—'

'Of course, of course, Sister. Your department entirely. Carry on.'

'Thank you, Elder.'

I watch as Sister Morningbright's hand sweeps gravel away from the earth in front of me. There's a slight shake in her fingers.

I have never seen her nervous or deferential before. But then, I've never seen her speak to men before.

I feel like I'm just watching what's happening. I can't feel anything. I'm just kind of floating in my body, seeing her fingers dig into the earth and haul up a handful. There are little chunks of stone in it, and I am sure I can see the shiny, wriggly back of some kind of insect. Feeling crashes back into me, and I feel hot sick rise in my throat.

'What's her name?'

Sister Morningbright's hand freezes.

'I – I – your pardon, Hand of God?'

One pair of shoes steps closer to the fence. I can see the cuffs of his trousers: a crisp, spotless black.

'It's quite a simple question. What is her name?'

'Catherine, Hand of God,' says Sister Morningbright, stuttering over the 'C'. Some of the earth in her hand crumbles away and patters to the ground. The insect is still in the centre of her hand, half buried, back legs waving.

'Catherine.'

My name is in his mouth. He says it softly, like he's satisfied with it. 'Catherine.'

The moment stretches. I stop breathing.

'Proceed, then.'

A silence, then: 'Thank you, Hand of God.' Her hand holding the mud clenches, and the strong fingers of her other hand claw at my mouth. I shake my head, try to clamp my lips, but her nails hook into my skin and the bright pain makes me open up. Her fingers worm in, pulling my jaw so far open that it feels like it will tear off in her hand.

'You know what we do to girls with filthy mouths,' she says, and she sounds more confident now. She's back on familiar territory.

I'm pinned under her arm, against her chest. The threads of the flame-and-circle stitched on her dress scrape my cheek. I try to shake my head out of her grip, but she hooks her fingers behind my front teeth and wrenches my head up and back.

My gaze is dragged up with my head, and I find myself looking at the Elder and the Hand of God. They are huge and dark against

7

the bright sky, criss-crossed by the wire of the fence. The Elder has his hands clasped together in front of him, and is nodding. His face is sunk into a thick neck, his tongue running over his lips.

The Hand of God has one hand on the fence, his fingers curling through the holes. He is looking at me with his head on one side. He sees me staring right at him, but he doesn't seem angry. He's just watching.

Wet, foul earth is crammed into my mouth. There's mud up my nose. I try to spit, but more is pushed in and I feel it filling my mouth, gritting in my teeth, clagging up my throat.

More earth, strong fingers against my cheeks, holding it in. I'm gagging but there's nowhere for the sick to go, it's filling my throat, I can't breathe.

I can't breathe.

I'm going to die.

She's going to kill me.

Her hand disappears, and I fall forward, retching and digging the mud out with my fingers, and I'm coughing and choking and on my hands and knees, and I breathe in finally but the air is full of little bits of grit and then stinging bile is coming up and rushing out. I spit and spit but the mud is everywhere, between all my teeth, in my throat.

I blink away the tears in my eyes and see the mud and sick on the ground between my hands. A little many-legged insect is struggling weakly in the middle of the puddle, its body slick with vomit.

'This is what we do to girls with filthy mouths,' Sister Morningbright is saying behind me. 'We make them eat their words.'

I look at the wriggling bug, at how pathetic and broken it is. This is how the Hand of God must see me. This is how they all must see me.

2

Now

A hand falls onto my shoulder and I wheel around. Fatima jumps back.

'Christ, Zoe!'

'Sorry – sorry.' A wave of dizziness washes over me. I steady myself with a hand on a stack of boxes. 'You gave me a fright.'

Fatima lowers her hands, but is still looking at me warily. Over her shoulder, I can see through the little back room out to the cafe. There is a soft hum of chatter, clinking cutlery, a trill from the bell over the door as a customer leaves. All the usual mid-afternoon coffee-shop sounds.

Fatima shows me her phone screen. There is a bright yellow taxi icon, and a cheery message underneath, saying 'I'm on my way!'

'You're going home,' she says, slipping the mobile back into the pocket of her apron.

'What?'

'Zoe, you've barely kept on your feet all day. You've been pale and coughing and . . . sort of out of it, to be honest. I texted Meg and she said I was to send you home. The taxi's on her. The evening shift are coming in soon, I can manage until then.'

'Ah no, I can't leave you on your own—' I start coughing.

'Janey Mac, Zoe. You're a living health hazard. I'll be fine. The taxi'll be here any minute, just feck off and don't for the love of god come in tomorrow.'

'I'm off for a couple of days anyway,' I say, giving in and pulling on my jacket.

'Good! Go hibernate. Stay warm. Drink lots of fluids.' Fatima hands me my scarf and before I know it, I am being bundled into a taxi. She watches as it pulls away, and I give her two fingers out of the back window. She gives me two fingers back, laughing, and as the car turns the corner I see her ducking back inside.

The brightly painted letters on the sign saying 'The Underpass Cafe' and the fogged-over windows hung with twinkling lights smear and blur as rain hits the taxi windows. Although I never supposed that a tiny, book-filled cafe in a nondescript corner of Dublin would become like a home to me, or its owner like a mother, it has and she is. In the six years I've worked here, I've never had to be sent home. I feel like crying, all of a sudden. I really must be sick. I don't ever cry.

I place my palms flat against my thighs, try to breathe deeply. I'm all right. Everything is okay. I tap my fingertips, one after the other, and count to four along with the taps.

> One – It's only a cold, I'll feel fine soon
> Two – Fatima and Meg are concerned, not angry
> Three – It's okay to rest sometimes
> Four – My shift was almost over anyway, so it's not like
>   I've hugely inconvenienced anyone

Okay. That's better. Those are four true things, even if number two and three are particularly hard to accept. I just hate not being useful.

I close my eyes, and repeat my list of four, letting the pattering of the rain on the taxi roof soothe and wash over me.

A tapping noise pulls me up out of a half doze. The driver is peering through the Perspex partition at me. I heave open the door and stumble out into a gust of wind. He winds his window down. 'You all right there, love? You're not lookin too grand,' he says.

Something is wrong with his face. What is wrong with his face? I don't feel right. This isn't just being sick. This is . . .

Distantly, I feel rain soaking through the knees of my jeans. The driver's voice comes into focus, like when static blurs into words on a radio. He's asking me if I'm all right.

I am not all right. I can't get a grip on what direction anything is in – the ground, the sky, anything. It's as though the world has lurched to the side and then turned upside down. Everything is in the wrong place.

I use the door of the cab to pull myself up. The driver is unbuckling his seat belt, about to get out and help me, but I wave to show I'm okay and stumble away into the rain, feeling like I've just stepped off a boat that was on choppy seas. I don't look at the driver's face again.

The door to my building is standing open, but that's not new. The part of the city it's in isn't great, but my little flat is my sanctuary. It's small, and too cold in the winter and too hot in the summer, but it's my own place, filled with my own things, and I know that as soon as I get inside, I'll feel much better.

I can't quite see right. It's like there's shadows where there shouldn't be, too many of them and at strange angles. I steady myself with a hand on the bannister and drag myself up the stairs to my flat.

I'll be okay once I get inside. I might not get into bed right away. I might strip off my soaked jeans, make a cup of tea in my favourite mug, the giant stripy blue one Meg gave me, wrap myself in my cosy winter blanket with the constellations on it and curl up on my squashy old couch. I'll nap there, and then later maybe read my book. If I feel like eating I might even order takeaway instead of cooking, as a treat.

Everything will be fine if I can just get inside.

I have to pause on the way up the stairs. Black spots waft in from the edge of my vision. I need to sit down.

My key catches in the door instead of clicking through smoothly. I must have forgotten to lock it this morning. I try the Yale lock, and that's on properly at least. I push open the door and drop my keys and phone into the bowl on the little table just inside, and hang up my jacket and scarf. I shuffle down the dim hallway to the kitchen. I'll put the kettle on first, then get into my pyjamas . . .

There is a man sitting at my kitchen table.

He is dressed all in black, with a black overcoat folded neatly over the chair beside him. His hair is greyer than it was, but it is still recognisably him. He is tracing a design on the tabletop with one of his fingers, and he looks up as I come in.

'Hello, Catherine,' he says.

My legs can't hold me, and I drop to the ground. There is a rushing noise in my ears, and everything is overbright. This is not happening. He cannot be here.

He is speaking, his mouth is moving, but I can't hear what he's saying.

He stands and moves towards me, and I want to get up and run, I want to open my mouth and scream, but the black spots are back, crowding into my vision, flowing and merging into the darkness of him, until the last of the light is gone and they have blotted out everything.

3

THEN

It always seems to be dark in the Scripture room, no matter how bright it is outside. Today it is blazing sunshine and Sister Morningbright has decided to take class outside, but since the incident at the Training Grounds, I'm banned from going outside unless it's to the Nutrition Hall or to Worship. So when she looked out of the window earlier and pulled her collar away from her sweaty neck with one finger and announced in a sugary voice to the Daughters that it was SUCH a nice day that they would go outside and continue learning Father's words in the sun, she had to come up with something for me to do instead.

'Give this room a proper clean, Catherine – and I mean a *proper* clean,' she said as she stood at the door, watching all the girls file out with their heads bent and their hands clasped in front of them. Several of them still managed to look up at me as they passed to give me a face that meant *you* don't get to enjoy the sunshine. I kept my hands folded in front of me too, head down, and tried to look appropriately humbled. Even after the door clicked shut behind her and the noise of the Daughters' footsteps trooping down the stairs had faded, I kept my face carefully blank. When it had been silent in the classroom for two whole minutes, I let myself smile.

I can hear them through the open windows now, Sister Morningbright's voice reciting the lesson, then the chorus of girls chanting the reply.

'We are Father's precious Children and these are His words.'
'We are Father's precious Children and these are His words.'

'What is the chief Duty of Women?'

'To Serve and be Fruitful.'

I decide to start with dusting, because it's the least strenuous thing I can think of doing. I flap a yellow cloth at some of the framed Scriptures on the wall: *Watch Thou for Transgressions* beside the big window, then *A Woman's Silence is her Glory* next to the chalkboard, and *Lead us, Father, to the Perfect World to Come!* above the light switch. There's a huge wooden flame-and-circle mounted on the opposite wall, above *Hold Tight to My Words, Children, Lest ye Become a Recreant*, which probably needs some kind of polish or something because it's shiny. The one stitched to my tunic, over my heart, is getting a bit worn, and the butter-yellow flame has threads trailing over the sky blue of the circle. I'll need to sort that before one of the Sisters notices.

I didn't see any polish in the cupboard when I fetched the rest of the cleaning stuff earlier, but I don't suppose there's any harm in checking again.

The corridor outside is even quieter than the classroom. The whole building must be empty. Our group was the only one doing Scripture just now – everyone else is working. The whole building belongs to me, just for a moment.

I tiptoe up the stairs, not wanting to disturb the silence. The cleaning things are kept in a cupboard on the same level as the dormitories, above the classrooms. All the doors are closed, so the corridor is dark and cool. I trail my hand along the plaster of the wall as I go, mainly because it's the sort of thing you're not supposed to do. The wall is painted a uriney sort of yellow, flaking in places. I go past my dormitory, which is nearest the stairs, then past the next one, which is for the older girls. That one is Amy's dormitory.

She is the only person in the whole world who likes me even a little bit. But even she isn't talking to me anymore.

The cleaning cupboard is opposite the Ablutions Room. I pull the door shut behind me, so I'm in total darkness. No one else knows exactly where I am right at this very moment. The thrill of it makes me want to giggle, or jump, or something. It feels almost Transgressive.

Something brushes my face in the darkness, and I flap a hand in front of me. It's a cord, swinging from the ceiling. I give it a tug and the little space is flooded with light. Squinting up, I can see a single bulb hanging from the ceiling, beside a trapdoor. A lone moth floats lazily up from somewhere among the shelves and starts dancing around the light.

I find a box with a can of polish and some cloths and balance it in one hand as I turn the light back off and close the cupboard door. Then I open the door again, a little, so the moth can get out.

I hover in front of the door to the Ablutions Room, instead of going straight downstairs. There's no point in going in. Amy hasn't left me a message for weeks now, not since the latest group of the Awakened arrived. Not since Teneil arrived.

Teneil came at the beginning of the summer, when the sky was starting to stay bright later and later. I didn't take much notice at first – she's fifteen, older than me by three years; we aren't in any of the same classes or chore groups – and anyway we're not supposed to pay any particular attention to the recently Awakened.

But a few weeks after Teneil arrived, things started to go wrong between Amy and me. Since we are in adjoining dormitories, we both use the same Ablutions Room, and we have this secret way of communicating using our washbags.

Amy and I hang our washbags up on their nails in the Ablutions Room with our names facing out, so they are easy to find. The nails run along the walls on either side of the space, then rows of showerheads that spit freezing water line the far edge of the room, across acres of chilly tile. Cubicles for the necessary face them, and down the middle is a double row of back-to-back sinks.

The Ablutions Room is busy three times a day – morning ablutions, afternoon necessary break and evening ablutions. Daughters in their nighties or tunics shift from foot to foot in the icy air, the noise of the pipes clattering overhead as we line up in silent rows to make our ablutions or do a necessary. Two Sisters wait, one at each end of the room, looming brown pillars above our heads. At times, you can get in when no one is there, but you have to be clever. You volunteer to take a message, or to do cleanup duty in the dormitories, and you sneak in when no one is looking. Then, the room is much bigger, and you can hear the bright lights fizzing, and the tiles repeat your steps back to you. You have to be quick, and you have to look over your shoulder the whole time. Getting caught somewhere you oughtn't be is a Transgression.

If Amy and I want to leave each other a message, we grab the other's bag when we get a chance – when no one else is looking, or when we can snatch a moment on our own – take it into a cubicle and unscrew the handle of the hairbrush kept inside. The hairbrush handle is hollow – a perfect space for tucking a tightly folded scrap of paper with a note scribbled on it. Once you've screwed the handle back on, there's no way to see that there is a secret in there. We hang the bags back up with the name facing the wall – then you know that there is a message waiting for you.

The messages are never really anything important. Sometimes Amy'll just write things like 'Sit besid me at lunch tomoro', or 'Thers baby foxs in the kichen garden'. Sometimes it is just 'Ru ok?' when she's noticed or heard I've gotten into trouble again. Unscrewing the handle of my hairbrush in an alone moment, hidden inside a necessary cubicle or behind a pale plastic shower curtain before I've turned the water on, and seeing a message packed in there is like having a warm hand reach into my chest and curl around my heart.

The first time Amy left me a secret note was last year, after the Bad Night when we'd both been pulled out of our beds and brought up to the Big House. The morning after, I was in the kitchens, marble-eyed with lack of sleep, wearing my arms away trying to scrub burnt mashed potato off a big pot. A load of new dishes to wash clattered down on the draining board, and I looked up to see Amy. I almost dropped my scourer. I hadn't slept since I'd been marched back to my dormitory early that morning, and the whole strange night already seemed like the kind of dream you have when you're ill and fevered. But there was the girl who had been there too, sleep-eyed and scared like I had been, who'd gone through it all with me.

The girl leaned forward, as if to straighten a wobbling tower of greasy dishes, and spoke into my ear. Washbag, she'd said.

Hairbrush. Unscrew. Then she was gone, and my heart was jumping and jumping against my ribs.

The first chance I got – after chores but before dinner, during the necessary break – I took my washbag into a cubicle and pulled the hairbrush out. I turned it over in my hands. I'd never tried to unscrew the handle before, but it turned out to be easy – a couple of twists and it came right off. Inside was some tightly rolled paper. I pinched it out and spread it open on my knee. The paper was whitish, with faint, blue-ruled lines. From one of our exercise books, where we copied out the Scriptures. The blocky letters spilled diagonally across the neat horizontal lines.

Ur my blood sister. We cant tell anywon what hapned last nite but you can tok to me if you want. I cood see you wer scard becos I was to. Rite a note bak put in my brush lik this. My name is AMY.

We'd never really spoken before, and I don't think I knew that she was my blood sister before that night either. You're not supposed to care about your blood family; we are all Father's Children, and that's more important than any blood. But I can't help it: there is something about knowing that Amy is connected to me, really connected, that makes it special. But I know it's wrong. I have added 'loves blood sister more than other Sisters' to the swelling list of Transgressions I keep tucked in my head.

Amy isn't like the others. She doesn't care that I have trouble being modest or can't remember Scripture or don't have hair that lies flat properly. She winks at me when we're on chore duty together. She lets our hands brush when we pass in the corridor. She knows what happened on the Bad Night.

But since Teneil came, there haven't been any messages waiting for me in my hairbrush, not for weeks. I kept leaving messages for her for a while, but she never answered. The last one she didn't even read – I know because when I unscrewed the handle to leave a new message, I saw with a cold sick feeling that the old one was still there. And I'd left that one days earlier.

I still check my own brush now and then, but I think Amy has forgotten about me.

I could check just now. Maybe she's found the last message and has left a new one for me. We're blood sisters, and Teneil is only her friend. It has to mean something, otherwise why would she have even bothered with me all this time?

I put the box of cloths and polish down on the floor, and ease open the door to the Ablutions Room. I'm breathing like I've just run up and down the stairs, and there's a twinge from my back as the fabric of my tunic scrapes across one of my stripes. I don't want to have to Atone again. But, more than that, I want to believe that Amy hasn't totally forgotten me.

'Catherine!'

I leap away from the Ablutions Room door. The voice comes from below again, reaching me from the stairwell. 'Where is that . . . *Catherine*?'

'I'm here, Sister!' I say, thumping down the steps, my heart hammering in time. It's not Sister Morningbright, it's another one – one of the younger Sisters who works mainly in the kitchen. She gestures at me impatiently.

'What in Father's name were you doing up there?'

'Just getting some polish, Sister—' I realise my hands are empty. I left the polish upstairs. Right beside the open Ablutions Room door. 'I . . . I just—'

'There's no time for that now,' she says, and ushers me towards the stairs that lead down to the ground floor, where the Sisters have their rooms.

I feel light-headed. How much trouble am I in now?

'Sister, I really was—' I start, but she silences me with a wave of her hand.

'Don't talk in the corridor, Daughter,' she says.

I feel sick. How are they even going to make me Atone when I've still got the marks from the last time? Would they just do it over the same bit, or would they find somewhere else on my body?

We get to the bottom of the stairs and the Sister pushes me towards the main doors, which are open. Outside, Daughters are filing along the path in neat, silent rows. Not just the group that were doing Scripture outside – all the Daughters. Sisters, too. All walking along the path that leads away from the women's building to the rest of Home.

'Go on, hurry *up*,' says the Sister, and I trot forward. So I'm not in proper trouble, after all? Something else is going on. Was this something I was supposed to know about?

I see Amy, taller than the other girls around her, and, before I can think about it too much, I fall in beside her. She is looking down, lips pinched together, skin tight over her cheekbones, and doesn't look over at me. I can feel myself shrivelling, but I try.

'Amy,' I whisper.

She doesn't answer, just gives a tiny shake of her head. I try again.

'Amy? What's happening?'

She shakes her head again, and this time, it dislodges a tear which rolls down her cheek. I have never seen her cry before. Not even during the Bad Night.

'What's wrong?' I say, fighting to keep my voice low. 'Amy? What's going on?'

She turns to me this time, just a little, and I see that her lower lip is split and swollen. 'Don't . . .' she says, then her eyes flash behind me and she looks forward again. One of the Sisters stalks past, cane smacking against her palm.

I keep my left hand against my middle, so if someone was glancing over it would look like my hands were folded neatly in front of me, and I stretch my right out to Amy. But she just pushes it away.

'Stay away from me, Catherine,' she says.

Her elbow smacks me in the side and I stumble away from her. A mass of brown-clothed girls flows past me until I am shoved back into line by a Sister, the imprint of Amy's elbow lodged in my ribs like a stone in my throat. I try to keep sight of her up ahead, but my eyes are wet and spilling over and everything is blurring together so that I lose her completely.

4

Now

I open my eyes, and I see him. The Hand of God. The world slips from under me. He can't be here. How can he be here? He is sitting on a kitchen chair, but we're not in the kitchen. We're in my bedroom. He regards me calmly. 'You're awake,' he says.

I'm in my bed, under the covers. 'I carried you in here,' he says. Disgust and fear rise like bile in my throat. I'm still dressed, in my jeans and Underpass Cafe T-shirt. I move my feet and realise I still even have my trainers on. But he's picked me up. He's *touched* me . . .

He is looking at me with a sort of clinical detachment that makes me feel like an insect under a microscope. His face is as long and thin as ever, but the lines around his mouth are deeper than I remember.

'I need to talk to you,' he says.

I stare at him. His voice is conversational, as though all this – what he's done, where he is, what's happening – is perfectly normal and fine.

The fainting-fogginess is still lingering around the edges of my mind. It's like I've come up out of a dream, but the cafe is the dream, Dublin is the dream, my whole life for the past six years is the dream and I've finally woken up to the reality that I never escaped, never left it all behind, not really.

I feel like I'll start coughing if I speak, and I don't want to. I don't want to show him any more weakness. If only I wasn't so ill. If only his sudden, awful presence didn't make me feel four inches tall.

He waits for me to respond, still looking at me as though I am some kind of disappointing failed experiment, which I suppose, to him, I am. My hand is near the edge of my bed. There is a large knife taped underneath the bed frame. I can reach down, pull it free of the tape and have it through his lung in three seconds. Right between the fifth and sixth ribs. I move as though I am resettling myself further up on the bed, letting my hand drift nearer to the knife as I do so.

His face stays blank as he takes the knife from inside his jacket. I go cold, feeling absurdly like a child caught doing something naughty. He places the knife down on my bedside table, exactly between us. It is a test, a taunt, and an insult, all in one. I stare at it, feeling sick deep down in my stomach. My head swims.

'Rather obvious, don't you think?' he says.

I pull everything I have together in order to force the next words out. My throat is still dry and raw, so the words come out in a croak. 'Get out.'

'Catherine—'

'Stop,' I say, knotting my fingers in the bedclothes, 'calling me that. Get out. Get out.'

'Ah yes. It's "Zoe" now, isn't it?' His sarcasm drips the inverted commas into place. I feel my cheeks get hot. I want out of this bed.

'Zoe, coffee-shop waitress,' he says. His gaze drifts down to my T-shirt, and I fight the urge to pull the covers up to my neck. I make myself glare back at him. He looks around my room – the threadbare carpet, the battered furniture, the peeling wallpaper. 'How wonderful this new life of yours is. So worth leaving your family for.'

'You're not my family,' I say. This seems to strike him as funny, and he laughs. A hot little coal of humiliation and hatred flares to life in my chest. 'Fuck you,' I tell him.

He backhands me across my jaw. My head cracks into the headboard. Pain flares through my skull.

'Watch your mouth,' he says. He stands up. I flinch, hating myself for it but unable to stop. 'The Sullied world is degenerate,' he says, 'and its impact on you is clear. You have a filthy mouth

21

for a girl.' He leans over me, and I throw my arm across my face. My jaw smarts and the back of my head aches. I can feel his breath on my skin as he whispers, 'You remember what we do to girls with filthy mouths, don't you?'

I keep my arm up, hiding behind it.

'Don't you, Catherine?'

My eyes are hot and prickling. I will not cry in front of him. 'What do you want?' I mean it to come out tough, but I sound pathetic. I still feel sick and shivery, and my head is ringing from his strike.

The chair creaks as he sits himself back down. I lower my arm. My jaw throbs. He is smoothing his tie and tucking his shirt in where part of it has pulled out of his trousers. The knuckles on the hand he struck me with are reddening.

'I want what I've always wanted,' he says. I shake my head.

'I don't know what that is.'

'Of course you do.'

I don't. I have no idea. This is like some riddle, some test I've never studied for. I want to bury my face in my hands, but I can't take my eyes off him.

'Do you feel well enough to stand?' He gets up and holds out a hand. I want to get up, want to be on my own two feet, but I won't let him help me. I push the covers back and swing my feet down. He steps back as I get up, dropping his hand with a shrug.

My vision greys for a moment, but it passes and I'm fine. I'm fine.

'Shall we?' he says, gesturing out of the open bedroom door. That sense of unreality is back, and stronger this time. He is acting like a solicitous friend, someone caring and concerned. But he just struck me. This is the man who broke in here and attacked me. That is what is happening. That is the truth.

He follows me to the kitchen, where I sink into one of the chairs, feeling dizzy again. My phone. It's in the bowl by the front door. I can get to it, run outside. Call the Guards . . .

He sets a glass of water on the table in front of me, sits down opposite. I stare at the water. I could dump it over his head. I could throw it in his face and run.

I just need to wait for this dizziness to pass.

22

He folds his hands on the table. 'You asked me what I want, Catherine,' he says. 'I want you to come Home with me. Back to the Children.' This is so absurd that I almost laugh.

'You think this makes me want to come back with you? Breaking in and attacking me?'

His eyebrows draw together. 'I haven't attacked you.'

No, of course he wouldn't see that as attacking me. He was 'correcting' me. For my own good. All of a sudden, my fear is gone and I just feel angry. I feel as though I have been lit on fire. 'I will never. Never. Come back with you.'

'You will return Home with me.'

'You will have to drag me there. I'll scream. I'll fight. You'll have to knock me out. And if you do get me back then I will never stop trying to escape.' I think about the busy street outside. The cars, the people – surely someone would stop him if they saw me being dragged out? Someone would step in, or say something, surely . . .

'Oh, I'm not going to force you, Catherine,' he says. 'I have never forced you to do anything. I never will.' He reaches into his inside pocket and pulls out a white rectangle, holds it up. It is the back of a photograph. 'I'm going to show you this, and you're going to come back with me of your own free will.'

He's insane. 'And if I refuse?'

'Then I'll leave.'

I stare at him. He's found me, after all this time. There's no way he's going to walk out of here without me.

He turns the photograph around. Time and sound leak out of the world, until all that exists is the picture in front of me. I reach out and he lets me take it.

'This is fake.'

'No.'

I believe him, despite myself. He never lies, exactly. I hold the picture so tightly that the shiny surface bends and warps around my fingers. I run my thumb over the smooth image, over the two faces. It seems real. Can it be real?

I can feel the Hand of God's eyes on me. I keep mine on the figures in the picture.

All of my earlier fire has gone, sputtered out. I know that I have to go with him.

The sense I had when I first came to, that the past few years of my life have just been a dream, returns, but stronger. Of course, says a dull little voice in my skull. Of course this life wasn't real. Of course this was all just a little fantasy he let me play out for a while. Of course I'll go back with him.

I can't go back with him.

But the photograph – I have to.

What do I do?

I try to speak, cough, clear my throat and try again. 'When was this taken?'

He blinks once, slowly, like a shutter sliding over a camera lens in slow motion.

He so rarely answered direct questions. But I have so many things I need answers to.

And here is an answer, held in my hand. A picture of a woman, older now, with a sharper face and more deeply set eyes, but I would know her anywhere.

Amy. My sister. The one who loved me. The one who helped me escape. The one who disappeared.

She is standing with her head slightly tilted down, her gaze not quite meeting the camera. There is a man next to her, his hand a claw on her shoulder. I would know his face anywhere, too.

Amy is wearing a red dress, floor-length with a high collar and long sleeves. I've only ever seen one other person wear that dress. There is only one thing it can mean.

I try again. 'How long has Amy been back with the Children?'

Blank, blank stare.

I cannot keep my voice calm. 'How long has she been married to Father?'

5

THEN

The Guards and their dogs are lined up outside the Worship Hall as we file in silently. The dogs strain at their leads, jowls dripping and tongues lolling. I've never seen the Guards anywhere except outside the Big House or at the Gate before.

We troop up the stairs to the female section of the Hall, a cramped and dust-smelling half floor with railings. There are never enough seats up here, which is why the younger Daughters mostly sit cross-legged down at the front. Generally this isn't too bad, as you can look out through the railings and get a good view of what is going on. I always want to sit with my legs dangling out over the space, ten or twelve feet above the chairs and heads below, but it would probably be immodest, like most things seem to be, so you have to sit with your legs crossed neatly under your skirt.

The mood in the Hall is dark and quiet, which – more than anything else – underscores how unusual this all is. Normally, when there are both men and women in the Hall, it is a time of celebration. Usually when the Hall is this full, there's a buzz and a crackle in the air, and everyone is happier and more relaxed, and you get away with maybe being a tiny bit louder and giddier than usual. But today, there's not much talking; just the odd hushed voice here and there as people settle themselves in their seats. I still have no idea why we're all gathering like this.

Earlier, as we all shuffled through the main doors, I heard two Daughters behind me whispering, so low I could barely hear it. *It's Teneil*, one said to the other. *That new girl. She went mad during*

Rejuvenation – did you hear? Refused to take part, screamed at the Sisters.

There is no escaping Rejuvenation. Every week, every single girl and woman has to stand in the middle of a group (different groups every time, so you're always telling new people), list their Transgressions and be cleansed by the righteous anger of the others. Even if you're dog-sick, you get dragged from your bed and put up there in your nightie, and you still have to do Rejuvenation. I hate it, which is just one of the many reasons that I am a bad person.

She kicked and screamed, a girl on the stairs had said, her voice low but excited. *The Sisters had to drag her away. And that Amy girl, her friend – she tried to* attack *the Sisters. Tried to get them off of Teneil.*

So that was why Amy's lip had been split. She'd tried to protect Teneil. The thought of attacking a Sister makes me feel weak.

Teneil was wild, a girl behind me was whispering as I sat down. *Like a demon.*

They say she's possessed, another was hissing to my side.

They say she's evil.

I am up right at the front, pressed up against the railings. When I look about, I see that Amy is sitting on the floor by the rail like me, a few girls to my right. She doesn't look at me. Below us, the last of the Brothers are taking their seats, the Warriors having already taken their positions on the benches at the back of the Hall.

I can just about see Amy without moving my head if I look right out of the corner of my eye. Wisps of hair have escaped from her pins, and they snake around her face, lit up by the slants of sunlight from the windows. The split part of her mouth is on the far side of me, but what I can see of the rest of her lips looks bitten.

The low sound of movement from beneath us goes quiet from the front of the Hall to the back, like wind rolling across a field of tall grass. Heads turn to the dais.

The door behind the dais opens, and the Vessels step out. They are dressed like always: in long, plain white dresses that cover them from their throats to their wrists to their ankles. Their hair is tied back into a knot at the back of their head, and they keep their eyes on their clasped hands as they troop the short distance around the dais to the special box at its side. There is a strip of curtain hiding them from the view of the Brothers in the bottom gallery once they have sat down, but from the female section we can see the tops of their bowed heads.

It's rare to see the Vessels. Usually you see them once a year at the Harvest, when Father makes His choice of new Vessels from the Daughters who've come of age. The Vessels accept the new girls into their ranks by tying a white sash around the waist of their brown smock, and then they all disappear into the door behind the dais. The next time you see them, the new girls are dressed in the long white dresses and you can't tell them apart from the others anymore.

Once the Vessels have all filed into the pew box and sat down, the door behind the dais opens again. The Brothers and Elders below me rise to their feet and the Sisters behind me sink to their knees. I can't help my breath rushing out of me. Father is coming!

But it's not the graceful, white-bearded figure of Father who appears. It is a woman in a red dress, with a tall, blond boy in white next to her.

It's blasphemous, but I can't help gasping. It's all right, though – everyone around me has done the same. We are all one in this moment. I can feel it. Electricity crackles in the air between us all as we kneel or stand, barely containing ourselves. It is Father's wife and the Seed of the Children.

Father has many Vessels, but only one wife, and she bore His only son, the Seed who will carry on Father's legacy when Father is taken to the perfect world to come.

I've only seen the Seed once before. Amy has too. The Bad Night. I manage to tear my eyes away from Father's wife and the Seed long enough to peer around the girls next to me at Amy. She is looking down, tight-lipped, red spots of colour bruising her cheeks. She has grabbed hold of the bannisters and her knuckles are white. She still doesn't look back at me.

It's so unusual to see Father's wife and the Seed that no one knows what to do. We only kneel or stand to greet Father, but as everyone had already moved to greet Him in expectation, no one seems to know whether or not they should go back to sitting. And why are they here? Can all this really be happening because of what Teneil did? What Amy did?

Father's wife stands aside to allow the Seed to take the first of the two gold chairs at the side of the dais. Sometimes the more senior Elders sit there during services, but all the Elders are in the first row of the men's pews below. The boy sits, smoothing the front of his loose shirt down as he does. He is maybe four or five years older than I am. I can't see his face properly from this angle, but I remember his cool, pale blue eyes. I remember shrinking as those eyes settled on me.

As his mother sits, the boy glances up to the female section. I can almost hear the hearts of every girl in the front row slamming to a stop as he trails his gaze along us, then fixes on one girl. I already know who he is looking at. Everyone does. The girl to my left presses into my side as she cranes around me to look at Amy. The heads of every girl and woman in the gallery have swivelled around to stare at her, mine included. I feel what that white-hot scrutiny must be like for her, and my guts cramp in sympathy. She is staring straight ahead at nothing, unmoving, not even seeming to breathe.

The pressure from the crush of girls trying to get a look at Amy has pushed me forward, and my left knee is jammed uncomfortably against a bannister. I try to shift it, but we are packed in so tight that I can't move an inch.

Almost no one notices the door behind the dais opening again. Then I hear one of the Sisters hissing, 'Daughters!' to send our attention back down there.

Father.

Instantly the pressure on my knee is released as the crowd shifts its attention to the dais and the girls shuffle back to their original positions, herded by pokes and slaps from the Sisters behind us.

We generally see Father about once a month, when He speaks at the Sowing. But the last women's Sowing He'd spoken at was only two weeks ago.

I sneak another look at Amy. She is still staring straight ahead, instead of looking down at Father like everyone else, and won't meet my eye. Father steps up on the dais and turns to face everyone. He raises His hands, up and out to the side like an embrace meant for everyone in the room.

'My Children,' He says.

'Praise Father, who makes us Fruitful and will bring the perfect world to come,' I chant along with everyone else.

'Be seated,' He says. His voice is soft, but it carries through the entire Hall. There is a subdued murmur as everyone sits back down, then silence again. Father waits, His eyes drifting over the faces in front of Him.

'Children,' Father says. 'Children, there is grave danger in our midst.'

A rumble of whispers and shuffling feet. The girls sitting next to me grab each other's hands. It's so hot, jammed among the mass of bodies. I can feel sweat prickling at the small of my back.

Father waits once more for quiet. He's so tall, taller than anyone I've ever seen. His white robe glows, making everything else look dull in comparison. His hair is white too, and so long that you can't tell where it ends and His beard starts. His eyes in His pale face are blue, like the Seed's, except much brighter. His gaze sweeps over the room, and the power of it crackles in the air.

'Danger!' He cries, and we all jump. 'Evil!' Father clasps His hands. 'A poison planted among us!' At this, another rumble, louder this time. A half-stifled scream comes from one of the Sisters behind me. Father looks up at the balcony.

'Do not despair, My Daughters,' He says. 'Do not despair, for evil cannot defeat your Father. Your Father will protect His Children! They may try – they may try again and again, but we shall not, we cannot be broken. Our faith will not be compromised, nor our spirits quenched. You will see here today, My Children, how evil itself is overcome in the face of your Pure and untainted faith in Me.'

'Thanks be to our Father!' one of the Elders below shouts. The prayer is taken up by other throats below us, and even by some of the Sisters around me. I grip the railing. The old wood is slippery with sweat under my hand.

'Today you will witness a miracle! Children, today you will see what happens when our faith – when our very way of life – is tested. When our lives are threatened. By My grace and glory, I will defeat this evil. By My grace and glory, I will remove evil from the world! I will bring the perfect world to come!'

'Thanks be to our Father!' The call is being chanted now, voices raised in cries of prayer and praise. People are up out of their seats, hands in the air, feet stamping, arms waving. I am kicked in the elbow by the girl jumping up and down next to me, so I pull myself up too.

Below, the Brothers and Elders are turning to the back of the Hall, under the gallery and out of my view. Their cries get even louder, turn jeering and harsh. I am shoved against the railing as the Sisters and girls behind me push forward, jostling to peer down into the Hall.

It is Teneil. Grasping her elbow, leading her up the aisle, is a man dressed all in black.

'It's the Hand of God!' says a girl behind me. She is silenced with a cuff to the head from one of the Sisters within reach, and silence begins to roll out through the crowd, rippling outwards from the Hand of God as though he carries it with him.

Teneil looks dazed, like she's just woken up, but at the same time exhausted, as though she hasn't slept in days. Whenever I've seen her before – sauntering past tight-lipped Sisters in the corridors, or in the Nutrition Hall, sitting next to Amy, their heads close together and a Sister nearby, watching – she's always seemed so calm, so together. She has curly brown hair that's always escaping its pins, against the modesty rules, and she always holds her head up high, walks with her arms swinging and her back straight. Amy looks at her the way I suppose I look at Amy.

I caught Teneil's eye once, when she was sitting eating lunch with Amy. I was wandering past their table, maybe staring a bit . . . then she glanced up, and held my gaze. Her eyes were a bright green, startling against the soft golden-brown of her skin, and made me think of the algae-covered pond round the back of the dormitories. You can't see to the bottom through all the green on top of the water, but I've always been sure that it's really, treacherously deep. The Sisters have always told us to stay away from it, that it's dangerous. I looked away first.

Now, her hair is a mess, and her smock crumpled and stained. She trips over her feet and is hauled upright and marched on by the Hand of God. When they reach the dais, he lets her fall down in front of Father. Teneil looks up blearily, towards the balcony. Her eyes slip over our faces, back and forth like she's searching for someone.

Still squashed up against the bannisters, I look over again at Amy. She is gripping the top of the railing with both hands, leaning so far forward that she looks like she might tip right over it. Her eyes are fixed on Teneil.

Father cuts through the silence. 'This poor child, Children, this poor child has been propagated with evil. It has rooted deep in her soul. It is only through the power of your faith in Me that she can be healed. Your faith, wielded by Me, channelled through My Hand' – here He grasps the Hand of God's shoulder – 'can bring her out of the darkness and into My light.'

Teneil doesn't seem to be hearing him. She is still looking desperately up at the balcony.

'This child, My Children . . . this child is beset by demons.'

Brothers and Sisters cry out in shock. One of the girls behind me sobs.

'They hide under her skin, My Children. The demons. You can see how they twist beneath her face. But have faith, Children, for I—'

'Mum!' A scream has erupted from Teneil. She draws in a deep, wobbly breath. 'Mum, please!'

'Be silent, demons!' Father gestures to the Hand of God, who clips Teneil on the head.

'Mum!'

'See how they try to trick us, Children? Do you see what they are doing? They are preventing this child from achieving perfection! Preventing her from achieving salvation! She must be saved!'

'Save her!'

'Save her, Father!'

'Save her, please!'

Teneil tries to get up, but she's unsteady and she lurches sideways. So quickly that I jump, the Hand of God seizes her by the shoulders. Teneil screams, thrashes. The Hand of God places one palm on her forehead. She shakes her head violently, knocking his hand away. He takes a firmer grip of her shoulder and puts his hand back on her head again. It swallows her up, his palm resting just above her eyebrows and his longest finger reaching right to the back of her head. She looks very little.

'Mum!' Teneil screams again. She whips her head back and forth, but the Hand of God keeps his grip this time. Father holds on to the Hand of God's shoulder, His other hand upraised towards us all.

'Demons, begone from this child!' Father commands. The Hand of God presses hard on Teneil's head, so that her neck is forced back. I look for Amy again, but the girls next to me are leaning forward and blocking my view of her. The crowd behind me surges, and my ribs press painfully against the bannisters. The hot breath of the girl behind me washes over my neck. Below, on the dais, Father is still gripping the Hand of God's shoulder. Father draws breath. 'Demons, I command you—'

The Hand of God rocks backwards, almost falling. Teneil kicked him! Gasps and cries explode around me as everyone registers what she has done.

Teneil scrambles to her feet and staggers forward, missing the step down from the dais and sprawling to the floor.

'Mum!' she screams from her hands and knees. 'Mum, please, stop them!'

I am swept to the side, crushed into the girls to my left. A group of Sisters are escorting a tall woman with dark eyes and elegant, braided hair through the crowd to the railing. Teneil, who has been wildly searching the balcony, her eyes scanning desperately from side to side, sees her and sobs. 'Mum!'

The woman leans forward. Behind Teneil, the Hand of God makes to pick her up, but Father keeps a hold of his shoulder and pulls him back. Father raises His other hand to command silence. The noise in the Hall dies, leaving Teneil's ragged breathing to gasp out into the space all alone. The Sisters surrounding the tall woman hold her shoulders and arms with their hands. They are keeping her up. She is almost falling. But when she speaks, her voice is clear and calm.

'You are not my daughter,' she says.

Teneil's face is a frozen, horrified mask.

'You are a demon, and—' The woman stops, closes her eyes. One Sister leans in and whispers in her ear. She gathers herself, opens her eyes again to stare straight down at Teneil. '—and you must be Purified.'

The woman steps back into the crowd of Sisters, hands and arms leading her in and swallowing her up. She disappears.

'Mummy!' Teneil is screeching now. 'Mummy, please, Mummy, help me!'

Brothers from nearby pews surround her, lift her up and bring her back to the dais. She thrashes and bucks, kicking and flailing until they manage to get her pinned down, one man on each arm and leg. Jammed between the railing and the elbows and shoulders of the girls next to me, hot and light-headed, I feel sick. Father raises His voice above Teneil's shrieks.

'You see how strong the evil is? How desperately it attempts to defy My will?'

The Hand of God kneels over her, straddling her torso, and places his hand on her head again. Father grips both of his shoulders. 'Begone, demons!'

'Thanks be to our Father!' The call rings out through the Hall. I try to see Teneil's face. Can there really be demons in there? She has stopped screaming, and her mouth is lolling open. Before one of the men pinning her arm down shifts and blocks my view, I think I see her eyes roll up in her head.

'Demons, begone from this child and make her whole!' Father cries. 'I have the strength to Purify this child! I have the strength to save her! Demons, I cast you out!' The Hand of God pulls Teneil to a half-sitting position, grasps her shoulders and shakes her once, hard. Her head snaps back.

'I cast you out!' Father repeats, and the Hand of God shakes her again. Teneil's head flops.

'I cast you OUT!' The Hand of God shakes her a final time, then lets go. She falls back, her head smacking the wooden floor of the dais loud enough to send the noise of it through the Hall, then lies still.

The Hand of God leans over her, head turned so his ear rests against her lips, his chest heaving with exertion. He looks up at Father, who has let go of his shoulders. His face is pale and his lips tight.

They stay like that for a few moments as the noise dies away and a waiting silence fills the room. Then the Hand of God stands, smooths his shirt back into his trousers where it has come untucked, and bows his head to Father. Father throws His arms in the air.

'Children, I have saved her!'

Cheers and praises break out. Hands are raised, feet are stamped, knees are fallen to. The railing presses into my chest, and I can barely breathe for the bodies packed in around me. In all the commotion, I see the Hand of God gesturing at some Brothers. They scoop Teneil up and carry her very quickly out of the door behind the dais. The last I see of her is one drooping arm, flopping up and down with the steps of the men carrying her.

6

Now

'You want me to take her away?' I say, incredulous. I am sitting across from the Hand of God, the photograph of Amy and Father on the table between us.

'That's all, Catherine. I'm not here to interfere in your life. I'm not here to force you back. I'm simply here so you can reunite with your sister. That's what you want, isn't it?'

I stare at him. He meets my gaze as steadily as he always did.

'Why do you want her gone?' I say. 'And, I mean – what if she doesn't want to leave?'

The Hand of God shakes his head. 'She'll leave when she sees you.'

'But why do you want her to go?' I press. He looks at me for a moment without answering. I almost quail, but will myself not to. I am not lying half-conscious in my bed. I am not the child he remembers. I will not defer to him the way I always did.

'Amy is in some danger,' he says eventually.

'What? What danger?' Again, that maddening pause before he replies. And he is so still – normal people shift in their seats, glance about, fidget or gesture. But he sits like he is carved from stone. I'd forgotten how unsettling it is.

'I don't want to bore you with internal politicking among the Children,' he says at length.

'Bore me,' I say, and there is movement, finally – a slight upward quirk of one of his eyebrows.

'How you've grown, Catherine,' he says. I close my hands into fists under the table.

'Zoe.'

'Oh,' he says, and this time he half smiles. 'But I'll always think of you as my Catherine. As my—'

'Tell me why Amy is in danger.' It must be the first time I've ever interrupted him. I shove away the little shadow-me, the memory of who I was as a child, which is gibbering in fear over this disrespect. But that isn't me anymore, and he needs to know it.

But he doesn't seem angry. Just faintly amused. 'There are some among the upper echelons of the Children – some Elders – who do not approve of her marriage. Who would prefer that she be . . . removed.'

'So the Elders sent you? So I could take her away?' Something catches in my throat and I cough into my sleeve.

The line of his mouth firms. 'I do not act at the Elders' bidding,' he says.

Right. Of course. There'd always been some tension between him and a lot of the Elders. He occupied a strange position in the hierarchy of the Children, sort of above and to the side of the other powerful men. All under Father, of course. 'Why . . . I mean, why don't they just tell her to leave, or something? Banish her?'

'They cannot instruct her to do anything. Given her position. And she is . . . disinclined to leave of her own free will. I fear that they may be moved to do something rather rash. It wouldn't be the first time.'

I try to sort through all this information. My head is starting to ache. 'So . . . Amy is married to Father. The Elders don't like it, but they can't force her to leave, and she doesn't want to. You think that they'll . . . what, harm her? If she doesn't go?' I swallow, rub my aching throat.

The Hand of God pushes the glass of water towards me. 'Drink. Yes. I think Amy may come to some harm.'

I don't want to seem like I am following orders, but my throat feels stuffed with broken glass. I take a sip of the water. 'So why do you care?'

He raises his eyebrows. 'Why would you assume I wouldn't? You think I want a young woman to come to harm? You believe that of me?'

My thoughts feel like a tangled ball of string. 'I . . .'

'I don't know what kind of monster you've made me out to be, Catherine,' he says. 'I don't know what you've told yourself about us . . . about me. But you must remember that I only ever sought to protect you.'

Nausea lurches in my stomach. I pull myself to my feet. He stands too.

'I'm going to the bathroom,' I say. He inclines his head, like he's giving me permission. I shuffle away, his gaze hot on the back of my neck.

I shut the bathroom door firmly, then lock it for good measure. I don't think he'd try to come in here after me, but it still feels better to have a lock – however flimsy – between him and me.

I grip the edges of the sink and try to breathe normally. I don't feel like I've taken a proper breath since I walked in and saw him sitting at my kitchen table. It feels like it happened days ago, but it can only have been an hour, at most.

I could slip out and grab my phone from the hall table. I know that if I texted Meg, she'd come over right away, no questions asked. She's not just a boss, or even just a friend. She's been a guide and a protector and a teacher to me since I came to this country.

But how can I bring her into this? How can I put her in the path of a man like the Hand of God? To him, she'd just be an obstacle to overcome. And I know what he does to obstacles.

I sit on the toilet seat, put my face in my hands. He wants me to go with him to Home. 'Home.' I haven't been back in six years. I can barely even remember it.

That's only sort of half true. I remember bits. Flashes. Disconnected memories of cooking and cleaning and sewing and all sorts of other menial tasks. Classes chanting 'Scripture'. Services in the big hall. Meals in an echoing canteen. Sleeping in a cold, narrow dormitory with a dozen other girls. The angry, cruel Sisters.

There is more. I know that. I can feel other memories, sometimes, pressing against my mind like a figure behind a curtain, threatening to come out. But even if I wanted to draw that curtain aside and look at them, I'm not sure I could, anymore. I've spent so much time forgetting.

I remember him, of course. The Hand of God. Father's Hand. He was someone I was equally fascinated by and terrified of as a kid, when I was with the Daughters. Then all the stuff with Amy happened, and after that he took a particular interest in me. I don't know why, except that he used to tell me I was special, that I was different. But that was a lie, like everything else.

And then of course I left, just over a year or so after Amy disappeared. And it was only because of Amy that I was able to escape in the first place. That's why I have to go back. I owe it to her.

I can't believe she's back there. Why would she return, after all this time? And to marry Father?

Father – the man in the picture – is young, just a few years older than Amy herself. He's not the 'Father' who was there when I was. That Father is dead, and now his son, who used to be the Seed, is Father. I cannot think of any reason why Amy would want to have anything to do with him. The thought of her being married to him makes me feel utterly sick. Why would she go back? Why would she marry him?

Perhaps she felt alone, and that's why she went back.

Maybe she went back because she couldn't manage what the world was like Outside.

Or maybe – and this makes me feel cold to my very core – she went back to find me. I escaped some time after her, and we never found each other. Perhaps she hadn't ever known I'd left. Maybe she'd thought I was still there.

The Hand of God hasn't told me why she returned, or perhaps he doesn't know. He just wants her gone.

I run the tap, splash water on my face. He can't really be concerned for Amy's safety. Why would he be? What's in it for him?

An excuse, maybe? A reason to come and get me, after all this time?

But why wait until now? And how did he find me? How long had he known where I was?

I wipe my face with a towel, look up at the mirror. There I am – paler than usual, with my dark cloud of curls loose around my face. My head was shaved the last time the Hand of God saw me. He'd been the one to do it.

There is a red mark on my jaw, beside my chin. I touch it, feel a dull throb of pain.

That is the truth. That bruise. That mark, and the rest of the marks on my body, most of which I can't even remember getting, because there are so many. That is the truth of the Children, and of the Hand of God. That is what they do to women. Whatever else he's telling me, I do believe that Amy is in danger.

It doesn't matter what his game is. The Elders want Amy gone, and he does too, for whatever reason. But it doesn't matter why he's doing this, because the outcome is what I want, too. So I will go back to the Children with him, and I will tell Amy that she's in danger, and I'll take her away – take her home with me. That's what I've always wanted, to see her again, to be a family, a proper family. She got me out, all those years ago. Now I have to return the favour.

7

THEN

Nobody has said my name in weeks. Not since that day with Teneil, who hasn't been seen since. Any mention of her is totally forbidden, because you can't talk about people after they've gone. There's a big black cloud over her name, and there might as well be one over mine, too.

I am washing up before bed in the big chilly Ablutions Room – all alone because somehow I ended up at the back of the queue, even though I joined it early on – and I'm staring at my washbag in the mirror, which I can see behind me hanging on its nail. It's badly made, even by the standards of the other girls' ones. You do them when you're little and just learning to sew – one for you, with your name stitched in big letters on the front, and one for one of the boys, when you've learned how to sew better. The boy I made a shower bag for is called JEREMY. I don't know which one he is, but sometimes when I hear a group of Warriors distantly in the Training Grounds, I still try to imagine which boy keeps his things in a shower bag with crooked letters spelling his name (and a messy bit where I did an extra E instead of a Y and Sister Amity had to unpick it).

I started to feel quite fond of my one when I was associating it with Amy's messages. But now I can see that it's falling apart, drooping and lumpy, with loose stitching everywhere. Not something anyone would ever want.

Not that it matters to everyone else that Amy still doesn't want me, even though Teneil's gone now. I have been tainted by my association with her. You'd think I couldn't be less liked – I'd certainly thought so – but apparently it was possible to sink to an even lower status than I already had. Since Teneil is now not-to-be-mentioned, Amy (as her friend, and because she waded in when the Sisters grabbed Teneil) is being shunned – not officially, they wouldn't be allowed to do anything to Amy officially – but no one is speaking to her or even really looking at her. And because the other Daughters know that Amy is my blood sister, I have been dragged into the whole thing.

It's my fault that they all know that we're blood sisters. I told Angela last year. I was going through this period of trying to make her like me, because I thought it might make my life easier. I thought if we could be friends then maybe she'd stop point-ing out to the Sisters when I'd done something wrong, or getting the others to laugh at me, or pinching me when I was working next to her. I'd watched the other Daughters, and had noticed that the ones who were particular friends would go off and whis-per together in corners, pointedly staring at anyone who got too close. They were exchanging secrets. Secrets, I thought, were how you got to be friends with someone. So I told Angela about Amy. Stupid me, because of course I shouldn't have known about it, and of course Angela went straight to the Sisters, and of course that meant I had to Atone. And Amy too, because that's how it works.

The moment the words were out of my mouth I wanted to reach out and cram them back in, but of course I couldn't. It felt like I'd let something precious go, or smashed something I was supposed to keep safe. The piggy little gleam in Angela's eyes when she realised what I'd told her just made it worse. Amy forgave me, but I still feel terrible about it.

Anyway, I've given up trying to be friends with Angela now. I've given up trying to have any friends at all except Amy. Except then she got Teneil and stopped bothering with me. And even though Teneil's gone now, Amy hasn't tried to speak to me again.

I could have managed the shunning if only Amy was talking to me again. But she's not, and neither is anyone else. I didn't have friends except Amy really, before this, but at least other people acknowledged that I was alive. Now, I am starting to feel as though I don't exist.

The soap in my hair drips into my eyes, making them sting, so I take up a palmful of cold water from the sink and scrub my face with it. I can't face fully submerging myself under the shower. Since there is no Sister here, I can get away with a quick wash in the sink.

I don't want to look at my reflection in the mirror, so I avoid my own gaze and instead look at my washbag again, hanging uselessly behind me.

I get this urge to tear it off the nail and rip it, pull it all to pieces. But then I see Amy's reflection appear behind me in the mirror through strands of my soapy hair. Her lip has healed, but otherwise she doesn't look any better than she did on the bad day with Teneil.

I plunge my hair back into the freezing stream of water from the tap and scrub vigorously. I let it flood my ears. If I ignore Amy, she'll have to go away.

I hear her saying something through the rush of water. I push my head further under the tap and let it flow around the back of my neck. It sends a shiver right down to the soles of my feet.

A hand pulls at my arm, and my head knocks into the tap. 'Ow!' I straighten up, clamping a hand over where it hurts. Freezing water pours from my hair and down my shoulders, dampening my vest. Amy lets go and stands back.

'Sorry,' she says.

This is so unexpected that I don't say anything. I don't think she's ever apologised to me before. I'm not certain anyone ever has. I scrape my hair back off my forehead and shoulders and twist it into a rope. Water skooshes out of it like a sponge.

'Is your head okay?'

'It's fine,' I say. I don't know what else to say, and she seems to have ground to a halt, so I tie my hair up using the band around my wrist. My vest is soaking – I'll have to hang it on the back of a chair or something to dry or the Room Leader will go spare.

'Look,' says Amy, then stops.

'I should go to bed,' I say. I start to gather up my things, but my washbag isn't on its nail. Amy turns and picks it up from the bench behind her.

'Don't go – just give me a minute, okay?'

'I'll get in trouble if I'm late for bed.' I snatch the bag from her. Then it all comes out in a rush. 'I'm already in trouble because of you! I don't need any more!'

'You're in trouble?' She actually looks surprised. I feel a fresh sweep of pain. How can she not have noticed?

'Of course I'm in trouble! You had to go and be Te— *her* friend, and look what's happened! Now no one wants to talk to me!'

'Okay, listen—'

'You're not even supposed to be here, and if you get caught, I'll get in trouble as well, so it's not fair—'

'Catherine, listen . . .' Amy reaches out for my hand, but I move out of her way.

'What do you want?'

She looks at me, and she looks scared and unhappy, and then her face just . . . drops. 'It's all right. It doesn't matter.' She turns to go. I nearly throw all my things on the floor in frustration, and the only thing that stops me is that it would make a huge clatter and definitely alert someone that we are in here.

'So you come in here and risk getting me into even more trouble and then you're just going?'

'You don't want to talk to me!' Amy hisses.

I want to pull her hair out. 'Well, just say what you've come here for!'

Amy lets out an angry sigh. 'I came . . . I just came here to give you something.'

'What?'

'Here.' She holds out a scrap of paper, rolled into a cylinder.

'What is it?'

'It's . . . it's something for you. If you ever want to . . . to do what I've done.'

I go cold. 'What have you done?'

'Nothing! Nothing. Just take it, and don't ever tell anyone I gave it to you.' She pushes the paper into my hand and curls my fingers over it. She holds on, her warm and dry hand covering my freezing and damp one. 'Just keep it, all right? Promise me.'

43

'Amy—'

'Promise me, Catherine!'

'I promise,' I say. I can feel the slip of paper scrunched up small in my wet palm. Amy's face is very close to mine – the closest we've been in as long as I can remember. Her eyes are large and open and, this close up, she doesn't seem as different, as distant as she has lately. Something about this makes me want to promise her whatever she wants.

'Amy, are you okay?'

'I'm fine.' She moves back and whatever it is that existed between us for that moment stretches and snaps and is gone. A mask clicks back down over her face. She turns very quickly and leaves without looking back.

The door to the washroom shuts behind her and I am left in the cold, echoing room by myself. I can feel chilly water pooling in the small of my back, and my toes feel numb. I open my hand and look down at the scrap of paper. My hand is still wet from washing my hair, and the note has clumped and stuck into a little ball. I unpeel it carefully, but it is no use. There is just a blur of blue, smudged ink. Whatever was written there is unreadable, and Amy is gone.

8

Now

There is a small scuffed patch on the arm of the chair, just where my fingers rest. I've been worrying away at it since I sat down. Every time I want to laugh, or roll my eyes, or storm out, I just pick away at that little scuffed patch instead.

The chair looks like it would be comfortable, but after an hour in it my back feels like it's about to break. The upholstery is hospital green, smooth and slick except for that little rough patch on the edge of the left armrest. It was already there when I started, worn away by some other inhabitant of this chair and of this endless, circular time.

'Catherine? Would you like to answer my question?'

I force my head into a nod. 'Yes, Sister. I'm just thinking about my answer.'

The woman opposite me smiles. Sister Innocence has kind eyes and a soft voice. Her hair, white against her dark skin, is gathered into a neat bun. She has little half-moon wire-rimmed glasses perched on her nose. She looks like a sweet grandmother.

It's an act, though. And it's not going to work on me. I know what she's doing, what all this is supposed to accomplish. But I'm not the kind of person she's used to. I'm not joining the Children. I'm not buying into their bullshit. I know who I am and what I'm here to do.

One – My name is Zoe
Two – I am here to rescue my sister Amy
Three – Nothing anyone says here is true
Four –

What is my fourth thing? It could be that I am sat in the world's most uncomfortable chair. It could be that I still feel absolutely rotten and can't stop coughing, and a night spent in the passenger seat of the Hand of God's car hasn't helped matters. It could be that Innocence's cloying, self-satisfied smile makes me want to answer every question she asks me with the truth, instead of carefully curated answers that will make it seem like I am a penitent returning member of the Children.

Why did you decide to return to us, Catherine?

Because a psychotic bastard appeared in my kitchen yesterday when I was semi-delirious with the flu and sent me on a rescue mission that, now I think about it, doesn't make a whole fucking lot of sense, Sister.

I actually said something about feeling lost and adrift in a modern world full of 'Transgressions' and corruption. But I imagined saying the other thing really hard. Then I had a coughing fit.

I can do better than this. The four true things list doesn't work unless I am really, truly honest with myself.

> Four – I have not seen the Hand of God since we arrived early this morning
>
> Or
>
> Four – Being taken through the Gate back into the compound was so disorientating that I had to close my eyes and breathe slowly until I was certain I wouldn't throw up
>
> Or
>
> Four – I still have no idea why the Hand of God really wanted me to come back, but I know it's definitely not out of an abundance of concern for my sister's safety

I've got to stop thinking of him as 'the Hand of God'. It's a nonsense title from a batshit insane cult, whose beliefs are no longer mine. However, I have no idea what his name actually is. He was always just 'the Hand of God'.

I'll think of him as 'Hand'. It sounds like it could be a name. It reminds me of *Treasure Island*, which Meg lent me a few years ago. Israel Hands. He was a villain.

Hand had made it seem, when we were still in Dublin, like he would take me directly to Amy, and I'd speak to her and then we'd leave. Easy. Simple. I'd be back home before anyone knew I'd even gone anywhere.

I'd thought about taking Amy back with me, bringing her to the cafe, introducing her to Meg and the rest of them. *This is my sister*, I'd say. *She's come to stay with me.* It felt so warm, that thought. So perfect. So possible.

It hasn't turned out to be exactly that straightforward.

'Catherine?' Innocence's smile is, as ever, patient and calm.

Oh, help. What did she ask me?

'I . . . I don't know quite how to answer,' I say, casting my eyes down. I rub my fingers over the little worn patch on the armrest. My head feels like it's full of static.

'Let's put it a different way, then,' she says, shifting in her chair and crossing her legs at the ankle. She smooths down her brown skirt. It is the same as the one I am wearing – full, ankle-length, no pockets (which is driving me mad) – except mine is grey, as befits one of the newly Awakened. I so rarely wear dresses or skirts these days – I much prefer jeans – and the wrongness of this garment on me hums in my bones.

There's no other option, though. I'm 'Catherine', therefore I wear female clothing. It's such a suffocating box. It took me a long time, in the world outside, to accept that there was more than one way to be a woman. But there are no shades of identity here.

Innocence is the only one apart from Hand to know the truth about me. Or some of the truth. That I am not just another recently Awakened recruit, that I was previously one of the Children, that I left and have now, apparently, returned. I don't remember her from my days here, so I'm pretty sure that she wasn't here then. She doesn't seem to know about Amy, and obviously doesn't know about the plan Hand and I have.

Over my knee lies a grey cloth mask, except this kind has long ties at the back instead of ear loops. I vaguely remember seeing some people wear these when I was a kid. The newly Awakened, who, as part of their integration into Home, had to wear these face masks as a visual reminder that they could not talk, and that you weren't supposed to talk to them. After a while, once they were deemed fully integrated, they would be allowed to take them off, to wear the same colour clothes as the rest of the Children, to talk to others and be talked to.

The mask has the added consequence that no one has recognised me. I've only seen a few other Sisters today, and, of those, maybe a small number were sort of familiar, but it's been so long I can't remember names or really any particulars. Just a vague sense of recognition.

The mask was the first thing I took out of the bag Hand gave me, when he pulled over to the side of the road just before we reached Home. We hadn't really spoken in the car up to that point. I was exhausted, feeling unwell, and I fell asleep on the drive to the ferry port in Belfast, barely kept awake on the crossing, and remained in a kind of half-dazed stupor as he drove through the night towards Home. We'd been in the car for around six hours by then, and I was stiff and sore and half asleep when I registered that we were slowing and he was pulling in.

He stopped the car in what looked to me like a random spot on a country road, empty apart from us. We'd passed through Glasgow a couple of hours after driving off the ferry, but after that it had been ever smaller and quieter roads, and fewer signs of life apart from the odd cluster of houses.

I looked around blearily. Grey hills in the pre-dawn light. 'Where are we?'

'Here.' He handed me a canvas bag he'd taken from the back seat. I reached in and took out the grey face mask.

'What is this?'

'This is how you see Amy.'

I'm only allowed to take the mask off when I'm with Sister Innocence. The rest of today I've had to keep it on.

'Of course you can't simply walk back through the Gate and see her,' he said, raising an eyebrow, as though I was painfully stupid. I stared down at the mask and felt a cold spike of worry settle into my guts. 'I will take you to her, but it won't be possible during the day. There are too many people about. You will have to wait until night.'

'But why do I have to wear this stuff?' I pulled the rest of the grey clothes out of the bag.

'You cannot be seen at Home in Outside attire,' Hand said. 'You will have to appear as one of the recently Awakened. I have arranged for one of the Sisters to meet you when we arrive, and take you to get changed into these. She'll take your clothes, and any personal items, so you can leave anything you don't want her to have with me for now.'

I had a small bag with me, sitting at my feet, with my phone, spare clothes and passport in it. I gripped it with one hand and said, 'Can't I just—'

'Would you like me to take you back?'

'Sorry?'

'Shall I take you back? I can't go the whole way, but I'll take you to the nearest town. You can get a bus from there.' He released the handbrake, began to turn the car around.

'Wait! Wait.'

He looked at me levelly. 'I've gone to quite some trouble to ensure Amy's safety, Catherine. All you have to do is put these on.'

I looked down at the pile of grey in my lap again, feeling sick. I nodded. He pointed the car in its original direction and we moved off.

'I will come for you tonight and take you to Amy. You must . . .' he waved his hand '. . . just play along until then.'

I can't stop thinking about Meg. Will she realise I've gone? She knows I'm unwell – she'll probably call or drop by or something. She usually would. What's she going to do when she can't get in touch with me? She has a key, so she'll let herself into my flat, but I won't be there.

If it were me looking for a friend, and I was worried, that's the point I might call the Guards. But Meg knows that she can't do that for me. She'll probably ring around a few people, put out feelers.

She'll be worried sick.

But it's better that she doesn't know where I am, or who I'm with. The further I can keep her – keep Dublin, and my whole,

49

real, actual life – safely away from Hand and the Children, the better. And I'll be back before long, anyway. She'll understand.

Deep breaths. I wish I had my notebook. What could I list right now?

Reasons Why This Whole Thing is Probably a Terrible Fucking Idea:

> One – Meg is going to be worried and upset
> Two – I don't know why (or when) my sister returned Home
> Three – I don't know for sure if she'll agree to leave with me
> Four – I don't even know if it's my responsibility to get her to leave

No, that's wrong. Of course it's my responsibility. She got me out. Amy got me out, and I need to do the same for her now.

I only need to wait until tonight. I can manage that. I am not the child that I was, and I know exactly what and who these people are now. And it's just until tonight.

It's just until tonight kept me going when Hand dropped me at the door to the women's building and drove off again, leaving me in the company of a thin-lipped, silent Sister. It kept me going when I took off my clothes in the freezing bathroom and put on the grey dress and tied the mask over my face. It kept me going when I had to spend two hours cleaning one of the dormitories this morning with a dozen other silent women, then sat among them while they ate dry toast and drank water for breakfast (I was allowed to lift my mask quickly to slip bites of food into my mouth, but I didn't bother. I wasn't hungry). And it's kept me going through this last, endless hour of my 'Revival Session' with Innocence.

She fixes me with a penetrating gaze, and it takes everything I have not to wriggle about uncomfortably. Shit. She's been talking this entire time, and I haven't listened to a word.

I take a shuddery breath, which I only have to half fake, and give her a watery smile. 'I'm so sorry, Sister, I just find this . . . thinking about my past . . . so hard,' I say. I cough into my elbow

50

and continue. 'I just feel so bad about leaving. So guilty.' I'm laying it on thick, but this is exactly the sort of crap she wants to hear. I know what these people are like.

Innocence presses the tips of her fingers together and raises them to her chin. 'What action would you say you feel most guilty about, after leaving the Children?'

'It's . . . hard to say,' I say slowly. 'Obviously, leaving was such a huge Transgression that everything I did afterwards was tainted by that.'

She nods. 'Of course. But what do you consider to be the thing that took you furthest from our Father's light?'

I know what she's doing. I read about this stuff after I left. I'm currently experiencing one of the later stages of cult indoctrination. By Hand taking me straight here, to the Children's compound, I've skipped the early stages, as administered by the Children's little outreach groups. They run all sorts of 'classes' and 'courses' and 'support groups', where people are enticed in with lovely but vague promises about improving their lives. I've even seen flame-and-circle signs and banners in Dublin, especially in the last couple of years. Successive global financial and health crises and everything that accompanies them have made people more desperate for something to cling on to – and the Children were perfectly poised to capitalise on that. I've looked at their website, where – hidden among all the well-being, self-improvement crap – there are tell-tale signs of the Children's true nature. Stuff about 'returning to basics' and 'the natural roles of men and women' and 'seeding the Fruit of the future'. It attracts the sort of people who feel like there's something reassuring about clear, defined roles for 'the sexes'. The sort of people who want to believe that they know 'the truth' and others don't. The sort of people who feel like they need something 'more', but can't put their finger on exactly what that 'more' is. And when some poor sap goes along to the sessions the Children run, they are sucked into a smoothly efficient machine. The whole, oh, here's our lovely little group, where we welcome you and make you feel great, now don't you want to figure out what's wrong in your life? Sign right here and we'll help you sort it right out . . . yes, right here, and here, and here . . . initial here . . .

I clear my throat. 'I suppose I feel most guilt about . . . living immodestly?'

Cults pull you in with kindness and belonging, and then make you commit financially and emotionally, so by the time you realise something is wrong, they hit you with the guilt and the emotional blackmail. That's the stage I'm at now. The recently Awakened, the ones who have sold their houses and given up their jobs and signed documents they were never really allowed to read, arrive at Home and are given lots of group sessions, called 'Revivals'. It's only once they've completed these sessions that they're deemed fully 'Awakened' and allowed to join the Children proper. There was a steady trickle of these people back when I was here, but from what little I saw this morning, there are more now. There is construction of a new building adjoining the women's dormitories, and I heard distant building work going on elsewhere, when I was briefly outside on the way to the Nutrition Hall for the good old bread-and-water breakfast buffet. The last few years have plunged more people than ever into poverty, but the Children have been making bank.

Innocence raises her eyebrows encouragingly. 'Yeah,' I say. 'Living immodestly is what I feel most guilty about.'

She leans forward, chin propped on her hand. 'Immodest in what way, Catherine?'

Innocence has explained that I'm getting one-to-one Revival sessions, presumably because, as a previous leaver, it's a bit risky to allow me near the rest of the recently Awakened. That's fine. It's not like I'll be here after today. I just have to make it through the rest of this session and whatever Camp Cult activity is planned for the afternoon (Floor Scrubbing! Sock Mending! Cabbage Hoeing!), and then Hand will come and get me.

'Well . . . I talked to men.' Innocence nods, indicating that I should continue. 'I worked in a coffee shop, and a lot of the customers and other staff were men. So I had to talk to them.'

'And how did that make you feel, Catherine?' Innocence must have been a psychiatrist or something before she got snapped up by the Children. Which makes no sense. She's clearly intelligent; how can she swallow all the Children's bullshit?

'How do you mean?'

'Did it make you feel . . . important?' Innocence clasps her hands together, index fingers extended and pressed against her chin. 'Did it make you feel special?'

I know where this is going. But I have to play along, just for now.

'I . . . yes,' I say. I look down at my feet and swallow. I wonder if I can even dredge up a few tears. My fingers worry at the worn patch on the chair. 'I did feel special.'

'And did you feel . . . feelings . . . for any of these men?'

I almost laugh. Nothing could be further from the truth, but I'm not going to go there with her. 'Sometimes. One or two,' I say.

'And did you allow these men to know you, Catherine?'

If I say no, that I'd never allowed a man to know me, will Innocence believe me? If I say yes, will there be some bullshit punishment ritual I have to go through?

'No, Sister,' I say, looking up. 'I never fell so far from Father's eyes that I allowed . . . that.'

Innocence smiles at me. She looks . . . triumphant? Did I pick the right option?

She tilts her head to one side, looking like an old, wise bird. She takes off her glasses and taps her teeth with one of the stems. 'Oh, Catherine,' she says. 'You know that you must be truly honest with me.'

Shit. Should have gone for option two. I open my mouth, but she keeps going before I can get a word out.

'You were – inadvertently, I think – telling the truth when you said that you never fell far from Father's eye. We are, of course, all within Father's eye. Even if we don't think we are. Even if we think we can't be seen.'

I nod. 'Of course,' I say, trying to look contrite. I want to grab her shoulders and scream I DON'T CARE, I DON'T CARE ABOUT ANY OF THIS in her face. I scrape at the arm of the chair with my fingernails.

'So, Catherine, I'll ask you again.' Innocence smiles broadly, encouragingly. 'What action do you feel the most guilt about since you left? What is your greatest Transgression, after your apostasy?'

'I . . . I courted the attentions of men?' I say, and even to my ears it sounds like a question. Innocence shakes her head. I plough on. 'I mean . . . I spent time with men. With a man, I mean. Once. Alone. I—' She's shaking her head again. I stop. What does she want from me? Does she want me to say I put it about with every man in a ten-mile radius of the Underpass Cafe?

Innocence reaches to the desk beside her, opens a drawer and pulls out a slim brown folder. She lays it on her knees. I watch her, feeling like I'm looking at a trap ready to spring. She taps the folder with one finger.

'You know what's in here, Catherine,' she says.

'I don't,' I say, letting an edge of impatience creep into my voice. I'm done being deferential. I don't have to scrape and quiver. I don't have to care about whatever this is. I'm out of here in a few hours.

'You do. Because you know the truth. And Father's eye saw the truth. I have it here. So you have one more chance to tell me. To absolve yourself.'

I stare at the folder. It's a trick. It's full of blank paper. I'm supposed to feel worried and guilty, and to panic and come out with something incriminating. She's fishing. She doesn't know anything.

And yet . . . Hand knew exactly where to find me. He knew where I lived and worked.

A cold hand settles on the back of my neck. How long have they been watching me? How long has Hand known exactly where I was?

When I asked him how he'd found me, in Dublin before we left, he'd just said, *We never lost you.*

Innocence shakes her head, looking regretful. 'I'm sorry that you've forced me to this, Catherine,' she says.

It doesn't matter what's in there. They can't do anything to me. I'm not really one of them. I'll be gone by tonight. Me and Amy, we'll be gone.

She opens the folder and slides out a glossy photograph, placing it on the low table between us. It's bigger than the one Hand had of Amy and Father, and is a little blurry, which makes it look like it's been cropped and blown up from a wider image, but the detail is clear enough. It's the Underpass Cafe. The sight of it twists my heart. The picture looks like it's been taken from about hip-height – so a camera placed on one of the tables, maybe? There's the main bar. There are the pastry tiers, and the register with the cash drawer that's always getting stuck, and the chalkboard behind – out of focus, but I can see the day's specials written on it in Meg's looping script.

And there I am behind the counter, tea towel draped over my shoulder and a pencil behind one ear. I am leaning forward, my elbows propped on the bar, and I am smiling. I look happy. Just so simply, uncomplicatedly happy.

Opposite me, on the customer side, is a young woman. She's wearing low-slung jeans, a vest top that shows the tattooed flowers that tumble from shoulder to shoulder across her back, and her hair is gathered on the top of her head in her customary Afro puff. Her back is to the camera, but I can see her face as though it's in front of me. Deep, beautiful brown eyes, and a wide smile that makes her cheeks fold into dimples.

Innocence pulls another picture out of the folder. It is almost identical to the first, except the girl across the counter has pushed herself up on her tiptoes in order to lean across and press her lips against mine. One of my hands is resting on the back of her neck.

I stare at the images, feeling dizzy. Two years ago. Those pictures must have been taken around two years ago. They've known where I was for that long?

Innocence returns her hands to her lap, shakes her head regretfully. 'You must know how wrong this is, Catherine,' she says.

I could leave, now. I could just stand up and say that I'm leaving. She can't keep me here. I've done nothing wrong, and I'm not a prisoner, and she can't keep me here.

The door behind me opens, and I twist around in the chair. Two men, dressed in the dark green uniform of Father's Guards, step into the room.

Innocence stands up. 'It isn't enough to Revive you, Catherine,' she says. 'I had hoped that you might not be so very lost – that you might be truthful with me. But you've concealed this, throughout our session together. You are not ready to be called Awakened.'

I look up at her. I am gripping the arms of the chair so tightly that my fingers have punched right through the worn little patch in the upholstery. I can feel the rough, prickly material coiled underneath. Behind me, I hear the men step closer.

'You cannot be Awakened, Catherine, until you are Purified.'

9

THEN

A hand is gripping my shoulder and shaking me. I fight my way up from a dark, watery dream where Amy was yelling at me through puddles and mirrors, telling me something very important, but I couldn't make out a word.

I am shaken again, roughly. I push the hair out of my eyes and squint. It's dark, and I can't see who's there. Have I somehow missed the bell and overslept? But no, that can't be it – it's too dark to be morning.

'Amy?' I say. There is a little gasp above me, then I am yanked up out of the bed.

'Get up, Catherine,' someone hisses. It's one of the Sisters. She pushes me to the dormitory door. I'm still only in my nightgown, with bare feet. The shadowy shapes of girls in the other beds are around me, some half sitting up as I am hustled out of the room and down the unlit corridor.

'What's happening?' I ask. The Sister has my upper arm gripped firmly, her fingers digging in. She doesn't look at me. I'm too scared to ask again.

We go down the main staircase. I trip and almost fall, but the Sister still has a grip on my arm, so I just dangle from her fist into empty air for a second, heart dropping, until she hauls me back to my feet and pushes me on. I am propelled down another flight, past the main hallway, through more corridors and past the Sisters' sleeping quarters on the ground floor.

I dare another look up at the Sister. In the moonlight filtering through the windows, I see her lips are clamped into a thin, straight line. She is staring straight ahead. She looks furious.

What have I done now?

We get to a door at the end of the corridor, which she unlocks and pushes me through. There are stairs behind it, leading down. I've never been through this door before, but I know what it is. I know where we are going, now. She is taking me to the Atonement Room.

I've Transgressed before, but it's been for things like being forgetful, or not being properly modest, or not concentrating in lessons. The Atonement for these is stripes, and sometimes extra chores. The worst one I've ever had was when I was caught looking at the Warriors and swearing, and that was bad enough. The Atonement Room is for much, much worse Transgressions. It's for blasphemers and questioners. It's for those who are disrespectful or rude. It's for the worst, worst things you can do.

I try to think as I'm dragged down the stairs. They're narrow, and twist down into the earth. The Sister's hand is a pincer on my shoulder now; her nails are biting into the skin at the back of my neck. What could I have done?

I try to say a prayer, but I've never been good at them. I can't focus for long enough to get through them. My mind wanders and slides off the words. Tonight, it's more hopeless than ever.

At the bottom of the stairs are three doors. They all have big, heavy locks on the outside. The cold here has seeped into every part of me.

The Sister knocks on the first one, and it is opened from the inside. A man looks out and down at me. He is tall, and has a thick beard – grey, with dark brown streaks down the sides. Elder Butchart. I didn't think it was possible to be any more scared than I already am, but the sight of his face makes every part of me seize up. He sits up on the dais with Father. He leads Worship when Father isn't there. He was in that room on the Bad Night.

His pale eyes flick over me, then up to the Sister. He nods, and she leaves. I feel like I might be sick, or faint.

Elder Butchart steps to the side, and points. 'In. Now.'

I obey. The floor is freezing stone, and my nightie is thin. I start to shiver.

Elder Butchart closes the door slowly. There's a single, bright lightbulb hanging above me, so bright that I need to blink my eyes and squint to see after the darkness of the corridor. I shift from foot to icy foot and pull the sleeves of my nightie over my hands.

Elder Butchart is still facing the closed door. 'Tell me what you know,' he says, without turning around.

I open and close my mouth like a fish. What I know about what?

He turns around, finally. His face is terrifying. It's all knotted and twisted around his mouth and eyes. 'Well?' he says.

I have no idea what to say. He grabs me by the shoulders and gives me a hard shake. My eyes and teeth feel like they're being flung back into my skull.

'Where. Is. Amy?' A shake with every word. He lets me go and I stumble back.

'Amy?'

He looks, if possible, even more furious. 'You stupid little girl. Where has she gone?'

'I – I don't know!' I'm trying to get a grip on what he's saying. Amy. Amy is gone. Missing. Hiding somewhere?

There is a stinging whack on my cheek. He has slapped me. I put my hand to my face and concentrate on not crying. It's always worse when you cry.

'Lying to me is a Transgression, Catherine. You understand? Your soul will burn. Now tell me the truth. I will know if you are lying.'

The room goes wobbly with the tears I can't hold back anymore. The Elders can read your mind. They know when you're thinking bad things. 'Please, Elder, I am telling the truth!' Another slap, and this time my head rocks back and the room slips and I am on my knees on the cold floor.

'Don't lie to me, Catherine. You have no idea of the gravity of the situation. Father Himself is taking a personal interest in this.'

Father is taking an interest in Amy?

'Amy was seen entering the Ablutions Room on your floor before lights out tonight. You were the last out. She must have come to see you. What did she tell you? Were you planning this together? Where did she go?' The Elder's voice is rising and rising, and he pulls me up by the collar of my nightie. I dangle from his grip like a rabbit I saw in the teeth of a dog once.

'She didn't tell me anything!' I say. Is that true? She said something – something strange – what had she said? I can't remember, not while he's shaking me like this . . . I can't breathe . . .

I hear the door open, and swift footsteps, and then I'm on the floor again. I pull my collar away from my burning throat and cough out shards of air. There is a low, calm voice speaking quietly, the beginning of a shout from the Elder, then quick, angry footsteps and a slammed door. I look up at my rescuer.

It is the Hand of God.

I look down again, quickly. You're not allowed to look in his eyes. I will be in even more trouble now because I looked right in his eyes. He is staring down at me, impossibly tall and thin in his black clothes. He's almost as tall as Father.

'Catherine?' He sounds . . . gentle, almost. Certainly not angry, like the Elder.

I don't say anything. I don't know how you're supposed to address the Hand of God, and I don't want to get hit again.

A rustle of cloth, and I hear the Hand of God's voice again. 'It's all right, Catherine,' he says. He's squatted down on his heels. I feel his hand on my shoulder, and I flinch back without meaning to. 'It's all right – it's okay,' he says. 'I'm not going to hurt you, Catherine. I'm here to help you.'

A handkerchief appears under my nose. It is white, and folded neatly. I stare at it. He shakes it slightly. 'Go on. Take it.'

I take it from him, careful not to let my fingers touch his. It would be wrong, surely. He acts as Father's hands for interacting with things-of-the-world that would corrupt Father's perfection. To touch the Hand of God would be like touching Father, which is a huge Transgression, unless you're one of Father's Vessels. Or His wife. But the Hand of God just touched me, so . . . it is all so confusing.

I blot the tears away from my hot face. His hand is back on my shoulder, patting it and sort of rubbing up and down. It feels good. I can't think when anyone's ever touched me like that. I feel a little heat build in my chest.

'Thank you,' I say, before I remember I probably shouldn't speak to him. But he doesn't get angry. Instead, his hand moves from my shoulder to my chin, which he tilts up. He plucks the handkerchief from my fingers and gently wipes my cheeks. I can barely breathe.

'Catherine, look at me,' he says. I can't disobey.

He has kind eyes. I never knew that. They are grey, and soft. He smiles, and I feel that little heat in my chest spread out to every part of my body.

'That's better,' he says. He tucks the handkerchief back inside his jacket. 'Now, Catherine, I need you to help me, and then I can help you.'

I nod, and he smiles more widely. I will do anything for him.

'Good. That's good, Catherine. Now, Amy came to see you earlier, didn't she?' I nod again. 'Great. You're doing really well. Now, Catherine, I need you to tell me exactly what happened when she came to see you. It's very important we find her.'

The Hand of God is waiting for me to answer. 'Nothing happened, really – she just—' What had she said? 'She just wanted to talk to me.'

'About what?'

What had Amy said? It seems ages ago now. I try to remember. I had been so annoyed with her.

I remember the sodden little strip of paper, and the promise I'd made.

I had promised her. I'd promised not to say anything.

But what did I owe her? She was only my blood sister. And she'd got me into trouble. And the Hand of God himself was asking me to help him.

I open my mouth, and stop. The Hand of God nods encouragingly.

'She – she said—'

The Elders know when you're lying. The Hand of God does, too. They can see into your mind and tell if you're hiding things.

I'd promised. I'd promised. And the note she gave me is unreadable, anyway. There is nothing I can tell him, not really.

And she is my blood sister. That means something, even if I'm not sure why.

'She said that she wanted to talk,' I say. 'But I told her that she shouldn't be in the Ablutions Room, and she got annoyed and – went away.' I'm not lying – not exactly. The Hand of God's face is blank. He stands up and turns away. The warm feeling that I'd had when he wiped my tears away seeps out of my body.

'Are you sure that's all that she said, Catherine?' he says, not looking at me. I am gripped by a sudden, desperate desire to tell the truth. To tell him exactly what Amy told me, about the note, about how she was planning to do something, to spill my guts completely – but I find I can't. I can't betray her.

'That's all,' I say in a small voice.

The Hand of God nods to himself, then opens the door of the small cell and leaves without looking at me again, shutting the door quietly but firmly behind him. I feel like my stomach is filling up with freezing, sloshing water.

What have I done?

I try not to remember what happened after the Hand of God left me in the Atonement Room. I haven't seen him or Amy since. It's been months and months. The weather got colder and now it's warmer again, and when I'm working in the kitchen gardens, I have a constant film of sweat between me and my clothes. I haven't been back in the Atonement Room, but I have been constantly in one kind of trouble or another. The latest thing I'm in trouble over is the tomatoes.

Sister Morningbright saw me in the back corner of the greenhouse this afternoon, shoving a tomato into my mouth. I was supposed to be picking them, and I was, but I got hungry – I'm banned from eating for two days as another Atonement, for some other Transgression I can't even remember now – and I wedged myself in what I thought was a blind corner and ate one, then another. I was starting on a third when there was a skewer of pain in my ear, and I was hauled backwards. I was dragged out of the greenhouse, Sister Morningbright's fingers jerking me along by my ear so that I honestly thought she'd tear it straight off.

She made me throw up until nothing came up anymore, then told me to clear all the weeds from the path with my fingers. Everyone else has been in bed for hours now, and I haven't even done half of it. My fingers are sore and stiff, and the entire left side of my head is a glowing ball of pain, radiating out from my ear. I can barely even see the path now the lights from the Nutrition Hall have gone out.

It's only the latest thing. There will be another thing, and another, because I can't seem to stop getting into trouble. There is something wrong with me, and probably with Amy too, because why else would she have run off? She didn't even tell me what she was doing. She didn't even take me with her. That's how worthless I am.

There's steps on the path behind me. Oh, Father. It'll be Sister Morningbright. I'm not even close to done yet. I turn, saying, 'I'm going as fast as I can, Sister—' to see, instead, the tall, dark figure of the Hand of God.

I shut up and drop my head immediately. This is it. This is the moment I will be cast out. I have caused too much trouble, and they are going to get rid of me. Like my stupid, selfish sister, I will never reach the perfect world to come. Why else would the Hand of God come to see me after all this time?

'Catherine.'

I keep my eyes down.

I hear him move forward, then his hand reaches into my field of vision and takes hold of my chin, just like he had in the Atonement Room. He tilts my head up, carefully, until I am looking up at him. He is standing very close, reaching down to me. It is hard to breathe.

'Don't be afraid of me, child,' he says. His thumb strokes from the edge of my lips to my cheekbone. I feel a sort of shiver low in my stomach. He drops his hand. 'Sister Morningbright doesn't like you, does she?'

This is so unexpected that I can't stop my mouth from falling open. 'She knows you're different,' he says.

'Different?' I say stupidly. I have to stop myself from slapping a hand over my mouth.

'She treats you very badly,' he says. He gestures to my ear. I put my hand up to it. The pain had receded in my shock and fear, but now it is throbbing again. 'Let me see,' he says. He takes hold of my hand and lowers himself to his heels. His breath tickles my skin, and I feel that shiver again. His fingers brush against my ear, circle it and come to rest just underneath. 'She has torn the skin a little here,' he says. 'No permanent damage, though, I think.' I look at him, and he at me, and his gaze is as full and as clear as the sky.

Has he forgiven me?

'How would you like to not have to deal with Sister Morningbright again? Or any of them?'

There is a sound behind him and I jump to my feet. He stands up slowly, casual and calm, as Sister Morningbright hovers behind him, gaping. Her gaze drops from him, swings to me. I have a sudden, mad desire to laugh.

'Sister?' he says. There is just the faintest hint of irritation in his voice, as though she has interrupted something important.

'I . . . forgive me, Hand of God, I—' She looks at me, and her eyes go hard. 'Is there some matter to be attended to with this child?'

'It doesn't concern you, Sister.'

Sister Morningbright's mouth opens and closes. Her skin begins to flush, a dark red rising from the line of her collar. 'The . . . the girl . . .'

The Hand of God doesn't say anything. He raises one eyebrow, just the smallest bit, and she deflates.

'I have taken Catherine under my governance, Sister. See that her duties are attended to by some other girl. She belongs to me now.' And with that, he sweeps past her and strides towards the kitchen garden gate.

The Sister gawps after him. I am so taken with seeing her all at sea that I quite forget to follow the Hand of God. I just stare at the woman who has done so much to make my life a misery. Sister Morningbright turns back to me, and the shock on her face gives way to fury.

Nothing in my life so far has given me as much pleasure as what I do next, which is to walk after the Hand of God, straight past Sister Morningbright, and let the garden gate bang shut behind me.

I trot after the Hand of God, who is disappearing down the dark path, away from the Nutrition Hall and all the women's buildings. His words to Sister Morningbright are a bright flame deep in my chest.

She belongs to me now.

10

Now

They'll be coming back soon. Who knows when, exactly? There's no way to tell the time in this cell. If only they'd shut that fucking lightbulb off. The glare of it is burnt onto my eyeballs. And it's so cold in here.

A treacherous little part of me wants Hand to come and get me. Like he did before. Swoop in and rescue me.

Wait. No. That's not right. Hand left me. I was in the Atonement Room after Amy disappeared, shivering in my nightdress, disorientated and confused, trying to process what he was saying about Amy – then I lied to him and he left. He didn't rescue me then. I'm getting mixed up with the other time, the time he came and told me he was taking me away from the Sisters.

It doesn't matter. I don't want Hand to rescue me. He lied. He must have known this would happen. Planned the whole thing. Lured me back with that story about rescuing Amy, convinced me to act like I was rejoining the Children. Pretended he was going to come and get me, take me to her. Stupid. I'm so fucking *stupid*.

I'm going to get out myself. The next time they come. I won't sit through another of their Purifications. I won't let them tell me that what Adi and I had was wrong.

It's so cold in here I can barely think. I just want to sleep.

I can't let myself sleep.

Adi. Adi. Think about Adi.

Her smile was the first thing I noticed about her. So wide and sunny. Infectious. She'd been coming into the Underpass Cafe for a couple of weeks, and I looked forward to seeing her because of her smile and the friendly way she chatted. I loved the fact that she always left a tip of coins stacked neatly by height into a little tower.

One day, one otherwise unimportant Wednesday or Monday, she came in, rushing to get out of the rain, shaking raindrops from her brightly patterned umbrella.

'Bucketing down out there,' I said. My small talk with customers was largely weather based. It was a safe and inexhaustible topic to occupy the gaps around the standard script of what drink they were ordering and the here-you-go-grand-thanks-cheers-now-grand.

Adi grinned. I didn't know her name, then. I thought of her as 'big smile and tip girl'. 'Sure, the wind would blow you off your feet. I only just made it.'

I smiled and started making her black coffee. Meg appeared at my back with a tray of pastries to replenish the morning's ravages.

'Shame it's so rainy anyway. With the screening tonight,' Adi said. I raised my eyebrows, and she nodded at one of the fliers pinned to the board above the coffee machine. I glanced over my shoulder. Open-air film screening, Stephen's Green.

'*Withnail and I*,' I read. 'Were you planning to go see it?'

'Ah, yeah. It's a classic. Be good craic, down there with a picnic blanket and a couple of cans. Don't want to mix your drinks, of course.' She grinned, like someone who had just made a joke. I had learned to pick up on these moments when someone made a joke, even when I didn't get it, so that I could react like I did. I laughed, and Adi grinned even more broadly. Meg started to hum as she shovelled pastries onto the tier.

'Be rained out now, I suppose,' I said, capping the drink and passing it over. She always sat in, but had her drink in a takeaway cup.

Adi shrugged. 'They do these screenings every so often. They might reschedule this one.' She rummaged in her pocket for money. 'Would you fancy it?' she said, nodding at the flier again.

I looked back at the flier, as though it had somehow changed in the minute and a half since I'd last looked at it. 'The screening? Not really my kind of thing.'

A beat, then Adi smiled, but at what seemed a lower wattage than usual. After she'd handed over the money and gone to a table, Meg started wiping down the counter by the cash register.

'I just did that,' I said.

'I know,' she said. 'My cleaning the counter is but a subtle pretext for talking to you.'

'Okay,' I said. Meg carefully buffed an invisible speck.

'Adi's nice, isn't she?' she said.

'Who's Adi?'

Meg sighed. 'The girl you just served, Zoe. Adunni.'

'Adunni?' I'd never heard the name before.

'Lovely name, isn't it? Nigerian. Yoruba. By way of Galway. Adi for short.'

'Oh. Yeah, she's nice. She always leaves a tip.'

'Sign of an excellent person. She works at the gallery down the road. Just moved here a few weeks ago after finishing her degree in art history. Doing a Masters now, so she is. Doesn't know many people, though. She got a cat. I said get a dog, because that way you meet people taking them for walks and whatnot, but she got a cat. What can you do?' Meg addressed this last comment to Madra, the cafe's mascot, who was happily asleep under the counter after being fed into a near coma by the morning customers.

It never failed to amaze me how Meg could know every detail about anyone who came to the cafe. I could just about manage talking about the weather to a few people every day, while she seemed to breezily act as a mixture of psychologist, confidante and confessor to almost everyone who came through the door.

'Right,' I nodded. I wasn't sure why she was telling me about this girl in such detail, but then most things people said were a mystery to me. I tended to nod along until they stopped talking.

'So, Zoe,' said Meg. 'Despite her ignoring my excellent advice about strategic pet ownership, Adi seems like a grand individual who's in need of some companionship.'

'Definitely,' I said.

'Yes.' Meg waited expectantly. I rearranged some napkins, and Meg rubbed one of her eyebrows with her index finger. 'She reminds me of someone,' Meg continued. 'Someone else I know. A grand individual. In need of companionship.'

'Me?'

68

'Ah!' said Meg. 'Light breaks, dawn has come upon us, the slumberer awakens. Yes, Zoe. You. Go on your break.'

'Now?' I looked at the clock. It was only eleven twenty.

'Yes, now. Go take a couple of these delicious cinnamon roll things over and sit at her table and chat to her about the films. And admit to her that you've never seen bloody *Withnail and I*,' she added as I obediently stacked pastries on a plate and skirted around the counter. I was so used to just doing what I was told that I forgot to even be nervous until I got to the table and Adi looked up from her paperback and raised her eyebrows. I could see Meg over her shoulder, who gave me a thumbs up and a big grin.

'I've never seen *Withnail and I*,' I said.

'Oh. Right,' said Adi. Behind her, Meg propped her elbows on the counter and buried her face in her hands.

'Would you like a delicious cinnamon roll thing?' I held out the plate.

Adi grinned broadly. 'Sure, I never say no to a delicious cinnamon roll thing.'

I wonder what Adi is doing now. She'll be living some great life somewhere. She always had it so together. Knew who she was and where she was going. That's one of the things I loved about her. Or didn't love, exactly – it was almost like I wanted that about her. Wanted it for myself. She was so self-assured. There was an Adi-shaped hole in the universe, and she'd stepped right into it. But there was no Catherine-shaped hole.

Jesus. Jesus. *Zoe*. Zoe-shaped hole. My name is Zoe.

One – My name is Zoe
Two – I have made a terrible mistake
Three – Fuck Amy, fuck everything, I need to leave
Four –

What's a fourth? Come on. Come on.

Adi. Adi is a true thing. Adi and I were a true thing. And I won't let them make me believe otherwise.

11

THEN

It is raining so hard that it feels like thousands of tiny rocks are pummelling my back. The ground is so wet and muddy that my hands have sunk into it almost up to the wrists. I can't feel them anymore. They ached with the cold at first, but now they are just lumps of numb, useless meat at the end of my arms. I lower my body down once more, feeling my T-shirt and shorts sop into the muddy rainwater. They are heavy with it, hanging away from my body so that the wind rages under them and rakes along my skin. I push myself back up.

My arms are rotten, brittle twigs that are ready to snap. I just want to stop. I want to let myself fall down on the ground and let the mud well up over my face. But I can't. I have to keep doing the press-ups until Elder Thomas comes back for me.

I lower myself again. My toes – long ago gone numb, like my hands – have sunk into the mud, and skate backwards so that I lose my balance and crash down onto my left side. Freezing water splashes up inside my clothes, and I rest my head on my forearm and catch a sob in my throat. How long have I been doing this?

The swelling around my eye feels tight and stiff, hot despite the cold rain. I touch it, and there is a flare of pain that streaks down the side of my face and into my teeth. I feel sick. I would be sick, but there's nothing in my stomach. I retch anyway. The ground tilts and I dig my fingers into the mud, hold on as the world wheels around me.

I tip over and lie on my back. Rain sheets across my face. I open my mouth and let some of the water fall in. I can feel the freezing mud cake the back of my freshly shaved head.

A thud on my side registers dully. I open my eyes and squint against the rain to see one of the Warriors pull his leg back and deliver another kick to my ribs. I'm so numb I feel the impact, but no pain.

Another face looms into view. His mouth is open. Shouting something. I have to concentrate to hear it over the wind.

'Get up, abomination!'

I raise myself up on my elbows, but my arms give out and I fall back into the mud. Hands reach down and snatch me up, pulling my collar, my arms, dragging me over the exercise field over to the shelter of the Pavilion. They let me go and I stumble, my knees scraping on the concrete. It's a little quieter here, away from the scream of the wind. The rain drums relentlessly on the roof. Shadows move and gather around me, and I realise that I am surrounded by all fifteen of the Warriors in my troop. Boys' faces, with shaved heads like mine, wearing shorts and T-shirts like mine. But they are clean and only a little rain-wet, while I am soaking and filthy.

'I'm . . . I'm supposed to—' I begin.

'We know, abomination,' says Caleb. He is the Corporal of our troop. Troop 16. The only troop in the Warriors to have an abomination among their number.

One of the boys raps on the back of my head. 'Stand to attention when the Corporal is addressing you, abomination.'

I drag myself to my feet. Caleb, easily a foot taller than me, regards me with disgust. 'Elder Thomas said you can stop now.' I feel a wave of exhaustion. Thank Father. 'But he said that your effort was so pathetic that you'll have to do the push-ups after training tomorrow night too. During dinner. Again.'

The boys laugh. My throat tightens and a buzzing, rushing sound rises in my ears. I make fists. Caleb notices and laughs.

'You want to go again, abomination?' He lifts his eyebrows at the assembled Warriors, who hoot with laughter. Caleb points to my swollen eye. 'You were lucky that that was all you got. If Elder Thomas hadn't made me stop . . .'

I want to tear his throat out. But Caleb is much, much stronger than me. During combat training today, he knocked me to the ground, pinned my shoulders with his knees and rained a flurry of quick, hard jabs down on my face in under three seconds. I didn't stand a chance. But Elder Thomas still punished my 'lack of effort' with push-ups instead of dinner.

'I'm so sick of her being in our troop,' mutters one of the boys behind me.

'It's not a *her*,' Caleb says. 'It's an *it*, remember?' More laughter.

Tears prickle my eyes. But it would be unthinkable to cry in front of them. I push out from the circle of boys and head for my quarters, which are not the same as theirs. A volley of outraged shouts swell behind me. Running feet, then I am knocked forward, my hands and knees scraping against the concrete of the Pavilion floor. Boys fall on top of me, crushing my breath out, pinning down my legs, my arms.

'You weren't dismissed, abomination!'

'We haven't given you permission to leave!'

'It thinks it can do what it wants!'

I struggle, but it's no use. I can't move under the suffocating weight of the boys. My face is pressed painfully into the concrete. I wrench my head to the side and gasp in air.

'Move – move!' Caleb's voice. He sounds excited – delighted, almost. 'Hold it! Hold it down!' The weight on top of me shifts, moves to my shoulders. A hand pushes the side of my head, forcing it to stay pressed onto the ground.

Something has changed in the air behind me. There isn't any talking, just panting and rustling that I barely hear over the drumming of the rain. Then a new pressure – someone lying on my back. Hot breath on the back of my neck. Hands scrabbling at my shorts. I try to reach behind me, knock the hands away, but my arms are pinned and fingers dig into my wrists.

A voice, quiet, panicked. 'Caleb—'

'Shut up! Shut up.' Caleb's voice, behind me. His hands tug at my shorts again. The material is wet, stuck to my skin. He is panting, speaking in short bursts. 'I'm going to . . . going to teach it a lesson—'

His hand worms down under the waistband of my shorts, scrapes along my skin. A bone-deep panic fills me, and I buck and twist, try to push the boys off me. They press down harder, holding me down. I open my mouth and scream.

'Shut it up!' Caleb hisses. He pulls my shorts down. I feel the soaked material as it is dragged along my skin and bunches at the tops of my thighs. I scream again, and a hand clamps over my mouth. And then something pushes against me, something hard and hot. I scream against the hand over my mouth, so loud and long that my throat tears apart. The something hard is pushing and pushing between my legs, and it hurts . . .

All at once, the pressure on me lifts, and I am free. The hands are gone from my mouth and my body, and Caleb's awful weight leaves my back. I feel cold air across my backside, and I reach back and frantically tug my shorts up. There is something wet there. When I pull my hand back, I see red.

A voice, cold and furious. 'Get. Up.'

I get to my feet. My whole body is shaking. I feel small inside. I don't know what just happened to me, but I feel small – so small – and sick. Something very, very wrong happened. I want to scour the skin from my body, I want to tear furrows in my scalp with my fingernails, I want to tuck myself into a ball in a corner somewhere and scream and scream.

The boys are standing back, looking chastened. Caleb is tucking his T-shirt back into his shorts. The sight of him turns me to water.

A hand on my shoulder spins me around. I flinch and shrink away from it. I don't want anyone to touch me, ever again.

It is Elder Thomas. He glares at me. 'What do you think you're doing?'

I can't say anything. I don't understand what he's asking. What was I doing?

The Elder pushes his face close to mine. I take a step back, without meaning to. 'I'm asking you a question, Acolyte. What do you think you're doing?'

There are no words inside me. He sighs, a rush of hot, exasperated air, and lifts his gaze to the boys behind me. 'Well? Corporal, perhaps you can enlighten me?'

'I . . . I don't know, Elder.' His voice, everything about him, makes my skin creep from my bones. 'It – the Acolyte – was mocking us, mocking you, saying that the Atonement you gave it was stupid – and we knew we needed to stop it – teach it its place—'

I should defend myself, but I can't. I just watch the Elder as he nods and lifts a hand to cut Caleb off. 'I see,' he says. He turns back to me, and his eyes are full of disgust. 'You are an abomination, Acolyte. Far be it from me to question the orders of the Hand of God, but your presence here makes a mockery of the Father-given mission of the Warriors. We have tolerated you – your incompetence, your deviancy, your distraction – but we cannot be expected to tolerate your disrespect. Apologise. Apologise for your disrespect, and apologise for tempting them.'

My head is full of the roar of the rain on the roof. 'Tempting them?' I repeat.

'Look at yourself!' Elder Thomas bellows. I flinch. 'Look at you!'

I look down at myself. My sopping wet T-shirt and shorts cling to my skin. The T-shirt, white where it isn't streaked with mud, has gone see-through. I can see my chest wrap through it. I look up at Elder Thomas. My hands automatically cross over my chest.

'Transgressive,' he says. There is something other than disgust in the way he is looking at me, something that was present as well in Caleb's hot, excited voice as he told the boys to hold me down. I am flayed, exposed under that gaze.

'Transgressive,' he repeats, his eyes running up and down my body, but never alighting on my face. 'A Transgressive temptation.' Tears rise, and, this time, I can't stop them spilling out and down my cheeks. Elder Thomas grabs my shoulders and twists me around so I'm forced to look at the boys. They are faceless blurs through a shimmering film.

'Apologise to them.' The Elder's fingers dig into my neck.

'I . . . I'm—' A sob breaks my voice. The Elder shakes me. 'I'm sorry,' I say. He shakes me again, harder. 'I'm sorry!' I repeat. 'I'm sorry, I'm sorry, I'm—' I'm crying too much to speak. I barely register the Elder dismissing the boys, who file away silently. When I next open my eyes, I am alone in the Pavilion. Elder Thomas is gone. The rain has stopped.

I go back to my room. It is on the far side of the Warrior Barracks, but I can't make myself walk past them. I go the long way, past the kitchen gardens and the dark, silent Nutrition Hall, around the looming Fruitfulness Hall, taking stiff, painful step after step, until I reach the private residence of the Hand of God. A self-contained set of rooms with its own entrance, it is in the east wing of the Elders' House.

I go in through the dark back corridor to my little room. It is on the ground floor, a windowless box room only a little bigger than my narrow bed. It is dark upstairs – I don't think the Hand of God is here. I haven't seen him in weeks, although I do hear him sometimes, moving around in his room above mine late at night, or slamming the front door as he leaves in the early hours.

I take my washbag from the hook behind my door and lock myself in the small Ablutions Room. Clean. I need to get clean. Clean and warm. It'll be okay if I can just get clean and warm.

I don't look in the mirror. I don't want to meet my eyes. I'll be okay if I can just get clean.

I strip off my sodden clothes. A sudden, sickening flash as I pull my shorts down – hands scrabbling, hot breath, hold it down, hold it down – but I keep moving and it goes as quickly as it came. I turn the shower on and open my washbag while the water heats up. I need soap . . .

My searching hands find and pull out my hairbrush. I stare at it. It is blue plastic, with a round rubber handle and black bristles. Some of my hair, a dull, mousy brown, is caught in its teeth. I laugh. I don't mean to. But then I laugh again. Why have I kept this?

The Hand of God shaved my head when he brought me here, when he first took me away from the Sisters and installed me in his residence, told me I'd be joining Troop 16. He told me to collect anything I needed from the dormitory, then took me to his quarters, where he gave me a new room, and new clothes, and a new name. He told me I belonged to him now. He cut off my hair and shaved what was left down to bristles.

So why in Father's name did I keep my hairbrush?

I know why, of course.

Anger streams over me and I clench my fist around the brush. I raise it and throw it as hard as I can into the corner, and I kick the washbag away from me too, the old, worn bag with the ghost of unpicked stitches spelling out a name that isn't mine anymore, then I crumple on the tiles, arms around my head, and I sob and sob.

When I stop crying, the little room has filled with steam from the shower. I feel hollowed out. The automatic part of my brain takes over again, and like a mechanism that has been wound up and set to go I stand up, pick up my washbag, look around for the hairbrush. It's lying in two pieces in the corner, the rubber handle broken away from the bristles. I pick both up, and out of old habit I look inside the hollow of the handle, where Amy used to leave me her notes. But that wasn't me, of course. That was Catherine. The Hand of God explained that I was never really Catherine. I amwaswillalwaysbe his Acolyte, his instrument, and I am not a girl or a boy, I am an it, and I don't have any blood family . . .

There is a note inside the handle.

I stare at it, the little ball of white paper. Had I – had Catherine – left an old note in there? Or – this possibility stops my heart – is it a new note? One I've never read?

Like someone in a dream, I slowly and carefully prise the note out. My clumsy fingers make it difficult, but I get it out and smooth the paper. Remembering how the last note from Amy had got wet and been unreadable, I hold only the tiniest corner of it. There, on the paper, is her handwriting. Tiny blocky letters, skewing across the lines of the page as they always did, then a long, incomprehensible number.

The Phoenix Initiative
07729476183

What in Father's name does it mean? I've never seen the word 'phoenix' before, which looks unpronounceable, and I've read almost every book the Hand of God has in his library. And what is that long number? None of it makes any sense. Why did Amy leave me this nonsense?

A burst of rage again. I want to slam this useless scrap of paper down into the pool of water collecting on the tiles. I want to smash it against the floor and rip it to shreds. She could have left me anything, anything at all – the reason she left, where she had gone, why she hadn't told me what she was planning – but she just left these nonsense words and a string of random numbers. Nothing. Nothing that can help me.

I should show this to the Hand of God. Confess properly about what happened that night in the Ablutions Room. Make up for the time I lied to him about it.

I owe her nothing. She was Catherine's blood sister, after all. She is nothing to the Acolyte.

I imagine handing the note to him, explaining where I found it. He'd be pleased, so pleased that he wouldn't be angry that I'd lied to him before.

He'd known that I was lying, of course. They always know. The Elders and the Hand of God. They can tell what's in your head. I'd been punished for it, and I'd continued to be punished for months and months. Then, that night in the kitchen garden, he'd come for me. Brought me here. Changed every part of me into something else. Then left me alone.

Maybe if I showed him the note he'd talk to me again. He'd tell me what in Father's name I'm supposed to be doing here with him.

I see it, like it's happening in the air in front of me. I hand him the paper, show him the broken brush. He reads the paper, smiles. Reaches out and touches my cheek, like he hasn't in so long. He tells me that Father will be so happy that I've discovered some-thing that will help them find Amy. He smiles at me with his kind grey eyes.

The last remaining scrap of Catherine, of who I was, is burnt away with that smile. He walks away, holding Amy's last message to me, and only the Acolyte is left.

I breathe out, a long, steady stream of air, and I clutch the slip of paper in my fist.

12

Now

Meg had patiently coached me for my first outing with Adi. I'd been asked to a film and a drink afterwards.

'You're not wearing that,' said Meg flatly.

'What's wrong with this?' I said.

'It's your work T-shirt, Zoe,' Meg said. 'You can't be wearing your work T-shirt out on a . . . out to the films.'

'Why not?' I frowned down at it. Black, printed with the Underpass Cafe logo of a book and a gently steaming cup of coffee, it was soft and comfortably shapeless from many washings. It was my favourite piece of clothing.

'You just can't. What else have you got?'

I thought. I had two pairs of jeans, one of which I was currently wearing, three Underpass Cafe tops (two T-shirts and one sleeveless one for hot days, which I hadn't ever quite brought myself to wear) and a grey hoodie I wore to and from work.

'Nothing else, really.'

Meg looked at me with her head on one side. We were in the back room, drinking a last cup of tea before locking up. She had her feet up on a box of unsorted books, one arm thrown across the back of the sofa. I was sitting on the broad windowsill, curled up on the cushion I kept there for that purpose. It was my favourite nook.

'Zoe, what do you wear when you're not working?'

'My pyjamas?'

79

Meg pursed her lips. 'You're on afternoon shift tomorrow, aren't you? Meet me in front of Trinity at ten. We're going to do a bit of shopping.'

Fatima was there with Meg next morning when I arrived at the university gates. Although it was early, the place was already getting busy with tourists, milling around the arched entrance and posing for selfies. It was spring – still too cold to go around in short sleeves, but warm enough that the green pitches around the back of the university would be peppered with people having their lunch outside in a couple of hours. Fatima waved when she saw me, looking a little embarrassed.

'Meg asked me along,' she said. 'Hey, Zoe.'

'Hey,' I said shyly. Fatima was new, but already knew the place better than half the other students we had working there. She was crisp and efficient and I thought she would likely be running the world someday. I was a little in awe of her, even though she was younger than me.

'Sure I dunno what the young wans is wearing these days,' said Meg, ramping up her accent. 'Teema is here in a special advisory capacity.'

Fatima looked at me and shrugged. 'Any excuse for a bit of a shop. C'mon.'

By the third shop, I felt like crying. Fatima kept saying with increasing desperation, 'This? Do you like this, Zoe?' and I'd shrug and mumble something and stare at my scuffed trainers while Fatima and Meg looked at each other. I didn't know what to do with all these clothes. They were bright and patterned and there were so many different styles. I just wanted to wear my T-shirt. I liked my T-shirt.

Eventually, in a shop so dizzyingly big that it was like a ware-house, Fatima steered me into a curtained-off cubicle with a little bench inside it and told me to wait there. I sat, avoiding my gaze in the mirror and burning with embarrassment. Fatima was so willowy and elegant – she even made the Underpass Cafe T-shirt look stylish. She wore it with black trousers that clung to her legs, or a short skirt with brightly coloured tights, or jeans that were like mine except with rips in them that were somehow cool, rather than things to be mended carefully. I would never look like her. This whole thing was a waste of time.

Fatima brushed back the curtain and swung in, dumping a pile of clothes in my lap. 'I feel like what you need is more of a personal shopper sort of experience,' she said, tucking her hair behind her ears. 'So I'm going to bring you things to try on, and you let me know what you think.'

I looked down at the pile of fabrics in my arms. I felt like panicking. Did she want me to change in front of her?

'Zoe?' I looked up. Fatima glanced over her shoulder, then tugged the curtain back across the cubicle opening. It was in a corridor of similar cubicles, and although we were still technically in that huge, busy shop, it was quiet and calm in here. The thick carpet muffled footsteps, and the people in the other cubicles talked in softer voices than they did outside.

Fatima knelt down next to me. 'Listen. It's okay to be a bit anxious about it all. Before I came to uni, you should have seen me. I wore, like, the worst stuff. Like big shapeless T-shirts and baggy joggers and that. I had these thick plastic hairbands in, like, a variety of hideous neon colours, and I swear to God, for a while I wore two of them at once. I thought it was like a unique fashion statement or something. I looked like I was wearing a safety helmet.'

'But you're so . . . you know—' I waved a hand at her.

'What? I dress well?'

'Yeah.'

'D'you know how I learnt how to dress like this?' said Fatima. 'Honestly, now.' She settled herself back on her heels. 'And you're not to go telling anyone this. I got this fashion magazine, right, out of my older sister's room, and I picked one of the models that I liked the look of and I bought the entire outfit she was wearing. Not the actual stuff: the high-street version, you know?' I nodded like I understood. 'And then I did the same with a couple of other ones. I had, like, three outfits for going to uni. So I turned up here and any time I saw a girl in lectures or in town or whatever who looked good, I went and got something like what she was wearing. And then eventually I just sort of . . . evolved my own style.' She shrugged one shoulder. 'Sure, all the best artists learn by copying.'

I smiled and felt a little better. 'It's okay to be anxious and that, Zoe,' she said. 'And you don't have to get anything you don't want, or that doesn't make you feel good. You can try these on, and then not show me if you'd rather not. No pressure, all right?'

I nodded. She stood up and smacked the pile of clothes in my arms. 'Get those on you.' She swung out of the cubicle, and I pulled the first item out of the pile. A soft grey T-shirt. I smiled.

Half an hour later, I walked out of the shop weighed down by two carrier bags of new clothes. Meg had insisted on paying, and, when I protested, said she'd take it out of me in unwaged overtime. Her eyes had been bright, so I knew it was a joke.

Fatima left, waving over her shoulder as she slipped into the stream of tourists and office workers out for lunch. She had picked out three new T-shirts for me – the grey one, a white one and a stripy blue one – a pair of black jeans with cool rips, and a sort of light, floaty scarf thing. When I pointed out that it wouldn't do anything to keep me warm, she told me that that wasn't the point, and arranged it around my neck to hang in wide loops. 'It completes your look,' she informed me.

In the other bag, I had something that made my heart race. A dress. It was brightly patterned, low cut and not very long at all. Fatima had seen my expression and added a thick pair of purple tights, which helped, but it was still such a risky piece of clothing. Looking in the mirror (with the curtain firmly drawn across) and turning side to side, I saw myself and thought I looked . . . like a girl. A normal girl.

'You're pretty, you know, Zoe,' Fatima had said, slinging the scarf around my shoulders and fiddling with it ('It's a versatile piece'). 'Here, look.' Gently, she pulled away the band holding back my unruly hair. She gathered some of it up and lifted it to the top of my head, leaving strands to frame my face. 'See, you look so nice like this. It just takes a bit of styling, you know?'

It's what girls wear, I thought. Fatima knows this stuff. It's what you wear when you're a girl, and going out.

Walking back to the cafe, Meg strolling beside me, the bags bumping against my legs, I felt a strange, light sensation. A sort of internal lifting. I'm happy, I realised. I feel happy.

I wondered what Adi would make of my clothes, and the light feeling inside expanded to fill every part of me.

If only I could turn that fucking lightbulb off. I'd smash it if I could, but it's inside a cage on the ceiling. And there's nothing in here to use as a weapon.

If I'm going to get out, I'll have to take them by surprise. I can do it. I have a plan.

The door opens inwards, which means I can stand behind it out of sight. I can push it hard when they next come in. There's always at least two of them. If I push hard enough, the door should smack the one in front hard enough to knock them back into the other. If I'm quick, I can run out and push past both of them before they know what's happening. The Atonement Room is in the basement of the women's building, so there's a long, narrow staircase leading to the ground floor at the far end of this corridor. They don't lock the door at the top of the stairs – why would they when the Atonement Room is locked already? So if I'm fast enough, I can get past them and up the stairs and out of the building. Outside. I'll run to the woods beside the building, disappear into them. Climb over the boundary wall. Get away.

I haven't eaten in . . . I'm not sure. I was hungry, but then I stopped being hungry, in that way you do when you haven't eaten for so long that your stomach stops really registering it. But I feel like smoke – as though I'll disappear if someone so much as waves a hand at me. How can I knock over two people and run out of here when I feel like I'll pass out just from standing?

I can't think like that. I can do this. I have to. I can't stay locked in here anymore.

The Purifications. They put out a table with paper and a pen and instructed me to describe anything Adi and I ever did together. They ordered me to kneel on the floor of the cell, and Innocence sat in the chair they brought in for her and told me in that calm, reasonable voice how Transgressive I've been. I refused at first, but then they brought the buckets of cold water in, and one of the Guards wrapped my hair around his fist and held it so tight that I couldn't pull away, and kept my face under the water until I was sure my lungs would explode, and then they let me out long enough to gasp in some air, then they did it again and again, and even when I said that I'd do what they wanted, whatever they wanted, they kept at it.

When they finally finished and I was gulping in air, feeling like my chest was full of broken glass, the Guard held my jaw in one hand, my hair in the other, and hauled me up to look at Innocence in her chair. I couldn't stop shaking. The Guard's body pressed against my back caused an old, sickly, familiar terror to rise in me. Innocence looked at me over the top of her oh-granny-what-big-teeth-you-have half-moon glasses and smiled. 'You really must co-operate with us, Catherine,' she said gently. 'Father just wants your soul to be free of Transgressions. To be Pure again, a Pure and fertile soil for His cultivation.' She leaned forward, flicked her eyes over my shoulder, and I felt the Guard push himself against me. 'We don't want it to come to this, Catherine, but you should be aware that there are other ways to Purify a female of these unnatural impulses.'

I haven't refused again. I'm not brave. I'm not a hero. I don't even know about Amy anymore. I just want to get out. I just want to go home.

I don't know when they'll next come, but I have to be ready. I have to wait behind the door and be ready.

The night that Adi had arranged to meet me, I wore the risky dress and the floaty scarf, and almost immediately regretted it.

I stood awkwardly near the gates to the park, trying to look as though I wasn't desperately scanning the faces of everyone nearby. The film screening had been rescheduled to the following weekend, and it was chilly but dry. There was a steady stream of people into the park, clutching picnic blankets and clinking carrier bags, laughing and talking loudly in their little groups. The wind caught a few strands of my hair and blew it into my face. I pushed it out of the way. I hadn't gone for the style Fatima suggested – I had limits – but I'd at least dragged a brush through it and left it loose, which was a big departure from my usual ponytail.

I felt stiff and uncomfortable in the dress with my hair down. I kept tugging at the hemline, trying to stretch it a bit further to my knees. This was a mistake. She wasn't going to meet me, and I felt so wrong in these clothes, and . . .

'Zoe!' I turned, and there she was, waving and threading her way through the crowd. Relief washed over me. Adi pointed at the ticket booth, and I moved forward to meet her at the end of the queue.

'You're looking well!' she said. When I first got to Dublin, I thought that when people said this they meant I appeared in good health, but it actually means that they think you look nice. I tugged at the dress again.

'I . . . yes. I mean. Thanks?' I said. She laughed.

'I like your hair like that. God, I didn't realise it was so long!'

'Oh . . . yeah.' I shoved it away from my neck. 'Yeah, it is . . . long.'

Meg had patiently schooled me in how to do small talk. Her lessons were mainly to do with how to talk to customers, but it was all talk, wasn't it? One thing she'd mentioned was that if someone compliments you, it's good to compliment them back on something. I looked at Adi, who was wearing pretty much what she always wore. A thick overcoat and brightly coloured glasses. Jeans. God, I wished I had worn jeans.

'That's a nice . . . necklace,' I said. She looked pleased. She touched the green and white charm hanging around her neck.

'Ah, this? Thanks – my mammy gave it to me.'

I nodded. 'Cool,' I said. 'Cool' is a useful filler word. It covers most eventualities, except when someone tells you something sad. I tried to think of something to add. 'Do your parents live in Dublin?'

'No, Mammy and Daddy are in Galway, with my sisters.'

'Oh, yeah?' I said, which is another useful filler.

'I brought us a blanket,' said Adi, half lifting a rolled bundle under her arm. 'And I've a couple of bits in the bag here, look—'

She shrugged her backpack onto one shoulder and unzipped it for me to peer in. 'I didn't know if you'd want cans or what, so I got water as well and some oranges.'

'I should have brought something,' I said, panicking.

'Ah here, no worries. I've enough, sure.'

I was saved from trying to think of something else to say because we reached the front of the line and had to negotiate the whole ticket-buying process. I bought Adi's, over her protests, because she'd brought the food and the blanket. She told me not to, but I knew that it was okay to do it anyway because she said no in the way that people in the Underpass Cafe do when they're with friends and one gets the bill. They say 'ah, no, ah now you won't, don't be daft, here I'll get it, don't you dare', and sometimes it seems quite heated, but actually it's all part of being polite. I didn't get it at first, but, after seeing it several times a day for a few years, I had developed quite a good handle on the whole weird social dance of who's-paying-the-bill. The better you're friends, the more you protest.

We got ourselves settled on the blanket on a spot at the edge of the crowd. It was getting dark, but the park was lit with strings of glowing yellow bulbs, and bright lanterns sat around the screen at the front. As we waited for the film to start, Adi chatted comfortably about her job, and her cat, and Cork where she'd studied, and her family, and other open-air screenings and gigs she'd been to, and I was happy to sit and nod and take it all in. She didn't seem to expect me to talk much, which was a relief. I was just sort of in awe about how easy she found it to chatter so endlessly, and so entertainingly.

I don't remember much about the film. It was funny, except I didn't get a lot of the jokes, and a lot of the time the crowd was chattering or shouting out lines from the film instead of listening quietly like in the cinema, so I didn't follow much of the plot. I didn't mind, though. I felt lit up inside, like one of the lanterns, by being out and with a friend and taking part in something so unlike my usual life. The glowing feeling lingered as I strolled to the bus stop with Adi, managing to contribute to her chatter here and there. The feeling flared when she put her number into my phone and mentioned a band she wanted to see the following week ('You should come too, you'd like them!'). It lasted as I got the bus home by myself, and went into my little flat alone, and wrapped myself in my blanket in my cold bed.

I have a friend, I thought. I have a friend, and I was out with them tonight. I'm seeing them again next week. I have a friend.

I went to sleep, wrapped around that warm little coal of a thought.

They unlock the door. I've been so lost in my own head that I barely have time to register the *chunk-clunk* of the key turning in the lock before I remember what I'm planning to do. I'm already in position, so all I have to do is press my back into the wall and hold my hands up in front of me like I'm warding off an attacker.

The door swings in towards me, and I push it back as hard as I can. There is a jarring thump along my arms as it slams into the person on the other side.

I lurch around the door and there is a confusion of arms and legs and shouts as I tangle with whoever is there and we fall-scramble-fight into the corridor. My head is stuffed with clouds, and my vision greys over as I push myself to my feet and crawl-pull-stagger forward.

The door at the top of the stairs is open. There's no one between me and it.

My foot is tugged, sharp, and I'm winded as I hit the floor. Hands claw up my legs and dig into my arms as I'm lifted-dragged-hauled up and thrown-pushed-heaved back into the cell. My head connects with the floor and I want to get up, to throw myself at the door before they can get it closed, but nothing is working at the speed it's supposed to and it's all I can do to pull myself onto one elbow as the door is slammed shut and *clunk-chunk* locked and I've failed, I've failed, I've failed to get out.

I'm hitting the door with my fists and screaming. I don't remember getting up from the floor, but I'm leaning against the door and my throat is raw from screaming. I slide down to my knees, black spots crowding out my vision. There is a line of light under the door. Voices snatch at my ears from the other side.

'—clearly not working.'

'—stricter measures need to be—'

'—by the grace of Father, we will—'

'Bring me the Hand of God!' I didn't mean to say it, but I'm screaming it at the door. 'Bring me the Hand of God! Bring me the Hand of God!'

I listen, but it's quiet outside. The line of light under the door is gone. How long has it been dark outside? How long have I been yelling?

How long have I been in here?

How long am I going to be in here?

13

THEN

I don't get out of bed the morning after the night I discovered Amy's message. It's the first time I've ever not risen at the distant tolling of the Rising Bell, and it should feel terrifying to disobey that call. But I don't feel terrified. I don't feel anything at all.

I turn over in my narrow bed and stare at the wall. Grey light creeps in from under the door, and I can hear, far off, the noise of people beginning the day.

I should be washing and dressing now. I should be putting on my uniform and going to muster with the Warriors by the Pavilion in about ten minutes. I should be standing shoulder to shoulder with the boys in my unit and keeping my face still and blank as they jostle and jab and kick me while the Elders pretend not to see.

They'll notice I'm missing fairly soon. Will they send someone to get me?

I'm not worried about that. They can't get in here. No one is allowed in the Hand of God's private rooms apart from me and him. Not even the Elders. So if they want me, they have to get the Hand of God to get me out.

Good luck to them. I haven't seen him in weeks.

I shift in bed and my ribs let out a kick of pain. My vision blurs for a moment, black clouding in from the sides then fading back. I bite the inside of my cheeks until it is over.

Last night . . .

Abruptly, a black curtain is pulled across my mind. My thought stops as though the curtain has cut it in half.

Last night I . . .

The black curtain stays. I can't complete the thought. I probe at it, like you push at a sore tooth with the tip of your tongue. I try to bring up images from last night, and all at once I am lying, cold from the rain, with the weight of panting boys pinning me down. I push myself up in bed and the cold and the weight vanishes, but the room I am in, already small, is shrinking. The wall behind my bed slides soundlessly towards me. I watch it, my heart wild. I put a hand out and feel the rough brick smack against my palm. My arm is fully extended, I can see that, I can see that my elbow doesn't bend in with the oncoming movement of the wall, but still I can see the wall moving closer.

What is happening to me?

I have gone mad.

It takes every scrap of courage I have to close my eyes, when all I want to do is scramble out of bed and run for the door. But I do close my eyes, and I keep my palm pressed to the wall, and I can feel that it isn't moving. It isn't moving. I don't know what's happening, but somehow my mind is playing tricks on me. The wall is not getting any closer.

I force myself to breathe in and out slowly. In. Out. In. The brick is cool and textured under my palm. Out. In. I can feel the narrow dips between bricks, where the cement is. Out. In. There is a chipped edge, right under my index finger. Out. I press on it, the sharp little edge, and the spike of pain cuts through my panic. I press my finger on it again, concentrating on that sharp clear pain, and pushing everything else away.

When I open my eyes, the wall stays where it is. I shuffle backwards on my bed until I reach the end, keeping my eyes trained on the wall like it is a dog about to attack. I get to the door without it beginning that awful silent slide towards me once more.

I go to the shower. I want to wash again.

The Hand of God finds me in his library, practising my writing. It's one of the tasks he's given me to do in his absence, to sit with an exercise book open in front of me and copy out the books in his library. I don't know why he wants me to do this, but then I don't know why he wants me to do anything.

A couple of times over the last two days I have caught the walls beginning to move in towards me again. Each time, I resist the urge to flee (because where would I go?) and I stand, eyes closed, my left hand against the wall, digging the sharp fingernail of my right thumb into the soft skin of my left wrist. I concentrate on the pain and stillness of the wall until my breath and heart calm down, then I open my eyes and get on with whatever I'm doing.

In the past forty-eight hours, I've found a lot to do in this set of rooms. I'm allowed access to my box room, the small Ablutions Room, the kitchen and the library. I have scrubbed every inch of the Ablutions Room. There are machines for washing and drying clothes in the kitchen, smaller than the ones in the laundry where I (where Catherine) used to work occasionally, so I have washed and dried all of my clothing and bedding. I have polished my boots to a brilliant shine, scoured the kitchen (which was already gleaming, as it's entirely unused by either me or the Hand of God) and dusted every surface in the library. I have performed all the sit-ups and push-ups that my glowing body can tolerate. There is nothing here to eat, but I don't want to anyway. I feel hollowed out, clean and empty. My stomach doesn't even rumble anymore. I have memorised two pages of *Preparations for the Perfect World to Come*, and I have copied out three pages of *The Life of Father* in my exercise book in careful, neat handwriting. No one has come for me. No Elders have banged on the door and demanded I come out. There have been no shouted orders, no painful reprisals. It has been quiet and calm and, despite the pain and the creeping horror of the walls moving in on me at times, in some ways I have not felt so at ease ever in my life. Living in the Hand of God's residence has meant that I've had a room with a door I can close, and an Ablutions Room with a door I can lock if I want, but now I've realised I have all this space to myself as well. No one is going to dare to come in here except for the Hand of God and me. I am safe.

I am sitting at my little desk in the corner of the library. There is a larger desk in front of the window, for the Hand of God. There is a fireplace on one wall, and another wall holds a set of bookshelves, dark shiny wood to match the room's panelling. There are seventeen books on those shelves, the largest number of books I have ever seen. It's embarrassing to admit it, but until the Hand of God showed me his library, I thought that the Scriptures, which I (which *Catherine*) used to copy out in lessons with Sister Morningbright, was the only book that existed. I'd never seen any others. But of course Father has written more.

It's late afternoon, but it is still bright enough to work in here without turning the lamps on. The sun has painted orange bars across the room, and it's warm in their light. I have almost finished the page I am working on from *The Life of Father* when the door handle clicks and the Hand of God steps into the room.

I push my chair back and stand to attention. The Hand of God's eyes flicker when he sees me, but his face stays still. I know what I must look like. I've avoided looking in the mirror, but I can feel the tight, puffy skin around my left eye, and the tender patches where bruises have spread across my cheek and forehead.

He regards me steadily. I stay at attention, like he's taught me.

'Who?' he says eventually.

'Corporal Caleb.' The name feels like hot breath on my neck and weight on my back until the black curtain falls and cuts the sensations off.

The Hand of God nods. He crosses the room, sits in his chair. 'Elder Thomas tells me it was a fight. That the Corporal was reprimanding your lack of diligence and you attacked him.'

The unfairness of it registers, but only dully, like thumps on numb skin.

'Is that what happened, Acolyte?'

What to say? I shouldn't contradict an Elder. But I can't lie to the Hand of God. Not again, not to his face.

'No, Hand of God.' He nods, but doesn't look at me or speak. I think this means I should continue, but I can't get any more words out. I open and close my mouth like a fish.

'Tell me exactly what Caleb did, Acolyte,' he says into the silence. I twist my hands into fists behind my back. Mortifyingly, tears jab at my eyes. I take a deep breath, then another. He waits.

'I was returning to your quarters when . . . the Corporal and the other boys knocked me down. They held me down and—' I stop. The terrible weight is on my back again, forcing the breath from my lungs.

'And?' The Hand of God waits.

'And . . . then the Corporal . . . he . . . he told the others to—' I grind to a halt again. I can't say it. I can't. I remember how Elder Thomas told me I'd tempted the boys, and I want to wrap my arms around myself, hide under the covers, huddle under the scalding water of the shower. Anything but admit what happened out loud to the only person who cares about me.

But does he care about you? a sour little voice bubbles up in my head. *Does he care? He left. He left you to fend for yourself, and he hasn't told you anything.*

I push it away. If he doesn't care about me, who does? Certainly not Amy. She left me/Catherine. The Hand of God came back. He took me away from the Sisters. He gave me a new life.

I close my eyes and it all comes out in a rush. 'The Corporal told the others to hold me down and then he pulled down my shorts and he leant on me and sort of pushed at me and . . . and I was injured.'

I open my eyes. The light from the sun is behind him, lighting up the strands of his hair so he looks almost like he's glowing. I wait, my heart thumping.

'Injured in what way?' he says finally.

I cast about. There's no word for that part of the body. 'Injured . . . injured under my shorts,' I say.

The Hand of God gets to his feet with a screech of chair legs and comes towards me. I feel the edge of my little desk bump into the backs of my thighs as I retreat.

'Under your shorts,' he says. It's not a question, but I nod.

'Show me,' he says.

I can't stop my mouth from dropping open. I want to take another step back, but there is nowhere to go.

'I . . . I can't. I mean,' I say, seeing his eyebrows draw together, 'I cleaned it up . . . the injury . . . all the blood. I . . . I cleaned it up.'

He reaches out his hand and rests it on my lower stomach. I can feel it burning, even through my heavy jumper and shirt. His fingers press against me. The air in my lungs solidifies.

'No one – *no one* may touch you. Do you understand?' he says. 'You are my Acolyte, and you belong to me. Do you understand?'

I manage to nod. He removes his hand, and I feel like my knees are going to give out. He spins on his heel and leaves the room, calling, 'With me,' over his shoulder as he goes.

I follow him.

14

Now

I've been given some food, at least. Some kind of stew. I thought about throwing it at the wall, but I couldn't, in the end. I ate it.

Hand hasn't come. Of course he hasn't.

No one else has come in either since I attempted to escape. They've just slid the food through the hatch in the door. I don't know what they're planning to do with me.

Sometimes I think about Dublin, and the cafe, and Meg, and I want to be there so much that I feel like smashing my brains out on the wall for being so stupid. I don't even know anymore if it was my choice to return. I don't feel like it was. I feel light and insubstantial, like I was blown here by the wind, with no more control over my movements than a leaf.

Did I return because of Amy? Or am I here because Hand whistled and I came to heel?

I have to stop thinking like this. It doesn't matter why I'm here. It matters that I get out of this cage.

What will I do if I get out of here?

As I see it, my options are:

One – Leave Home (if they let me) and go home
Two – Stay and keep trying to get to Amy

I don't know which one I want more, anymore.

I wish I had my notebook. Back when I first arrived in Dublin, a half-feral, unsocialised mess of a thing, Meg got me a special notebook and suggested that, when I needed to calm myself, I write down four true things. Four things I know to be absolutely, unquestionably true. I could use that right now. I generally always have a notebook on the go, in a bag or near me so that I can grab it when I need to. I've done it ever since that day she first suggested it to me.

It was a grey, blustery day, and the rain pouring down the cafe windows was so constant that it was like someone was outside with a hose trained on them. Customers came rushing in, scarves wound around their faces or collars pulled up, shoes leaving trails of puddles on the floor that I would periodically mop up. I wasn't serving yet – I was still too scared to speak to anyone except Meg – so my responsibilities consisted mainly of cleaning the floor and tables, and collecting and washing dishes. Meg had patiently coached me to ask her questions when I was unsure of something, or even just curious, after noticing that when I got confused about how to carry out a task she'd set me, I'd just sort of quietly panic in a corner instead of asking for help. I was getting better at it, but it still felt strange – almost illicit – to ask questions whenever I wanted.

Meg had just started getting me to help a bit with some of the baking she did in the little kitchen area at the back, as well. That morning, I chopped bright, sticky cherries into halves and stirred them into a claggy mess of dough that rose, under Meg's watchful eye, into soft, fluffy cherry scones. I had one for my break (break! I still couldn't believe that time was set aside simply for doing nothing, every day) and slathered it in butter, which melted and dripped onto my fingers as I ate. I'd never had anything so delicious.

It was a busy morning, and when it finally calmed down, Meg took her break at the same time as me, leaving the other server to deal with the trickle of late-morning customers. I sat, curled up on the cushion on the windowsill, licking the last of the butter from my fingers and watching as Meg sat on the sagging back-room sofa and scribbled in a notebook. It wasn't like the exercise books I'd been used to writing in: its covers were hard, like the books on the shelves out in the cafe, and covered with a soft green material with shiny gold embossed leaves. I'd seen Meg note things in it now and then, but I'd never seen inside.

Meg glanced up and saw me staring, and I looked away, cheeks hot. 'Sorry,' I mumbled. I brushed crumbs from my legs. From the corner of my eye, I saw Meg close the notebook on her finger and lean back comfortably into the sofa.

'Not a bother,' said Meg, in the strange voice that almost everyone here had. I still had to concentrate hard to understand what some people were saying.

It was almost the end of my break. I slid down from the windowsill and picked up my apron from where I'd hung it on the back of a chair.

'Come here to me, Zoe,' said Meg. I looked at her, and she patted the seat next to her, so I knew she wanted me to sit down with her. Sometimes she said that phrase and it didn't mean 'come and sit next to me', it meant 'listen to this – I have something to tell you'. It had taken me several weeks to figure that one out, but I was secretly proud of myself for doing so.

I perched next to her on the sofa, and Meg tapped her notebook with a finger. 'Did you wonder what I was doing there?' she said. I twisted my hands together. Meg held the notebook out.

'Want to see?'

I took it carefully. My fingers made a soft rasp on the material of the cover. I ran my finger over the gold leaves, which caught the last of the light from the wet afternoon outside.

'You like it?' she asked. I nodded. 'Would you like one?'

I felt rather than saw myself, sat at a tiny, cramped little table, surrounded by girls in brown tunics, endlessly copying out Father's Scripture. My hand ached, as though it had been curled around a pencil for hours. I shook my head.

'No?'

'I . . . I mean, I'd have nothing – nothing to write in it,' I said, holding the book out to her. Meg took it, leafed through the pages.

'Oh, there's loads you could be writing in it, Zoe,' she said. 'See here – I jot down things I need to order in for the cafe, or sometimes I write a little to-do list, or I note down something that's happened that I want to remember—'

I peeked at the pages as she flipped through them. Here and there among the various lines of scribbled writing – I couldn't read it, all the letters were mushed up and joining together strangely – were little sketches, drawings that I recognised as customers' faces, cups of steaming coffee, the view from the windows at the front of the cafe . . .

'These are amazing,' I said, and Meg laughed.

'Just scribbles, so they are,' she said, but she said it in a happy way. People like it when you say nice things about them, I'd noticed, even if they seem to protest or argue after you've said it. I pointed at the top of one of the pages.

'What are those?'

'Which?'

'Those . . . fours?'

Every few pages, there were little lists of things, always four items long, and surrounded by a sketched box. I could read the numbers all right, but the words after them were in Meg's indecipherable scrawl.

'Ah, those. My four true things,' said Meg.

'Four true things?'

'Yeah, it's a bit self-helpy, I suppose, but it works for me. What I do, Zoe, when I'm . . . oh, a bit tired out or fed up or worried, or something, is I sit myself down with my notebook here and a big old cup of coffee, and I write down four things that I know to be absolutely, unquestionably true.'

I stared at the little list, surrounded by its boxed lines. Later on, I'd realise this was the right point in a conversation to say 'oh?' or 'is that right?', but back then, when I was unsure what to say I just kept silent.

'So writing those four true things down, Zoe,' Meg continued patiently, 'makes me feel better. It reminds me of things that matter and helps me forget things that don't.'

We were on the most recent page in her notebook, the one she'd just been writing in. I looked up at her face, which was already becoming familiar to me. The folded lines at the corners of her eyes that got bigger when she smiled, the smooth skin over her cheekbones, the easy curve of her lips. 'Are you a bit tired out or worried just now?' I said, then wondered if it was okay to ask that sort of thing. But Meg smiled.

'Well, I'm not just now, Zoe. I was a bit when I first sat down, after the morning we've had, and – well, bills and things I always worry about, I suppose – but I wrote down my four true things and I'm fine now.' She tapped the list with a finger. I squinted at it. 'Would you like to know what it says?'

I nodded. I couldn't think of four things that I knew to be absolutely true. I could hardly think of one.

Meg held up the notebook and read out her list. 'One. My name is Meg,' she began. 'Two. The weather outside is fierce awful. Three. I know I'm getting on, for I've a funny squeaky noise in my knees when I bend them, and it reminds me of the time my dad stepped on my poor hamster. Four. My friend is sitting on the windowsill nearby me.' She shut the book with a snap and grinned at me. I smiled back, and felt brave enough to ask another question.

'Why was your first true thing "my name is Meg"?' I asked.

'Well,' said Meg. 'I was reminding myself that I know who I am, even if other people don't – or won't – accept it.'

I didn't quite know what to say to that, so I looked around and caught sight of the clock. My break was over, but I didn't want to stop having this conversation. Meg had written that I was her friend. It made me feel as warm as the cherry scones when they were first out of the oven. 'Did you know I chose my own name?' said Meg.

I looked back at her. 'Really?'

'Really. Just as you did. My old name is dead to me now – my deadname,' she said, like it was all one word.

'Deadname,' I repeated. 'Like, you killed your past self off.' I liked that idea.

'Hm. I wouldn't say exactly,' Meg said. She stood up and stretched. 'More like pruning a flower so a new bud can grow. It's not a violent thing. You can love what you were, and still grow beyond it.'

I thought about that. *Love what you were*. It wasn't something that had ever occurred to me before.

'Shall we?' Meg smiled, gesturing out at the quiet hum of the cafe. I smiled back. It reminded me of how I'd felt with Amy, sometimes: like there was someone who understood me, who'd gone through the same things. Though Meg hadn't, of course; but we had both chosen new names for ourselves. We had that in common.

'Meg?' I said, as we left the cosy back room for the cafe.

'Mm?'

'What's a hamster?'

She'd come in the next day with a notebook for me, not exactly like hers but just as fine. It was midnight blue, and instead of gold leaves there were little stars scattered over the cover. Inside, Meg had written (in careful, wide-spaced letters that I could actually read): 'For Zoe, for her true things. With all my heart, from Meg.'

That first notebook is tattered and old now, lying at the bottom of a cardboard box half full of similar ones I scribbled in over the six years I was in Dublin. I never really got into the habit of writing down to-do lists, or things that had happened that day, as Meg did. I only filled them with things I knew to be absolutely, unquestionably true.

Right now, even if I had my notebook, I have no idea what I'd put into it.

I roll onto my back. The floor is cold and hard, and if I lie in one position for too long, I start to feel like I've been pummelled on that side. I press the heels of my hands into my eyes to block out that incessant burning light.

'Catherine?'

Hand's voice! Is he outside?

I drop my hands. He's here. Hand is here, in front of me, kneeling down, looking into my eyes with such kindness that I almost cry.

I blink, and the cell is empty. I push myself up onto my knees, topple back into the corner.

There is no one here.

I feel like I've been grabbed and shaken, violently. I heard his voice. I *heard* it, then I saw him. But I am alone in here.

What is going on? Am I going mad? Is this what it feels like?

My eyes sweep the cell. Grey, bare concrete floor and pitted brick walls. Glaring lightbulb in cage on ceiling. Heavy wooden door. Nothing else.

100

Did I fall asleep? Did he come in while I was sleeping, or did I dream it?

I press my hands into my eyes again. Bright colours swirl in the darkness behind my eyelids, and his voice comes again. 'Do you know what my job is, Catherine?'

I drop my hands. Empty. The cell is empty.

I'm hallucinating. I must be. Lack of food, isolation, stress – my mind is responding to this by hallucinating Hand coming to rescue me, like he did before.

No. He *didn't* rescue me when I was locked in here before, after Amy left. A Sister pulled me out of bed, dumped me in the Atonement Room, he came in, I lied to him, and he . . .

He came back. He did come back, later on. Jesus. I'd forgotten. How did I forget that? He came back, after . . . who knows how long. I was lying on the floor, half out of my mind, and I opened my eyes to find him crouched in front of me.

'Catherine?' I had blinked up at him, trying to focus.

'Do you know what my job is, Catherine?'

'You're the Hand of God,' I said, and I say it now, as Zoe, but also then, as Catherine. I see him prop his elbows on his bended knees, so his hands with their long, pale fingers dangle between his legs.

'That's my title. But do you know what my job is?'

'You are Father's Hand. You interact with things-of-the-world that would corrupt Him,' I say/said. My child-voice, Catherine's voice, is thready and clotted with half-swallowed blood.

Hand nods. 'That's right. But what does it mean, Catherine?'

'I don't know,' I whisper/ed.

'The Children will inherit the perfect world to come,' Hand says. 'But for the world to be perfect, it has to be free of evil. Do you understand?'

I nod/ded.

'It's my job to rid the world of evil,' Hand whispers.

I close my eyes. Tears squeeze out, hot on my skin. He's going to kill me. I am evil and he's here to rid the world of me.

'Not you, Catherine,' he says, reading my mind. 'Not you. You're not evil. You lied to me, and you are justly Atoning for that, but you're not evil. You are special.'

101

I keep my eyes closed.

'You are very, very special.'

I open my eyes. Hand is gone. He was never here. He was gone, back then, too. I'd passed out, maybe, or fallen asleep, and when I awoke he was gone. But the door to the cell was open, and a Sister was waiting outside. She took me back upstairs, to my dormitory. I was free.

How could I have forgotten that? The first time he told me I was 'special'. It started even earlier than I thought.

If I forgot that, what else have I forgotten?

The dark curtain in my mind, the one that is drawn across when I think back to more than just the barest details of being a child, is there, as always. But this time, I have the awful, vertiginous feeling that if I tried to pull it back, to peer around it at what lies behind, I might be able to. That being here, back in this place, is enough to make that curtain dissolve, if I really want it to.

I don't want it to.

Adi. Think about Adi.

I try to grab onto a specific memory, but moments slide through my mind like sand pouring through my fingers. I just have flashes and impressions. Factual information. Okay. That's fine. All right. Start with that. What do I know about Adi?

One – She was left-handed
Two – Her sisters were identical twins
Three – Her favourite artist was Nnenna Okore
Four – Her cat was called Michael Burnham, or Burnie
   for short

This is ridiculous. It's like a list of facts about a pen pal. I knew this woman, knew her so well. Think. Think.

Adi gently tipping a spoonful of hot, fragrant pepper soup into my mouth. Adi sending me a picture of her smooshing her cat's face. Adi hooking an arm through mine as we wandered through a streetlamp-lit Dublin after a gig.

Okay. Memories. Those are memories. They're not all gone.

They'd been trying to make me forget. It was part of the Purifications. They made me stand until I felt like I'd drop, and they told me to recount my memories of her, or write them down, then they told me to repeat Father's words about impurity, over and over, to replace my memories of Adi with Father's words. They'd done it first after the cold water and the Guard's body against mine, and I hadn't had it in me to do anything but tell them the truth. Then I had to tell them the same things, again and again. Over and over.

'It's not love, Catherine,' Innocence says, peering at me over her glasses. 'It can't be love, because it's not sanctioned by Father. It's not between a man and a Sister who has been chosen to suit him. It's not real.'

A nudge in my side. 'Zoe, you're starin, love,' said Meg. I looked away from the two women who were both sitting squashed on one of the window seats, two steaming mugs and a plate of strawberries with two forks abandoned on the table in front of them. One had her arm around the other, twining a strand of her hair around a finger. Their faces were very close, and they were laying little kisses on each other's lips, soft, like dropping petals in water. Meg handed me a box of teabags. 'Put these out, will you?'

I started filling the jars we kept our different types of tea in, my cheeks flaming hot. Meg helped. The cafe was quiet, the two women the only customers sitting in apart from an old man named Michael, a regular who had nodded off in his usual spot. I had been at the Underpass Cafe for almost five months.

'Meg,' I said under my breath. She inclined her head to show she was listening. 'They . . . those . . . they're both women,' I whispered. Meg flipped up the lid of the jar of rosehip tea and scooped in fresh teabags.

'And have you been told that's wrong?' she asked. I thought about it.

'I don't think I've ever been told about it,' I said.

'Well, that's brilliant then, Zoe,' said Meg, snapping the jar closed. 'Then you've no preconceptions. Isn't that a wonderful thing, to have a clear mind and a heart untainted by other people's hatred?'

'Yes?' I said. Meg patted my shoulder and turned to greet a new customer, and I sneaked another look at the two women. The one with her arm around the other had leaned her head back against the wall and was looking out of the foggy window to the street outside. The other woman had her head tucked up under the first woman's chin, and was eating strawberries with her fingers. I watched her face, content and comfortable, and wondered how it would feel to be held like that.

'And is this when you first realised you had these impure inclinations?' Innocence says, leaning forward, one hand gripping a sheet of paper covered in my handwriting. I look at the words on the paper, my words, warping under her fingers.

'Thanks, that was great!'

'Off, are you? See you again, so.' Meg smiled from her station behind the coffee machine at the young man, who was fumbling in his pocket for the right change. He handed the money to me, his hand soft and a bit damp. I began dropping the coins into the various slots in the till, then glanced up and realised his hand was still outstretched. He was holding out a slip of paper. I took it, and he flashed a quick, panicky smile and disappeared through the door, the bell jingling in his wake. I had been at the Underpass Cafe for two years.

I looked at the slip of paper. There was a number scrawled on it, and a name.

'Goin to call him?' asked Meg.

'Uh . . .' I rubbed my head. 'Does he want me to?'

'I'd say him givin you his number is a fair sign that he would like you to.' Meg leaned on the bar, her tea towel slung over one shoulder. Her hair was currently a resplendent orange going red at the tips, so that she looked like an exotic bird that had caught fire. 'Do you want to?'

I looked at the number again, feeling hopeless. 'He's always really nice . . .'

'Nice is good,' said Meg sagely.

'And he seemed kind of nervous.'

'He did, all right.'

'So I suppose I . . . should?' I looked up at Meg, who raised an eyebrow.

'There's no should about these things, Zoe,' said Meg. She pressed her hands into the small of her back and stretched. 'Ooft. Come here to me. What do you think of him?'

I shrugged.

'Like, does he—' Meg twirled her hands in the air '—make you, I don't know, feel sort of happy and excited when you see him?'

'Uh—'

'Do you feel pleased that he gave you his number?'

'I—'

'Do you relish the opportunity to spend time with him?'

'Um. Should I?'

'There's no should in feelings, Zoe. You either do or you don't.'

'But—' I twisted my hands together. 'But what would be the normal thing to think? To feel?'

Meg reached out and took my shoulder. 'Oh, Zoe,' she said. 'Oh, sweetheart.'

'Again. And Father will choose for him a female, of good stock, and she shall be Fruitful and bring forth a Warrior or Daughter for Father. Again. Again.'

'You must expiate these poisonous impulses, Catherine.' Innocence's glasses flash with the light from the ever-burning bulb above me. 'You must tell us everything. You must get it all out.'

Adi lying back on the grass, paperback propped over her nose and eyes. I'm rolling onto my side on the blanket, and the hot sun is like butter on my skin. 'Are you awake?' I'm saying. She is making a comfortable sound, sleepy and content. I'm leaning over her, and I am very gently pressing a kiss onto her mouth. Her lips are curving upwards, so I'm leaning over and doing it again. Soft, like dropping petals in water. It is my first real kiss, and it is perfect.

'And that was the first time, Catherine? The first instance of physical Transgression between the two of you? You instigated it, is that what you're confessing?'

Sheets tangling around my legs. Fingers on my skin. Breath in my mouth. Gasps and whispers and low laughter.

'What you did is Transgressive, you know that, don't you, Catherine? You understand that?'

Lying in her arms.

'Again.'

Oh, Adi. I'm sorry. I'm so, so sorry.

15

THEN

'Again,' he says. I move back into position and raise my arms. I can barely keep them in the air. They feel like they weigh a hundred pounds.

The Hand of God moves behind me.

I breathe in and try to focus. Knowing that he is behind me makes the hairs on my neck stand up.

A weight on my back, hands pressing my face into the concrete. Darkness, rain and scrabbling fingers.

I squeeze my hands into fists and will the images away, will that black curtain to swing into place.

The Hand of God moves in front of me, striding as though he is just walking past without noticing me. I step behind him and hook my foot through his legs, around his calf. I pull my leg back towards me, and his foot slips backwards and he stumbles. I wrap my arm around his throat, throw my weight into dragging him to the floor. He falls to one knee, and I realise, dizzy with it, that I almost have him. Then he twists to the side, knocks away my arm and clips me on the side of my jaw. I fall back, pain lighting up my face.

The floor mat in the Training Centre is cool against my hot skin. It's dark outside, and rain is pelting the windows set high up in the walls. It's almost soothing. I could just lie here.

'Again.'

One of the windows is cracked. A breeze is whistling through, lifting the knotted ropes hanging from the ceiling, making them dance. Part of the Warrior training is climbing them. I can't do it.

'Again, I said!' A muted impact on my side. He's kicked me. I really should get up, but my body is so, so heavy.

Someone is slapping my face. I try to raise my hand, but I'm so tired.

I am not on the mat anymore. I am lying on the floorboards, on my side, one hand tucked under my head. I don't remember moving.

The Hand of God is crouched on his heels, looking at me. He gets up and moves out of my sight. Footsteps recede, then rushing water, then footsteps approach. He crouches down again and holds a glass of water to my lips. I push myself up a little to sip at it, then grey washes over and I rock back. The water runs down my cheek.

I wait until my vision comes back, then try to get up again. A hand presses me back.

'Not yet.'

I settle back onto my side. The Hand of God is staring at me.

'When was the last time you ate properly?'

I try to think. I had lunch in the mess with the Warriors the day that . . . that day. Since then, I haven't left the Hand of God's quarters. I haven't had much of an appetite, anyway.

'The body is a machine, Acolyte,' says the Hand of God. 'It requires fuel, and maintenance. If you deprive it of either, it will cease to function optimally. Understood?'

I nod. 'I'm sorry,' I say. My voice is rusty.

'Can you stand now?'

I nod again. 'I . . . think so.'

I get up. Grey fizzes at the edge of my vision, but I stay still, breathing slowly, and it abates. The Hand of God hands me the glass, and I tip the water down my throat. I am suddenly ravenous.

'I will have one of the Sisters leave some food for you at the residence. You are to eat, sleep and report to me tomorrow morning at dawn,' the Hand of God says. He moves towards the door, then pauses. 'This has been disappointing. Don't disappoint me tomorrow.'

He leaves. The heavy door of the Training Centre bangs shut behind him.

I am waiting around the corner of the Men's Quarters, on the far side of the Training Centre. It's a quiet little spot, away from any of the main paths, so no one can see me.

I shift my grip on the baton. There is tape wrapped around the tapered edge, and I can feel the frayed edges of it catch on my skin. It feels good. Solid, and real. I hold it firmly in my right hand. The thicker end rests on my left palm.

The Hand of God and I have practised what to do over and over. I know how to hold this, how to use it. I've felt the judder up the bones of my arms when I swing it, hard, into a punchbag. I can imagine bringing it down on real, living flesh, doing it again and again until it buckles and crushes and splits apart beneath me. The Hand of God told me to picture it in my head, every detail, to think about doing it over and over. It would make me stronger, he said.

He was right. I do feel strong.

I wish I'd felt like this before. I wish I'd had this baton before, and the Hand of God's training. I'd have used this on Angela, and Sister Morningbright, and all the rest of them.

Cold blue eyes flash in my mind, and instead of forcing the image of the Bad Night out of my head like I usually do, I think about swinging the baton straight into those icy eyes, again and again, until they are swollen then smashed then closed forever.

I shouldn't think like this, because the blue eyes belong to the Seed, who is Father's son, but it doesn't matter because it feels so good to think about it. I would have done it, if I could. I would have brought the baton down hard, over and over, then I would have grabbed Amy's hand and taken her out of there. I wouldn't have let them take me away. I wouldn't have left her alone in there with him.

I almost don't hear the footsteps coming around the corner. But I come back to myself in time.

Pressure on my back. Scrabbling fingers. Hot breath on my neck.

The baton in my hand.

He comes around the corner, and before he can fully register my presence, I have whipped the baton out and connected, hard, with his stomach. The impact jars my arm, but I was ready for that, and he crumples, pitches forward. I raise the baton high above my head and bring it down on his back. There is a dull thud, and a huffed, bitten-off yelp. He reaches for my legs, but I step back easily and bring the baton down again. And again.

When I finish, Caleb is lying in a ball at my feet. He has one arm over his face, and one splayed at an odd angle. He is breathing in screamy little puffs, and one wide eye peers at me from behind his arm. His fingers are shaking. I look down at him the same way I'd look at an insect I'd stepped on.

I place my boot on his hip, and push. He tips onto his back and lets out a shriek. He tries to put his hands up in front of him, but he can't quite move the left one.

I raise the baton again, and he begins to babble. 'Don't . . . don't . . . oh, Father . . . no, please—'

I think about what the Hand of God told me. To finish, he said, hit him between the legs. Hard as you can.

I heft the baton, and Caleb moans. I am looking between his legs, so I see it when a dark stain blossoms and begins to spread. I let the baton drop to my side. And I laugh.

I laugh, and laugh, and laugh, so hard that I have to bend down and prop my hands on my knees. My stomach aches and my eyes are streaming. I haven't felt this giddily happy in such a long time.

I wipe the tears away from my eyes. My cheeks ache. Caleb is still staring up at me from behind his shaking arm, but I can see the bright red flush of his cheeks against the pallor of his skin. I can see the embarrassment, and the shame, and the fear in his eyes. I know, somehow, that laughing at him has done more damage than striking him between his legs could have.

I look at his quivering fingers and feel a ghost-scrabble of those fingers at the back of my neck. I swing the baton up again, so fast I barely know I'm doing it, and whack it as hard as I can into his side. His mouth stretches open and he looks like he's screaming, but he doesn't make any noise.

This feeling: this hatred, this anger – this is strength. This is fierce, and powerful – more powerful than any love I've ever felt for Father, or for the Hand of God, or even for Amy, because I am the Acolyte and I have never loved Amy, only Catherine loved Amy. I am the Acolyte and all I am is hate.

The feeling obliterates any lingering sense of the happiness I felt when I was laughing. It clouds everything, and all at once I feel that I could drop the baton and use my fingers and teeth to take Caleb to bits, to tear him apart until only a bloody smear and scraps of flesh were left.

The feeling subsides as quickly as it arrived, and I just feel sick. I want to sit under the pounding hot water of the shower again, and let it burn out any and all thoughts in my head. I'm sick of thinking, and of feeling. I want to be nothing.

Hand had told me to speak to Caleb at the end, to tell him that he was never to touch me, never to even look at me again, because I belonged to the Hand of God. He'd told me what to say, had practised it with me over and over. His hand cupping the back of my neck, his face close to mine, mouthing the words along with me.

'Again. Say it again.'

'I belong to the Hand of God. You must never—'

'You *will* never—'

'You *will* never touch me again.'

'Again.'

'I belong to the Hand of God. I belong to the Hand of God. I belong to the Hand of God.'

But I can't muster the energy to do it. I turn on my heel and leave Caleb there, the cold wind rushing past the bare skin of my ears and neck.

16

NOW

I dig the hoe into the earth, neatly turning over the soil around rows and rows of sickly green cabbages.

I don't scream, though I want to.

My long skirts swing around my ankles, and the stiff, buttoned shoes I'm wearing are nipping my toes.

I don't look up at the sky. If I do, I will see all the space around me and I will want to run.

I don't know what they'll do if they see me running. I suppose they'll stop me. I suppose they'll take me back to the Atonement Room.

If I avoid thinking about the Atonement Room, and about what happened there, then my hands don't shake.

I've been having nightmares.

When I finally get hold of Amy, I don't know if she'll recognise this person.

'Sister Catherine?'

I stand up, pressing my hand into the small of my back.

It's a small, nervous-looking girl. She flinches when my gaze lands on her, a quick double-blink of her eyes accompanied by her chin tucking down into her neck. The movement looks compulsive. 'Yes?'

'Sister Grace is looking for you. She said to come to the Fruitfulness Hall as soon as you can.'

'Oh, okay. Thanks.' That quick, compulsive movement again, as though the girl is ducking from a blow, then she spins and hurries off. I stare after her as she picks her way through the rows of cabbages, huddled against the wind. Why would someone in the Fruitfulness Hall want me?

Sisters are helpful, and punctual, and never question anything. Sisters will drop everything if a senior Sister requests her presence, so that's exactly what I do.

The Sister overseeing the work in the garden watches me as I put the hoe away.

'Sister Catherine?' she says. I keep my eyes down.

'I've been requested at the Fruitfulness Hall, Sister.'

'Very well.'

I skirt past her and make my way to the garden gate. The other Sisters don't look up as I go. You don't look up here. I think I'd forgotten that. I'd forgotten a lot.

I'm remembering, now.

The Fruitfulness Hall is between the Worship Hall and the Men's Quarters, on the far side of Home from the women's building. To get there, I could go around the front of the Nutrition Hall, from which the Big House is visible. Or I could go around the back, and pass by Hand's residence.

I should go the front way. I have a reason to be on the move, and they only let me out of the Atonement Room because they think I'm broken. They don't expect me to do anything I haven't been told to. I could go to the Big House right now.

I haven't moved faster than a sedate walking pace, but my heart is going like I've just sprinted here. It's daytime. Someone would see. And how could I get into the Big House? There's Guards at the door, and high hedges all around its private gardens. I'd never manage to sneak in right now.

Another time, then. It's fine. It's all right. I'll figure out another way to get there. It's only been a couple of days since they took me out of the Atonement Room, since they let me rejoin the Sisters. I don't even have to wear the face mask anymore. I just need more time to make a plan.

And it's not because I'm afraid to do something unsanctioned. It's not because I can't. They're wrong. I'm not broken.

I just need more time.

I take the path around the back of the Nutrition Hall. I can see Hand's quarters from here.

Why would you think the Hand of God would come to see you?

I flinch and shake my head, like the memory of Innocence's voice is an insect I can duck away from. I can't, though. Her voice continues, a relentless buzz in my ear.

Why on earth would you think that, Catherine?

The Hand of God brought me here, but it was a mistake, it was a mistake, he was supposed to come and get me, you're not supposed to be keeping me here, I'm not supposed to be in here!

From this distance, Hand's quarters are dark, and look empty. I don't know where he is. It doesn't matter where he is.

This is all a delusion, Catherine. It's an indication of how deeply your mind has been poisoned by the Sullied world. The Hand of God is Father's Hand. Why would he have anything to do with you?

He brought me back . . .

Now, you know that's not true, Catherine, don't you? Of course the Hand of God didn't bring you back. You came back yourself.

It doesn't matter what he did or didn't do. I don't need him. I never did.

You will never be able to rejoin the Children unless you accept some basic truths, Catherine. You felt immense guilt over your impurity, your Transgressions, and you returned to us. You must forget all this nonsense about the Hand of God.

I told Innocence what she wanted to hear. Of course I'd come back of my own accord. Of course the Hand of God wasn't coming to get me out. And that was true, at least. He didn't come and get me out. I got out by myself. I did it by agreeing to everything she said. I went through all of it, all over again, every Purification she wanted. I just wanted to get back outside.

It didn't work, though. I know what's true. I held on to the truth, the real truth, *my* truth, hammered it diamond-hard, kept my fist clenched around it, held on to it to keep me tethered. The Hand of God brought me back here, then abandoned me. That is the truth. It's clear he never meant to help me find Amy in the first place. It's fine. I'll get to her without him.

There's a drumbeat of a thought in the back of my head that matches my footsteps as I make my way along the empty path. *Stu-pid, stu-pid, stu-pid.* I am so, so stupid. It wasn't even hard for Hand to lure me back. I just trotted along after him.

I still don't know why he did it at that particular moment. The images Innocence had of me in the cafe show that they knew where I was for a couple of years before Hand came to get me. So why only come and get me now?

I don't know. I don't know. I am too stupid to work it out. My thoughts are like logs half submerged in muddy water, lately. I can't get them moving anymore.

I'll be fine, though. I'm leaving here, after I find Amy. I just need to figure out how to get to her. And until then, I'm just playing along.

I'm just playing along.

I've never actually been inside the Fruitfulness Hall, though of course, as a kid, I'd passed it from time to time. I'd heard the sounds that came from there – the high, mewling cries of the Fruit, and, sometimes, the howls and screams from the Sisters.

I suppose I must have been in there at one time, now I think about it. But of course I wouldn't remember.

The door to the building is under a concrete overhang, casting it into shadow. I pause for a moment, looking up. There are a couple of storeys, and every window has dark, heavy blinds drawn across it. You can't see in.

The door bangs open, and a harassed-looking woman with a severe brow peers out. She has skin like unbaked dough. Sister Grace. 'Catherine?' she demands. I nod. 'Thank Father. You've been ages. I thought that stupid girl had got lost on the way to the gardens.'

She turns and stalks back inside, and I follow along behind. Inside, the floors are bare and polished, and my boots squeak against them. The air is full of some sweet, chalky smell. In a room above us I can hear a low, insistent crying. Sister Grace keeps talking as we pass doors on both sides of the corridor, all firmly shut. 'We're very short today, very short, which is why I asked for someone. Sister Ascension has been sick as a dog all week, and of course two of my other girls are sick as well now—'

I let her voice fade out as I trudge behind her along the dim corridor. I want to drive my fist into the neat bun on the back of her head. I don't care, I want to shout. I don't care, I don't care about any of this, I'm not one of you, I just want Amy, I just want Amy and to go *home*.

But I don't. I don't do any of it.

'—So I asked for someone and they said they could spare you. The cabbages will survive without you for a few hours, I dare say.' Sister Grace sniffs, takes out a brace of keys from a deep pocket, unlocks a door and gestures at me impatiently to go inside.

I step through. The room is full of Fruit. Children – babies really, I suppose – are two to a cot, all wearing blue or pink all-in-ones. It is quiet; much quieter than I would have supposed a room full of very young children would be. As I look around, one of the babies grabs onto the cot bars, hauls herself to her feet, and stretches her arms out towards us.

'You'll want to cut that out, for a start,' says Sister Grace. She crosses the room and firmly deposits the baby back onto its bottom. The baby's chin wobbles, and her chubby little fists open and close. She makes a series of insistent sounds. Sister Grace turns away and hoicks an eyebrow at me.

'So I'll just leave you to it?' she says.

I stare at her. 'I . . . sorry?'

'You've looked after children before, haven't you?' she says. I shake my head, and she throws up her hands. 'For Father's sake! I told them . . . Okay, look, it's not difficult. You feed them now, change them in an hour and put out the lights after that. Feed and change again when they wake up. I'll be back in a few hours. I've a Sister upstairs waiting to deliver her Fruit, and barely anyone here to help me at all.' Before I can respond, she steps past me, slams the door and I hear her keys turn in the lock.

Behind me, the babies begin to wail.

17

Then

The click of the door to my little box room wakes me. Pale light from the corridor spills in, making a silhouette of the figure in the doorway. I push myself up, rubbing a hand across my eyes.

'Get up, Acolyte,' says the Hand of God. He withdraws, but leaves the door ajar behind him. I drag myself out of bed and pull on my clothes, shivering. How early is it?

I hop into the corridor, tugging on my boots as I go. The front door is open, letting an icy gust whip inside. I can hear a car engine rumbling.

I step out. The Hand of God is sitting in the driver's seat of his big black car. Through the window, I see him gesture to the seat beside him.

I've never been in a car before. How do you get in?

There is a sort of dip with a latch above it set into the door, which I give an experimental tug. It clunks open, and I feel a wash of warm air from inside.

The Hand of God is tapping his fingers on the wheel. I slide onto the seat next to him and pull the car door shut using the handle on the inside. The seat is smooth and shiny. In front of me, there is a ledge with illuminated symbols and circles, and a perplexing array of buttons and levers. The Hand of God does something with one of the levers, then turns the wheel and the car begins to move. I grab onto the side of my seat, and he glances over, amused.

'Belt,' he says. I look down at the belt on my trousers, thinking perhaps I'd forgotten to put it on.

'Seat belt,' he says. I don't know what he means. The Hand of God reaches across me, behind my left shoulder. There is an unzipping sort of sound as he pulls a long grey strap down and across my body. He pushes the metal tab at the end of it into a black and red case down beside my right hip, and it makes a loud clunking noise. The strap sits snug against me, holding me back into the seat. When I look over at him, I see he has a similar belt secured across his body as well.

I look out of the window to my side. The scenery spins past. I feel a wobble of nausea in my stomach, and a strange sensation, almost like falling inside my head.

'Look forward,' says the Hand of God, and I do, through the big window at the front of the car. The ground outside looks like it's moving less fast than it did outside the side window. The nausea recedes.

I feel a hot blast of air on my cheek. There is a little vent in front of me, set into the ledge. Hot air is steadily coming out of it. It feels amazing. I raise my hand and let the heat wash over my fingers.

There is a noise from outside, the screech of metal on metal, loud enough that I hear it over the sound of the car. I look up and see the huge Gate ahead swinging open. A Guard beside it waves us through.

My mouth drops open, and I twist around in my seat to look behind me at the Gate, and the Wall, receding. Getting smaller. The car twists to the side, we round a corner, and they disappear behind a screen of trees.

We have left Home.

I feel dizzy, like I did when I first looked out of the car window. Home. I'm outside Home. I've left it, I've passed through the Gate. I can't even see Home anymore!

I gulp for air.

'This is your first time Outside, Acolyte,' the Hand of God says. It's not a question. He knows it is. I nod anyway, unable to speak. I am too busy looking around me.

It's the same, and it's not. The same trees, with a few red and orange leaves still clinging to their branches. The same scrubby grass on the side of the road. The same slate-grey sky.

But it's new trees. It's new grass. It's even, somehow, a new sky.

The car rounds another corner and a landscape unrolls in front of me. I've never seen so much . . . space.

The road cuts through a wide area, flattish where we are but climbing up to hillsides at either end. It's just vast. No buildings, no paths, no high stone walls, just endless land stretching away in every direction. I feel dizzy with it.

Home is pretty large, of course – there are nine buildings, including the Big House, and then there's the kitchen gardens and the Pavilion and the Training Grounds and the woods – it's enormous. It's the whole world. But here is another world, and it was right outside the Wall the whole time.

I've thought about the Outside before, of course. I'd just never seriously considered that I would ever see it. What would be the point? The Children have all they need at Home. Why would I ever go to the Outside? And yet . . . I used to spend all my time in Scripture lessons staring at the distant forest from Sister Morningbright's window. I knew that people did come in and out of the Gate. Supply vans come in regularly, and the newly Awakened arrive from Outside, and of course the Hand of God comes and goes as he pleases.

And Amy. Amy was in the Outside.

For a brief, mad moment I think that the Hand of God is taking me to see Amy. Then I realise how silly that is. Amy disappeared. They don't know where she is. If they knew, they'd bring her back.

The car follows the curve of the road into a dense forest. Trees bracket the road, and the weak light grows even dimmer, filtered through rafters of branches.

'What is the Hand of God's purpose?'

The question stumps me for a moment, because even though I know the answer, my mind is so full of these new trees, this new sky, these new thoughts.

'The Hand of God acts as Father's hands. He interacts with things-of-the-world . . .' I begin to recite. The Hand of God's head shake cuts me off. I flounder, but then something peeks out from behind the curtain in my mind.

119

'The Hand of God rids the world of evil,' I whisper. 'So that the Children can inherit the perfect world to come.'

He nods. 'Do you know why I chose you as my Acolyte?'

I stay quiet. He has never referred to that time in the cell before. We've never talked about why he took me away from the Sisters.

'You are special. I knew it as soon as I saw you, when you were very little. But I knew that you needed to grow first. To ripen. So I watched you. And when the time was right, I took you. You have a gift, my little Acolyte. A gift that only I could see in you. And it will help me in my sacred duty.'

I try to think what to say. Do I thank him? But I don't understand what gift I'm supposed to have. I don't have any gifts. I'm nothing special. I'm not properly modest and demure, like Angela. I'm not strong or fast, like the Warriors of God. I'm not a girl anymore, or a boy either. I'm nothing.

I can't ask what it is he thinks I can do. If I ask, he might realise that I'm not who he thinks I am. He might send me back to the Sisters. I might lose him, too.

'I'm happy to serve the will of Father,' I say eventually, because that standard phrase seems safest. But the Hand of God doesn't respond. It's as though I haven't said anything at all.

I've done something wrong. I am always doing something wrong. I have to try harder to be what he wants me to be.

'I'm glad you chose me,' I say aloud before I can stop myself. I want to slap a hand over my mouth. I shouldn't ever talk first. This time, though, the Hand of God glances over at me, and he seems pleased.

'Are you tired, Acolyte?'

'I'm fine.'

'We have a long journey ahead of us. Close your eyes.'

18

Now

'Shit, shit, *shit*. Please, *please* stop crying,' I say. The sniffling baby boy in my arms seems to consider this, then opens his mouth and screams, this time even louder than before.

I don't know what's wrong with him. He's been howling for what seems like hours. My eardrums feel like they've been stabbed.

The babies were quiet initially, just watching me dully as I pawed through the cupboard, trying to figure out how to feed them. There was no food, but there were lots of bottles, and boxes of powdered formula. I tried to remember what I'd seen people with small children do at the cafe. I'd seen them dump powder into bottles, then ask for hot water to be poured on top. Hot water. I needed to heat water.

There was a kettle on the counter, which I filled from the tap and switched on. But how much to put in? How much powder did you need?

I picked up the box and scanned it for instructions. There was a table on the side, with different amounts for different ages. What ages were these kids?

I looked at them helplessly. They could stand, mostly, if they hung on to the bars of the cots, but didn't seem able to walk, and didn't have much hair. One of the boys nearest to me caught my eye, and his mouth dropped open, showing clean pink gums. No teeth. What did that mean?

I had no idea. I decided to pick the middle amount and hope it was right.

I lined up bottles, one for each baby. Eight in total. I tipped scoops of powder in, spilling a lot of it over the counter. The babies were still silent, gazing at me or just looking at the bars in their cots. It didn't seem right. Babies cried, didn't they? Or sort of wiggled and squeaked.

I waited for the kettle to boil. My hands were shaking. They'd been doing that lately. I gripped them together to stop it, avoided the weird blank stares of the babies, tried to breathe and forget that Sister Grace had locked the door.

She'd be back, though. It wasn't like the Atonement Room. She'd be back to let me out.

The kettle boiled, I started to pour in the water, then stopped. Babies couldn't drink boiling water.

I had a flash from the cafe – a young father, eyes dark-ringed and shirt buttoned up all wrong, rolling up his sleeve and dribbling milk from a bottle onto the skin on the inside of his wrist.

I poured steaming water into each bottle, then filled the rest from the cold tap. I started screwing the caps on. In my hurry, I knocked one with my elbow and it went flying, milk gushing out onto the counter, the floor and down my skirt. I groaned. This was worse than rush hour at the cafe.

I grabbed a bottle and held it out to the nearest cot. One of the babies raised his arms, and I was about to give it to him when I remembered the skin test. I pulled it back and shook it against my wrist. Lukewarm milk splashed me. Was that fine? It was probably fine.

I gave the baby the bottle. Sticking the teat firmly in his mouth, he tilted his head back and began drinking contentedly.

A few minutes later, all the babies except one were sitting or lying in their cots with bottles grasped in their chubby hands. I still had to remake the bottle I'd knocked over, and the last baby – a boy with wispy brown curls – was making his displeasure at this incompetence clear. By the time I'd managed to make a new bottle, it was too late. He batted away my hands every time I tried to stick the bottle in his mouth, and flung himself down in the cot, kicking his legs frantically and screaming.

122

I covered my face with my hands. Breathe, I told myself. Just breathe. That was when I reached into the cot to pick him up, thinking that it would soothe him, but I am still holding him and he doesn't appear to have calmed down yet.

His little face is bright red, and his hands are knotted into fists, and his entire body is like a tightly drawn wire. I am walking up and down, patting his back, making shushing noises like I've seen harried parents do in the cafe, but it's not helping. I want nothing more than to put him down, walk out of the door and slam it on my way out. But it's locked. It's locked, and I can't leave.

For a moment, I wonder if shaking the baby sharply would make him stop crying.

For a moment, I am a child, I am in the Worship Hall, and I see a dark head of curly hair snapping back, slim shoulders gripped by big hands. I feel the wood of the bannister pressing against my legs. I hear the prayers shrieked by a hall full of throats. I see the head snap back again.

The images disappear as quickly as they came, and the desire to shake the boy goes with them. I press the hot, taut body of the baby boy against my chest. Of course I can't shake him. That would hurt him. I can't hurt him.

One of his flailing hands lands in my hair, and he grasps onto it and pulls it, hard.

'Ah, *fuck*,' I say. Tears spring to my eyes. The boy's cries trail off, and he looks at me with a comical expression of surprise. Then, with the air of one conducting an important experiment, he tugs my hair again.

'*Shit*,' I say. His flushed, teary face breaks into a delighted grin, and he chuckles. He pulls my hair again. I swear loudly, and he laughs like a bubbling fountain. Nervously, I tickle him under his arm. He lets go of my hair – thankfully – and twists back, laughing. Then he tucks himself into my chest, and settles his head under my chin. I stroke his back, and he lets out a sigh. He tilts his head back and looks up at me. His eyes are a bright green, like a still pond.

I grab the bottle from the counter beside me and hold it up in front of him. He reaches for it, making little *eh eh eh* noises, so

I joggle him into a cradle position in my arms and give him the bottle. Contented milk drinking ensues.

'This isn't so bad,' I tell him. I stroke his soft little cheek with a finger, and he gazes up at me with those deep eyes. The silence is a balm after all the shrieking. I feel like I could sleep for a week.

His eyes are so striking. So green.

Eight babies for one person to look after. They must barely get touched. That can't be a normal way to grow up, surely. It must be why these babies seem so strange. They barely make any noise, apart from this little one.

I was one of these babies, once. It makes a shudder run through me to think of it, being here, being so . . . unloved. I don't remember anyone touching me when I was little, except to push or hit me. Until Amy, of course. She used to squeeze my hand sometimes, when we could get away with it. That little bit of physical contact had been so exquisitely painful, but I had wanted more of it. So much more. I wanted to be burnt up by it.

Hand had hit me plenty of times, when I wasn't performing whatever ridiculous task he'd given me to his satisfaction – slaps, kicks, shoves – but he'd touched me gently, too. His fingers were always skating across my cheek, his thumb rubbing across my lips, his hand cupping my chin. It makes me feel sick now, but at the time I wanted those little moments of contact more than anything. I must have been such an easy mark.

A sound like someone trying to get the last drops from a milkshake through a straw catches my attention. One of the babies in the cot beside me drains her bottle, regards its emptiness for a moment, tries to drink from it again, and – finding that no more milk has magically appeared – flings it at the bars and starts to wail.

19

THEN

'Acolyte? Wake up.'

I had thought I would be too excited to sleep, too mesmerised by the world spinning past the car windows to stop looking at it, but I must have nodded off all the same. My neck is stiff, sore where I've leaned against the door to doze. I stretch as much as I can within the confines of the seat and look outside. What I see makes me sit bolt upright.

We are stopped at the side of a long road that goes so far in either direction that I can't see where it begins or ends. It is enormous, so wide that two cars can pass on either side of each other. There are dozens of cars, all tearing past us impossibly quickly. They are going so fast that each time one of them passes, our car shakes.

The Hand of God presses the red button beside his hip, and the seat belt retracts with a shuddering noise. 'I'm going to get us some food,' he says, nodding out of the window. 'We have some way to go yet.'

I look to my left. There is a small white van, with one side of it all opened up. Inside I can see two people, and above there is a sign with bright red letters. BURGERS CHIPS CANS.

The Hand of God reaches into the inside pocket of his jacket and pulls out a small brown leather square. He lifts one edge of it, and it opens like a book. Inside there are little slits with strips of plastic poking out of them. He pulls the top of the little leather square open, and I see there is a sort of hidden pocket along the edge. It is filled with long patterned pieces of paper, blue-green, reddish brown and purple. He scissors one piece of paper out between finger and thumb and shows it to me.

'This is called "money",' he says. 'Have you heard of it before?'

I have a dim memory of 'money' being mentioned in some sermon or other. I was never entirely sure what it was, only that it was a thing they had on the Outside and it was, like all Outside things, bad.

'It's . . . evil?' I say. The Hand of God nods.

'It's idolatry,' he says, and I'm on firmer ground here. I know what idolatry is, and why it's bad. 'The Sullied worship it. They exchange it for things that the Earth gives us for free. It is just one of the reasons they will not enter the perfect world to come.'

It occurs to me to ask why, if money is so bad, he has so much of it in his little leather square. I don't, though.

'However,' he continues, tucking the money back into its little slot, 'if we are to enter into the Outside in order to Purify it, Acolyte, we must, at times, make use of their Transgressive affections. We do not Transgress ourselves by doing so,' he adds, looking at me directly. 'We are about our sacred duty, and nothing we do as part of that duty can therefore be a Transgression.'

I glow. We. Our. He is counting me as part of this important thing he is doing. Perhaps I am special, in some way.

'We can exchange this,' he holds up the leather square, 'with those Sullied people,' here he nods at the two people in the strange van, 'for food.' I can't help it – I laugh.

'We give them paper, and they'll give us food?' I say. His face breaks into a smile, and I glow even brighter. He laughs along with me.

'Ridiculous, isn't it?' he says. 'We give them no sweat from our brows, no work from our bodies, nothing of any real value at all, and they hand over whatever we desire.'

'Where do we get money?' The Hand of God shakes his head.

'That is the most ridiculous part, little Acolyte,' he says. 'They give it to us themselves.'

'The Sullied give it to us?'

'To the Children. They send it to us, and some of them, if they send us enough, if they give us all the money they have,

126

they become Unsullied. They become like us. Those are the newly Awakened, those who come to us from Outside.'

'They become Unsullied when they give us all their money?' I say slowly. 'Because . . . because then they aren't Transgressing anymore?'

'Good!' the Hand of God says. 'There is more to it than that, of course, but that's a big part of it. They must give up all Transgressive things-of-the-world before they can be Awoken. Before they can join us.'

'Then we use it to help us create the perfect world to come.' He nods.

'Exactly so. And that's why it's not Transgressive for us. Now. Watch closely.' He opens the car door and steps out. The roar of cars from outside is momentarily louder before the door closes again, and I watch as he walks towards the open van, his black coat whipping behind him in the wind.

He reaches the van and one of the figures inside says something. He replies, points at something inside the van, and the Sullied person nods and turns away.

I feel dizzy. The Hand of God is actually talking to a Sullied person! Someone who lives outside of Father's light. I try to get a good look at them. One is turned away, busying themselves doing something in the back of the van. The other is leaning against the counter, which comes up to about mid-chest height. He's male, young, with straight dark hair under a white netted cap. He is wearing a white apron, like the other person in the van. He has something in his hands that is glowing, lighting up his face from underneath. He is staring at this glowing thing and occasionally stroking it with a finger, and completely ignoring the Hand of God in front of him. The sheer rudeness of this is breathtaking. But perhaps he is so far from Father's light that he doesn't even realise he's being unforgivably disrespectful.

The other Sullied person in the van turns and hands a white bag to the Hand of God, who passes the money to her. She is older than the boy and her hair is more grey than black. She reaches into her pocket, but the Hand of God raises a hand and shakes his head. The woman's face creases into a smile, and she nods and raises her own hand back. She has the same sort of smile as Sister Assumption, the sort of smile where you can see a person's gums as well as their teeth. She looks just like us.

The Sullied look just like the Unsullied. Realising this is almost like getting whacked in the chest. I grip onto the handle on the inside of the car door as the Hand of God turns and walks back to the car, the white bag swinging from one hand. But of course they look just like us. Once the newly Awakened are properly part of Home, once they're not in their grey clothing and masks anymore, you can't always tell them apart from the rest of the Children if you don't already know who is who. So why should the Unsullied look different?

I can't shake the uneasy feeling the thought has given me, though. There is another blast of noise and cold air as the door opens and the Hand of God gets in. There is a smell, too, a hot, meaty sort of smell. My stomach shifts, rumbles.

'Here,' he says, reaching into the bag and passing me something wrapped in a white paper napkin. I unwrap it. It is two pieces of puffy bread, and a thick piece of meat in the middle. I pull up the top bit of bread and look under it. There is lettuce and tomato, which I recognise, but there is also a pinkish sort of sauce spread across them.

'Eat,' he says, and the car engine roars on. He turns the wheel while taking his own similarly napkin-wrapped food out of the bag, and begins to drive while biting down on it.

I open my mouth and sink my teeth into the top and bottom layers of the puffy bread. My mouth floods with saliva at once, almost painfully. The bread is soft and fluffy, and the lettuce and tomato crunch crisply as I bite down. The meat is hot and juicy, and tastes different from anything I've had before. It almost tastes like smoke. I swallow, and something smarts at the back of my throat. It's a kind of perfumed burning sensation, and it's not totally unpleasant. The sauce?

'Good?' the Hand of God says, and I nod.

'Good,' I say, and take my second bite.

20

Now

A hand on my shoulder, and a shake. 'Sister Catherine?'

It's dark when I open my eyes, so I can't properly see the woman waking me up. She is a shadow in the dim room, and I don't recognise her voice. It's not Sister Grace.

'Sister Catherine? You can go now,' she says. She reaches to her side and clicks on a small lamp, and a soft glow lights her dark skin. She is young, maybe in her twenties, and has hair braided into neat rows on her head. There is a distant noise that, for a second, I almost don't recognise – a drawn-out trill, repeated. A phone, ringing somewhere in the building.

The woman glances back over her shoulder, steps swiftly to the door and closes it softly, then gestures to me. 'You'd better not let Sister Grace catch you doing that,' she says, plucking the sleeping baby from my arms. The baby, a girl, stretches like a cat and I'm afraid she'll wake, but the woman tucks her against her chest and pats her back until she quiets.

I rub my eyes and look around. The light doesn't appear to have disturbed the rest of the babies, who are sleeping in a variety of poses, up to and including one baby that seems to be fast asleep while propped only on her head and knees, with her bottom firmly in the air. After the bottles, I'd turned off the light to try and get them to go to sleep, which worked for some but seemed to enrage several others. Eventually, they all quietened except for one, and I finally attempted to get that baby to sleep by holding her up on my shoulder while sitting in the uncomfortable hard-backed chair in the corner of the room. It worked after a while, and I thought the groaning stiffness in my back (between the weight of the baby on my arm and the rigid chair) would keep me awake, but apparently I'd been exhausted enough to fall asleep too.

The woman gently and expertly rolls the sleeping baby into a crib, where she settles down without a peep. I look at her in disbelief. 'How did you do that?'

She laughs a little, then glances over her shoulder again. 'It's just practice.' She hesitates, then leans closer, dropping her voice. 'I do it too, sometimes,' she says. 'Give them a wee cuddle, I mean. Sister Grace doesn't like us to, but sometimes it's the only thing that will calm them.'

'Are we not supposed to cuddle them at all, then?'

'Mm, no. Not really. It's not good for them.' I look at the sleeping forms around me, so small and so still, chests rising and falling, little fists clenched by parted lips. I think about their dull stares, and about how the ones I picked up felt against my chest. How they leaned into me, settling against me like I was a mould.

The woman turns to the door. 'I'll let you away now, then?' she says. One part of me is relieved – I can't remember the last time I was so tired, the last time I felt such a desire to be utterly and completely on my own – but a part of me is almost reluctant to go. I have a weird impulse to pat one of the babies' backs as I leave, or to stroke a cheek or head, but I can't, of course. I smile at the other Sister as I go, and I realise as the door clicks softly shut behind me that I haven't asked her name.

The corridor is as empty as it was when I arrived. I hurry out, wanting to put this place behind me. The air outside is crisp and cold, and I wrap my arms around myself as I step into it. The sleeves of this dress are thin and threadbare, and going a bit at one elbow. I'll have to mend it.

I look up at the window to the baby room as I pass.

It's not normal. I know that. Not natural. Babies are supposed to be held, and cuddled, and caressed. Not left to claw at the air as distant bodies pass them, only occasionally touching them to change or feed them.

I spin on my heel and hurry away from the Fruitfulness Hall. It sickens me. The grey stone and dark windows and blank eyes of the babies.

The wind ploughs around the corner of the building and I tuck my chin into the collar of my dress. It doesn't provide much protection from the cold. It'll be warmer when I get to the Nutrition Hall. I'll get some soup and . . .

I slow, stop. I'm staring across the scrubby strip of grass between the Fruitfulness Hall and the Men's Quarters. A row of bins lines the back of the building, and the lid of one is hanging open and banging in the wind. The stink of the open bin claws at me.

I should run along. Hurry back to the Nutrition Hall like a good little Sister. Sister Catherine. Get my bowl of watery soup, go do evening Worship and Ablutions with the rest of the brown-clothed women, tuck myself under the threadbare sheet in the narrow bed in the dormitory full of other mice, and get a good sleep so I can do it all again tomorrow. Like I have the last two nights, since they finally let me out of the Atonement Room.

I close my eyes. What am I doing?

What am I *doing*?

I am here to find Amy. I left Dublin – left my whole *life* – and came here with Hand to get Amy. Then he said I couldn't see her right away. Then they said I needed to be Purified.

Then that room, and endless, circular time, and the bright, shrieking light, and the constant, awful Purifications. Then giving up completely, and doing it, doing all of it, everything they asked, no matter how many times. Agreeing that I was delusional. Agreeing that I was impure. Agreeing that Adi and I . . .

I clench my fists, feel a hot prickle of tears threatening to come out. I had to do it, to get out. I know that. I didn't mean any of it. I didn't. So it doesn't matter what I said to them, because it wasn't true. None of it.

It still feels like a betrayal.

And then 'Sister Catherine'. Sister Catherine, who did what she was told, not because she was playing along just so she could get to Amy, but because . . .

Be honest. Why not? Who followed orders because she was scared.

Scared that if she didn't, she'd be taken back to that room. Scared that if she didn't, she'd never get to see Amy. Scared that if she didn't, maybe she'd figure out that she couldn't.

I am not Sister Catherine. Sister Catherine is a mask I have put on, that I have had to put on to rescue my sister. But no one else is here right now. No one is watching me. Here, I am still Zoe.

What would Zoe do?

I think about Meg. Zoe, when she's not sure about something, goes to Meg. Thinking of Meg, her kind eyes and quick smile and wild-coloured hair, makes me miss her so much that it's like a fish hook in my heart. I would give anything to hear her voice. To be able to call her, and hear her voice, and listen to her say my name, my real name.

God knows what she thinks has happened to me. It's been – fucking hell, how many days has it been now? I don't know exactly, because I've not tried to work it out, because to do that I'd have to think about how long I was in that icebox, and my mind just runs and hides from that.

Something tugs at my memory. Something recent. A noise, familiar but strange, when I was in the baby room. A phone, ringing.

Zoe would talk to Meg. So, Zoe is going to talk to Meg.

Putting the Men's Quarters behind me, I turn and make my way back to the Fruitfulness Hall.

21

THEN

The forest floor hits my back. It's not raining anymore, but the ground is still damp, and wet earth squelches under my elbows as I push myself up. The Hand of God is watching me, head slightly to one side, face expressionless. Shame suffuses me. This has got to be the tenth time that he has gone through this combination with me, and every time I end up on my back. He's even stopped saying 'again' in that dry, disappointed way after I crash to the ground. He just tilts his head to one side and stares until I get up.

I heave myself to my feet. At first, my body was cramped and achy from the long car ride, and my muscles didn't move as quickly as I wanted them to. Now, I'm smarting from a dozen different bruises, my head has been stuffed with dirty cotton, and my left hip feels like it's grinding in its socket. I want to have a long, burning hot shower. I want to roll into bed and sleep for a week.

But the Hand of God chose me. Me. And he took me here – Outside! – on a special mission. So it doesn't matter how I feel. It only matters that I do what he tells me, that I do what he wants. I square my shoulders and face him.

The Hand of God steps forward until he's so close we're almost touching. My skin tingles, waiting for what happens next.

It's been the same the last ten times. His hand shoots out, grips me around the neck, and thrusts me back against a tree trunk. I am to let him do this.

As soon as I feel the impact of my back hitting the tree, I am to move. I reach up, grasp his thumb, and bend it back towards him.

His arm bends at the elbow, giving me enough room to brace against the tree, push him back with my other hand, then duck under his arm.

At least, that's what's supposed to happen. But I can't get past the part where I bend his thumb back. His grip is too strong. I tug and tug, and his fingers bite deeper into my neck, and when greyish fog begins to cloud my vision, I tap his shoulder frantically with my free hand to show that, once again, I have failed. It is then that he pushes me away from the tree and lets me fall to the ground.

I roll onto my side and cough. I can still feel the impression of his fingers in my neck. It's as though I'm a piece of clay that he is pinching and poking and shaping.

I drag myself to my feet again. Dread feels like a barrel full of polluted water in my chest. How long is he going to make me do this? Why did we come all the way out here?

He didn't explain, when we arrived. Just shook me awake and said, 'We're here.'

I looked around sleepily, expecting . . . I don't know what I expected. Something more than what I saw, which was a small, gravelled area in a thick forest. There were no other cars, only a narrow road that led to where the Hand of God had stopped. We must have driven up it, because there was no other road that I could see. Trees surrounded us, pressed in on us. The sky through the waving branches was grey and dull. I couldn't tell what time it was.

The Hand of God turned the engine off, and the silence flooded in. I couldn't hear any other cars. He opened the door and stepped out. I automatically reached for the door handle to follow him, but my foot hesitated before it touched the ground.

This was the Outside. I had never set foot anywhere but the hallowed ground of Home. This was different. This was other. This was new.

Some part of me believed that I would be tainted if I stepped on Outside ground. If I allowed myself contact with the world that wasn't Home.

But Amy was Outside. Did I believe that Amy was tainted?

I didn't know. For all I knew, she might be.

I remembered the Hand of God holding money out towards me. Showing me those dull-coloured strips of paper that the Sullied people so prized.

We are about our sacred duty, and nothing we do as part of that duty can therefore be a Transgression.

I could, then, touch the filthy money that the Sullied used, and walk upon the ground Outside, and not be tainted by it. I was acting as Father's instrument, and the Hand of God and I had a special mission. Nothing we did in the service of that mission could be wrong.

I whooshed air into my lungs and stepped out of the car, my boots crunching on gravel that sounded just like the gravel we had at Home. The wind felt the same as when I was training in the woods inside our walls. Soft, because the trees had broken it into ribbons.

Something was different, though. Something about the air, the wind. The smell of it – it was some new scent I hadn't come across before. Something woody, and fresh, and vegetable.

'Pine trees,' the Hand of God said. I must have been sniffing the air like a dog. My cheeks flooded with heat. What a stupid thing to do.

I closed the car door and followed him into the forest, down a wandering path beaten into the earth by many feet. We came to a small clearing, the one we are in now, and he told me what he wanted me to practise.

'It's important that you can do this, Acolyte,' he said, placing one hand on my shoulder. 'I won't go easy on you. You have to be able to defend yourself against a fully-grown man.' I nodded eagerly. I would show him I was special. I was worthy of this mission. I could do what he needed me to do.

But I have disappointed him.

Shame and pain and embarrassment twist into a hot, flickery mess in my gut. I have to do this. I have to.

This time, when he grabs me by the throat, before I know what I'm doing, my own hand extends and my fingers claw into his throat. His eyes widen in surprise and his grip falters for a second, just an instant, but it's enough for me to jerk his thumb back and to push him away so that I can slip out under his arm.

I did it! I feel giddy with the sheer relief of finally accomplishing what he set out for me to do, so much so that I almost laugh. The giddiness drains as he turns and I see the red marks of my fingers on his neck. What have I done?

The Hand of God appraises me. I wait, shrinking. Then he nods.

'You're ready,' he says.

22

Now

My footsteps echo as I step back inside the Fruitfulness Hall. I can hear a baby crying from behind a door. Briefly, I feel again the weight of the children from earlier in my arms. It's a strange feeling – part longing, part terror. I haven't ever wanted my own child (and the hours locked in a room with a pack of hungry babies has, if anything, only solidified this) but for a moment I let myself imagine what it would be like, to have a little baby made of me. A little person I would keep and look after. A blood relative.

Voices echo from the other end of the corridor, and I hare up the staircase – as quickly as I can manage in these ridiculous skirts – away from them. The staircase twists around, so by the time I'm halfway up it I can't be seen from the floor below. The voices get louder and closer, two women talking ('—low on nappies, and talcum as well.' 'Well, we asked for some last week, but of course they never—') – and then a door opens and shuts, and their voices are gone.

I look around. The second-floor corridor is dark and quiet, lined like the one below with closed doors. I step closer to one, trying to walk as quietly as it's possible to walk in these hard-soled shoes on polished wooden floors. The nearest door has a little brass holder at eye level, a slip of paper tucked in it with '002364' printed in careful letters. An office? An office is a likely place for a phone. But I have no way of knowing if it's occupied.

What is the best thing to do? If I just go about opening random doors, I'll be found and ejected fairly quickly. And in trouble.

Back in that room.

No. No one knows I'm here. I'm not in trouble. I'm not going to be found.

Come on. Focus. I am standing in the middle of a corridor, somewhere I'm clearly not meant to be, and I need a plan if I'm not going to get caught.

I could hide. I could find a cupboard or something, and hide until night, when it would be quieter and I could sneak about a bit more freely.

But then, will it be any quieter later on? Babies don't sleep all the way through the night, do they? So there will still be Sisters up and about at all hours.

I have not thought this through.

Voices again. Coming up the stairs.

Oh, shit. I spin around, looking for somewhere to run. There's only the doors. The corridor is too long for me to make it to the turn at the end before those voices get here.

I grab the handle of the door beside me, the one with the number, and I pull it open, step inside, and shut it gently just in time. The voices and footsteps get louder as they near the door outside. My skin freezes over until they pass and get quieter again. I breathe, for what seems the first time in minutes.

'What are you doing?'

The door hits my back. There is a woman in here. She is leaning on a bed, feet splayed on the floor and upper body propped up on her arms. A green hospital gown strains over her swollen belly, and she is glaring at me through strings of lank, sweaty hair.

My mouth opens and closes. The woman's face fogs, then clears. 'Catherine?'

23

THEN

We are back in the car. The Hand of God put his hand on my shoulder as we were walking back in the fading light, just rested it there and held on, and I almost burst with it. As we reached the gravelled area, he gave me a little squeeze then took his hand away, but it was like an imprint remained, glowing.

He reaches behind him to grab a small package from a bag in the back seat of the car. It is black, stiff fabric, about as long as my forearm, with a little pop-button flap at the top. He holds it out to me. As I extend my hand, he leans over and gently takes hold of my chin. 'This is a present for you, little Acolyte,' he says. 'This is to help you assist me in my work.'

My skin is singing where he is touching it. I nod, unable to speak. Those girls, Angela and the rest, they would feel so stupid if they could see me now. If they could see how important I am. If they could see how much I matter.

And what would Amy think?

I push this invading thought away. It doesn't matter what Amy would think. She left.

The Hand of God places the object in my hands, and nods for me to open it. I push my thumb under the flap and lift, and it pops open. Inside, I can just see the polished black of a handle. I draw it out, slowly, and the blade makes a soft *sssshhhh* sound as it emerges into the last of the day's light.

I have never held anything so fine. The handle is smooth and almost warm to the touch, and moulded with grips for my fingers. It's not made for an adult man's hands; it's like it was made to measure for me only. My fingers settle into the grooves as though they'd always been meant to. I open my hand and let the knife rest on my palm, feeling the weight and balance of it.

'Thank you,' I say.

'You're very welcome,' he says, and I can hear the smile in his voice even before I look at him and see those kind grey eyes gazing at me softly.

He plucks the knife from me, and slides the blade under his right thigh. 'You conceal it like this,' he says. 'On the far side of them. Then, when it's time—'

So fast I barely see it, the tip of the knife is against my ribs. The Hand of God's hand is curled around the back of my neck, a pincer-grip that I couldn't break if I tried. 'Here,' he says into my ear. His breath is hot, and works its way under my collar. He presses the knife point in a little harder, and I bite down on a yelp. 'Between the fifth and sixth ribs.' I feel a hot little trickle under my shirt. It pools at my waistband. It will stain. I'll have to wash it. I'll have to . . .

The Hand of God releases me, and I thump back against the seat. The wet streak under my shirt feels sticky. He spins the knife in his hand, holds the handle out to me. 'You try,' he says.

Unbidden, an image comes of me holding the knife with the blade buried up to the hilt in the Hand of God's side. Sick burns the back of my throat. The place where the blade pricked my skin is a bright point of fire.

'Do it,' he says, and his eyes are alive with something I don't understand.

I slide the knife under my thigh, like he showed me. On my left side, the far side from

them who is them what does he want me to do

him. I swallow, the spit scratching down my throat. My hands are shaking. I grab the knife and

amy would do it she'd do it she'd stick it right in him open the door and run run and find her

swing it towards the Hand of God. The knife tip stops just against the fabric of his coat. I look at it wavering in my hands, as the point catches on black threads.

'Good,' he says, but his voice is far away. Then his hand grasps mine, the one without the knife, and he pulls it up and places it on the back of his neck. 'But like this,' he says, and grips my hand, making me press down. His skin is hot. I can feel the hair that has been shaved short at the nape of his neck. 'Pull down,' he says. I do, and our faces get closer. I train my eyes on the knife. His voice comes from somewhere above me. 'When you put it in at first, there will be resistance. The knife needs to get through fabric, then skin and muscle. You have to follow through. Pulling down on their neck will help you to brace yourself and drive the knife home.'

I am watching this from somewhere at the back of my mind, seeing from a distance the girl

not a girl not a girl not anymore

and the man wrapped together in the car, hearing only faintly the instructions the man is giving, feeling only as if through layers and layers of cloth what the man's body is doing.

From this far back in my mind, I don't have to wonder about what he wants me to do. Who he wants me to do it to. I don't have to worry that it's real. I don't have to do anything at all.

24

Now

I stare at the woman.

'It is you, isn't it? It's Catherine?' she says, heaving herself up. Standing straight, I see just how big her belly is. The green gown is stretched across it, and there are dark pools of dampness under her armpits and at the neck. Her legs are bare.

'What are you doing here?' she says, and with that I know who it is. That sneering *you*.

'Hello, Angela,' I say, and she visibly blanches.

'It's not Angela anymore, of course,' she says stiffly. Of course. Stupid. She'll have been Named by now.

'Right. Sorry – sorry. Sister . . . ?'

Angela's eyes narrow. 'Verity,' she says. 'Why are you here?' Her hands drop to her stomach. She cups it, holds it in that protective way pregnant women do. 'Are you here to . . . are you—' She looks scared, all of a sudden.

'No, no,' I say, even though I have no idea what she's worried that I'm here to do. I smile reassuringly, but it clearly doesn't have the intended effect because she blinks and takes a step backwards. I suppose I must look a little wild, or something, what with having burst in here.

'It's, uh, been a long time,' I say. Angela raises her eyebrows, then lets out a little laugh.

'Yes,' she says. 'A long time. Where in Father's name—' She stops talking, then lets out a huff through clenched teeth, like she's been kicked in the gut. She gropes forward and leans on the bed again.

142

'Are you . . . is everything—' I feel like punching myself in the face. I'm talking to her as though she's still the popular perfect girl, and I'm the odd kid with no friends. We're not children anymore. I stand up a little straighter.

'It's. Been. *Hours*,' Angela grunts. She raises her head, sweaty strings of hair pasted across her skin. 'And they keep saying that's normal. They—' She pauses, and her eyes roll up in her head. Her body slips sideways, and, before I know what I'm doing, I've darted forward and caught her.

She is heavier than me, and we almost topple over until I grab a hold of the bedrail with one hand and half heave, half lower her down onto the mattress. I swing her legs up and brush the hair away from her eyes. Her skin is clammy. Her eyes are closed, and she's breathing in a throaty kind of way, almost snoring.

'Angela?' I say, patting her cheek. 'An— I mean, Sister Verity? Sister? Can you open your eyes?'

Her eyelids flicker. I look around the room. Apart from the bed, it's almost totally empty except for a sink in the corner by the cupboard. There's no glass anywhere I can see, so I wet my sleeve with cold water then dab at Angela's forehead. Her skin is flushed, but feels cold.

Her eyes peel open and look up and past me.

'Don't feel good—' she whispers.

'Don't worry, I'll, um, I'll—' What am I going to do? She's in labour or something, and she's not well. I can't help with that. She needs the Sisters.

I can't get them. I can't reveal that I'm in here.

Even if she dies? They do die, women in childbirth. They can die. Is me not getting in trouble worth more than Angela's life? Her baby's life?

That freezing, overbright room slides into my mind. I shake the image away, and I'm left with a coldness I didn't know I had. Angela isn't dying. She'll be fine. They'll be checking on her regularly, so it's fine. It's fine. I don't need to get anyone.

I poke about in the cupboard. There's shelves and shelves of medical-looking stuff – bandages and cardboard bedpans and things – and I find a box with some dusty glass tumblers in it.

143

I rinse and fill one glass from the cracked sink in the corner and hold it to Angela's lips. When she's had a little, I wet a corner of the sheet and use it to dab the sweat away from her face. She sighs.

When she speaks, it's so quiet and un-Angela that I almost ask her to repeat it. But I heard it, quiet like a voice being wisped away by the wind. 'Thank you—'

I look at her and feel terrible. 'An— Sister Verity,' I say. 'I need to ask you something.'

'Where did you go?' she says, still in that whisper-voice. 'You just disappeared one day. They said – they all said that you and that girl – your blood sister – that you'd both Transgressed, and you were Atoning. But then you didn't come back—'

'I . . . it's complicated,' I say.

'Some of the girls said they saw you. But it couldn't have been you, with the Warriors. With the Hand of God.'

'Right, no,' I say. 'Couldn't have been.'

'And then they said you'd both been taken into the Big House. Well, her, of course. That was always the plan, wasn't it?'

'What do you mean?' I say.

'But I knew you wouldn't be there,' she continues. I'm not sure she can really hear me. 'Why would He want you? But her—'

'Amy?' I say.

'But then of course I was chosen,' she says, and this time she looks properly at me. 'I was chosen. And when I got to the Big House, she wasn't there. So I thought . . . I thought maybe it would be me—'

Of course. Of *course*. Sister Verity. Her name was changed to one beginning with a V. Angela is Father's Vessel. This is his child.

'But she's there now,' Angela says, and she laughs, a horrible, bubbling little girl's laugh that is grotesquely out of place coming from her red, strained face. 'She came back, and they said she'd never left, and now she's there at His side, and me . . . and I'm just—'

Her body snaps rigid, and tendons stand out like cables in her throat. A strangled sound escapes from her mouth.

My hand feels warm. I look down, and see blood pooling from under Angela's leg, reaching the place my hand is resting on the mattress.

144

I have to get out of here. I have to get help.

Angela is a Vessel. Angela is in the Big House, where Amy must be, with Father. She's the only person I've seen so far with any real connection to Amy.

Outside, the corridor is quiet. I look up and down. It's hopeless – this whole mission to find a phone was ridiculous from the start.

I need to get out of here.

I look back over my shoulder, at Angela straining and grunting on the bed.

It's not my job to help her. There's people here for that. They must check in on her soon. They have to. It's Father's baby. It's the Fruit of the Children. Of course they will be checking on her.

I look out at the silent corridor again. I can slip down the stairs and get away. She'll be fine.

She'll be fine.

25

THEN

I know what I have to do.

It's easy. Just like he taught me. Just like we've been practising.

The knife is under my left thigh, the handle just poking out a little bit. Sitting in the driver's seat, you wouldn't ever know it was there. The handle is reassuringly solid and firm. The blade is a cool slice of moonlight under my leg.

The Hand of God is standing outside the car, near the trees, talking to a man. A Sullied man. I can barely see them both in the gloom, but there is just enough light to see the Hand of God gesturing towards the car (towards me) and the Sullied man turning and staring, then nodding.

We'd waited until it got dark, and then the car had arrived, its headlights puncturing the night, and parked on the far side of the clearing. The Hand of God had told me to be ready, then he got out to speak to the man in the car.

The Hand of God turns and leads the man towards me.

This is it. It's happening. It's really happening.

I stare down at my lap, at my hands pressed flat to my legs. I try to breathe slow. I only need to remember what I've been taught, and he said it would all be fine.

The clunk of the car door opening, a blast of cold wind, and the creak of the seat as the man sits down. The car sinks a little on its wheels, he's so big and heavy.

The Hand of God's voice. 'I'll be waiting here.'

The Sullied man's. 'Okay, yeah.' The door slams shut, and it's just me and this man in here. I've never been so close to a Sullied person. It's like the air is contaminated.

He shifts in the seat, clears his throat.

I keep looking down. I push my left thigh down onto the seat, feeling the knife there.

'Who's he, then? Your dad, or what?'

I don't know what to do. Do I answer him? The Hand of God didn't tell me what to do if he spoke to me.

'Hmm?' Another creak from the seat as the man shifts his weight. Out of the corner of my eye I see that he's twisted himself around to face me. He's puffing a bit, this big man, as though even this small amount of exertion is enough to tire him. I nod, quickly, then shake my head. I just don't want him to move any closer.

He laughs, then, a short wheezy sound. 'Well, that clears that up,' he says. 'Don't worry, all right? I don't want to hurt you. I'm not here for that.'

I press my leg down onto the knife.

'I like you. I like the look of you,' he says. 'Thought you were a boy at first. Then couldn't tell if you were a girl. I like that. I like that.'

His fingers brush my leg. It's the right leg, the one without the knife under it, but I flinch away. I can't help it.

'It's all right, it's all right,' he croons, and the seat creaks again as he shuffles closer. His breath strokes my cheek. I'm jammed right up against the car door, and the knife has slipped right under my leg. I can't easily grab the handle anymore.

His fingers worm across the fabric of my trousers, moving around and then up and in. He'll feel the knife! I grab his hand and shove it away, and, in doing so, look at him properly for the first time. He has a moon-face, raw-looking skin on his cheeks, pale, watery eyes. He throws his weight against me, and the breath is knocked out of my lungs. He pins my right wrist over my body. I can't move either arm. Fingers dig into my chin and he shoves my head up and back. He's panting hard now, a dog after running down a rabbit.

'Bitch,' he's saying. 'Little bitch, you little bitch—'

I can't move. I can't move. I open my mouth to scream, but he pushes his face onto mine and I feel his soft wet mouth and my scream locks in my throat.

There is space, suddenly, and I fall back into it. Above me, the Hand of God reaches into the car and drags the man out. For a moment, the world is full of legs and arms and the kick and thud of two men fighting over and on me, then the pressure is gone and they move away

wet, screamy noises and a frantic rustling, somewhere in front of me. I'm sitting with my back to a tree and I ache all over

'—must do it now.' I look at the knife in my hand, and I look up at the Hand of God. 'You've failed me once already tonight, Acolyte. Don't—'

hands feel damp and hot. In the dark, I can't see what's all over them, but it's drying quickly, making the skin under it feel

headlights, swooping past, then darkness. My cheek is stinging and hot, like it's been slapped. I am so, so tired. I need to wake up.

I need to wake up.

26

NOW

From where I'm crouching, I can't see anything much except for the swirling motes in the shaft of light coming from the skylight. I can hear what's going on down there pretty well, though I wish I couldn't.

I probably should have left when I had the chance. I was going to, if I'm honest with myself. Angela had made my childhood a lonely, bitter place, and I owed her nothing. There were other people in the building, and surely they would check on her eventually. Why did I need to get involved?

But I couldn't do it. I don't know why. Maybe because this place makes monsters of us all. Maybe because it wasn't a spiteful little girl on the bed behind me, but a woman in pain, a woman who had been abandoned when she needed help.

So I held the door open a crack, and in a high, wavery voice shouted, 'Help! Help! The baby's coming!'

I pushed the door shut and dashed into the cupboard, closing the door behind me. I could wait in there until it was all over.

Moving backwards, I bumped into one of the shelves. Something metallic clinked. Some kind of long, pincer-like implement. Probably something to do with childbirth. Urgh.

Sometimes, I am a complete idiot.

The cupboard was full of medical equipment. Medical equipment. The Sisters were going to open it, weren't they?

It occurred to me that, yet again, I hadn't really thought things through.

I threw my head back and bit down on a groan. Then I noticed the hatch set into the ceiling.

The shelves were sturdy enough that I could haul myself up them like a ladder, and although there was a latch on the trap-door, there was no padlock. I pushed up until the hatch rose and tipped, crashing into the darkness overhead. Noisy, so noisy. Were they coming? How long had it been since I yelled? How quickly would the Sisters respond?

Had they even heard me?

I grabbed a hold of the sides of the hatch and heaved, my arms screaming. I pulled myself through, eased the hatch closed, then lay, panting and aching.

I was in some kind of attic space, with low beams and dusty air. There was no real floor, just boards with puffy fibreglass spilling out between them. A skylight set in the eaves behind me let some of the waning light in.

I strained my ears. Underneath me, there was the muffled sound of Angela's high, whistling breaths.

Nothing else, though. No running feet or yelling, no sound of anyone coming to check on her. Shit. Had I not yelled loud enough? Had no one heard?

I was trying to figure out what to do when, finally, I heard the sound of a door opening.

'Now what's . . . yelling about, Sister—?' I held my breath so I could hear what the woman was saying. I could only just about get every other word. A pause. Footsteps. Another pause. Come on.

'Well, looks . . . coming,' said the voice. I'd expected whoever turned up to be panicked, or at the very least have some urgency about them. But whoever this was sounded only mildly irritated, as though Angela was interrupting her nice tea break with some trivial matter.

The footsteps receded, and the door closed again. Were they just going to leave her?

Long minutes passed. I was getting frantic. Angela's moans filled the space around me. What the hell was wrong with them? She was obviously in trouble.

An almost physical sensation of relief filled me as the door opened again and what sounded like several pairs of feet trooped in.

'Okay, Sisters . . . move on . . . prepare Sister—'

I covered my face in my hands. Finally.

Since then, it's been a buzz of activity below. Footsteps, the door banging, voices issuing instructions. Angela screaming.

How long does it take to have a baby? It seems like it's been hours.

I am aching. I am curled up on the boards beside the hatch, so I can hear as much as possible. The skylight went dim and then black, and I can barely see anything anymore.

I will surely be missed, by now.

I'll have to come up with some story. Something to explain my absence. The Sisters at the kitchen garden will know I was called away to help at the Fruitfulness Hall, so I could just pretend that I was needed for longer than I really was.

But they talk to each other. They talk, and keep tabs, and someone is always watching.

I cannot see how I can explain away what I was doing this whole time. Half an hour might go unnoticed, but all this time certainly won't. And I can't go back to that room.

Meg and the Underpass Cafe surface in my head. I feel almost sick for them. I never meant for things to go so far – to get so embedded in the Children again. It was like I started running downhill, and once I realised I had gone too far, it was too steep to stop.

This enforced inactivity is reminding me too much of the Atonement Room. I want to walk up and down to take my mind off it, to keep warm, but even though it's noisy I might be heard downstairs. I can't be caught up here.

An animal shriek from underneath me. A snapped, 'Hold. Still!'

God, I feel sick. What if I left it too late to call for help for Angela?

But if I hadn't, no one would have come. I have to remember that. I did the right thing.

I did something, for a change. I made a choice. Freely. With no Sisters hovering over my head, I made two choices today. To try to contact Meg, and to help Angela.

But now I need to get to Amy. I need to, or all this will have been for nothing. So far, Angela is the closest I've gotten to her.

Another scream. I press my hands over my ears.

> One – My name is Zoe
> Two – I still want to find Amy
> Three –

Screaming that goes on for so long that it seems inhuman. The sound drills through my fingers, fills my head.

> Three –
> Three –

For fuck's sake, come up with a third true thing

> Three – I have a life waiting for me at home. Meg, and
> the cafe, and Adi—

I dig my fingers into my hair. I *don't* have Adi. I haven't had Adi for almost two years. Not since . . .

I try to remember a good memory with her. Adi waving as she leaves—

And Father will choose for him a female, of good stock

I press my knuckles against my eyes. Adi. Adi laughing as—

and she shall be Fruitful and bring forth a Warrior or Daughter for Father

> Adi. Adi reaching out—

And Father will choose for him a female

It didn't work, what they did. It didn't. Those memories are still there. They are. It's just when I try to call them up, when I

152

try to see her body, her face, her smile, they stutter and stop and I'm back in the Atonement Room and the voice saying the words coming from my mouth is not mine.

I didn't give them all my memories. There's others, ones they didn't get.

The last time I saw her, for example. They didn't ask about that.

I've avoided thinking about that night for so long, but I sink into that memory now gratefully. It's there, whole and untainted. Sharp and cold.

Adi is waiting for me to react. She raises her eyebrows and spreads her hands. 'So—?'

The screen of her phone times out and goes black. I don't open it again, although I know her code. I know what the email she's showed me says.

'Congratulations,' I say. 'I'm so proud of you.' It sounds false even to me. Adi takes her phone away and grabs my hand.

'Zoe, I want you to come with me.' She beams.

'To Paris?'

'Yes!' She looks so excited. I feel like I'm being torn apart.

'Adi, I . . . I can't go to Paris.'

'I know it's a lot. I know. But – God, Zoe, Paris! Haven't you ever wanted to live there?'

She's so, so happy. She should be happy. She's wanted a job like this for so long. And I know that she wants to travel. The chance to work at a prestigious gallery in France is perfect for her.

'It's not that simple,' I say, letting go of her hand and turning back to the peppers I'd been chopping. I pick up the knife and slice it down. 'I have a job here. I don't speak French – what could I do there?' I keep my eyes on the peppers, the knife dipping into the red flesh and cutting it apart, over and over.

I feel Adi's disappointment. She's a fixer. She'll try to figure this out, as though it's a puzzle with a correct answer. But, of course, she's missing half the information.

'You could learn French, Zoe. I'd help you. And I'm sure there's jobs you could do while you're learning the language. I mean, what's the point of not even trying?'

She doesn't know that I only have a fake passport. She doesn't know that I might not even exist as a person, legally speaking. I don't know if the Children registered my birth. I've managed so far because my employment at the cafe isn't strictly above board, and I only get away with that because Meg is sympathetic.

'Jesus, Zoe! It's like you're not even bothered that I'll be leaving!'

She doesn't know that I have to stay in Dublin, in case Amy comes looking for me.

'It's not that,' I say, sweeping the chopped peppers into the pan. Oil spits and flares. 'I have a life here.'

The argument swirls and repeats and spreads its tendrils into old wounds, until Adi is shouting that she doesn't know me, she doesn't know anything about me, I won't tell her anything, I won't ever let her in, while she has opened herself up completely.

What can I say? She's not wrong. But I can't tell her the truth. No one, not even Meg, knows everything about me. I don't know everything about me.

Later, I use a knife to attempt to chip the blackened, burnt remains of the peppers from the pan. I can't get rid of it all, so I dump the pan in the bin.

There's another cry from below, except it's not low and full of pain like Angela's have been. It's a high wail. A baby.

I press my ear to the crack of the hatch. Over the baby's cries, I can just hear another voice, drowsy and halting. 'Can I . . . can I hold—'

A door opens and closes, and the cries get quieter and quieter until they fade altogether.

There's more noise down below, feet tramping about and low voices, and then an age later, the door shuts for the last time and there's silence. I wait for a count of one hundred, then gently ease the trapdoor open and slip down into the cupboard. The room beyond it is dim and quiet.

I can barely make out the humped shape of Angela in the bed. The room stinks of bleach, and there's another scent underneath it – a meaty, metallic stench.

I tiptoe around to the head of the bed. There's just enough light to see that Angela is staring straight ahead, but glassily, as though she's not really looking at anything in the room. Tears have scored their way down her cheeks to soak the pillow under her. She is crying, but completely silently.

I try to get in her eyeline, but I'm not sure if she's really seeing me.

'Angela?' I whisper. There is no response.

'Angela?' I repeat. 'Was it a boy or a girl?'

Her eyes flicker and focus on me. 'The baby,' I try again. 'What did you have?'

She shakes her head. 'They took it away,' she whispers. Her voice is raw and clogged. 'They wouldn't . . . wouldn't tell . . . I never . . . held . . .'

I find myself leaning forward, throwing my arm around her and pressing my forehead to her flaming skin. Her fingers lock around my neck and she buries her face in my shoulder. I stroke and rub her back like Meg has done for me, like I did for the babies downstairs, and I listen to her bury her wail in the folds of my clothes.

27

THEN

There is a click behind me, and I am in the Ablutions Room in Hand's quarters. The door has just shut.

I have a feeling like time has just leapt from one point to another without going through the space in between. Weren't we just in the car?

In the woods?

In . . .

A dark curtain closes over the rest of that thought. I can't – won't – look behind it.

I catch sight of myself in the mirror. I look like a completely different person. A person with fishbelly-white skin under streaks of mud and dirt. I raise a hand to my face, and then recoil. My hand – both of my hands – are caked in something that is dried and flaking.

I get the taps on and hold my hands under the blast of water. Soap. I need soap.

I scrub and scrub, sloughing off the crust on my skin. My fingernails are full of it too, half-moons that come out almost solid as I hook my thumbnail under each nail and drag it along, gouging out the muck underneath.

When my hands seem clean, I turn my attention to my face. My skin is gritty to the touch, and there are crumbs of mud and tiny bits of bark and leaves caught in the fuzz of my hair. I get my whole head under the tap and rub furiously with the soap, building up a lather that foams over my mouth and nose and I can't quite breathe and I wonder if I could suffocate like this, trying desperately to be clean, and it doesn't seem such a bad ending.

'—know what to do, now do it.' The hot, slippery feeling of the knife in my hand. The choking sounds beside my feet

I am on my knees, throwing up in the toilet bowl, still with soap stinging my eyes. I spit and spit but the taste doesn't leave my mouth and my stomach heaves again and it all rushes up and out of me.

When I feel like I can stand again, I put my head back under the tap and rinse off the soap and let the water flood into my mouth. The vomit taste washes around my mouth and then dilutes, leaving only the burning in the back of my throat. My teeth ache with the cold, but it's beautiful and I want it to fill me, to freeze me.

What have I done?

I can't let go of the thought once I've had it. What have I done? What have I done?

A hand on my shoulder. I wrench my head out of the stream of water to see the Hand of God in the mirror behind me. I gasp, dripping, and he leans past me to turn off the tap. His hands look clean, but under his nails there are the same black half-moons that were under mine. His face is free from any dirt, but his suit, normally so neat and pressed, is rumpled and shining with dark stains.

He leans into the shower cubicle. The sudden spray of water hitting the tiles makes me jump. He shrugs off his jacket and hands it to me.

'I'll need my clothes laundered,' he says, loosening his tie. It's not until he starts unbuttoning his shirt – the usually immaculate white marred by dark streaks down the front and at the cuffs – that I realise that he is going to undress in front of me. I spin around, cheeks burning. There is rustling behind me, and his bare arm appears, reaching around me to deposit more clothes onto the pile in my arms. His breath is hot on the back of my neck as his shirt, his trousers, his socks, and – Father preserve me – his underthings appear. I flip the tail of his shirt up over the top of the pile to hide them, and hurry out of the bathroom. He calls me back, and I pause at the door, steam curling past me into the dark hallway.

'My shoes. Clean them as well. Then see to your own clothes.' The bare arm again, curling around me to drop his black shoes on top of his clothes. Then the door closes behind me and I can breathe again.

Kneeling on the floor of the little kitchen, I pack his clothes into the washing machine. The shirt and tie can't go in. I'll need to handwash those.

I press the button and the rumbling burr of the machine billows through the kitchen, drowning out the sound of the shower from down the hall. I run cold water into the sink and submerge his shirt in the basin. Something glows in the air in front of me, and a heart-stopping second later I realise I'm seeing my own face reflected in the window. Pale dawn light makes me a ghost.

'—at his face. You see it?'

I manage to get the sopping shirt up and out of the sink just in time for whatever is left in my stomach to rush out again. I grip the edge of the sink, feeling water from the shirt drip over the counter onto my feet, and try to breathe deeply and calmly.

'Look at his face.'

There's nothing left, but I retch and retch into the sink anyway. The images are coming up just like the vomit, vile and unstoppable.

'His face. Do you see it? Do you see what's truly there?' The Hand of God has the man's hair gripped in one hand, and is holding up his chin with the other. The man is breathing in little screamy gasps, and a line of blood is trickling down from one nostril. I watch it reach the Hand of God's fingers, and well up to streak over and down them.

'Acolyte. Look at him. Look.'

I look at the man, at his sweating, blood-streaked face, at his wild eyes, at his slack, wet mouth.

'Do you see it?'

I feel like I'm floating outside of my body. I should be cold, I should be in pain, I should be scared. But I'm not. I'm nothing.

'Tell me what you see.'

I look up at the Hand of God. He is calm, steady, a high wall against strong winds.

I look down at the man, and his *face*, there's something wrong with his *face*, and my knees hit the earth, and I pin my hands to my eyes. Someone is yelling, screaming, 'No, no, no!' over and over.

'What do you see? What do you see?'

I keep my hands over my eyes. My stomach tilts and turns. The ground goes with it. I put a hand over my mouth, and the 'No, no, no' stops. There is, for a moment, silence in the forest.

'Acolyte? What do you see?'

I shake my head. I can't look again. The image is there, though, floating inside my closed eyelids. There was something else in the man's face, something hiding under his skin, looking out through his eyes. I saw it. I know I saw it.

I unpeel my hand from my lips. 'Him,' I manage to gasp. 'Him. The man. He's evil. He's evil! He's a demon!'

The wind rushes through the trees and blows right through me. I wish I could go with it, be borne away like a leaf caught in a draft. But I am here, kneeling in a dark forest far from home. The man I love most in the world is holding a knife towards me, handle first.

'You know what you have to do.'

28

Now

I have prepared carefully for this moment. It is not going to be easy to pull off, partly because I don't think I'm a particularly convincing actor, but mainly because as soon as I start, I am going to want to punch myself very hard in the face.

I need an explanation for where I've been all this time. And I need to play it carefully. I'm not going back to the Atonement Room, not for anything, but I can't just leave either. Angela is my only hope of getting anywhere near Amy. So I need to avoid punishment, and I need access to the Fruitfulness Hall again.

It's late when I slip out of Angela's room, leaving her in a fitful sleep behind me, and creep downstairs and out the main door. The building is quiet, and I don't see anyone. But behind closed doors, I hear babies crying.

Outside, it's pitch-black. The paths between buildings aren't lit, because once dinner time is over, you're supposed to go back to the dormitories and stay there for the rest of the night. So I have to wait for my eyes to adjust to the weak light from the moon before I can pick my way back towards the women's dormitories.

I take the long way there – behind the Men's Quarters and the Warrior Barracks – so that I can leave the path and get into the woods. I roll about on the ground, making sure to get leaves and twigs and stuff all over my dress and in my hair. I dig my fingers into the earth, then rake them backwards and forwards until I feel a sharp pain under my nails. I gather up a handful of mud and rub it down one side of my face.

The next part is a little harder. I pat about on the ground until I find a good-sized stone, then I take a deep breath, count to three, and bring it down sharply against my cheekbone. The pain bites into my skull, radiates down my jaw. I gingerly feel the spot I've hit. It smarts, but not enough. Again.

This plan rests almost entirely on me looking pathetic and vulnerable. I need to appear weak. I am relying heavily on the Sisters' reaction to that, counting on them responding to me in the way that predators do to sick or injured animals on the periphery of a flock.

Sometimes I wonder how conscious it all is for them. The cruelty. The intimidation and gaslighting and constant social pressure. I read a few books about cults, back in Dublin. I hadn't initially gone looking for books on the subject, but one afternoon I'd been unpacking boxes of books – recently picked up by Meg from a family donating their deceased father's library – when a title caught my eye.

'A professor of sociology,' Meg said, dumping the last box of books on the limited floor space in the staff room, and rising to stretch her arms out. 'Lot of dry stuff, I'd imagine, but see if you can fish out anything good.'

I'd been part of the Underpass Cafe for almost two years by then, and Meg was drip-feeding me more and more responsibility. She'd only recently finished teaching me how to complete online stock orders using the – I later realised – ancient desktop computer in the tiny back office ('Then you move the mouse . . . the mouse, Zoe . . . that yoke, the thing by your hand . . .'), and I was by then an expert in answering the phone and talking to people that I couldn't see.

Choosing which books to stock was an important role. Customers came to the Underpass Cafe for our eclectic stock of second-hand books as much as they came for the cakes and coffees. Meg began my literary education almost as soon as I arrived by gifting me a copy of *Treasure Island* (her favourite book growing up), but then had to backtrack somewhat when she realised I assumed it was an absolutely true historical document. I had come to accept that there were more books in the world – vastly more – than those written by Father, but up until that point I hadn't understood that books could contain lies.

Meg supplied me with a variety of non-fiction after that, about world history and various cultures, and some biographies of well-known people: Mary Wollstonecraft, Maya Angelou, and Janelle Monáe, to start with. In this way, I got something like an education.

I sometimes scribbled down quotes to talk over with her in my notebook – I was, by then, onto I think my second or third. Writing down Mary Wollstonecraft's 'I do not wish women to have power over men; but over themselves' made me feel almost sick with the Transgressiveness of it. I was copying out her words just as I had copied out Father's, but they were the complete opposite.

I asked Meg once, over our after-closing tea and mildly stale cakes, why she mostly gave me women's biographies. 'We're largely taught men's history, Zoe,' she said. 'And white men's history, at that. But here I have a unique chance to impress the whole of the world on you, not just one narrow part of it.'

I was looking down at my notebook, at Mary Wollstonecraft's quote, and tracing my pen over the word 'woman'. 'Is it also because you think I'm a woman?' I asked quietly.

Meg, who had been idly sweeping the crumbs from her slice of carrot cake into a little pile, looked up at me. She was lit from behind, in the buzzing glow of the neon sign that said UNDERPASS CAFE behind the bar. The rest of the cafe was dark, so her face was mostly in shadow but her curly hair was picked out.

'Do you think you're a woman?' she said. I shrugged, glad that the light was dim so it wouldn't be as obvious that my cheeks were burning. 'You're whatever you think you are, Zoe.'

I stared down at the tabletop. The faint marks of the wet cloth I'd run over its shiny surface earlier were still there. 'What if I think I'm nothing?' I whispered.

Meg's hand slid across the tabletop and waited, open. I inched my fingers over to hers, and she closed her warm hand around mine. 'You are not nothing,' she said. 'No one is nothing. You can be a man or a woman or whatever you want, Zoe, but you'll never be nothing.'

I felt hot and cold at the same time. I'd existed in some kind of non-space ever since Hand had taken me from the Sisters, taken my name and shaved my head. It had all seemed to make sense when he explained it then. Of course I couldn't be a proper woman. I wasn't like what a woman was supposed to be. But then I hadn't managed to be a boy, either. The Warriors hadn't accepted it. And by then, I didn't even know if I still wanted to be a boy. Their world was just as narrow as the world the females inhabited, but in a different way. Then I was just 'the Acolyte', and that had seemed enough for a while – but I wasn't the Acolyte now. And I had let my hair grow, and it fell to my shoulders in a wavy tumble, and customers at the cafe called me 'love' or 'darlin' or 'dear', but I hated wearing dresses, and felt uncomfortable in anything that showed a hint of my shape. So what did that mean?

I said some of this to Meg, who told me that I was the only one who knew what I was, and it might take some time to figure out, but that was okay. Then she told me that there was more than one way to be a woman, and I didn't have to listen to anyone else about what that meant for me. Then she got up from her seat, ran her hands along a shelf at the back of the cafe, and plucked out a copy of *Orlando*. In this way, I began the literary stage of my education.

By the time I opened the boxes of books from the sociologist, I was on my way to being well-read, and, furthermore, had a good idea of what sold and what didn't. I stacked the books from the sociologist in two piles: To Shelve, and Definitely Not. Meg had been right; a lot of it was dry, textbook-style stuff, or impenetrable scholarly tomes. The To Shelve pile was pretty small, and I had almost gotten to the bottom of the first box when I pulled out a book called *Cults: A Spotter's Guide*.

I knew what cults were. I'd heard the word when Meg had used it the few times we talked a bit about where I came from. I knew, by then, that Father's Children was a cult.

I could feel my heartbeat in my fingers as I opened the book. On the inside cover, a note had been handwritten.

To my dear father-in-law – thought this would be right up your street! Jarlath, Christmas '17.

It looked quite different to the other books – the cover was bright and almost jaunty, and the text inside was quite large, with lots of pictures. The spine had never been cracked. I flipped through, and saw images of strange symbols, a photo of hundreds of couples dressed in white, a mugshot of a man with wild hair and eyes that drilled through you. One picture, full page and in colour, showed a large house from above, like it had been taken from an aeroplane. Around it were bright dots of colour that I realised, on closer inspection, were people, lying in their dozens on the ground.

I flipped back to the contents page.

Introduction
1. What is a cult, anyway?
2. How they get you
3. How they keep you
4. How they play the tax man
5. How to tell if your new best friend is actually trying to get you into a cult
6. De-programming: How it works and if it works
7. Case Study – Aum Shinrikyo
8. Case Study – The 'Moonies'
9. Case Study – Heaven's Gate
10. Case Study – Multi-level Marketing
Acknowledgements

By that point, I had stopped thinking of books as Transgressive objects. I no longer automatically rejected what they told me about history and the world if they contradicted Father's teachings. I didn't feel guilty when I became so involved in a story that the characters became almost more important to me than real people and felt more real than anything that had ever happened to me.

But this book . . . this book felt illicit. It felt secret. It felt dangerous. And so, for the first time, I didn't tell Meg when I took a book home. I tucked it into my backpack, and that night I sat up at my kitchen table with my notebook and my pen ready, and I read the entire thing. In the end, I didn't touch my notebook once. I didn't put the book down, even when I needed to go to the bathroom. I continued to read it as I walked along the corridor, and fumbled for the light switch, and hiked my trousers down and up one-handed.

It was as though someone had reached into my past and written it all down. It didn't all fit, of course. I'd never experienced 'love-bombing', or any of the other indoctrination methods that cults use to entice their victims. I'd been born into my cage. But there were so many other things that rang jarringly true. It was like the book's writer had plucked elements from my life and scattered them through the pages.

Mind control is used to inspire terror in cult members. The members are taught to believe that the leaders and elite know and see all, creating deep-seated fear . . .

Escapees often reflect that they cannot understand what led them to do the things they did under the influence of the cult. Their mindset was wholly controlled, so that behaviour which once might have seemed outlandish, extreme or even abhorrent became normalised . . .

Methods by which the cult ensures compliance include isolation from mainstream society, punishment, confession, removal of privacy and freedom, enforced dress codes . . .

Reading almost every page was like someone throwing a bucket of cold water over me. It was here. It was all here. Everything that had happened to me, everything that the Children had done, everything Father had said and wrote . . . it was all here.

It was all so fucking unoriginal.

I was angry, mostly. Angry at just how stupid I'd been, at just how stupid we'd all been. How could we have been taken in with all that nonsense? The Elders can read minds? Father is God? What the fuck.

I wondered if Father really knew what he was doing, or if he was just as deluded as the rest of us. But really, it was textbook, what he'd created. A group of mindless, lost people, all enforcing his batshit philosophy.

Is there a playbook somewhere? Like, when a woman becomes one of the senior Sisters, do they take her aside and say, here, this is how you make all these girls and women do what they're told? Or do they just sort of absorb it?

Or maybe the ones who have an aptitude for that sort of cruelty are the ones that are chosen to become senior Sisters in the first place. I certainly remember the figures from my childhood, Sister Morningbright especially, seemed to enjoy what they were doing. There was never a reprimand or punishment doled out that wasn't accompanied by her smug satisfaction.

I haven't seen her since I came back. Maybe she's dead. I hope so.

As I walk back towards the women's dormitory, I try to cry. It's not easy. I don't cry often, and even though I pinch the tender skin inside my elbow and try to work up tears, I just can't get going. So I think about Meg, and the Underpass Cafe, and my little flat—

This does actually make the tears come. My nest, my sanctuary. The place I'd retreat to at night, the place Meg would visit with food, where we'd watch movies, the place I'd been safe for so long. I want to be there so badly.

By the time I get to the dormitory, I have tears running down my cheeks and my eyes feel swollen. Perfect.

From the main entrance of the women's dormitories, I can see the Wall and the Gate. Just visible beyond them, in the farthest corner of Home, is the Big House. It's lit up, like it always was, the glow from its many windows spilling out over the high hedges that surround it.

I can't worry about how the hell I'll get in there. Not right now. Things are moving, finally. I've got a way to Amy.

Right. Action.

The door makes a loud creak as it opens, which is good. I need to be seen.

The entry hall is dim, with light from the open common room door casting a rectangular spotlight on the floor and wall further down the passage. It's where the Sisters gather in the evenings to sew and mend things, and you're allowed to chat a little. No one comes out, so I push the main door shut, letting it bang closed as though by accident.

It works. A face pokes out from the common room, one of the other Sisters. She sees the state of me, and her jaw drops open. She withdraws hurriedly, and I limp towards the stairs. I hear a voice behind me as I put my hand on the bannister. It's the dormitory leader, Sister Justice.

'Sister Catherine? Where in Father's name—' She stops as I turn, and she sees my teary, dirty face.

'I . . . I'm sorry, Sister . . . I . . . I just need to . . . I'll go wash—' I gulp down a sob.

Sister Justice looks at me for a moment, her mouth a thin hard line.

There is a murmur behind her, and we both look around to see several Sisters clustered at the door to the common room, peering out. Sister Justice grasps my elbow firmly and flaps a hand to dispel the other women.

'Back inside! Back to your industry!' she says, and they melt back into the room, but as slowly as they can get away with. I get it. Not much happens when you are one of the Children. Life is all routine and ritual and round and round it goes. Any break from the norm is a welcome distraction.

Sister Justice marches me down the hall, towards a door that she unlocks with a key on a chain hanging at her belt. She sweeps me in, and only when the light comes on do I realise that we must be in her room. Dormitory leaders are the only women who get their own rooms.

It's austere, like everything for women here. A single bed, a desk, and a straight-backed chair. A bare bulb streaming light from the centre of the ceiling. A tiny window, looking out onto the brick wall of the adjoining dormitory building.

Sister Justice sits me down on her bed. 'Wait there,' she says crisply. She trots out and closes the door behind her. I listen, but she doesn't lock it. That's probably a good sign.

I wait long enough to get anxious that she's fetching one of the Elders, and that my ruse hasn't worked at all.

167

Long minutes later, the door opens and Sister Justice returns, this time carrying a bowl of water and a small green zippered bag with a white cross on it. She sits down at the table, unzips the bag, and plucks out a pair of scissors, a roll of bandage, and a couple of antiseptic pads. I sit in silence, twisting my hands together and squeezing out a couple more tears.

She doesn't look at me when she starts speaking. 'Where were you when it happened?'

I stare at her, and shake my head. She sighs, stops preparing the first aid stuff, and looks at me properly. 'It's all right,' she says, and I'm caught off guard by how gentle her voice is. 'You can tell me.'

'Coming back from the Fruitfulness Hall, Sister,' I whisper. She nods, and opens one of the antiseptic pads.

She dabs the pad on my cheekbone. I flinch, and she murmurs, 'Sorry.' I just about manage to stop my mouth from falling open. I don't remember her from when I was a kid. Is she new? Maybe Sisters are softer these days.

I catch myself. No one here can be trusted. I am a sucker for people treating me with a bit of kindness, like a dog that's been kicked all its life but still creeps up, ever hopeful, to the next human who offers it a scrap. But I must remember what the people here are like.

Sister Justice unwraps the next antiseptic pad and gently picks up one of my hands. She swipes softly at the tips of my fingers, where raking them through the earth has broken my nails and scraped away some of the skin. I don't have to fake flinching – it smarts like hell.

'When was this?' she says, in that same gentle voice.

'Just after I was released from my duties there, Sister,' I say. 'I don't know what time – it – it was – still light . . .' I let my voice choke off. She nods for me to continue.

'I don't . . . I didn't quite see . . . who he was . . .' I say. Then I bury my face in my hands and cry.

There is a creak as the Sister moves from the chair to sit beside me on the bed. The mattress dips towards her weight and I find myself leaning against her, with her arm around my shoulders.

She is patting my arm, and for a moment it's so like being with Meg again that I cry for real.

'That's good,' she's saying. 'That's good, that's good.' I think she's talking about crying, about 'letting it all out', until she says, 'Now you must forget this ever happened.'

I blink up at her and she smooths my hair away from my hot face. 'That's right. It's good you didn't see . . . whoever it was, because then you won't have to worry about being silly when you see him at Worship, will you?'

I stare at her.

'That's right. Now we're going to clean you up, and you're going to get into some fresh nightclothes, and you're not to be a silly girl anymore, are you?' I shake my head.

'That's right.' She pats my arm briskly, returns to the chair, and snips a bit of bandage off. She tapes it to my cheekbone, and her movements are slow and careful.

'Men have their appetites,' she says as she wets a cloth in the bowl of water and begins cleaning my face. She isn't making eye contact, and her voice is distracted, almost as though she's talking to herself. 'Men have their appetites, yes they do. It's how they're made. As Daughters of Father, it's our job to keep ourselves Pure until we're called upon. We need to give aid and comfort and support to men, not condemn them. No, that's not our place.'

For fuck's sake. I expected something like this, I suppose, but hearing it is something else again.

A tail-end of a memory. Freezing rain, and a circle of hostile eyes. A powerful feeling of shame, and of being somehow unclean, somehow spoiled. An Elder squeezing the back of my neck. Apologise.

I curl my hands into fists. I will not feel this shame. I will not. This place is diseased. It's not normal to treat people like this.

I block out the rest of Sister Justice's rambling, but zone back in long enough to smile and nod gratefully when she pats my hand and tells me that I can go.

I'm shuffling to the door when I remember. 'Oh, Sister . . .'

'Yes?' She doesn't look up from where she's repacking the first aid kit.

I let some petulance creep around the edges of my voice. 'It's just . . . I don't think I should . . . well, I think it might be best if I'm not sent to work at the Fruitfulness Hall again? Just, you know – I don't think it would be a good idea.'

Sister Justice looks around. Her eyebrows hike up to her hairline. 'Is that right?' she says slowly.

Jackpot.

29

THEN

The Hand of God and I were continuing my training last night, so my arms and back are aching. Not as much as they used to, though. I'm getting stronger. I'm embarrassed when I remember what I was like way back when I first joined the Warriors of God: I could barely manage a push-up, couldn't run for longer than a minute, and had no idea how to handle a weapon.

I've moved far beyond them, now. I hear them sometimes when I'm working at my desk in the Hand of God's study, when they are doing their forms and drills and bouts in the field, their silly little yells and cries making them sound like scrapping puppies. They've never been in a true battle. They don't know what it is to fight evil for Father. I do. I've done it so many times now.

And the women? I haven't heard a female voice since the Hand of God took me from the Sisters. There are none of their buildings in this part of Home, and women keep their voices low when they are working in the gardens. When I leave Home with the Hand of God, it is only men we find at the Transgressive places deep in the woods. Women Transgress too, but their evil is smaller, more domestic. Sullied men's evil travels, and infects, and pollutes widely. It's why it's so important to rid the world of it. It's why the work the Hand of God and I do is so important. It's why I'm so important.

It hasn't been easy. I had to get past the weakness in me at the start, the doubt about my true purpose, but with the Hand of God's guidance I got there. I left behind everything that tied me to my old, polluted self, and I began anew.

My body knew I was transforming. I woke up one morning last month and there was blood coming from me. I thought I was dying at first; that maybe something was wrong, that I'd been injured somehow. But when I told the Hand of God, he told me that it was all the Transgressions leaving my body. I would bleed for several days, and then it would stop. For the first two days, it felt like my guts were being pulled down out of me with the blood, but I bore the pain because I knew it was making me cleaner, purer. And it was like the Hand of God said: after a few days, the bleeding stopped.

The Hand of God left a mark in one of the pages of Father's books, where he must have known I would find it. I'm reading them and copying them all out, after all. It's *Father's Journey*, which tells the story of how Father received His Seven Visions and rose up against the false gods in the world Outside and established Home as a place of safety for all the Unsullied. In Father's Third Vision, He is visited by a being described as 'constructed of Pure light, too bright to look at'. The passage, which I recite sometimes when I can't sleep, goes as follows:

IV. Then, in My Despair, I was bequeathed My Third Vision. A being, constructed of Pure light, too bright to look at, appeared to Me. The being spoke in a Language unheard for Millennia, yet I understood the meaning Perfectly.

V. It was the Language of the Angels, for the Being was neither Man nor female, but an Angel composed of Energy and Grace and Purity, after My own Image.

I especially like the fifth verse. I repeat it over and over, until I can almost believe that it is written on the inside of my mouth.

. . . the Being was neither Man nor female, but an Angel . . .

The Hand of God had lightly underlined that section in pencil. I believe he left it there so I could find it, and understand myself better.

I asked him, during one of the long drives we have taken on the way to our work, what the purpose of angels is. He smiled and looked ahead at the road, but I could see he was pleased at the question. He likes when I ask good questions.

'Angels are soldiers,' he said. 'Angels will help us to win our war.'

'Our war?' I knew what he was talking about, but he likes to tell me anyway. I like to hear it.

'The war,' he nodded. 'Our constant fight against the forces of evil. The war that the Warriors train for, and that you and I are fighting even now.'

'The war that will secure the perfect world to come,' I said.

'The war that will enable us to build our perfect world, yes.'

I love it when he says *our*.

'I'll do anything to help make the perfect world,' I said carefully. 'I am your instrument.'

The proper phrase is 'I am His instrument' – Father's. It could have been a mistake, a slip of the tongue. I could pretend it was, if he got angry.

But he didn't get angry. His hand left the wheel and gripped my shoulder. For a moment, I was constructed entirely of light.

'You are my Acolyte,' he said. 'You are my soldier.'

He put his hand back on the wheel. The sun was setting over the far peaks, and the endless fields that lined the road glowed golden in the late light. A breeze gently stirred the few trees that we passed. My knife lay solid and heavy in my lap, ready for the night's work.

I knew that what the Hand of God meant, but hadn't said, was that I was his Angel.

30

Now

The morning after I'd returned to the dormitory with my mud-and-blood makeup routine, I was shaken awake even earlier than the other women, and crisply told to get up by Sister Justice. Once I was in my dress, cold water from my basin bath still dribbling down from my hair, I was informed that I would no longer be needed in the kitchen gardens, but rather, was being assigned to the Fruitfulness Hall indefinitely. I'd done such a good job last time, she told me, looking me dead in the eye, that I had been requested back. I was to report to the same room as yesterday, at once.

I did my best to look affronted, then sick and fearful, just to make Sister Justice feel like she'd got her squalid little win. She'd like me more if she thought I was broken.

I want to tear this whole place down. The women here have conspired to send a young woman who, as far as they know, was violently assaulted, to walk frequently back and forth along the path where it happened. Unprotected. And they did it because I had the temerity to ask them not to. It's what I wanted and expected them to do, but that doesn't mean it's not appalling.

I'm getting through the hours by imagining dropping a lit match behind me when Amy and I finally leave.

It's so frustrating being in the baby room. Each time, I'm locked in, with no opportunity to sneak upstairs to Angela. When my shift is over, I'm escorted to the main door, and one of the Sisters watches as I walk away. I am not kidding myself that they are doing this for my safety. They're doing it because they want me to know I don't have any freedom.

Being in the baby room has, inevitably, made me think about my own mother. I try not to, on the whole. We were never encouraged to think about having mothers when we were kids – we were all Father's Children, and that was enough. But Amy and I must have come from someone.

Did I know her? I had, occasionally, wondered if any of the Sisters were my mother. There was one Sister – I forget her name, she taught us sewing – who was kind and patient, and sometimes, when I couldn't sleep, I'd let myself imagine that she was my mother, and she would pull Amy and I aside one day and whisper the secret to us and she would stop Sister Morningbright being so mean to me and I would stop getting into trouble so much. But even as a kid, I knew that this was just a fantasy. The Sister didn't look anything like either me or Amy, for one thing. Not that Amy and I looked much like each other, either.

Most of the babies are asleep at the moment. It's their second nap of the day. One of them started to stir, his high little cries making the others wriggle in their sleep, dangerously close to waking, so I started stroking his back gently. It soothed him, but now whenever I stop, he stirs again. I have spent almost forty-five minutes perched on a chair beside him, my arm hanging into the cot, and my back is killing me. If anyone comes in, I will have to take my arm out of there quickly. That other Sister said touching the babies too much 'spoils them'.

That's got to warp a kid. But it's what must have been done to most of the Children – all the ones who grew up here, anyway. I knew from the research I'd done while living in Dublin that the cult has been going for almost fifty years by now, and established itself in the compound known as 'Home' thirty-five years ago, following the donation of the grounds and some of the original buildings by an aristocratic inductee into the cult, who passed away pretty speedily afterwards. Discounting the Awakened, who were brought here as children or adults, that meant that all the Children under the age of thirty-five had been brought up this way.

I started to do my research after I read that first book on cults. It wasn't the kind of thing most books the Underpass Cafe ended up with were about – we did do a line in non-fiction, but it was more biography or world history-type stuff – so I mostly looked online.

By that point, I had a dim grasp of how to use the internet for email, to search for information, and for social media (Meg took pictures of artfully arranged food and drink and stacks of books, 'posted' them, and then people – many of whom never even came to the cafe – would click a heart or a thumb to show their appreciation. I was uncertain of the point of all this). Up to then, the most searching I'd ever done online was for directions to the homes of people who wanted us to pick up large amounts of books they were donating.

I had a second-hand smartphone, given to me by a boy called Fiachra – a lanky teenager who worked for an hour most days after school, sweeping and dishwashing and sneaking cookies to his friends who came in and giggled at him in his apron. He'd got a new phone for his birthday, he said, and given I didn't have a phone, did I want his old one? I'd noticed that almost everybody had a phone, and it was occasionally a source of incredulity among the other staff and customers when they discovered that I didn't have one – or any social media, or even an email address.

'It's so old-school,' Fiachra said, about two months after he'd started at the cafe. He had asked if he could 'add me', and after a couple of confusing minutes, we'd established that I was from the Stone Age. 'It's just – I've like literally never met anyone who doesn't have a phone or anything. I mean, my granny has one. She plays Scrabble on it.' His tone was half amazement, half scorn. I'd resolved to get a phone then. I needed to disappear into normality.

They were expensive, though, and most – all – of my wages went on my tiny flat, and food, and transport. So when Fiachra casually offered me his phone, I jumped at the offer. (He subsequently provided me with instruction on how to use the damn thing. 'It's not a bother,' he said airily. 'I gave the same lessons to my granny.')

One night after work, not long after I'd read *Cults: A Spotter's Guide*, I sat down again at my kitchen table, took out my phone, and typed 'the children' into the search bar. None of the results were what I was looking for. I added the word 'cult' after my initial search and pressed the little magnifying glass. The page went blank, then new results appeared. At the very top was a picture of Father.

I slammed the phone face down on the table. Then I picked it back up with my eyes closed, and blindly jabbed at the button to get rid of the page of search results. When I opened my eyes, the screen had gone back to its usual picture of Meg and I at the cafe, both with cappuccino moustaches. I looked so happy in that picture.

I pressed both hands flat on the table. It was fine. It was all fine. I counted fours and tapped my fingers until I got my breathing under control.

Back in my hand, the sleeping black screen of the phone looked like a pool so polluted I couldn't see into its depths. This phone – this flat, this life – had all been separate from everything I'd been before. So separate that I had almost made myself believe that I was a completely different person now, and everything that had come before had happened to someone else, or in a dream. But seeing that picture of Father floating on the screen in my hand brought those two lives abruptly crashing together.

Why was I bringing it all back? What was the point of all this? Why scrape up the past and get its dirt caught under my fingernails?

Because I have to, I thought. Because I need to know.

I opened the search results again, and made myself look at the picture of Father.

He looked younger than I'd ever seen him, with shorter hair and a neater beard. His eyes were the same, though. That cobalt-blue gaze, the whites showing all around the irises. He was staring directly at the camera, face half turned over his shoulder, as though he'd glanced back to see the photographer. You could only see a bit of his shoulder in the picture, but it looked like he was wearing a suit, not his usual robes.

I pressed the link at the top of the page, under the image of Father. It said: 'The Children: The UK's Fastest Growing Cult?'

It took me a while to read the whole thing. Bits of it I didn't understand, so I had to stop and look other things up to get a context. Every so often, a phrase or detail or image would smack me in the chest with sickening recognition, so that I had to stop and press my hands against my eyes and force myself to breathe slowly.

The article described the Children as 'the secretive, fundamentalist organisation headed by the reclusive guru "Father"', and said it had been 'hit in recent years with a number of disturbing allegations'. It had a 'magpie philosophy', the journalist said, which meant that the cult's creed borrowed from a variety of sources: 'Principally Christianity, both evangelical and of the old-school fire-and-brimstone variety, though the Children are avowedly not Christian themselves, believing as they do that their "Father" is a god himself – not God's resurrected or returned Son, but an actual deity generously deigning to be down here in the dirt with the rest of us.'

The first part of the article was mostly about the history of the cult, where it had sprung from, what Father had done before ('Accounts conflict, but the man who styles himself "the truth made flesh" has left behind him a trail of discarded identities and failed business ventures, before this final, and so far successful, grift . . .').

The second part of the article looked at why the Children were experiencing a boom in popularity in recent years. 'Fringe groups which attract people searching for meaning and belonging are nothing new, but have rarely been long-lived in the UK. So what has prompted an increasing number of people to give up their jobs, homes, and families, and pledge themselves to a bearded con man living on a far-flung Scottish country estate?' It didn't give any clear answers, but offered a lot of possibilities: something about 'economic distress' and 'top-heavy work-life balance' making people crave 'a simple and idyllic communal country lifestyle', which made me snort. And then there was a bit about 'rapidly changing cultural landscapes with swift cancellation for those not fluent in woke-ese' (I had to stop and look several

things up at that point) sparking a desire for 'a return to traditional values' and 'traditional gender roles', apparently.

There was a linked article at the bottom, about several promi-
nent public figures who were 'connected' to the Children – actors,
politicians, that kind of thing. I didn't know who any of the
people were, so it didn't interest me much.

Scrolling through more search results, I paused at one link,
hovered my finger over it, then pressed down. It took me to a
newspaper report dated five months previously. The headline was
'"Father", Leader of "The Children" Cult, Found Dead'.

Dead. Father was dead.

It shouldn't have been such a shock, really – he was pretty
old, after all. But the news was like a kick to the guts. Father just
was – he existed as a fact of nature, like the sky or the air. The
very possibility that he'd be capable of death – of no longer exist-
ing – had never occurred to me.

It doesn't matter, I told myself. He's nothing to you now. None
of them are. So it doesn't matter that he's dead. It doesn't.

I made myself read the full article, trying to ignore the way
my heart was racing. He was, of course, to be succeeded by his
son, now himself known as 'Father'. There was no image of the
new Father, but all of a sudden, there were cool blue eyes watching me, and air on my skin, and Amy shivering beside me, and I
switched off the phone and didn't look for any other information
for a long time.

I stretch, feeling my spine ripple with little pops. I am so stiff and
tired. The babies will wake up soon, and then the hysterical cycle
of changing and feeding and cleaning will start again. But there's
not much longer to go today. Someone will come in to relieve me
in a couple of hours, and I'll see if I can take my chance to sneak
upstairs and see Angela.

I hope to fuck she's still here.

I need a better plan, to be honest. So far I've relied on what
worked before, which was being able to double back and get
upstairs without being seen. But I'm watched every second I'm
not locked in the baby room.

But what can I do? They escort me out of the building. They watch me as I leave. Once I get back to the dormitory, it's chores then dinner then bed, and all that is under the pinpoint glare of Sister Justice. My bed in the dormitory is farthest from the door, so creeping out at night would certainly alert someone.

The only time I have when I am wholly alone and unseen is the walk between the buildings to get back to the dormitory. I need to use that somehow. But how?

31

THEN

The Hand of God told me that he wanted me to progress to the next stage of training. He said I needed to learn to climb. He didn't say why, but I knew there must be a good reason. There is always a reason for everything he tells me to do.

I started with trees in the woods at night – they were easy, with wide, sturdy branches that I could haul myself up. The next stage, climbing up the rope in the Training Centre, is harder. The Hand of God showed me how to do it – you trap the rope between your thighs, pull up with your arms, and hitch your legs along by sliding them up the rope. It looked so easy when he did it.

I have not found it so easy. In fact, so far, I have completely failed.

It is late, and I have been in the Training Centre for hours already. My shoulders and upper arm muscles are screaming at me, and the skin on my hands is raw and bleeding in patches. And I still can't make it any higher up than a couple of feet.

I grip it again, ignoring the open, wet places on my hands which sing at the touch of the rope. I bite my teeth together and haul myself up. My toes rise from the floor, and the rope scrapes between my thighs, and my eyes are drawing level with my knotted hands, and I try to reach one arm up, but everything is shaking and then there is a rush of air, a thump, and I am resting my forehead on the cool floor and trying not to throw up.

I can't do it. I can't do it, and he's going to be so disappointed in me. He's going to cast me away, just like Amy.

Amy did that to *Catherine*. I am *not* Catherine, I am the Acolyte. I am the *Acolyte* and the Hand of God loves me.

He loves what you can do for him, a little voice whispers. I push it away. It's Catherine's voice, not mine, and she doesn't exist anymore.

I am the Acolyte, and the Hand of God has chosen me personally to help him in his important work. Surely I can manage this small task he's set me. I've done everything else he's asked – I've shown him that I can even be trusted to dispatch evil on my own. I have done it almost half a dozen times now.

It's always the same. We drive somewhere far away from Home, to places in the woods where Sullied men go, thinking that they are going to be left alone with a child. I let them get close, then I use my knife, and the Hand of God and I take the bodies far into the trees, where he says that they will be left to rot, just as all the Sullied eventually rot.

These trips usually take place every three or so weeks. In between times, I continue my study of Father's writing, and when the Warriors are in bed, I use the Training Centre and the Pavilion to strengthen my body. I like training at night. It's quiet, and there's no one around. The Hand of God doesn't supervise me when I train – he knows he can trust me to work hard. So I have the space to myself, and it's bliss. Catherine never had any space to herself, but the Acolyte has echoing, cavernous gym halls, and star-studded skies stretching above grass fields. Catherine slept stuffed into a cold room with other girls who hated the sight of her, but the Acolyte has a room that no one else shares, with a door that shuts out the world. Catherine had no one, but the Acolyte belongs to the Hand of God.

Sometimes, I worry that it's all going to go away, like Amy went away from Catherine. But I know that if I work hard and do everything the Hand of God tells me, even if I don't always understand why I need to do it at first, then this life won't slip away through my fingers. I can hold on to it.

I need to think about this climbing task clearly. I am exhausted, and there's no point in doing any more tonight. I need to sleep, and eat, and try again tomorrow when I'm rested.

I lock up the Training Centre and make my way back to the Hand of God's residence. It is cold, and quiet, and so dark I can barely see my hand in front of my face. The only light comes from the moon and the scatter of stars far above.

Nausea ripples through me. My stomach feels like it's ripping itself in two. I'm bleeding again. The Hand of God told me that it was my Transgressions leaving me, the first time it happened, but then it happened again. And then again. I haven't told him that it's come back. I was supposed to be clean, and Pure. But every time the blood comes back, I feel like I'm full of grit under my skin. I feel stained.

I stop for a moment, tilt my head back and look up at the stars until I feel dizzy. The sky stretches so far above me. I used to think it just covered Home, and everything Outside was a sort of . . . blankness, I suppose. Just white-grey nothingness, filled with lost souls – the luckiest of whom would be found and Awakened and come Home.

But I've been out there now. I know that the sky hangs over endless forests and hills and roads ribboning through them, hours and hours of space and distance filled with demons hiding under the faces of men.

I suppose there's more to the world that I haven't seen, yet. I suppose those men must live somewhere. We've driven past places, sometimes, collections of buildings where all the Sullied must live. Sometimes there are just a few buildings, but sometimes there are hundreds and hundreds. It makes my head ache to think about there being that many people in the world.

Somewhere out there, among the Sullied, there must be a building where Amy is.

I'm near Home's boundary wall, here. It's just visible through the trees.

A mad idea takes hold of me. I climb a tree – I can manage that, at least – close to the Wall, I jump over, I run down the road and through the forest and I find the building Amy is in and . . .

And what? What would happen? Would she even recognise me, this shaven-headed, uniformed new person?

Why would I want to find her, anyway? She ran away. She left me.

She left *Catherine*.

But here, under the stars, with no one else but me in the whole world alive and breathing, it doesn't feel like there's much difference between me and Catherine at all.

32

Now

The light is fading, and I don't want to attempt this in the dark, so I need to get going if I'm going to do it.

I look up. The first-floor windows can only be fifteen or so feet off the ground.

I've done something like this before, I'm pretty sure. I have a vague memory of scrambling up and down trees all over the compound shortly before I escaped. I can't remember why – part of the nonsense Hand got me doing during his long absences. He was forever inventing crap for me to do, which of course I did faithfully. Learn to climb trees, then a rope, copy out all the shite from Father's writings, weapons training and hand-to-hand combat. All of it for no purpose whatsoever. None that I can remember, anyway.

I suppose it's about to come in useful now.

I overheard a couple of the Sisters talking as I was escorted out of the Fruitfulness Hall earlier, aching all over with tiredness after my endless shift with the babies. I caught a snatch of the conversation as they passed me on their way up the stairs, something about one of the rooms upstairs finally being free once the occupant is moved back to the Big House tomorrow. That's got to be Angela.

As soon as I was out of sight of the Sister watching me from the door of the Hall, I doubled back around the building until I was under what I'm fairly certain is Angela's window. Luckily, it's at a corner, which makes this easier.

The outside corners of the Fruitfulness Hall, like most of the buildings here, have large, thick blocks standing out from the rest of the bricks, sort of decorating the edge where two walls meet. They go all the way up, creating a kind of ladder – if you can keep a hold of a ladder with steps only as wide as your fingertips. The blocks are about as high as my knee, so I can reach between them. I just need to keep a grip until I get up to the shade-covered window on the first floor and knock on it. If Angela is in there, I'm reasonably sure she'll let me in. Or at least open the window to hear what I have to say. I haven't forgotten the way she held on to me after they took her baby away, her wails muffled by my shoulder, and I'm hoping she hasn't either.

If I've got it wrong, and it's not Angela's room, or if there's a Sister in there with her, or she's gone already . . .

Well, then it's time for plan B.

Which I will devise when it becomes necessary.

I feel a bit giddy as I begin to climb. I feel like myself, like I did when I first sneaked upstairs and found Angela. I need to hold on to this, this recklessness, this Zoe-ness.

Except Zoe is never that reckless, to be honest. She's quiet, and calm, and ordered, and reliable. She never hung off the sides of buildings on spurious chances.

Climbing the wall is hard. My skirts keep getting in the way – it's difficult to raise my leg, and when I do, I have to sort of shake the fabric away from my toes before I press them into the tiny ledge and push myself upwards. I suppose I could have taken my dress off and scaled the wall without it, but the possibility of being discovered is bad enough without being in my underpants as well.

The thought brings a wild giggle bubbling up in my chest, and for a second, I almost lose my grip. I claw my fingers into the stone and focus on calming down the thudding deep in my chest. I risk a look back and down over my shoulder. The ground must be six feet or so below – not too far, but enough that I get a swirl of vertigo and look back at the surface of the wall again quickly.

Deep breaths.

I focus on the stone as I climb. Off-white, mainly smooth surface with some pitted holes and crevices. The occasional damp patch of moss under my fingers, which are getting chilled and stiff. My shoulders, upper arms and legs are beginning to complain. Surely climbing wasn't this tough when I was a kid?

I glance up, and see the windowsill just above my head. It's about two feet in from the edge of the wall, but if I get a little further up and lean out just a wee bit, maybe I can peek in.

No such luck. The blind is firmly down, a grey veil over whoever – whatever – is inside.

My foot slips and, for a sickening moment, I feel the yawning emptiness behind and below me. I'm holding on to the stone, but only just, only just. I scrabble with the toe of my boot, trying to find the ledge I was trusting my weight to only a moment before. It's gone.

The wind picks up, and for a second I feel as though I'll simply be blown off the wall. But then my toe finds the edge of the block again, and I grip the wall like a crab, breathing, breathing.

I close my eyes and lean my forehead against the wall, right on the pointed edge. It feels like I could press my head forward and be split in two.

What would Meg say, if she saw this? Me in a ridiculous, prim brown dress, clinging on to a wall halfway up a building, on the off-chance that I might be able to talk through a window to someone who almost certainly never wants to see me again?

I imagine her far below, arms crossed, one eyebrow raised as she looks up at me.

'How are ye, Spiderwoman?'

'Grand so,' I whisper into the wall.

'Sure you're lookin it right enough.' She'd rub one eyebrow with her forefinger, like she always did when she was being patient under extreme provocation. 'And is it worth it, now? This death-defying stunt? To find someone you haven't seen in years, who, as far as you know, is here entirely of her own free will?'

I feel sick. Below, Imaginary Meg's brow creases in sympathy. 'Is any of this worth it, Zoe? Leaving your home, your life?

Putting yourself back in the path of a man like Hand? Going through . . . everything they've done to you?'

I know exactly what I'd say to her, so I do say it, whispering it to the wall but seeing her face. 'It is worth it. It's all worth it.'

There is silence from Meg. She's not down there anymore. She's not anywhere. There's only me.

And Amy.

I open my eyes, and carefully raise one hand, dragging my fingertips up the stone until I find the next ledge. Then I pull my opposite foot up, kick the skirts away, and nestle my toes into the foothold I find. I rise.

I draw level with the windowsill. I either do this now, or not at all.

Keeping a careful hold on the wall with my left hand, I stretch my right out and rap sharply on the window.

Nothing but the wind whistling past my ears. Don't look down. Nothing, nothing.

Do I try again?

Maybe the room is empty.

Maybe Angela is in the bed and too weak to get up.

Maybe she's not coming to the window to let me in because no sane person would expect a visitor to demand entrance that way.

I rap again, longer and more insistently this time. The force rocks me back a little, and I clamp onto the wall again with panicky fingers and toes. Fuck, fuck, fuck.

A muffled rattle, and through the pane of glass, I see the shade being jerked to the side. A pale slice of a face peers out, looks past me, forward and up. I wave. Angela notices me, and her mouth drops open in a way that would be comical if I wasn't clinging to the side of a building in what is increasingly feeling like a force ten gale. I jab my finger at the window and raise my eyebrows. Angela blinks, then fumbles with the latch and pulls the sash up a few inches.

'What are you doing?' she hisses, dropping heavily to her knees to speak through the gap.

'Just a social call,' I say. 'Mind pulling that up a bit further so I can get in?'

'What are . . . you're mad . . . Catherine, you can't climb in! It's too far!'

'I'll give it a go,' I say. Angela pushes at the window, then winces and drops a hand down – I think to hold her stomach.

'Are you all right?' I say. She gives me a flat look, then tries more carefully to push the sash up again. It doesn't budge.

'It's jammed – I can't open it,' she says. She glances back into the room behind her, and I freeze. She looks back and sees my face. 'It's all right, no one's there,' she says. Her eyes are bruised-looking, and the skin is drawn tight under her cheekbones. Her hair hangs in thin, greasy strings from her scalp. She leans forward slowly and carefully, like a woman carrying a heavy, shifting load on her back. She rests her arms on the windowsill. 'Why are you climbing up the side of the building?' she says conversationally.

'I want to see Amy,' I say. I'd meant to lead up to this request a bit more gradually, but I'd also planned to have this conversation while standing on solid ground, so here we are.

'She's not here,' Angela says, and laughs. It's a strange, dull sound, utterly without humour.

'Listen,' I say. 'I need to see her. I need to, Angela.' She blinks at the use of her old name. 'I came back to find her. I need to find her. It's like – it's like there's something torn out of my chest, like a piece of me is missing. I need to see her, I just need to. Can you help me?'

She stares at me, the windowpane covering the top half of her face. A gust of wind whips my skirts around my legs, and I carefully flex my aching fingers. My left hand is starting to shake.

'Do you work down there?' she asks, so quietly that the wind almost takes her words and I barely hear her.

'With the babies? Yes.'

'Get me my baby,' she says. 'Get me my baby, and I'll help you.'

33

THEN

It's late when I hear the door opening. It's not too unusual for the Hand of God to come in unexpectedly at odd times of the night, but I can hear two sets of footsteps, which is unusual.

I sit up. It's dark still, so I haven't overslept, but I don't have a clock in my little room so I've no idea what time it is. It feels very late, or very early.

'. . . convinced of the necessity of this.' The Hand of God's voice floats through my door. There's the sound of someone clearing their throat, and the front door closing.

'Merely a chat. Merely a brief chat. Is your, ah . . . ward upstairs?' Another man's voice, but one I can't quite place.

'No . . . let's go into . . .' The voices both dwindle as they move away, and a door opens and closes. That's the door to the Hand of God's study. I know the squeak.

I know I shouldn't, but I slip out of bed and pad in bare feet to my door. I ease it open and peek out into the hall. It's dark, and silent. A thin light glows from underneath the study door.

There's never been a visitor, in all the time I've been here. One of the Sisters comes and leaves food for us, but it's always when we're out, so I've never seen her. Other than the evidence of her brief presence, it's always just me and the Hand of God. This must be one of the Elders – no one else would dare to talk to the Hand of God – but why come here so late?

I shift from foot to foot in the cold pre-dawn darkness. The Hand of God didn't sound happy. I know that he doesn't think much of the Elders. He's said as much, when we're in the car sometimes. They are complacent, and indolent, and content in their opulence here at Home. They don't endanger themselves for Father, for the perfect world to come.

What should the Acolyte do, in this situation? Help, probably. I just mainly want to go back to my warm bed. But the Hand of God relies on me, and I want to prove myself to him, so I need to find a way to help somehow.

There's a floorboard in the middle of the hall that groans when you step on it, so I skirt it carefully as I move towards the study door. The voices inside are just a murmur, so I press my ear against the gap where the door meets the wall.

My breathing seems far too loud, and almost drowns out the low voices from inside. I try to breathe more quietly.

'. . . your frequent excursions.' That's the man.

Then the Hand of God, sounding clipped: 'My position as Hand requires that I protect the Children from Outside influences. Naturally, I cannot achieve that if all I do is cower at Home.'

A pause. 'Well, we're all very grateful for your protection.'

'I assume that's not why you're here at this hour. To convey your gratitude.'

'No. Quite apart from the difficulty of, ah, pinning you down at times, I thought . . . Father thought . . . it best if this chat was as discreet as possible.'

'You were sent?' The Hand of God sounds like Sister Morningbright used to sound when you gave her some excuse that she didn't believe for a minute.

'I act only in accordance with His wishes.' I can hear the capital letter. He, whoever it is, means Father.

A long silence. 'Of course you do.'

'Look, the issue is . . .' A creak, and footsteps crossing the room. I dart back to my room. Are they coming out?

A second. Another. No one opens the door, but even just a few steps away I can't hear what's going on in there.

My heartbeat shudders through every part of my body as I creep back and put my ear against the crack. The man is still talking. Where have I heard him before?

'. . . starting to get concerned. It's not natural, what you're doing with . . .'

'Who has expressed these concerns?' There's another creak, and electricity flashes through my veins even as I realise it's just the sound of one of them shifting in a chair.

'That's beside the point. The point is, concerns have been raised. Multiple concerns. From various sources.'

'What would you have me do? Alternatively? With a case such as this?'

'I simply—'

'No, please enlighten me. What would you suggest, as an alternative option?'

'I don't . . .' An exasperated sigh. 'Could things not simply have continued on as they were?'

'Quite impossible. The females were incapable. It needed to be removed to a place where it could cause no further harm, where it could be channelled.'

'And you were the only one who could, ah, "channel" it?'

Yet another pause, and this one sounds dangerous. When the Hand of God speaks, it sounds as though he's choosing his words carefully to avoid spitting them out. 'Where else could it be placed? It couldn't continue where it was. The experiment exposing it to the Warriors was unsuccessful. Therefore, it had to be wholly under my control.'

'Couldn't we . . . I don't know . . . have it . . . disposed of?'

'Disposed of?' The Hand of God's voice is flat.

'Must we keep such an aberration?'

'You'd suggest that? Even knowing the lineage?'

Silence, then in a shocked voice, 'You're not saying—'

'I am.'

This time, the other voice doesn't speak for so long that I want to fling open the door in impatience. My feet are aching with the cold. I shift my weight gently, so I don't make any noise.

'I . . . I wasn't fully aware.'

'I would hardly have expected you to be.'

'This does rather change things.'

'Yes. The progeny must be protected. We don't want to repeat the circumstances with the last Seed—'

'Yes, yes,' the man cuts in. 'I wasn't suggesting—'

'Not at all. The issue is quite different.'

'Yes. Yes, of course.'

A drawn-out creak, which I recognise as the sound of one of them getting up out of a chair. I skid back into my room and close the door just as the study door opens and their voices and feet move into the hall.

I fall back into bed and pull the covers up to my waist. They're moving to the front door. The man, whoever he is, is leaving.

I've heard his voice before, definitely. And what were they discussing? Something dangerous. A weapon? Something the women couldn't manage. But why would you give women something dangerous in the first place?

There were words I don't know, as well. Lin-ee-age and pro-jen-ey. How would they look written down? They must be in Father's books – everything is. I'll have to try and find out.

The front door shuts, and for a moment there is no sound but the blood thumping in my ears. Then footsteps, slow and steady, move down the hall. They come to my door, then stop.

Did I shut the door properly?

A handle, turning. I shut my eyes and try to breathe as though I'm sleeping. It feels like someone is sitting on my chest.

The quiet sound of my door opening, its passage disturbing the air. The darkness in the room lifts slightly, just enough that I can perceive it through my closed eyelids. I try desperately to keep my face still and relaxed, to keep my eyelids from fluttering.

The Hand of God, breathing. What's he doing? He's not moving. He's just standing there. Watching me? Does he know? Does he know that I listened in?

Maybe that was the wrong thing to do. Of course it was. I'm always doing the wrong thing.

Stay still, stay still.

Soft footsteps. They cross the tiny room in two steps, and then I feel breath brush my face. He's leaning over me.

Stay. Still.

I take breaths in and out through my nose, count the spaces between each one. My lungs swell in my chest, until they're so big it feels like my ribcage is going to burst open.

I can feel him, his face so close to mine. I can feel the heat from his skin. I can hear the liquid sound of him swallowing.

There is a tug at my waist. A light weight settles over my body. The covers. He's pulled the covers up to my chin.

His hands pat the blanket down around me. Then a dry hand against my forehead.

He moves away. His breath and heat and the little sounds of his body recede, then my door shuts, very quietly. I hear him walk upstairs, and the familiar creaks and groans of the floor above as he goes into his room and gets into bed.

I wait for the noises to stop before I open my eyes.

34

Now

Angela shuts the window, letting the shade drop down so the window looks once more like a blind eye.

Right.

I climb down, because what else can I do? I could rap on the window and try to get her to a) open it and b) understand that what she wants is impossible, but I have the feeling that it would be useless. She's told me her terms. If I want to see Amy, I have to get Angela her baby.

My feet meet solid ground and I sink onto it gratefully. I take a second to rest, sitting hunched with my back to the wall and the wind cooling the sweat on my forehead. But I can't rest long. I heave myself up. I need to get back into the Fruitfulness Hall. I need to find the newborn room, and Angela's baby.

My stomach sloshes, and I have to grip the side of the building and close my eyes until I don't feel like throwing up anymore.

I haven't eaten since – last night? I get up too early to have breakfast before I start my shift in the baby room, and they don't give me any food while I'm in there. So it must have been last night's dinner, which I hadn't had much of anyway. The food here is disgusting. Give me stale rolls from the Underpass Cafe any day.

I need to think carefully. I've managed on sheer dumb luck so far, but I need to make a plan. The baby rooms are all locked, and I was supposed to be back at the dormitory about half an hour ago. I can't just go storming in, steal a (potentially very noisy) baby, bring it to Angela, then . . . what? Was she planning to keep it? Escape herself? Did she want my help with that, too?

It's all too much right now. I have to make a plan.

I turn it over and over in my head as I trudge back to the dormitory and endure Sister Justice's pointed comments about my lateness. I claim to have been kept late at the Fruitfulness Hall, which she'll definitely check up on later, but I will deal with that when I have to. I eat as much dinner as I can stomach (some kind of greasy soup) and sit in the common room darning socks with the other women. I've been darning the same sock for about three days, but I think they've realised how terrible I am at it because they've stopped trying to make me hurry up and do more.

The common room has hard-backed chairs set around the walls, old and creaky and occasionally a bit treacherous when it comes to bearing your weight. The coveted ones sit either side of the fireplace, which is lit only when it's absolutely freezing outside. It's smoking dully just now, and the heat doesn't quite reach me in the far corner of the room. Sister Justice is sitting on one of the fireside chairs, and on the other side is a woman who I'm fairly sure was here as a child the same time as me. She's familiar, but I can't put a name to her. It doesn't matter – she hasn't tried to interact with me at all. Her name would be different now, anyway. She follows Sister Justice around like an adoring little shadow.

'Ow!' I look down at my hand. The needle has sunk into the pad at the tip of my thumb, and a bright bead of blood is welling up there. I stick it in my mouth and suck.

'Ooh. That looks nippy,' says a voice next to me. It's a young-ish Sister, with papery pale skin, watery blue eyes behind thick lenses, and a flickery little smile. I smile back.

'It's grand,' I say. We're allowed to speak a little during common room time, but I keep my voice low out of habit, and bend back to the sock.

'Oh – you're not Irish, are you?'

I look up. 'I . . . what makes you say that?' The Sister blinks rapidly behind her glasses. It makes her look like an anxious mole.

'It's just you said "grand". My grandfather was Irish and he was always saying it.' She laughs, a kind of trill that shuts off suddenly, then that on-off smile again.

'You're from Outside,' I say.

She drops her head, cheeks flushing a dull red. 'Sorry,' I say, feeling stupid. It's considered rude to draw attention to someone's previous status as a Sullied person, even though, as I remember, it was made passive-aggressively explicit to them as often as possible.

'It's just, I am, too,' I say. She looks up, the movement of her head birdlike in its quickness. I see from the corner of my eye that Sister Justice's head is swivelling in our direction, so I look back down at the sock. Beside me, the woman does the same.

'Sorry,' I say quietly, pushing the needle into the fabric at random and pulling the thread through. 'It's just it gets a bit lonely here, you know? When you haven't always been a part of it, I mean.'

'Oh, do you think so?' She bites off the end of her thread and neatly folds the darned sock into the basket at her feet. She picks up another one and turns it over in her hands in a businesslike way, assessing the worn patches. 'I find just the opposite,' she continues. 'Being a part of something here – it's like coming home. Well, I suppose it is Home!' That trilling, snapped-off laugh again. I force a smile, and jab my needle into the fucking sock. She's just another fanatic. The Awakened are worse than the ones who were born into it, I swear.

'Where do you work?' she asks. It's on the tip of my tongue to say 'the Underpass Cafe', but I manage to drag my thoughts back into order just in time.

'The Fruitfulness Hall,' I say.

'Oh! All those little ones! How sweet!'

I think of all those blank-eyed babies, and stab the sock again. 'Yep.'

'I'd love to work in there. I actually asked for it when I came here, but they said they needed Sisters in the laundry, but maybe a place would come up soon, so I keep hoping! I'm Sister Diligence, by the way,' she says.

'Sister Catherine,' I say.

'Oh – you haven't been Named yet? I was Named after only three months here. They said it was quite early, but—' Trill.

'By the grace of Father I'll be blessed soon with a Naming of my own, Sister,' I say, looking up and fixing her left ear with a beatific gaze. Her smile flickers and her eyes flutter and the effect is like someone rapidly opening and shutting blinds. I keep my stare fixed just slightly to a point beside her head until she looks hurriedly down at her darning again, letting out her weird little laugh as she does.

It's rare that I meet someone even more socially awkward than me. Sister Diligence – or whatever her name was/is really – is like someone who has had laughter painstakingly explained to her, in great detail, possibly with diagrams, but never actually heard a real human being laugh before finally giving it a go herself.

That's unfair of me, really. You don't end up somewhere like Home without something – possibly several things – going seriously wrong in your life at some point. I'd bet that no one has ever told Sister Diligence that she is worth something, which is why she feels so at home in a place that treats women like a mass servant class.

She is talking again. I tune in reluctantly.

'Not quite sure how it all works here exactly, but I suppose if I can't help look after the Fruit I would like a few of my own! More little Warriors for Father! What about yourself, Sister Catherine? Would you like to have lots of babies?'

And just like that, looking into the glassy puddle of Sister Diligence's eyes, I have my plan.

35

THEN

I've had a breakthrough. For the last few weeks, I've been following a regime of push-ups and handstands. I worked out that if I'm not strong enough to pull myself up a rope, then I need to get stronger. Now I can do one hundred and ten push-ups in a row, and I can hold myself in a handstand – not against a wall or anything – for fifteen seconds. My upper arms have a bulge in them that goes hard when I clench my fists. When the Hand of God came to me last night and asked me to show him my progress, I pulled myself straight up the rope without even using my legs.

He was pleased, I could tell. He didn't say anything, but he doesn't have to.

I have a new task now.

I haven't asked why – he'll tell me when I need to know. For now, I just need to show him I can do whatever he needs me to. I can be who he wants me to be, if I just try hard enough.

'There's an attic in the Worship Hall,' he said. I was standing to attention in his study, the Hand of God in his chair, chin over his steepled fingers. 'I've left the skylight unlatched. Tonight, you will gain entry to the attic, and prove that you have done it by retrieving the object I've left for you there.'

I nod.

'That will be all.'

It's night now, cold but clear, with a bright moon that casts everything in silver. It's late enough that everyone is in bed, and my footsteps are the only ones I hear, echoing back to me as I pass through the Pavilion. I can't remember the last time I saw this place busy. Probably when I was back with the Warriors, while we were out training.

I haven't been to the Worship Hall in so long – not since the Hand of God made me his Acolyte. I've never asked why I don't go anymore. I don't miss it. It was always long, and kind of boring. The way the Hand of God and I serve Father now is far better.

Frozen leaves crunch under my boots as I reach the back wall of the Hall. It's smooth and featureless, except for the different bricks on the corners of the building, which are bigger and thicker and stand out about an inch from the rest of the wall. Just enough for my fingers and toes to latch onto, and climb.

I blow onto my cold fingers, flex them a couple of times, then grab hold of the brick edges at shoulder height and begin to pull myself up. It's not too hard, especially if I don't look down. Just like climbing a tree.

Pretty soon I'm as high as I can get, which is about a foot underneath the top of the building. There is a lip that juts out over me about half a foot, but if I can pull myself over it, I'll be able to drop down onto the flat section of roof on the other side.

There's a small opening in the brick to my right. It's a pipe, poking out to let rainwater run off the flat roof. It goes right through to the other side.

Most of the buildings in Home are made similarly. There are a couple of newer ones, like the Nutrition Hall, or the dormitories for the Warriors, but mostly they are made along the same pattern. Pillared porches, the stepping-stone bricks up the corners of the walls, flat roofs at the back that rise to a slope. A few weeks ago, the Hand of God took me to the roof of our building. On the upper floor, where I hadn't previously been, there was a cupboard with a hatch set into the ceiling. The Hand of God indicated a ladder propped against the wall, which I unfolded, and we went up through a dusty and disused attic and out through a skylight to the flat roof.

I don't think I'd ever been so high. The wind pulled my hair – a little longer now, and in need of shaving again – back from my temples, and made my eyes water.

'What do you think?' the Hand of God had said. He leant on the low wall, and swept an arm out to indicate the space around us.

'It's – it's beautiful,' I said. But I wasn't thinking that. What I was thinking was, *it looks so small*. I could see the entirety of Home from this point. The Hand of God and I live near the back of Home, near the rear boundary wall. Ahead of us was the Nutrition Hall with the squat little laundry and tidy kitchen gardens attached, the Warrior Barracks and the Pavilion off to the side, even the female dormitories visible at the furthest end – all linked by neat paths and surrounded by well-kept lawns. Near the Gate, in sight of my (Catherine's) old classroom, was the Big House. It was partially hidden by the large hedges around the lawns bordering the house, but from this vantage point I could see it more clearly than I ever had. From here, it looked like a box I could pick up with one hand.

'It looks different once you've left, doesn't it?' said the Hand of God. I felt my cheeks grow hot. Of course he could tell what I was thinking.

'It does,' I agreed. I looked at the road winding out into the woods on the other side of the Gate. Beyond were hills and towns. Beyond were the demons.

'We have to protect it,' I said. I didn't mean to say it aloud, but I was thinking it so he knew anyway.

The Hand of God put his hand on my shoulder and turned me to face him. The wind made the sides of his suit jacket flap open. I had a thick jumper on, so I was all right, but he must have felt the chill. He didn't seem to, though. He never seemed to be cold, or tired, or hungry, or anything.

He met my eyes with his. 'That's what all this is about,' he said. 'Protecting Home. Everything I ask you to do, everything I tell you – it's all to protect what we have here.'

Before we climbed back in through the skylight, he pointed out the gutter pipes to me. There were four, spaced out along the low wall. On the roof side, the pipes were set into little dips in the stone, so that the water would collect there. The mouths of the pipes weren't quite flush with the dips; they poked out a few inches.

He pointed all this out, and I listened. I didn't understand why he was telling me, but I knew that I'd understand some day. He wouldn't say it unless it was important.

I put it together last night, when he gave me my task. I was thinking about how to get onto the Worship Hall roof. The building was secured at night, and I didn't have the key. Of course, I'd have to climb the wall. What was the point of getting me to master rope climbing if I wasn't going to use it? I remembered the lip at the top of the building. How could I possibly get over it? Then I remembered the conversation on the roof, and I remembered the pipes, and I knew that nothing the Hand of God does is without reason.

I keep doubting myself, doubting my fitness to be his Acolyte – even doubting him sometimes. But moments like this show me I just need to have faith in him and everything will work out.

I have a short rope wound crossways around my chest – over one shoulder and under the opposite arm. Shifting my weight carefully onto my left hand, I pull the rope over my head until I'm holding it coiled in my right. My knees are getting stiff in this position, so I gently stretch them. I can take my time.

The wind gusts against my back, but I've got a good grip around the wall and I'm not worried. I look at the pipe opening to my right, then up at the lip of the wall, and try to gauge the distance on the other side.

I press the rope against the wall and wiggle my fingers until I've got my hand through the loop at one end. It's just big enough to fit comfortably over my knuckles. There is another loop on the other end. That one is bigger, but it's a slipknot, so it will shrink to the right size.

I let the slack of the rope out, so it dangles down by my leg. The wind bumps it against my trousers. I keep my eyes on the pipe opening, and carefully swing my arm up so that the rope arcs out and over my head. The end with the slipknot falls to the far side of the lip, but when I give it a tug it slithers back to me.

No problem. I try again. And again. My fingers cramp in the cold and my shoulder starts to ache from throwing the rope over and over again.

I shake my arm, rotate my shoulder, and fling the rope up. This time it doesn't even make it to the other side of the lip. It knocks against the overhang and falls back towards my face. I flinch back, and my left foot slips. I grab onto the wall, fingers biting into the stone. There's a horrifying moment where my body keeps tilting left, and I feel the air snatch me away from the wall. Emptiness, whistling air, then the gut-shaking impact against my back.

No. I'm still holding on. My foot scrabbles back onto the foot-hold, and I press my face to the wall, and I'm not falling even though I still feel like I am.

I need to get onto solid ground. I need to get off this wall.

I look down for the rope. My hand is empty. I knock my fore-head against the brick and groan.

I'll need to go all the way back down for it.

I reach up over the lip. My hand claws about, but I can't reach the far edge. I grip onto the overhang and try to pull myself up using that, but my arm shakes so much that I have to stop.

I cling on to the wall with both hands again. I want to cry.

I can't even remember the last time I cried. Was it . . .

the woods, the wind, the moon-face
bitch you little bitch

No.

I blink away afterimages of the trees, a wet and open mouth, the feeling of dirt under my nails. The sound of that voice, and the sounds that came later.

That can't be right, anyway. I didn't cry then. Did I?

It doesn't matter. I have been commanded by the Hand of God. I have to do this.

I begin to climb down.

36

Now

Everyone is sleeping, as far as I can tell. This is probably the best time.

I swing my feet out from underneath the covers and slip them into my unlaced boots. I move between the rows of beds, catching sight as I go of Sister Diligence's sleeping face. Her glasses are on the table beside her, and moonlight falls over her, and she looks so much younger than I'd originally thought.

I ease the door handle down, and a dark figure rockets up from the bed beside it. Shit. I'm sure I didn't make any noise.

'Who's that? Where are you going?'

'It's – it's me, Sister.' I try to sound breathless.

'Who's "me"?' She leans forward. It's the woman I'm sure I recognise from when I was younger. She has a sharp nose and eyes set deep in her head, like someone has grabbed her nose and pulled it away from the rest of her face.

'It's Sister Catherine,' I say. 'I'm sorry, I just—'

'Sister Catherine,' she says, her voice loud enough that some of the women in the beds near us start to stir. 'You are not to be out of your bed. Get back now.'

'I need to see Sister Justice,' I say. 'Please, Sister, it's important.'

'What could possibly—' she pulls the blanket back and stands up. She puts a hand against the door, holding it closed '—be so important that you have to bother Sister Justice in the middle of the night?'

Some of the women are half sitting now, enjoying the show. This wasn't part of the plan. Why can't I move a single inch here without justifying myself to self-righteous, psychotically controlling women?

I feel like grabbing hold of the Sister's neatly plaited hair and smacking her face into the door frame. Instead, I take a deep, wobbly breath, and say, 'Please, Sister,' in a little voice.

'Well?' Her voice is loud. She knows she's waking everyone up. 'What's so very important, Sister Catherine?'

'I need medical attention,' I say.

'You need medical attention.' The Sister hoicks her eyebrows. 'You seem fine to me.'

Here goes. I bite my lip, look tragic and press my hand against my stomach. 'It's for the baby.'

Two minutes later I am waiting downstairs in the dark and empty common room; the Sister had goggled at me, and then, fingers biting into the meat of my arm, she had whisked me out of the room and downstairs so fast I almost fell. I had a kind of weird déjà vu as she pulled me along – another Sister, another dark and empty corridor, another time I'd been dragged after someone who was coldly, silently furious – but I couldn't remember the exact details. When it had happened, and why. It could have been for anything. I was in trouble a lot.

I can hear the hysterical buzz of the Sister's voice along the corridor. She's telling Sister Justice what happened. There's creaks from upstairs. Footsteps in the dormitory. They're probably taking the opportunity to have a good gossip now that the room leader is gone. It's fair enough. This is likely the most interesting thing to have happened here in months.

Pattering footsteps in the hall, and Sister Justice's face appears in the doorway, the other Sister's face hovering behind like a satellite.

'You may leave, Sister,' says Sister Justice. She nods behind her, and the other Sister stalks off, throwing a last triumphant look my way.

Sister Justice glares at me. 'What,' she says, her voice icily calm, 'is this nonsense about a baby?'

'I . . . I'm sorry, Sister . . . I didn't mean . . . it's just—' I wring my hands. She waits. 'I . . . think something's wrong with the baby.'

'*Your* baby?' There's disbelief writ large across her face, but some doubt is creeping around the corners.

'I . . . I've been having pains, Sister. They're getting really bad. And . . . regular.' I don't know anything about pregnancy really, but one of the servers at work was pregnant a couple of years ago. She'd had to go to hospital because of 'pains', I remember Meg telling me one day when she hadn't come in. She'd been fine, and the baby too, but she'd needed to stay in hospital for a while.

'I think something is wrong. I'm bleeding, too,' I finish limply. Sister Justice's mouth bends firmly downwards, then she shakes her head.

'No, it's quite impossible. You . . . it only happened . . . it was only a few days ago. You can't possibly be pregnant.'

'He . . . it wasn't the first time,' I say quietly, keeping my eyes on the floor. It doesn't really make much sense, this wild story of mine, but I'm betting on her being shocked and not thinking about it too deeply.

She steps towards me, puts her face near mine. I can smell her breath, peppermint with something sour underneath.

'You are a dirty little slut, aren't you?'

I look up, shocked. Her hand cracks out and smacks me cleanly across the face. I tilt backwards and hit one of the chairs on the way down. It overturns with a clatter. I press a hand to my cheek.

'They'll deal with you at the Fruitfulness Hall,' she hisses. 'Get out of my sight.' With that, she turns on her heel and leaves the room.

37

THEN

I tug the rope, and feel resistance. I tug again, a little harder. It holds.

I sob, pressing my face against the cool brick. It's done. I've done it.

I take a good grip with my right hand, and prepare to take my left away from the wall. This is it. If the rope gives, then I'll fall back and hit the ground two storeys below.

I can't. I can't – I won't – fail him.

I focus on the rope, and let go of the wall. I fumble, miss the rope, then get it. It swings to the side, and I brace my feet, fighting against the movement.

I'm almost there. I'm so close.

I pull, and sob again. My arms are so heavy. I'm so tired.

I am such a failure. Such a disappointment. He'll get rid of me. He'll leave. Just like . . .

No. *No*. That was *Catherine*. I am not Catherine. I am the Acolyte, and no one has left me. I have never disappointed him.

I pull and kick and scrabble and slither and everything is shaking and weak and then I am over and lying on the flat roof. My throat and lungs burn. My hands are red raw. I have no power, nothing left in me at all. I have never been this exhausted.

I open my eyes, and look up at the stars, and laugh. I laugh and laugh and then it turns into coughing and I'm on my hands and knees, retching, and stringy stuff is hanging in great threads from my mouth.

I need some water. I spit and spit the threads away. My mouth is full of grit. There's necessary cubicles in the Worship Hall, but I'm only supposed to go into the attic. But at this time of night it won't matter. No one will be there, and I can get in and out quickly.

I get up. I'm waiting for the world to tilt and spin, but it stays still as it's supposed to. It's a sign. I'm on the right path.

I pull the rope over the wall and leave it curled neatly beside the pipe. The skylight is a couple of feet away, left unlatched like the Hand of God said it would be. I pull it open and drop down onto an old table that's placed just below it.

The attic is so dark that even after my eyes adjust, I can barely see anything. There are piles of old chairs, spiky legs reaching up towards the rafters. Boxes stacked every which way. My stomach sinks. How on earth am I going to find whatever it is the Hand of God left me?

Something catches in my throat and I bark out a volley of coughs. I need to get water first. I'll worry about the task later. Where is the trapdoor?

The buildings are all the same. Where was the trapdoor in the Hand of God's attic?

I shuffle forward, hands held out in front of me. Something brushes my fingers. It's only a spiderweb. I swipe the air, feeling more strands tear and wrap around my skin. I rub my hands on my trousers. I feel little prickles on the back of my hand, and shake it violently. I don't mind spiders all that much, but I still don't particularly want them crawling all over me in the darkness.

My foot, stepping carefully across the floor, drops farther down than I expected it to. The trapdoor, set low into the boards. I kneel and my fingers find the handle. I heave it up, peer down, and wait for my eyes to adjust to the darkness. A little cupboard, the same as in the Hand of God's residence.

I turn around and let myself down, holding on to the edge of the hatch and dropping the last couple of feet. Something tickles my neck and I bring my fingers away to see a needle-legged spider skitter across my hand. I knock it away and rub at my neck. It feels like every inch of my exposed skin is crawling with spiders, but it's not, I know.

I open the cupboard door and peek out. Watery moonlight from a couple of windows shows me a pale carpet and a staircase at the far end. I don't recognise it. The only places I've ever been in the Worship Hall are the entrance and the women's balcony.

I pad towards the stairs. If I can find the main entrance, then I can find the necessary cubicles and get a drink. Then back to figure out what I need to take away with me from the attic.

I think of the piles of boxes and tangle of chair legs again, and push the despair away. I'll find it. I'll know what he's left me when I see it.

There is a door at the bottom of the staircase. It's the entrance hall! Recognition flows over me, warm like easing into a hot bath. I didn't expect to feel so happy to see this place, but I am. It's just so familiar, even though it's dark and silent instead of light and full of bustle like usual. I know exactly where everything is.

Directly opposite me is the portrait of Father, sitting comfortably on a rolling hill, with children clustered around His feet. He is smiling out at me, and even though it's so dark that the colours are all washed out to greys, I know His eyes are the exact colour of the sky behind Him.

To my right are the doors to the main hall. When you go through, the stairs to the women's balcony are on both sides, and the men's pews are straight ahead, leading to the dais where Father and the Elders sit.

There's another door just to the left of me. It leads to the necessary cubicles for the women. I don't know where the men's are. I slip through the door, and the light *tink-tinks* on automatically. I look around for a switch to turn it off, but there's no windows so no one will be able to see it. No one will be up at this time, anyway.

I slip into one of the cubicles and tug my trousers down. My legs are covered in bruises. I prod them experimentally as I pee. None of them are too bad. I had one a few months ago, after one of the trips with the Hand of God, that turned black and purple and went all the way from my hip to my knee. One of the demons had tried to fight back, but of course, we prevailed. When we got back Home, the Hand of God had rubbed some stuff on the bruise that made it smart at first, then was beautifully soothing and cooling.

I flush, and wince at how loud it sounds. Then I run the tap, and gulp down the water. It's warmish, and tastes a bit of metal, but it feels amazing. I drink so much my belly hurts, then take palmfuls of it and slosh it over my face and neck.

There's no towels, so I rub my face dry with my jumper. Drips trickle down my neck as I leave.

I pause with my hand outstretched to the handle of the door back upstairs. I really want to see the main hall. I don't know why, but I just want to. I want to go up to the women's balcony and sit cross-legged against the bannisters, and look down at the silent pews and see the moonlight filter in through the stained-glass windows.

It can't hurt. I've got time.

The doors to the main hall are large and dark, with great bronze handles set into them. Father's words are emblazoned in gold across the doors above head height: 'Let he who seeks the Truth come to Me'.

I slip through, and the doors swing shut silently behind me. The carpet is thick and lush like I remember, and the Hall smells of incense and sandalwood. I breathe it in, hold it in my lungs.

The stairs to the women's balcony are to my left and right. I always filed in up the right staircase, so I go up that one. I realise halfway up that I'm hugging the wall, the way I usually would because the Daughters go up in double file and it gets cramped. It feels strange to have all this space around me.

I reach the top and sink down by the railings at the front. Cross-legged, knees jammed right up. No warm bodies on either side, or behind.

The hall looks smaller without so many people in it. The pews below seem stunted without the rows and rows of white-shirted Brothers or uniformed Warriors filling them.

The light filtering through the stained glass at the far end is dappled, and paints in mottled greys and blues the dais and the covered section where the Vessels sit. I think of Father standing there, arms raised to us, His Children, as we sing to Him.

All at once, the Hall is filled with song. Voices raised, all at once, arms waving in the air, clapping and stamping during the good parts, swaying and moving exactly in time. The words, familiar and easy, spill from my lips so cleanly it barely feels like singing at all; more an opening of the soul.

Just like that, the singing stops. It's as though someone has clapped their hands over my ears. The hall rings with silence.

What was that?

It was just a memory. A strong memory. Not even one of mine.

I look at the door to the side of the dais, and all of a sudden another memory, the memory of an arm swinging from a limp body, comes to me. A man, carrying someone. What was her name?

Amy's friend. That girl.

Teneil.

I remember her pond-green eyes, nailing me to the spot that time I (Catherine) caught her eye. Her studied coolness as she strode through the corridors. Her voice cracking as she screamed for her mother.

What had happened to her? I – *Catherine* – had never seen her again after that day. Perhaps she'd been sent away. She hadn't wanted to be here, that was certain.

My fingers stroke the smooth wood of the bannisters. I have an urge to poke my legs through the gaps, to let my feet dangle above the pews below, so I slide them through – a little tricky with my boots – and swing them into the empty air.

I think about how incensed Sister Morningbright would be if she could see me, and I swing my feet harder.

Downstairs, the doors open.

I freeze. For a moment I think it must be the Hand of God coming to check on me, but then I hear the voice of a young man, sleepy and complaining.

'All right, then. Here we are. Perfect time for it, as per.'

I pull my feet back, but my left boot gets stuck between the bannisters. I pull and pull in a frenzy, a tiny animal in a trap, as another voice floats up from below.

211

'This is the time Father has decreed—'

'Well, we all must follow Father's decrees, mustn't we?'

My boot comes free and I fall back, knocking into the chair behind me. The legs screech, and I freeze, flattened against the floor.

'What was that?' The second voice. It's familiar. I hear footsteps below, coming further into the Hall, and I close my eyes as though that will make me less likely to be seen.

'These old buildings make all kinds of noises. Gives me the shivers, to be quite honest with you.' The young voice. 'Can we just get on with this?'

'Mm – yes, of course.'

I know where I've heard that voice. That night that the Hand of God had a visitor. It's him.

I risk opening my eyes. I can see, just over the edge of the balcony, two shadowy figures making their way to the dais. They're not looking this way. If I'm very careful, I can squirm backwards until I get to the furthest corner of the balcony. They'll definitely not see me from there. Then I just have to wait until they go, and I can get back up to the attic and away.

The two men climb the steps to the dais, and I begin to inch backwards, using my elbows and knees and toes to transport myself as soundlessly as possible. Then the lights overhead blaze on, and I freeze again.

'That's better. Right, what are we doing tonight?'

Oh, Father help me. If they look up, they'll definitely see me.

'Ah, ah, perhaps we'll . . . that's quite bright, you see, and—'

'Oh, fine.' The younger man sounds bored. The lights dim. The ones around the periphery of the Hall have been switched back off, leaving only a strip still lit above the dais. 'That better?'

Much better. The women's balcony is in shadow again. If they glance up, they shouldn't be able to see me, especially with the bright lights right above them, but if I move, I risk catching their eyes. I'll just have to stay as still as I can until they go.

'Thank you, yes, that's much—'

'More discreet?' the younger voice sneers.

'Discretion is rather important.' The older man sounds like he is repressing a sigh. 'Father did want your preparations to be as . . . unobtrusive as possible, young Seed. It's imperative that we don't sow any worry or discord among the Children.'

It is as though the ground has given way beneath me. The Seed. The young man below is the Seed of the Children.

I've never heard him speak before. On the Bad Night, he just looked at us, while we shivered and tried to keep ourselves covered up with our arms and hands.

I blink away the memory. It didn't happen to me, anyway. Not to the Acolyte.

Why is the Seed in the Worship Hall in the middle of the night?

The young man stretches, his arms reaching out to the stained glass above him, then he collapses in one graceful movement into Father's gold chair. He swings his legs up over the arms, crosses his feet at the ankles, and peers at the other man over steepled fingers. I can't see the colour of his eyes from back here, but I know they are blue, and cold.

'Father said to be unobtrusive, did He,' says the Seed. He stares at the man. 'He does seem to be saying rather a lot lately.'

'His communications have increased, it's true,' says the man. He takes his glasses off and begins polishing them with a hand-kerchief. He half turns away from the Seed, coughing lightly, and I recognise him finally. Elder Holland. He is the Elder who sits closest to Father – on His left side, of course. The Hand of God alone sits at Father's right.

Elder Holland holds his glasses up to the light and squints through them. 'Father has revealed to us the need for you to complete your preparations at this time. He has been most concerned that you feel yourself to be ready.'

'Has He?' The Seed taps his fingertips together. 'He might have mentioned it to me Himself.'

'Ah, now,' Elder Holland turns and replaces his glasses. 'We all miss Father. You more than anyone, I imagine,' he adds hurriedly as the Seed's head swings to regard him balefully. 'But He has been most clear that His seclusion is of vital importance at present. He will return to us when the time is right, I am sure.'

Father is in seclusion? And what preparations could the Seed be making?

213

'He doesn't even see Mother anymore. She told me that the Guards have stopped letting her through.'

'Father must remain in absolute isolation.'

'Apart from seeing you, of course,' the Seed says. He props an elbow on his knee and leans his forehead on his hand, looking at Elder Holland from a slant. 'He still sees you.'

'Shall we, ah . . . ?' Elder Holland gestures to the pews behind him. The Seed stretches again, like a cat. I suppress a shiver. His feet thump down to the floor – Elder Holland winces – and he uncurls himself, a flag unfurling in a lazy wind.

'What's on your – sorry, *Father's* – agenda tonight?'

'Father has asked that you enact the Harvest of the Vessels.'

The Harvest! Once a year, Father welcomes new Daughters to be Vessels for Himself and the Elders. All the girls from the right age group line up at the front of the Hall – the only time females are permitted to be there – and He chooses from among them. I think I always knew, even then, that I wouldn't be called that way. Father always chose the pale ones, the ones with golden hair and blue eyes. With my unruly brown curls and dark eyes, I wasn't the right sort of girl.

I wasn't any sort of girl.

A flash of the Bad Night again, those cold blue eyes, looking over me like someone idly surveying an insect they've caught under a glass. Amy next to me, shivering in the cold. The air on my skin.

I try to concentrate on what the Seed and Elder Holland are doing.

The Seed is standing with arms crossed at the front of the dais, Elder Holland pacing along the strip of floor where the Daughters line up. The lights above him reflects off the bald spot at the top of his head.

'. . . standing here, of course,' he's saying. 'At your word . . .' He gestures to the Seed.

'Your Father welcomes your humble supplication, My Daughters,' the Seed says mechanically. Elder Holland nods and twirls his hand towards the not-there girls.

'Precisely, and they will then kneel and await your decision . . .'

It's always the same. Father regards the Daughters, who kneel, trembling, with their eyes turned down and hands folded neatly in their laps. The hall waits, holding its breath. When Father finally moves, it's so silent that His footsteps are like thunderclaps. He steps towards a girl, tilts her chin up to look at Him, then takes her hand and guides her to her feet. She steps behind Him and the Vessels, clothed in their white, engulf her like a bird passing into a cloud. Sometimes He'll choose two or three, sometimes only one. Each girl merges into the crowd of the Vessels, and has a white sash tied around her dress. Then they all disappear silently through the door behind the dais.

After they've gone, Father returns to His chair, and when He sits and raises His arms, the Hall explodes into cheers and exultations. People whistle and clap and stamp their feet. 'Father bless the Vessels!' they shout. 'Father make the Vessels Fruitful! Bring us more Warriors for Father!'

I watch as the Seed moves forward, and transforms into Father. He stands straighter, tilts his head to the side, and places a finger contemplatively against his lips just as Father does. It's uncanny. I wonder if this is how Father looked when He was the Seed's age. It's funny to think of Father being young. Then the Seed moves down the steps to the floor – not loosely, like he was walking before, but gliding, as Father does – and places his hand under Elder Holland's chin. What is he doing? Then the Seed winks, and bursts into laughter. Elder Holland makes a harrumphing sound.

'Yes, very amusing, my Seed.'

'Chop, chop, Holland! Up on the dais! You're my Vessel now!' The Seed trips lightly back up the steps and slings himself back into Father's chair. Elder Holland smooths back the hair at the sides of his head.

'This is a most sacred ritual, my Seed—'

'Yes, yes, quite right. What next? I raise my arms, everyone starts hooting and squawking, dadadada, I leave. That's about it, isn't it? Shall we call it a night?' The Seed claps his hands together and looks at Elder Holland expectantly.

'Well, at that point, you would of course retire to your apartments with the new Vessel – or Vessels, of course, if there's a good crop that year—'

'And what of my wife?' The Seed's voice is sharp. 'What would she do?'

'I beg your pardon, my Seed?'

'It's just my mother, you see. She's never present at the Harvest. Or afterwards. I don't see her in the house for days. I've always wondered where she is, at that time. She's never mentioned it.' The Seed is studying his fingernails with what looks like great interest. Elder Holland clears his throat.

'Am I to understand that you wish to take a wife, then? Have you made a choice?'

'What?'

'I'm just wondering why you're asking, my Seed. Have you changed your mind with regards to marriage?'

The Seed's cheeks flush a dull red under the bright lights. 'I have not. I don't need to change my mind. You know I've already made my choice.'

I feel an itch at the back of my neck. I shift a little, trying to use the stiff collar of my shirt to scratch.

Elder Holland sighs. He sounds almost exasperated. 'Of course, but as I know Father has told you—'

'Father doesn't understand!'

Elder Holland's mouth drops open. He looks as shocked as I feel. How could Father, who knows everything, not understand something?

I feel another tickle, beside my ear. I dip my head so I can scratch it with my fingertips.

'Father told me to make a choice, years ago. I made it. I don't understand why He – why any of you – won't listen to me.'

'My dear Seed—'

'I don't see her anymore!' The Seed says, standing up. He points straight at me. I go cold. 'She's never there, with the females at Worship! They don't bring her to talk to me anymore! That little demon you gave me isn't enough! No one will tell me where she is, and . . .'

Elder Holland is trying to interject as the Seed continues to talk, his voice getting higher and higher. Something brushes my fingers, and I look down. It's a spider. Huge – bigger than the one upstairs – with the same needle-legs but a much larger body.

I flick my fingers, and it falls to the carpet a couple of inches away, then skitters back towards me. I shoo my fingers at it, and it freezes.

'I think I'm done for tonight!' the Seed is saying downstairs. He clatters down the stairs of the dais and strides towards the door. 'And tell my Father – when you see Him – that I'm not doing any more of these ridiculous preparations until they bring her to me!' There is a crash as the doors of the Hall slam shut.

Elder Holland, left behind in the ring of lights on the dais, pulls the handkerchief he'd used earlier to clean his glasses out of his pocket and dabs at his forehead and bald spot.

He tilts his head back, lets out a great whoosh of air, and says loudly, 'You entitled little shit.'

He pulls something out of his pocket, taps it and holds it to his ear. He speaks into it. I can't believe it – I've seen the Sullied use these Outside, but I've never seen one inside Home. The Hand of God says they're devices that the Sullied are obsessed with, and they use them to talk to each other and look at depraved material. I don't really understand what they are, but I know I don't like them. I don't like how they glow.

'Hi – yeah, we might have a bit of a problem,' Elder Holland says. He starts towards the doors as well, but more slowly than the Seed did. 'Yeah – well, who do you think? He's had a fucking hissy fit. I know. I know. Well, we might have another job for *him* to do now as well. We need to redouble our efforts to find—'

His voice cuts off as the doors to the Hall shut behind him. I look down at the floor beside my hand. The spider is gone.

217

38

Now

I'm feeling a mix of things as I trot towards the Fruitfulness Hall, my stupid nightgown whipping about my legs. I didn't dare go back up for my dress, so I just grabbed one of the enormous shawls hanging by the door and slipped out after Sister Justice left. The night air is cooling my still-smarting cheek.

I'm a bit giddy that my plan worked. Sort of. It went a bit further than I originally intended – I only wanted to convince Sister Justice that I was pregnant and possibly miscarrying, not an entire roomful of women through which gossip passes faster than alcohol through a first-year Trinity student – but I have achieved my aim. I'm out, on my own, at night, on the way to the Fruitfulness Hall. One tick for me.

The Fruitfulness Hall is a shape cut out in the darkness. The shades are drawn against the windows, as usual, but lights glow dimly around a few of them.

Obviously, I can't climb up the side of the building with an infant under my arm. I'll need to find some way of getting to Angela's room undetected from the inside.

And I need to find the baby first, of course.

The main door creaks as I ease it open. The corridor is, as usual, dimly lit and empty. I can see the room that they lock me in a few doors down to the side. But where are the newborns kept?

I hover in the doorway. What should I do? I can't just go opening random doors until I find the right baby.

'Sister Catherine?'

I start. 'Oh, um, sorry, I'm just—' I begin. Soft footsteps pad down the big staircase and I see a familiar face. She has a basket under her arm. It's the Sister who relieved me the first shift I had here, the one who said that she secretly cuddled the babies sometimes. I pull the shawl tighter around me. It hangs almost to my feet, so it's not immediately apparent that I'm in my nightie.

'Are you all right?' she says, shifting the basket to the other hip. It looks heavy. I see her eyes flicker to my cheek – red from the Sister's slap, with the cut from a few days ago still healing on it. I move forward and hold out my arms.

'Let me help with that,' I say. She waves a hand and smiles.

'Oh, it's no bother—'

'No, really, I'm happy to.' I grab one of the handles, and she rolls her shoulders back and grins.

'That is better, actually,' she says, and we laugh together. She starts off down the corridor, and I follow. The basket is full of soiled sheets and clothes, and the weird popcorn-smell of baby shit fugs into my nose.

'Laundry's just in here,' she says, and pushes a door open with her hip. I hear the quiet jangle of keys as she does.

The room behind the door is warm, with damp, heavy air. Three washing machines rumble away, and piles of neatly folded sheets and baby clothes and cloth nappies fill freestanding shelves at the back wall. The Sister takes the basket from me and tips it into an empty sink. I cross my arms, keeping the shawl wrapped around me.

'Got to rinse them off first,' she says, nodding at the fetid pile. She puts her hands into the small of her back and stretches. 'I take it you haven't had this duty yet?'

I shake my head, she rolls her eyes, and we laugh again. I feel almost like I could be friends with this woman, if I met her somewhere normal and not in a terrifying baby factory.

She turns the taps on and lets water rush into the sink. 'Were you on your way out?' she says.

'No, actually, I got called in to help out tonight,' I say.

She nods. 'Oh, yeah, that'll be because Sister Modesty got unwell earlier.' Her eyes drop to my shoulders, and she blinks. 'Are you . . . in your nightclothes?'

I look down and force a laugh. 'Yeah, they said it was a bit urgent. Because Sister . . .'

'Sister Modesty.'

'Right, Sister Modesty got unwell. What was wrong with her?'

She shrugs. 'Oh, we're always getting sick here. There's some bug at the moment that's just going right through all of us. It comes of working with the little ones. You're always picking up this or that. It'll happen to you soon.'

'Oh, good,' I say, and she grins at me as she starts to sluice the mustardy shit off a nappy.

'Anyway, it certainly wasn't urgent enough to have you traipse over here in your nightclothes,' she says. 'It's actually pretty quiet here tonight.'

'I've never asked your name, Sister . . . ?'

'Sister Kehinde,' she says. She waves a hand at me. 'I'd shake, but . . .'

I laugh. 'That means you're a twin, doesn't it? Your name?' I say.

'Now how do you know that?' she says.

'Oh, I had a . . . a friend who had twin sisters. Taiwo and Kehinde. She told me about the Yoruba tradition.'

Kehinde glances at me over her shoulder. 'Mostly when I introduce myself here, people say, oh, you aren't Named yet . . .' She perfectly imitates the faux-delicate way Sister Diligence responded to me earlier, and I nod emphatically.

'I know just what you mean,' I say.

'Well, yes, you aren't Named either,' she says.

'No,' I say, and I don't feel the need to parrot the platitudes I had to Sister Diligence earlier. I shrug. 'It does seem that some people get Named faster than others.'

'Mm,' she says. 'And some people get the night-time nappy-washing shift.'

I look at her hands plunging into the water. Even as a kid I'd noticed that the only girls chosen to be Vessels were white and fair. Most – almost all – of the senior Sisters are white. The same goes for the Brothers and Elders, as far as I can tell.

220

I want to ask Kehinde why she's here, why someone who seems so nice and normal has ended up in this place, but I know I can't. To be honest, lots of the women here seem nice and normal. Lots of them are intelligent. But they're here, all the same. Something missing in them is filled by this place, for whatever reason.

I clear my throat. 'I'm supposed to be helping with the, uh – the newborns tonight.' I wait, holding my breath, but Kehinde just nods.

'Room 12. It's just to the left out the door, actually. Here, I'll give you my keys if you want – I need to get this lot finished.' She tilts her hip towards me, and I unhook the key ring from her belt.

'Thanks – I'll get these back to you later,' I say. I go to the door, a rushing in my ears. That was far too easy.

'Sister Catherine?'

I pause. 'Yes?'

'You're wrong about the newborns,' she says, and I turn around with innocence painted on my face. Oh, no. She's going to tell me I'm actually supposed to be with the usual babies, and she'll come and check on me . . .

'How's that, Sister Kehinde?'

'There's only one newborn at the moment. Not "newborns".' She gives me a dry look. 'Easy night for some.'

I cough out a laugh and fumble with the door handle.

Keys to the newborn room. And the baby in there can only be Angela's. Two more ticks for me.

39

THEN

I heave myself back into the attic and collapse on the floorboards, huffing. There was no ladder I could see for the attic hatch, and I didn't want to waste even more time hunting about on the off-chance I'd find one, so I had to jump up and grab onto the lip of the trapdoor with my fingertips, then pull myself up. It took a couple of tries, but I made it. Thank Father for all those hours of push-ups and rope climbing.

I swipe an arm across my forehead and try to concentrate on the matter at hand. I need to find the object the Hand of God left for me. But scraps of what I overheard earlier keep drifting through my head, especially the moments when the Seed spoke so disrespectfully about Father, and when Elder Holland spoke into his handheld thing about – I suppose – the Seed. I turn over the new words and phrases. *Entitled little shit. Fucking hissy fit.* I have a feeling I shouldn't repeat these.

But perhaps I should? The thought stops me as I'm poking about among the piles of junk. Perhaps I should tell the Hand of God everything I heard?

Maybe – and this is an exciting thought – maybe I was supposed to overhear it all. Perhaps the Hand of God sent me here specifically to listen in, and report back . . .

But that can't be right. He couldn't have known that I would sneak into the hall, for one thing. No, I still have to find whatever it is.

This is hopeless. I can barely see anything, and there's so much rubbish in here. I kick a jumbled pile of chairs, which teeters, and

I have to grab it to stop it all crashing down. A jag of pain lights up the skin between my thumb and forefinger, and I hiss and stick it in my mouth. A splinter, probably. I'll have to wait until I get back to check it under a light.

I want to kick the pile again, but I can't. 'Entitled little shit,' I whisper. 'Fucking hissy fit.'

For some reason, I feel a bit better.

All right. I need to think about this logically. The Hand of God does not send me on ridiculous errands. He gives me tasks and challenges that he also provides the tools for me to overcome. I don't always know the tools when he's giving them to me, but they are always there.

So. I need to find something in this attic. He knew, obviously, that it was full of stuff. He knew I'd have to look for it in the dark. Therefore, it will likely be somewhere that I'll be able to see it in the available light. The available light is from the skylight, so I need to start looking around there.

And just like that, when I turn around, under the skylight I see the table, which I'd used as a foothold earlier when I'd climbed in. I hadn't looked properly at what was on it, but now I can see that an open book has been left on top of it. A book – of course it's got to be that. It's perfect.

I pick my way through the mess of boxes and old furniture and pick the book up carefully. I recognise it. The cover is stiff, dark-coloured leather, with 'RECORDS' written in heavy letters in a white rectangle at the top. I've seen the Hand of God writing in this book in his study. He keeps it locked in a drawer in his desk, and I've never had the chance to look at what's in it before. I squint at the writing on the pages inside. I can just about make it out. There's columns of names and numbers, but they look almost totally random to me. I leaf through some pages, but they're all the same. Just row after row of neat columns with names and numbers. Some kind of code?

I bring the page closer to my eyes. It's full of entries like 'Robert, 001894, Thomas', and 'Paul, 001234, 002894'. They all seem to be either two names and a number, or two numbers and a name. Dates, maybe, or times?

Is this what he wanted me to find? I look around the attic one more time, but nothing else leaps out at me. It's got to be this. It's a test, like everything else. I just have to work out what it all means.

A bird twitters outside. The sky is fading to grey. I need to get back.

I tuck the book inside my shirt. It rests cool against my skin. Getting a foot on the table, I pull myself up and through the skylight and out onto the roof, before remembering that I've left the trapdoor open.

I smack my forehead, and half consider just leaving it, but I know I shouldn't. It only takes a couple of minutes to go back in, close it and get back out onto the roof again, but the sky has lightened noticeably in that time.

I check the rope is secure around the pipe, hop up on the edge of the roof and prepare to lower myself down onto the wall. I can't think of any way to get the rope back with me, so I'll just have to throw it over the lip onto the flat part of the roof and leave it there.

I tug on the rope, testing its hold again, then scoot backwards on my hands and knees until I feel my feet go over the edge. I let myself down, and the lip of the roof scrapes against my torso and threatens to dislodge the book. I feel about with my toes until I get a foothold on the wall, then inch down the rope until I can let go and hold on to the wall again. It doesn't take long to get to the ground.

I stand at the bottom, looking up. I can't stop myself grinning. I did it. I completed the task I was set. Even though I don't understand why he needed the book, the Hand of God will make it all clear to me when he needs to. He always does.

I think again about telling him what I overheard the Seed and Elder Holland discussing. Will he be pleased, or angry? Either way, he'll know whatever I know, so I have to tell him.

Why tell him if he already knows?

That sounds like a thought Catherine would have had. But I am not Catherine, and I don't need to listen to her. I have all the answers.

The answer is, of course, that I need to show him that I'm loyal. I need to show him that he can trust me. So I need to tell him so that he can see that I don't hide anything.

So why didn't you tell him about listening to him and Elder Holland that night?

For once, I can't push Catherine's thoughts away.

40

Now

Room 12 is as close as Kehinde said. It just takes me a few steps and I'm there, looking at the little slip of paper tacked to the door with '12' written on it in blue ink.

I rehearse my story for whoever is in there. I'm here to relieve you, I know you're not expecting it, extra people on tonight, off you go for an early sleep, praise Father, etc.

Everything else has gone in my favour tonight, so I'm hoping this paper-thin story will too. I'm too tired to come up with a plan B. This is it.

I slide a few keys into the lock until I find one that turns. I ease the door open and peek around it.

Dark. I can't see a thing.

I blink a couple of times, and my eyes adjust. There is a lighter patch at the far end of the room – the covered window. Dark, box-like shapes in a couple of rows – the cots.

There's no one in here. Shit. Is this the right room?

I find the light switch and flick it on. A blaze floods the place, and I have to close my eyes against the glare.

There's a little snorting sound to my side, and I look down into the nearest cot to see a tiny baby, purse-mouthed in sleep and swaddled in a tight bundle. The light doesn't seem to be bothering it.

Jesus. They left the baby alone in a locked room?

Maybe they just have someone look in on it now and then. Newborns sleep more, don't they?

I have no way of knowing when someone is actually supposed to be in the room with the baby, so I should go sooner rather than later. Maybe I'll get it back before anyone realises it's gone.

I rummage quietly in the cupboards on the other side of the room until I find a bottle and some formula. I don't know how much newborns should have, so I just make the same as I do for the older babies. The kettle seems screamingly loud in the silence, and takes forever. I test the milk on the inside of my forearm. If the baby wakes up when I pick it up, I'll jam the bottle in its mouth and hope for the best.

I don't have any pockets in this stupid nightgown, so I fold the shawl and tie it around my waist to make a sort of sling for the bottle and keys to sit in. I would literally kill someone for pockets right now.

I click off the light and hover over the cot. I've never picked up a baby this little before. You have to watch their heads, or something. Will it wake up as soon as I pick it up?

I work my fingers under the baby's head and body, then lift it as gently as I can. The baby makes a squalling sort of noise, so I prop it on my shoulder and shush and pat and do the bouncing-in-place thing. It seems to work, because the baby settles down and lolls its head into my shoulder.

I get the baby steady with one arm, then ease the door open. The corridor is dark and empty.

Right. Quick as possible.

I walk as fast as I can without bouncing the baby too much, through the corridor and up the stairs towards Angela's room. I'm at the top of the stairs before I realise that I didn't lock Room 12 behind me, but I can't go back now.

The baby makes an unhappy sort of sound as I make my way to Angela's door, and I say, 'Shh, shh,' and pat its back. The baby's noise seems to reverberate off the walls, and I'm sure it travels all the way down the stairs.

I pat the baby's back harder. It tenses, and makes a sort of 'urp' noise. My shoulder feels wet. The baby gives a contented grunt and settles back again.

'Enjoy that, did you?' I mutter, and reach for the handle of Angela's door. Before I can get there, it flies open and Angela is there, hands outstretched.

'Give me my baby,' she says.

41

THEN

'Do you have it?' the Hand of God says.

I hold the book out to him. It is the next evening, and I have slept most of the day after getting back close to dawn and falling asleep without washing or even taking off my clothes.

I'd taken up my usual place at the little table in the Hand of God's study in the afternoon, and continued working on *Father's Precepts* until he arrived and took up his own place at his desk. He'd done some work for a while, making notes and such, until he put his things away, sat back in his chair, and asked for the book.

I retrieve it from the drawer in my desk. I hand it to him and stand at attention. He flicks through the book, then places it neatly in the exact middle of his desk.

'Did you read it?'

He'd left it open on the table, so I am fairly certain that the right answer is yes.

'I had a look at some of it,' I say.

'And?'

'It's a list of names and dates,' I say. He looks at me, waiting. 'There are numbers with each entry, but they aren't sequential,' I continue. 'I think they might be codes. Some entries have two codes, but others have two names.'

'And what did you notice about the names?' the Hand of God asks.

'I . . . I'm not sure,' I say. 'But some of the entries are in red. The red ones all have an "F" at the start, then a code number, then some have a name after, but some have another code number.'

The Hand of God opens the book, riffles through the pages, then spins the book around and points at a particular entry. It's one of the ones in red.

'Read this one out,' he says.

'F, 002736, S,' I say. He leafs back through several pages, then points at another red entry. This one has been scored out in heavy black pen, but it's still just about readable.

'And this one, Acolyte.'

'F, 002398, S,' I read. 'But it's scored out.'

The Hand of God claps the book closed and rises to slide it onto a shelf. 'Conclusions?' he asks, his back to me.

I fidget. 'It's a record of something that people have done?' I say. The Hand of God turns and tilts his head to one side.

'What you should have noticed,' he says, 'is that the names are all male.'

My guts twist. I've disappointed him. 'So it's a record of Brothers? And – Warriors, and Elders?'

'In a manner of speaking. You are correct that the numbers are a code. You know, of course, that females, upon becoming Vessels, are Named?' I nod. 'And that lesser Sisters are Named also. Females, therefore, have more than one name throughout their lives. It would not, therefore, make any sense to record their names. They are the numbers.'

'So the entries are of men and females?' I ask.

'The book records their unions,' the Hand of God says. 'Our Elders and Brothers are granted the sacred duty of procreation. They are allocated a female, and if their union is fruitful, then it is recorded here.' He taps the book's spine with a finger.

'If their union is fruitful' makes me think of the Fruitfulness Hall. The Fruit. Babies. I have never before really given any thought to where new people come from. Men create them with females, with a . . . union?

The Hand of God is waiting for me to say something, so I try to drag my scattered thoughts together. 'The entries with two names are when the . . . union . . . produces a boy? A Warrior?' I say. He smiles, and my stomach untwists a bit.

'Exactly so. And the entries with two codes?'

'When the union produces a Daughter!' I say, feeling as though I've won a game. The Hand of God reaches out and pats my cheek, and I could just melt.

'What, then, of the entries with an F?' he asks.

'The red ones?' I say. 'I suppose . . . the F must stand for something.'

He raises his eyebrows expectantly. I cast about.

'F is for . . . Father?' I say. It is the first word starting with F that comes to mind, but I don't truly consider the implications until the sentence is out of my mouth.

'F, 002736, S,' the Hand of God says.

'Father and the Seed,' I say, mouth dry. I think of the young man I saw last night, asking where his mother goes when Father is Harvesting the new Vessels. His mother is that code, that number. 'But what about the other entry?' I ask. 'The scored out one?'

'Precisely.' The Hand of God opens a desk drawer and takes out his car keys. 'We're going to go on a little trip.'

42

Now

I don't really know what to do with myself. Angela is on the bed, the baby in her arms, rocking it back and forth. It is still asleep. She strokes its cheek with one finger, so gently that I have to look away.

I go to the window and fiddle with the blind. Behind me I can hear the soft sounds of her murmuring to the baby, and the bed creaking as she rocks.

It's terrible, but part of me wants to say, 'Okay, I kept up my end of the bargain, now you tell me how to get to Amy.' I want to say, 'Give me the baby back, I need to get it downstairs before they realise it's missing.' But is that what she wanted? Just a moment with the baby? Or does she want to leave too, now, with her child? Am I going to have to somehow smuggle a woman who's recently given birth and a newborn out of here, as well as get to Amy and convince her to leave, too? I feel dizzy with it all. I can't be responsible for Angela and her baby. I'm barely responsible for myself.

It's on the tip of my tongue to ask her what she wants now, what she plans to do, but I stop myself. They took her baby from her. They took her baby the moment it was born, and this is the first time – days later – that she's seen it again. I will give her as long as I can.

I glance around to see the baby lying on the bed, and Angela neatly rewrapping the blankets around its little body.

'He's a boy,' she says. Her voice is flat. I'd have expected a Vessel to be jumping for joy that they'd produced another Warrior for Father, but there's nothing there. Just a dry statement of fact.

'Congratulations,' I say, and I know it's the wrong thing as soon as it's out of my mouth. She doesn't react, just tucks in the last corner of blanket.

'Have they given him a name yet?' she asks.

'I don't know,' I say. She stares down at him, the little boy, and traces his features. Her finger moves across his lips, and his mouth opens and tries to suck on it. His little face screws up and he lets out a wail.

'Oh – here,' I say, and hand her the milk bottle from my improvised sling. She takes it and looks at it blankly.

'I'd try feeding him myself,' she says, as his cries grow louder, 'but my milk's all gone by now.'

'Uh-huh,' I say. Fucking hell, someone is going to hear him. 'He's quite hungry, I think.'

'Yes.' Finally, Angela picks him up and pokes the bottle between his lips. He quietens immediately, and starts making little contented grunts as he drinks. His eyes open, and fix on Angela's face. He stares up at her, and she down at him, and I wish I could just close the door softly on them and leave.

'You needn't worry about anyone hearing,' Angela says, still gazing down at her boy. 'I don't think many people are here at all. You can scream and scream and nobody comes.'

I pull the chair up by her bed and look at the baby. 'He's so beautiful, Angela,' I say.

She nods. 'He is.'

I wait. The room is filled with the soft sound of the baby drinking.

'We don't have much to do with Father's wife, really, but we're all in the same house so I can tell you some things,' Angela says.

My heart leaps, but I keep my voice casual as I say, 'Thank you.'

'She goes into the gardens in the morning. Every morning. Really early. There's a bit of the garden, all surrounded by bushes, with a little pond. She sits by it, looking in. I don't know, at her reflection or something. She's always alone. I've seen out of the window. When I've still been awake. Sometimes we have to be up all night. So I've seen it.'

I try not to think about what she means by having to be 'up all night'. I try not to think about what her life must be like. I try not to think about what Amy's life must be like. At least she'll only have to deal with the attentions of Father, instead of who knows how many Elders as well. 'What time?' I ask. This is it. This is how I finally find Amy.

'It's deceitful, what she does.' She looks at me, the first time she's looked away from the baby since I brought him in. 'Are you going to take her away?'

I open my mouth, but I don't know what to say. Angela is looking at me with eyes that are red-rimmed but steady. 'I—'

'You went away, didn't you? After her. You both disappeared; her first, you later. They said that she went to live in the Big House, and you went with the Hand of God, that sometimes you and he both came in through the Gate covered in blood, but that was just a stupid rumour. You and Amy never properly fitted in here, so you both left. Then she was back, and now you're back. But you could just leave again, couldn't you? Both of you?'

'Angela, I—'

'It's Sister Verity,' she says. The baby has finished the milk, and she pulls the bottle out of his mouth. He yawns. 'And this is Father's son. Father's wife is barren. So if you get rid of her, then I can be Father's wife, and my son will be the Seed of the Children.'

She stands up, hands me her baby, and turns away.

'She's always in the garden early. Just about dawn. She always goes back inside before He wakes up.' She gets into bed and rolls to face the wall, not looking at either me or her son. I start to back away, the baby snug against my shoulder.

'Thank you,' I say. She doesn't move or respond. I slip out, and close the door behind me.

43

THEN

I've been thinking about the red entries that the Hand of God had me read from the book. They had both had the same letters – F and S, for Father and Seed – but different numbers.

Different women. But Father only has one wife.

I consider asking about this, but it doesn't seem right. I look out of the window instead.

We've only been in the car a couple of hours so far. Our usual trips last hours and hours, take us far away, but this doesn't feel like a usual trip.

We start to pass more and more houses, until there's no fields or trees to be seen at all and we're in the middle of innumerable tall grey buildings. It's raining, and Sullied people scurry past on the streets with their faces hidden under hoods or umbrellas. Some buildings are all windows in the front, and have bright signs on top. These are 'shops', the Hand of God has told me. Sullied people use their money to get things in them, mostly things that they don't need. It's called 'shopping'. When there's so many buildings around you that you feel swallowed up in them, that's called a 'city'.

The Hand of God pulls to a stop at a red light. Sullied people can't be trusted to know when to stop and go while driving, so they need lights to tell them. The Hand of God scratches his cheek and his nails make a rasping sound against the stubble there.

'You will likely find the place we visit tonight strange, little Acolyte,' he says. 'It's not something I've shown you before.'

'Not the woods?' I say. He smiles a little.

'Not the woods, no. It's . . . well, you could think of it as a kind of outpost.'

'An outpost,' I repeat. I haven't heard the term before.

'In a manner of speaking. You know that we draw new Children from among the Sullied, when they are worthy enough.' The light turns to green and the car begins to move forward again.

'They give us money,' I remember.

'That's right. But some also complete spiritual tasks for us, depending on their abilities and station. Tasks that are . . . useful for us. For the Children. Some Sullied people have positions that make them important in their society, for various reasons. We draw those people to us. And some very lucky Sullied people, if they are enough use to us, become truly Unsullied, and join the rest of the Children at Home.'

'All right,' I say. I think about the Awakened people I know at Home, which makes me think about Teneil, which makes me think about her arm flopping as the man carried her out of the hall, which makes me think about what I heard last night. I still haven't told the Hand of God any of it. But he knows what I know. Of course.

Doesn't he?

'So there are places in the world Outside, places where those Sullied who are working to become Unsullied gather and do good works. Outposts of the Children. We call those places "churches".'

'Churches,' I say, tasting the strange word. 'So today we are visiting churches?'

'A church. And yes, we are. First. Then our work will take us elsewhere.'

'Are we getting rid of a demon tonight?' I say, feeling a little thrill deep in the pit of my belly. It's a bit like excitement, but it's also a bit like feeling ill.

'Oh, yes. We will rid the world of a great evil tonight,' says the Hand of God. 'An evil that comes from the heart of the Children itself. And your actions tonight will prepare you for the greatest task of all, little Acolyte.'

'I won't let you down,' I say.

The Hand of God touches my shoulder. 'I know you won't,' he says.

I stare down at my fingers, twisting together in my lap. I should feel happy. Proud. He's trusting me with more of our important work. But I don't feel right. I can't stop thinking about how I haven't told him everything, and how that shouldn't matter – how he should know it, anyway. The Elders and the Hand of God can read minds. It's what we were always taught. They can tell when you're lying. The Hand of God knew I was lying that time in the Atonement Room, when I told him that Amy hadn't said anything important to me before she left. Of course he did. Because he knows everything I know.

The only possibility is that he knows I was listening that night – the fact that he came into my room and tucked me into bed suggests he knew I'd been up, anyway – and doesn't feel the need to talk about it. And it must be the same with what I saw in the Worship Hall last night. He'd bring it up if he wanted to know more.

That's it. That's got to be it.

Why, says a little voice in my head that sounds a lot like Catherine, *would he ever need you to open your mouth, if it was really true he could read minds? Why would he ever ask you to speak? He wouldn't. He wouldn't need you to ever talk, or to answer his questions.*

I think *shut up* as hard as I can, but the voice keeps going, relentless.

He'd know you were thinking this, it says. *He'd know that you were doubting him, right now.*

I look over at the Hand of God, panicked. But he's just looking ahead and navigating the car through more grey city streets. He doesn't look like he's noticed anything at all.

It's not true, the voice says. *And if that's not true . . .*

What else isn't true?

44

Now

I can't stay here, obviously. The truth about my 'miscarriage' will get back to Sister Justice when she finds out that I didn't seek any medical attention at the Fruitfulness Hall. Sooner or later, she'll check up on me and realise that my story was nonsense. And that would mean the Atonement Room again, and I'm never going back there. So I need to leave Home tonight, with or without Amy. It's quiet at night, so I'm pretty sure I can get to the Big House without being seen, and I'm also pretty sure I could get into the woods and over the boundary wall to leave, as well. I don't think they'd let Amy and me just walk out through the Gate.

The corridors of the Fruitfulness Hall are empty as I take Angela's baby back to the newborn room. He's sleepy after his feed, and it's tempting just to put him into his cot and leave, but there's a distinct smell coming from his nappy and I don't know how long it's going to be before someone actually comes to check on him. He makes a displeased squawking sound as I lay him down on the table to quickly unbutton his onesie and change him.

I wonder where Hand is. I haven't seen any sign of him since he dropped me at the front of the women's building days and days ago. He was often away, as far as I remember, doing whatever it is he did when he wasn't at Home.

You and he both came in through the Gate covered in blood. Angela had said that. So there were wild rumours about me and Hand then, when I was here. It's only natural, I suppose – it is weird that he took an interest in me and took me away from the Sisters. But he never took me out through the Gate. Not that I remember.

Well, there was that one time. The first and only time he took me out of Home, when we went to visit one of the Children's churches on the Outside. That was the first and last time I ever left Home.

That's right, isn't it?

That black curtain again, swinging down. I don't have time to look behind it. It doesn't matter what's behind it.

Clean and dry now, Angela's baby is lying with his cheek pressed to my shoulder, his breath slowing. Rubbing his back in slow circles, I tip him gently into his cot. He lies tucked in his swaddle, looking peacefully asleep, but I hear him start to complain as soon as I shut the door. I leave Kehinde's keys in the lock. Hopefully whoever is actually supposed to be looking after him will check in on him soon. He is clean and dry and fed and safely in his bed, and that is all I can do for him.

I wonder if Angela can hear him crying from her lonely room up above.

To the Big House, then. It's late enough that no one's about, like I expected, but I can't stop checking over my shoulder as I make my way there. The path takes me between the Worship Hall and the Nutrition Hall. The windows are all dark.

Walking like this, alone at night, seems familiar. All that skulking about that Hand got me to do, hidden away from everyone else – I do remember that. But that's all I remember, really. The physical training, the endless copying of Father's words from his bullshit books. I must have filled ten exercise books with that rambling nonsense about Purity and Transgressions. I wonder if there was a point to it all – something Hand was leading towards – or if he was just making it all up as he went along to keep me busy.

I reach the edge of the field that lies between the Worship Hall and the Big House, the only place in the whole of Home that is lit up. It blazes like a beacon, with its spotlights by the pillared front entrance and the bright rectangles of several windows visible above the high border hedges. I remember what Angela said – *sometimes we have to be up all night* – and wince.

I don't know how Amy can have gone willingly to that man, submitted to that cold blue gaze. What must have happened to her outside, for that to seem better than being free?

She must have been so lonely. I should have tried harder to find her.

I look at the house, glowing like some radioactive tumour in the darkness. I need to get into the garden at the back. Going through the front is a no-go. A mad idea flashes across my mind: to steal a white dress from the laundry and attempt to pass myself off as a Vessel. I snort. I think about stealing a Warrior uniform then, and finding some scissors to chop my hair off, the way Hand did when he first took me in.

Why on earth had he cut my hair, anyway?

Men and women have little – officially – to do with each other here. I suppose to have me under his direct control, he needed an excuse. If I was a girl, then I needed to be with the women. If I wasn't a girl, then I could be with him.

There was the other stuff as well. He told me that I was an 'it', which meant I wasn't a real person. So that was me totally cut off from everyone else. Then that I was special, which meant I was pathetically devoted to him. It's classic grooming.

I have to stop trying to figure out what the point of it all was. There was probably no point. Hand is a fanatic. They all are. He wanted a little doll to control, or someone to torture, or someone to love him, and if I ever knew why then it's lost behind that black curtain. It doesn't even matter why exactly he brought me back. It doesn't matter what a madman wants. The only thing that matters is that I finish what I've started. Finally.

The field is relatively dark, especially this close to the woods that border the grounds. I slip through the high grass and moisture soaks into the bottom of my nightgown. Trousers: the first thing I will do, when Amy and I get out of here, is put on some fucking trousers.

My heart sinks as I reach the hedge around the Big House gardens. It's very high – at least twelve feet. It's thick, too, and pressing on it experimentally shows it's completely impenetrable. Even right down at the ground it's a tangle of roots that I can't squeeze through.

Fuck. Right. Don't despair. I skirt the hedge, moving away from the front of the house. The grounds inside must be enormous. Hopefully that means that the bit of the garden that Amy visits every morning is quite secluded, although, of course, Angela said she saw her from a window. So I could be seen.

I'm not going to think about that yet. I need to find a way in first.

I am rounding a corner of the hedge when I hear a trickling noise. Water. There's a little stream ahead, spilling out from the woods and winding towards the hedge. I trot towards it. Angela had said that Amy sits by a pond. Could she have meant a stream?

I reach the place where the stream meets the hedge. It goes underneath, but it's deep-ish – certainly deep enough for me to get into if I lie flat.

I hunker down and stare into the gap underneath the hedge. It's dark, but I can just see neatly cut grass bordering the stream on the other side.

This is it. This is how I finally, *finally* get to Amy.

I stand up and strip off my nightgown, kick off my boots. I roll the nightgown and my shawl into balls, then tuck each of them inside my boots. I lean in underneath the hedge and wedge the boots into the branches as far through as I can reach. Then I take a deep breath, and lower myself down into the stream bed.

I yelp out a curse when the water bites my skin. It's paralysingly cold. I clench my fists, and force myself to stay in it.

I am wearing the underwear all the women have here – longish woollen shorts and a breast band. They don't offer much in the way of protection. I am going to get freezing and filthy and probably scratched to bits, but I can put the dry nightgown back on at the far end at least.

The stream bed is gritty and rocks jab into my chest and thighs. I start to pull myself forward, mouth and nose just above the line of the water. Twigs from the underside of the hedge claw at my scalp, and I have to stop and untangle my hair. It's ensnarled in a huge knot, and in the end I just yank my hair away, feeling several strands pull out at the root. Maybe I should have shaved my head.

The hedge can only be a couple of feet wide, but it seems much more. I drag myself along, hissing with the cold, thinking about a film I watched with Adi once. This prisoner breaks out and escapes through a sewage pipe. He crawls through a river of shit and comes out clean. I am crawling through a river of hedge and coming out scratched. I get the giggles thinking about it, which carries me through to the other side and out into the gardens of the Big House.

I haul myself out of the shallow stream bed and up onto the grass, numb and dripping. The garden reminds me of the grounds of a stately home I visited in Ireland, with neat patches of lawn connected by little paths and surrounded by well-tended trees and bushes and flowerbeds. The part I'm in is like a wide corridor, running between the hedge I've just *Shawshank Redemption*-ed myself through and a row of trees that somehow have been made to grow in a sort of lattice pattern, with their trunks twining around each other to make a kind of natural fence. The stream cuts through the trees and disappears on the other side.

It's still dark. I've got time until dawn. I should have long enough to explore the gardens and find the pond that Amy visits.

I shiver. My shorts and chest wrap are soaked with wet mud, and my back is scratched to hell. My hair feels like a ball of tangled wool. I reach back under the hedge and pull out my boots. I rub myself down with the shawl and pull the nightgown on. It takes me a couple of goes to get it on because I'm shivering so much, and my fingers have turned to sausages. At least the hedges have cut the wind off. I'm still damp, but a little warmer at least. I try to finger-comb all the hedge out of my hair, but it's hopeless so I just tie the soggy, muddy shawl over it. I suppose I might look quite alarming when Amy sees me. Although I suppose she'll be quite surprised however I look.

What am I going to say to her? I've thought about it a lot since I've been here. I'll tell her how I missed her, I'll tell her I'm sorry that I hadn't found her earlier, I'll tell her that I have a home we can both go to and be happy and safe there. I'll describe the Underpass Cafe. An image of me introducing her to Meg blossoms. *This is Amy*, I'd say. *This is my sister*.

I hug that image to myself, and set off into the gardens to find her.

45

Then

I don't know what I was expecting the 'church' to look like. Like the Worship Hall, I suppose. But it's so unlike it that when the Hand of God pulls into the car park of the drab little building, I assume that we're not there yet, and that he's stopped at some other place first.

'Here we are,' he says, and gets out of the car. He doesn't look back at me. He doesn't seem to notice that it takes me a few seconds to go after him.

As soon as I'm outside, I taste the horrible, dirty air and sneeze. The Outside is diseased.

The Hand of God strides towards what I assume is the entrance, so I follow. There's a banner above the main door, half hanging off, and I start when I recognise the familiar blue and yellow flame-and-circle. It looks so wrong here. There are big letters running along the banner, and reading them gives me a sick little jolt. 'Let he who seeks the Truth come to Me.' But these letters are nothing like the grand gold ones scrolling across the doors to the Worship Hall. These are in a babyish sort of script, and a sickly yellow colour.

Everything seems wrong now.

Let he who seeks the Truth come to Me. But this doesn't look like a place I'd find any kind of Truth I'd want.

The Hand of God pushes open the door, and I trail inside after him. There's a small area with some wonky-looking chairs, and various bits of curling paper tacked to the walls. Weak light spills through the glass set into double doors that lead further into the building, and we go through these and step into a hall that looks a bit like the Training Centre at Home, but without the ropes and things at the sides. The floor is the same shiny boards, and noise echoes in the same way.

There is a circle of people in a puddle of light in the middle of the hall, in front of a raised stage that is a bit like the dais in the Worship Hall, but larger and higher. The people are sitting in chairs, facing each other, but a few turn around to look as we enter. Some of them smile.

'This is a great honour, friends!' A man stands and holds his hands out towards us. 'Some of us have had the privilege before, but for those who haven't – this is the Hand of God!'

There is an astonished muttering, and the rest of the people stand. There are, I notice with a creeping sense of horror, men and females right next to each other.

The Hand of God isn't paying any attention to me. He steps forward and nods an acknowledgement of their greeting. The man comes out from the circle and he and the Hand of God actually grasp each other's hands. They shake and clap each other on the back.

I feel sick. I have seen people on the Outside look the Hand of God in the eye before, and even touch him on occasion – handing him back money, or the demons in the woods sometimes do the hand-shaking thing before he leads them to the car – but they are Sullied, and don't know any better. These are supposed to be Children – or practically Children.

One of the females in the circle smiles at me. She's wearing clothing that falls off her shoulders. I can see the top of her chest.

It's too hot in here. I need to get out.

The Hand of God is speaking quietly to the man, who is nodding enthusiastically.

'Of course, of course,' he's saying. 'He's waiting in the back for you. But before you speak to him, would you have a few words for us?' The man smiles hopefully. 'It's not every day we see the Hand of God!'

The Hand of God surveys the group. Some have actually sat down again, in his presence. Surely he'll refuse? He'll rebuke them, he'll show them how to behave properly?

'I'd be delighted,' he says.

It's like watching a dream. The Hand of God moves through the circle, to the middle of the chairs. The group sit down, a buzz of excitement in the air. The female with the immodest clothes gestures to me.

'And what about your little friend here?' she says. 'Your . . . son, is he? Will we get him a chair?'

She's talking to the Hand of God as though she's equal to him. She looked right at him, addressed him without being addressed first! She glances over at me again, smiling. I want to scratch her eyes out.

'My companion is fine,' says the Hand of God. He's not even looking in my direction. 'But I welcome your compassion, Sister.' He reaches out and takes her hand, squeezes it, releases it. She looks thrilled.

What is happening here?

'Friends, it is wonderful to see you here tonight. The world Outside grows ever more degenerate by the day. The world is poisoned, diseased. Corruption and decay are everywhere.'

The group is nodding. Some are even murmuring, 'Oh, yes,' or, 'It's true,' and things like that. The Hand of God moves, turning to look at each member of the circle.

'The false idols you have all been told to venerate – money, the government, celebrity – every day, they seem to grow more powerful. They hold more sway over the minds of our young. But those idols are falling, friends! The value of the money in your pocket has plummeted. The government, those corrupt politicians – well, we have seen clearly that they have no desire to keep their citizens safe, but care only for their own self-interest. Culture has stagnated, and offers only shock and spectacle, depravity and poison. Those idols are falling, collapsing – and what will be left when they are gone? Those degenerate institutions in which the credulous masses place their faith?'

The group are still nodding and muttering along. A few actually say, 'What? What will be left?' when the Hand of God pauses here.

'Faith itself will be left. Faith that humanity can return to its natural state, its Pure state – untethered from the toxicity of modern life, from the anaemic ideals that corrupt this world. That we can live together, in Purity, as men and women are meant to. Free from the shackles of commerce, of meaningless labour, of unions that are not fruitful for the body or the soul. And do you know how I know this is possible, friends?'

The group have gone silent, are staring up at him as though he is Father Himself. The Hand of God spreads his hands out to them. '*Because it is already happening*. The Children, at Home, are living this Pure and Unsullied life. It is not an easy life – it is hard work – but it is honest, and it is purposeful. At Home, you see the fruits of your labours, in this life and the next. You have a place, set out and made especially for you. You have a Family. My friends, my Children . . . I hope someday soon to welcome you into the heart of the Children, at Home.'

They burst into applause. I feel like I'm having a fever as they stand, move towards the Hand of God, then begin touching him. Hands reach out and touch his arms, his back, his shoulders, his chest. The Hand of God stands there, face grave, arms lightly outstretched, accepting it all.

I step back out of the light, further into the shadows by the door. This can't be real. None of it can be real.

The Hand of God, taller than any of them, looks over the tops of their heads, right at me. He finally meets my eyes, and as they continue to touch and pat and run their hands over him, he pins me to the wall with his gaze, and smiles.

46

NOW

I think I've found it: a large rectangular pond, mostly encircled by tall bushes so it's like a little hideaway. Anyone coming from the house won't be able to see it, although a corner of the house with a high window does overlook it. That must be the window Angela looks out of sometimes.

I haven't found any other ponds in the gardens, so it's got to be this one. There's a stone bench set into one of the bushes, in a sort of shallow recess with overhanging branches, hidden from the house. I set myself there. I don't know when dawn will be. A couple of hours, maybe?

I stretch the knots out of my spine. My shorts are still damp under the nightdress, and my feet are frozen lumps. I try to massage some life back into them.

I yawn. The bench is just long enough for me to lie down, if I curl up a bit. I tuck my legs under my nightgown, pillow my head on my forearm, and run through what I'll say to Amy when I see her.

I'm here to take you home. Our real home. I'm here to take you home. Our real home.

I must have dozed off, because it's light and I hear birds singing. There's a splash of water, and I look up to see a dog paddling in the pond. Its tongue lolls out of its mouth happily.

'Here, sweetheart.' Meg is beside me, holding out a steaming cup of tea. 'Get that into yourself, Zoe, sure you must be frozen solid.'

I'm not cold, but I take the tea anyway. Meg yells over her shoulder, 'Madra! Would you credit that mutt with any sense at all? Get out of the pond, for the love of . . .'

'I'm taking Amy home,' I say to Meg, but she keeps yelling at Madra. 'Can she come work in the cafe?'

'But you are Home,' says the Hand of God. He's on the bench, next to me. 'You've always been Home.'

Like a scene in a movie cutting from one thing to another, suddenly the garden is dark and empty. I'm lying down. I thought I was sitting up. I rub my face. My mouth feels cottony. I'm awake now, but I can't quite shake off the shreds of the dream. I look at the pond, half expecting to see the surface rippled from Madra's splashing, but it's dark and still like polished glass. I look along the length of my body lying on the bench. I'm alone.

'What are you doing here?' a voice says behind me.

I fall off the bench. I'd tried to put my hand down to push myself up, but at the unexpected sound of the voice, had missed the edge of the bench and instead toppled awkwardly onto the flagstone, jarring my wrist.

A woman steps towards me, making an impatient noise. She's wearing a nightgown, like mine but red. Her hair is piled on top of her head in a messy bun. She crosses her arms. 'Are you hurt? You're not supposed to be out here.'

I pull myself up, stand facing her. Fine lines appear on her forehead as she frowns. She looks me up and down.

'You're not—' she says, and steps back.

'Amy,' I say. 'It's me. It's your sister.'

47

THEN

The Hand of God is directed to a door at the back of the hall. He gestures for me to follow, and I do, keeping my head down so I don't have to see the stupid faces of the people, still milling around and twittering happily.

The door closes behind us, plunging us into silence. We're in a corridor, painted bile green. I look down at my boots.

'I warned you that it would be strange, little Acolyte,' says the Hand of God. I glance up. His eyes are bright, his cheeks flushed. He looks – younger, almost.

'I know,' I say.

'What's wrong?'

I shrug, scuff my boot against the worn brown carpet. I feel his hand on my cheek, and I let him lift my face. I look into his soft grey eyes, which usually always makes me feel better, but it's just not the same. Not after that. Not after everything I couldn't help thinking in the car. But I have to tell him something.

'It's just . . . they don't know anything! Those people – they think they're like us, but they don't even know anything! They shouldn't have looked at you, and that female talked to you, and they shouldn't have . . . they shouldn't—' I stop, look away, unable to say *touch you*.

The Hand of God's thumb strokes my cheek. 'I understand, little Acolyte,' he murmurs. 'Let me tell you a secret. Those people in there – they are sheep. Sheep are dumb animals, there to be herded. There to be sheared. But ultimately, they are there to be slaughtered.' I meet his eyes again. His thumb moves across my lips, and I feel a shiver deep inside. 'You are my Acolyte,' he whispers, and I love when he says that, when he calls me his, and I push every bit of doubt I have away and hang everything on his words. 'You are my special one, the only one with the power I need. You are the one who is going to help me save the world.'

I am a flower, opening up to the sun. He pats my cheek, moves his hand to my shoulder, squeezes it. 'Now,' he says. 'We must continue with our true purpose tonight.'

I follow him down the corridor. I can still feel the heat of his hand against my face, and it's good, so I try to concentrate on it, rather than the strange behaviour of the people in the hall. And the way he encouraged it. He stood there, reached out, and let all of them touch him. It was wrong.

But everything he does has a purpose. Even if I don't always understand that purpose right away. I have to remember that.

We reach a small room. There's a table and chairs inside, a sink and a fridge, and a man leaning against a counter, looking at the glowing handheld device that all the Sullied have. He stows it in his pocket as the Hand of God enters, and drops his eyes. He's oldish: grey hair dusts his temples, and thick jowls hang down. His suit is clean and sharp-looking. There is a little metal badge pinned to his lapel – the flame-and-circle. I've never seen that badge on a man outside of Home before.

'Gavin,' the Hand of God says.

'Hand of God,' the man – Gavin – says, keeping his eyes low. Finally, someone who knows how to act properly!

The Hand of God takes a seat and gestures for Gavin to take one too. I stay standing at the door. Gavin's eyes flick to me as he sits down, but he doesn't ask any questions.

'You have the address?' the Hand of God asks. Gavin takes a folded-over piece of paper from the inside pocket of his grey suit coat, and passes it over.

'Everything's arranged, sir. My team will be the ones to respond whenever the call comes in, and I can ensure the result you're looking for.'

'Excellent work,' the Hand of God says. 'You're doing the Children a great service, Gavin.'

'Honoured to, sir. The things he's been putting about – I've been itching to get something done. You've seen the latest?'

'I'm aware of what's been circulated. That's why your role is so important. We must fight fire with fire.'

'Absolutely, sir.' Gavin's eyes flick towards me again. I keep at attention. The Hand of God stands and rests a hand for a moment on Gavin's shoulder.

'I'll see you're rewarded for this. Your contribution to our purpose thus far has been incalculable. This only raises your star higher in my estimation.'

Gavin's jowls lift in a shy smile. It makes him look almost boyish. 'I'm honoured, sir. Truly honoured. And if I may say so, a few more of my lads will be coming onside soon. It's slow going, but me and a couple of the others at my rank have been working on them. They'll come to us, sir. They'll come all right.'

The Hand of God nods, grasps Gavin's shoulder tighter a moment, then releases it. 'The more of your people you can bring to the light, the more of our work can be done,' he says. Gavin nods fervently. I am dizzy with not understanding any of this. I feel hot, and fidgety.

The Hand of God moves to the door, and I follow him gladly, but Gavin calls out before we can leave.

'You'll need this, sir,' he says, holding out a plastic bag. The Hand of God gestures at me to take it.

I carry it back to the car – thankfully, we exit by a back door and not through the hall with all those people again. I can hear them singing, though, as we leave. It's a song I know from Worship. They've got the tune all wrong.

There is a light drizzle, and mist obscures the end of the street. The Hand of God indicates to me to look in the bag as he starts the car.

The bag is white, with bright red and blue letters on it. 'ShopMart', it says. Inside are two other plastic bags, but a different type – both are square and see-through. One holds a small flattish rectangular object, shiny metal, about the size of my thumb. The other holds a knife, just like the ones I've seen used in the kitchens at Home. Black handle, serrated blade, almost as long as my hand.

'You won't be using your usual knife this evening, I'm afraid,' says the Hand of God as he pulls out onto the road. 'This is going to be a bit different.'

48

Now

Amy looks at me, utterly shocked.

'It's me,' I say again. I raise a hand, and she takes a step backwards, lifting her own hand to her mouth. She shakes her head.

'No,' she says. 'No, no, no.'

'It's all right,' I say. 'Amy, it's okay—'

'Catherine?' she says.

'Yes. It's me, it's really me.' I'll tell her about my new name later. 'Amy, listen—'

'What are you doing here?' she says. She puts both hands to her head, holding it as though it might otherwise fly apart.

'I came back for you,' I say. What colour there is completely drains from Amy's face.

'You did *what*?'

'I came back for you,' I repeat. I feel eleven years old again, lumpy and ungainly in the face of my smart, beautiful sister. And she is beautiful. She's older, and the lines of her jaw and her cheeks have sharpened, but her eyes are the same.

'Why?' she says, and it sounds like a moan. 'Why, why, why, Catherine? Why would you come back for me? How did you even know I was here?'

I flounder. This isn't what I expected. I don't know what I expected. 'I needed to find you,' I say.

'Oh my god,' she says. She turns away and puts her face in her hands. 'Oh my god.'

'The Hand of God told me you were here,' I say. 'He came and got me—'

'He what?' she says, spinning around. 'He came for you?' She advances on me, and I step back, bumping against the bench.

'Yes, but I came back for you, not because of him,' I say. This is all going wrong. I'm not saying any of the things I want to.

'That . . . that fucking psychopath knew where you were?'

'He – he said they'd always known,' I say. She covers her face with her hands again and groans.

'Oh Jesus, oh Catherine, oh god, I thought you were out—'

'I was out! I mean I am. Look, Amy, you can come with me. We can go back . . .' I trail off as she stares at me. Then she laughs. It reminds me of Angela's laugh – totally devoid of humour or warmth. What is wrong with her?

'I'm not going anywhere with you,' she says.

'But, Amy—'

'No. No. You have to go, Catherine. You have to go *right now*. Do you understand?'

'But I came back for you!' I say. I step forward and grab her hands. She looks at me in amazement. 'I came back for you, and we can leave now, both of us, and we don't have to be alone, and . . .' I'm crying, great big snotty gulps like a little kid, and I can barely speak through them. 'Please . . . please, Amy . . . we can go . . . go home . . .'

Amy pulls me into a hug. I collapse into her, sobbing. She's warm and real and she's here and I've found her, I've found her.

Her hand strokes my back. This is home. This, this feeling, this belonging. This warmth and closeness. I thought I'd found my home in Ireland, but it's here, with her. It always has been.

Her arms wrap around me, squeeze tight. I tuck my forehead under her chin and let myself be held.

I try to raise my arms to hug her back, but the way she's wrapped herself around me pins them against my side. I feel her take a deep breath, and then she shouts, 'Guards!'

49

Then

'May I ask a question?' I say as the streets spin past.

'You may.'

'What does this have to do with the scored-out entry in the records book?'

The Hand of God nods in approval. 'It has everything to do with it. Now, little Acolyte, you might find some of what I'm about to tell you strange.'

'Everything tonight has been strange,' I say, and he laughs.

'Then you will be ready to hear this. Well. The book records, in black, the Warriors and Daughters born to Brothers and Elders. But the book contains a record of two Seeds born as well. Can a Seed be born to a Vessel?'

'No,' I say. 'The Seed is from Father and His wife.'

'Exactly. Now, what did you notice about the two numbers?'

'They were different. But . . .' I don't know how to say it.

'They were two different females. Two wives,' the Hand of God supplies.

'But . . . Father only has one wife,' I say in a small voice. The Hand of God glances at me, his face painted by passing streetlights.

'There was a previous wife. Many years ago. And that union produced the first Seed.'

'How can there be more than one Seed?' I say. A car horn blasts outside, and I jump.

'There isn't.'

I think about the scored-out entry. 'Did he . . . did the Seed . . . die?'

The Hand of God shakes his head. 'Sometimes, you have to tell people something in order to help them. Even if it's untrue. Sometimes, for their own good, they cannot know the truth.'

'A . . . a good lie?'

'A good lie. The first Seed was flawed. The bloodline was tainted. He rejected everything about us, about Home and the Children, and he became a Recreant.'

A spray of rain hits the window by the Hand of God's face.

'Hold fast to My words, Children, lest ye become a Recreant, lest ye fall from Perfection in Mine eyes,' I whisper. I'd copied those words from *Father's Precepts* only the other day. Recreants were listed alongside the other sources of evil in Father's sermons, were cited as sources of damnation by the Sisters in their lessons. They were the worst of us. Those who had seen the possibility of Father's Truth, the perfection of the world to come, and who had stepped away from it. They were cowards, and worse.

'We realised that from birth, something had been very wrong with him,' the Hand of God continues. 'He had been made wrongly.'

'By his mother?' I say, but he doesn't seem to hear me.

'The Children . . . you have to understand that they would have been upset to know this. They wouldn't have understood. So they were told that the first Seed and his mother had died in a sickness. There was a long period of mourning. This was all before you were born, little Acolyte. Then there was a new wife, and soon enough that union produced the second Seed. The current Seed.'

That explains why I've never heard of the first Seed. You don't speak about the dead after you've mourned them. They are in the perfect world to come, waiting for us, and speaking about them can call their souls back down. So you have to be careful never to mention them.

'What happened to the first wife?' I ask. Again, he doesn't seem to hear this question.

'The first Seed – the Recreant – disappeared into the Sullied world, and for a long time we didn't know where he was. But recently, he came out of hiding. He began talking to the press.'

'The press?'

'Yes, the press – they . . .' The Hand of God waves a hand. 'They disseminate information among the Sullied. Misinformation.'

I'm not really following, but I nod.

'The Recreant has been defaming the Children. He has been telling all sorts of lies about us, Acolyte. About how we live, and what we believe.' I think about what Gavin said. *The things he's been putting about – I've been itching to get something done.* I look down at the knife in my lap, still inside its translucent plastic bag.

'We have to stop him,' I say.

'Yes,' says the Hand of God. 'We have to stop him.'

50

Now

'Amy? What are you doing?' I struggle, but she holds me tightly against her. She shouts again.

'Guards! Guards!'

I try to push her away, and we both stumble to the side. Amy slips, and we fall against the stone bench, my ribs catching the edge. Pain sparks, bright against the night. She lets go and I scramble away, my hand pressed to my side.

'Amy . . . what are you—'

She is half sitting, half lying on the ground by the bench. Her hair has escaped her bun and fallen over her face. She screams, 'Guards!' and I know I need to run. This isn't her. This isn't Amy. She's changed too much. Something's been done to her. She's brainwashed. Father has brainwashed her.

I pull myself to my feet. I have to get away. Have to make another plan . . .

I run straight into the Guards. Strong arms grasp me. I twist and pull, but my arms are wrenched up my back and there's a sickening impact in my stomach and I just hang there, gasping.

'Don't hurt her!' Amy. She stands up. She seems totally different now. Her head is high, and her voice commanding.

'What's going on?' says one of the Guards.

'She's a security risk. I want her put out of the grounds.'

'We'll take her to the Atonement Room.' I feel the Guard holding my arm twisted up behind my back jerk on it, turning me away. Fingers of pain radiate through my shoulder. I can't go back in there, I can't, I can't . . .

'No! No,' says Amy. The Guards pause. 'No,' she says again. 'She can't stay in the grounds. Anywhere in the grounds. Take her through the Gate, up towards the main road. Leave her there.'

What?

'We should really—' begins one of the Guard. Amy glares at him.

'Do as I ask. This is your Father's will.'

'Father's will be done,' they respond in tandem. They turn away, and I pull against them.

'Amy, please! Don't do this! Please, just—'

An arm hooks around my throat and presses in, and I have to lean back to avoid choking. Amy recedes as they drag me away.

'Get her out! Get her away!' she's screaming, and her voice has lost its commanding edge. It sounds thicker, choked.

I let my feet tangle together and I almost fall. The Guard is pulled off-balance. The pressure eases off my neck and I twist and punch and bite, but something cracks into my jaw, hard, and before I hit the ground, I'm caught and lifted and the world careens drunkenly until I'm resting with my cheek against rough dark green material, my stomach aching from where a shoulder presses into it.

I get snatches of upside-down view as he carries me through the gardens. Flowers and benches and some kind of statue, a man with his arms raised, children about his feet . . . then the crunch of gravel, a volley of dog barks and a voice, hailing us.

'What in Father's name . . .'

'Here, get that door . . .'

A creak, juddering up steps, then I'm tipped to the side and dropped onto the floor. I manage to get my arm up to protect my head, but my hip and knee and elbow smack onto concrete hard enough that I cry out. A burst of pain in my ribs, and the foot retreats.

'Quiet, you. Just keep it shut. Close that door!'

The door shuts, and boots surround me. We're not in the Big House, I don't think. This looks like a little shed, or something. I'm lying near a desk, and there's a window above it letting in slants of light from outside. A Guard station?

'What's going on?'

'This one was in the gardens, with Father's wife. She told us to get rid of her.'

'Get rid of her? Like—'

'Like take her Outside. Up the road, dump her there.'

There's a silence.

'Father's name.'

'Right? Real pushy about it too, like. Trying to order us about.' A snort.

'What we gonna do, then?' says a younger, nervous voice.

'I don't think we can take her out. Not just on a female's say-so. Not even if she is Father's wife.'

'She said it was a security risk.'

'Security risk, is it? You know what that means.'

'Oh no. Are you joking?'

'I am not. If it's security, it goes straight to the top. We have to call in the Hand of God.'

I start laughing. I roll onto my back, hands clutching my stomach. Blurry faces peer down at me, glance at one another.

'He's going to kill me,' I say when I can talk through the laughter. Hand wanted me back with the Children, and he won't let me leave again. I know this with a cold certainty, the same way I know that the sky is blue, that water is wet, that my sister is forever lost to me. 'The Hand of God will murder me.' I start laughing again, then lunge for the door. Hands scrabble at me, bring me back down to the ground. One of the blurs looks at the other.

'Go and get him, for Father's sake,' he says. 'And you, get some rope. We need to tie this crazy bitch up.'

51

Then

We're parked outside a high building, across the street from a shop with boarded-up windows.

The Hand of God checks the paper Gavin gave him. 'Number 78,' he says. 'Put that in your pocket.' He points to the thumb-sized thing.

I pick it up, still in its little see-through bag. 'You're going to leave that in his flat,' the Hand of God says.

'This thing?'

'It's very important that you do.'

'What is it?'

'You won't understand. It's full of pictures.'

'Pictures?' I squint at the object. Does it fold out somehow?

'Incriminating pictures. Illegal. It must be found at the same time as the Recreant's body. Gavin will ensure that the information is leaked to the press, and the Recreant will be discredited. Nothing he has said about us will be remembered, only his perversion.'

There's so much I don't understand. I put the thing that is somehow full of pictures into my pocket.

'When you get out of the car, tuck the knife in your waistband, under your jumper. Keep the plastic bag wrapped around the handle, and don't touch the blade.'

I pluck at the top of the bag holding the knife. It's sealed, but two ends split apart and when I pull them, the bag opens. I carefully turn the bag inside out, keeping a hold on the handle through the plastic. The blade shines dully in the orange glow coming from the lights set into the side of the building.

'You can get in through that door there.' The Hand of God points to a shabby door; the top window is splintered and cracked and only half patched with a piece of wood. 'You'll find stairs leading up. On each floor, there are numbers. Keep going up until you see the seventies.'

'Aren't you coming with me?' I ask.

'No, little Acolyte. This is your task.' I hadn't realised my hand, still clutching the knife by its plastic-wrapped handle, was trembling until he covered it with his own, larger hand. 'You must do this alone. I will be here, waiting for you. Now listen. You find number 78, and you knock on the door. When the Recreant answers, you tell him that you've run away from the Children.'

'But I—'

'It's a lie, little Acolyte. But it's all right. It's a good lie. You are lying for a righteous cause. He won't be able to see the truth in your mind. He's too far from the light.'

How far am I from the light?

'You tell him you've run away from Home, and that you need his help. Ensure you get into his flat. One you're in, you must find a way to get behind him and draw the knife across his throat.'

I look down at the wickedly serrated edge of the knife. I feel sick. 'But we always—'

'I know. This has to be different. Across the throat. Once you've done it, you're going to put the knife into his hand. Then put the USB into his other hand.'

'The . . . you-ess-bee?' I feel light-headed.

'The object in your pocket. Try not to touch it when you get it out of the bag. Try not to touch anything in the flat at all. It's all contaminated. It's all unclean. When you leave, put your hand inside the plastic bag and use it to shut the door. Understand?'

'I . . . yes.'

'Repeat your instructions to me.'

'Go in that door,' I say. 'Find number 78. Tell him I've run away. Get inside, and behind him. Knife across the throat. Leave the knife and the other thing in his hands. Don't touch anything. Get out.'

'That's it. That's it exactly.' He brushes my cheek with his knuckles.

'What happens then?'

'You return to me and we go Home. His body will be discovered in the next day or two, and the police will be called. Gavin will take it from there.'

Gavin is the . . . "police"?'

The Hand of God nods. 'Gavin is a useful pet. Gavin arranges all our targets, all the demons. He sets up the meetings, and if the remains are found, he makes them . . . go away.' The Hand of God waves a hand in the air to illustrate how the bodies are made to disappear. 'Now it's time to go,' he says, and reaches across me to open the car door. I breathe in the dry smell of him in the brief moment that he's pressed against me, and desperately want to stay in the car. But I get out, and he pulls the door shut after me.

52

Now

I'm propped against a unit; the edge of a shelf is digging into the small of my back, and my hands and my ankles are bound painfully tight. Two Guards are left, I think the same two who got me in the garden. One is standing by the half-open door, arms crossed, keeping an eye outside. The other, younger one, leans back against the table, looking down at me.

'She's not a Vessel,' he says eventually.

'Yeah, well done,' the Guard at the door says, not bothering to look at him.

'So why would one of the Sisters be in the gardens at this time of night?' he says. His eyes trail over my damp and dirty night-gown, the snarl of my hair. The shawl has got lost somewhere along the way.

'That's what the Hand of God's going to find out, isn't it, Jeremy?' says the one by the door.

'Your name is Jeremy?' I say. I'm feeling giddy again. Nothing matters anymore. All this shit has been for nothing, and now I'm going to die. I laugh.

The one by the door looks around sharply, and the one by the table stands upright, looking affronted.

'You can't speak to us,' the younger Guard says, sounding awed.

'Did you have a washbag that said "Jeremy" on it?' I say, remembering the name I'd laboriously stitched several lifetimes ago. 'Did it have a crooked "e"?'

The young Guard goggles at me. The one by the door takes a couple of swift steps and kicks me. The toe of his boot sinks into my thigh, and it cramps, filling me with brilliant pain. I gasp.

'No talking,' he says. He retreats back to the door. The younger one moves backwards towards him, not taking his eyes off me.

I haven't thought about stitching that name on a washbag for . . . years, I suppose. How strange. I grew up next to this man, this Jeremy, but I never met him. We'd lived utterly separate lives, so close to each other. I think about him hanging his washbag up in the shower room, then I think about how Amy and I used to communicate with each other, and the thought of her twists in my chest like she's plunged a knife into it. She's gone.

'How'd she know about my washbag?' the younger Guard whispers to the man.

'Shut it.'

'No, but how'd she know—'

There's the crunch of boots on the gravel outside, and the man hisses, 'Sharpen up,' as they both straighten to attention, their heads respectfully bowed. The door opens fully, and the glare from the floodlit driveway is so bright I have to blink away sudden tears. A dark shape appears.

'Leave us.'

The Guards both shuffle out, and the figure steps into the hut.

'Long time,' I say to the Hand of God. 'No see.'

He tilts his head and, keeping his eyes on me, speaks to the Guards behind him. 'Go to your posts,' he says, and shuts the door behind him. There is the muffled crunch of their footsteps departing over the gravel.

Hand pulls the chair out from under the desk and sits in it. He leans forward, rests his elbows on his knees, and loosely clasps his hands together.

'You don't write,' I say. 'You don't call.'

He backhands me across the face. I fall to the side, my head knocking against a shelf. I can feel myself cowering, and I tear that little snivelling piece of me out and I spit on the floor.

'Get these ropes off me! Get these ropes off! You're a coward, you're a fucking coward—' He stands and places his boot on my throat. I thrash, and he pushes down harder.

'You remember what we do to girls with filthy mouths?'

My throat is being crushed. His face looms above, looking utterly blank.

Black spots dance in my vision. My ears ring.

This is it. This is it; this is how I die.

The weight on my throat lifts and I heave air into me. It burns, and I cough and hack.

'Do you hate this?' he says, and his voice is close. He's crouched down beside me. 'All of this?'

I stare at him through tears. What kind of trap is this?

'Well, Zoe? Do you?'

He lifts me up, pulls me back up to sitting. He reaches down and begins to untie my ankles. I watch him, repulsed by the touch of his fingers on my skin. 'Yes,' I manage to say. My voice sounds like it's been chipped away. 'Yes. I hate all of this. I hate you.'

'Do you want to finish it?'

'Finish what?' My ankles fall away from one another as he pulls the rope away. They ache with the sudden rush of blood. He reaches behind me, shifts me around until he can get to the rope around my wrists.

His breath tickles my ear as he says, 'Your task. Your purpose.'

'What are you talking about?' I just want to sleep.

'Ridding the world of evil,' he whispers. I want to laugh, but my throat hurts too much.

'That was all – just bullshit,' I say.

'Was it? Everything I taught you? Everything we did?' The tight band around my wrists slackens, then falls away. He moves my hands forward into my lap, still crouching behind me. His arms stay there, encircling me. I'm too tired to pull away.

'We never did anything,' I say.

'Never? What about all the demons you and I dispatched? All the children we saved?'

'We never dispatched any demons,' I say. I fix my eyes on the light through the window. It's like it's fading.

'Don't you remember? Don't you remember the knife? And the work? You did this . . .' His fingers, straight and pointed like a blade, jab into my ribs. I suck in a sharp breath. 'You put the blade here, just here, and you and I watched as the evil poured out of them.'

'I didn't,' I say. The light blurs, and my cheeks are wet. 'I've never hurt . . . stabbed anyone . . .'

'They weren't real,' he says. He presses his cheek against mine, rocks me like a child. 'They weren't really people. They were demons, and they were hurting children. With their perversions. We stopped them, you and I.'

I put my face in my hands. 'I didn't—'

'You would see the demon under their faces,' he says, his voice inside my head. 'You must remember. You would see it, and tell me.'

I see . . .

a pale moon-face, dark streaks painting the skin, mouth open and wobbling

being sick, so sick

hands wet and sticky, skin drying stiff

the knife, the knife, the knife, flashing in the moonlight

'I . . . I—' Something is building up inside me, something heavy and thick and cold, starting in my stomach and spreading, spreading, pressing against the inside of my skin.

the knife, flashing

'What did you do to me?'
'So you remember?'
'I . . .'

hands on me, all over me in the dark of a car

muscle and flesh resisting

smell of vomit and dead leaves

'It's not real,' I say. 'I don't remember any of it.'

But I do. The curtain has been ripped away, and I do. I do remember.

'We did the work that needed to be done,' he says.

'You made me a monster,' I say, and my voice is a little girl's.

'No, Acolyte. I helped you become who you are.' His fingers brush my lips, and I writhe and kick away from him. This place is too small. It's collapsing in on me. It's a coffin.

My knees hit the floor, the world tilts, and I spread my fingers on the ground to keep from falling off. 'I can't . . . I didn't . . . no . . . no, please . . .'

A lurch, and I'm off the ground and in his arms. I want to pull away but the world is spinning so madly that I can't. That cold heavy sickness is in every cell of my body.

'It's all right,' he's saying. 'It's all right. I've got you. I've got you.'

I let myself be carried out of the hut and into the light.

53

THEN

The stairs are endless, and they stink. Like necessary cubicles when they haven't been cleaned properly. I go up and up, counting the numbers displayed in peeling paint at each floor. 1–10. 11–20. 21–30. My legs are starting to ache by the time I get to 71–80.

I look back down the stairs. A light is broken further down, so there's an irregular flash on-off-on-off. I can't see the door I came in anymore.

It occurs to me that this is the first time I've truly been alone Outside. Even when the Hand of God is drawing the demons to us in the woods, he's only ever just outside the car. I've never been this alone before.

A rush of cold air makes the door beside the numbers 71–80 bang. I put my shoulders back and my chin up. I can do this. The Hand of God is counting on me.

The knife is awkward against my leg. It's unwieldy, not like my proper knife. The blade scrapes against my undershorts, catching and pulling at the little fibres, the teeth jabbing me. The handle, crackling in its plastic cover, presses against my stomach. It's going to be hard to get it out quickly and quietly.

Ahead of me is a low-ceilinged corridor, open on one side to the air. Orange lights glow in strips above doors on the other side, curtained windows between each one. The nearest door says '71'.

78 is most of the way along. Noise comes from behind some of the doors and windows, voices raised in conversation or laughter,

some strange kind of booming music from one. But 78 is silent, the window dark.

The door is painted yellow, but it's split and bubbled so that the wood underneath is visible in places. I touch the handle of the knife through my jumper, then raise my hand and knock.

It barely makes a sound. I swallow, and knock again, harder this time.

Find 78. Tell him I've run away. Get inside, and behind him.

There's no noise from behind the door, no light coming on at the window. I knock again.

Knife across the throat. Leave the knife and the other thing in his hands.

I strain my ears, but don't hear anything apart from the booming music a few doors down, still audible even here.

Don't touch anything. Get out.

There's a rattle, and the door opens a crack. A wedge of face appears, a man's with dark hair falling over his eyes. There's a chain bisecting his nose, running from behind the door to the door frame.

'Who is it?'

Find 78. Tell him I've run away.

'I'm . . . I mean, I'm from the Children,' I say. I see his eyes widen, and the door bangs shut. Oh, no. No no no. This isn't supposed to happen. I hammer on it with both hands.

'I've run away!' I say. 'I've run away from Home!'

The door opens again, fully this time. The man – could this really have been the Seed? – is standing there, peering out over my shoulder at the corridor. 'Shh! Quiet! You've left them?' he says, his voice low.

I nod.

'How'd you know to come here?' He looks wary. 'Did the Initiative send you?'

The Initiative? 'The Puh-hee-oh-nix Initiative?' I say, remembering the last message from Amy. The one I'd found in my hairbrush handle. The one I couldn't think where to hide, so I'd memorised it, and eaten it. That was another thing I'd never told the Hand of God.

'The what?'

'The Pee-hee-nix?' I say. The man's eyebrows disappear into his hair.

'Are you trying to say "Phoenix"?' he asks, his voice softening.

'Yes. That's it. Fee-nix Initiative,' I say. He glances behind me again and then steps back, holding the door wide.

'Right. Get in, get in.'

I step inside.

Get behind him.

Knife across the throat.

54

Now

I'm sitting in Hand's study. It's smaller, though of course it isn't really. My little desk in the corner has gone. There are more books on the shelves than I remember. What happened to all those exercise books I filled? Has he got them in an old cardboard box somewhere, shoved in the attic, *Acolyte's stuff* scrawled on it in Sharpie?

I should laugh. Zoe would laugh at that.

But I'm not Zoe. I never was. Zoe was a fiction, built to hide a monster.

I've had a shower. I've put on new clothes. Not a dress, thankfully: rough trousers, a dull grey shirt, and a green jumper. Warrior clothes. Hand even left an elastic band for me, for my hair.

I felt like I was watching a film while I did all that. As though I was sitting back in my head, just watching this person wash and dress as though they're normal. As though nothing is wrong. As though they haven't just discovered that they are evil.

It's not just discovered, though, is it? I knew all along. Somehow, I made myself forget. I drew that curtain over it all. But I always knew. Those little flashes I'd get when looking at men, sometimes, like there was something wrong with their faces – the sense that the world was slipping away from me, followed by feeling sick and scared. Always feeling ready to attack when I was startled. Keeping that knife under my bed in Dublin, knowing where to stab someone to kill them. The monster was never fully gone. I was only sleeping.

And now I'm Awakened.

The door opens behind me, and Hand appears at my side, then places a glass of water on the desk in front of me. I stare at it, at the little beads running down the side, pooling around the bottom. It's so unnervingly like the time he gave me a glass of water in my flat in Dublin that I have the sensation that I'm still there, that this is all a dream. But it is Dublin that was the dream. It's my whole life that was the dream.

I half register a scraping noise to my side. Hand is pulling his chair around the desk to sit beside me.

I should take that glass, smash it, and use the biggest shard to cut my throat. What else do I deserve?

'How are you feeling?'

I don't respond. What could I say?

'Do you remember what I asked you earlier?'

I can't speak.

'I asked: do you hate all this?'

Yes. I do hate it.

'I asked if you wanted to finish what we started.'

I turn my head to look at Hand properly. It seems to take an age. It feels like my head weighs a thousand tons. 'You want me to do it again.'

He shakes his head. 'Just one more. Just one more, and then it's all over,' he says.

I feel tears track down my face, collect and drip from my chin. How long have I been crying? 'Who?' I ask.

Hand leans close. 'Father,' he says.

I'm so surprised that it shakes me out of my stupor. 'Father? You want me to kill Father?'

'He's the same as all the others,' Hand says urgently. 'All the others we got rid of, all the evil we stopped. They hurt children, you remember? He is the same.'

I shake my head, close my eyes. I can't keep up with this.

'He learned it from his Father. The Father you remember, when you were here with me.' Hand's voice is low, relentless. 'That was your original mission, little Acolyte. To get rid of the evil poisoning the Children. The corruption of their bloodline. To return us to the path of perfection. To destroy their perversion forever.'

'You wanted me to kill Father?' I say, keeping my eyes closed. I feel his hands touch mine, clasp them. I don't pull away.

'Yes. Yes. That was what all of it was for, your training. So that when the time came, you could gain entry to his rooms, get rid of his evil, and return to me.'

I think about all that climbing he had me do. Scrambling up trees, then ropes – did he have me break in somewhere?

'Why couldn't you just walk me into the Big House?' I ask, opening my eyes. I study his face, the new lines by his mouth, the eyes that seem lighter than I remember. 'You can go anywhere, do anything. So why not just march me in, order everyone out? Why not do it yourself, even? And I need answers, not riddles. Tell me.'

He sits back, but keeps hold of my hands. 'The truth, little Acolyte, is that I couldn't be seen to have anything to do with his death,' he says. 'I would be visible elsewhere, while you did it. No suspicion would fall on me.'

'And what then?' I say. 'The Seed would just take over from Father.' A creeping suspicion. 'Did – was I supposed to kill the Seed, too?'

Hand nods. I think about those pale blue eyes, and feel sick.

'Did you – did you kill him? Father? The old Father?'

Hand's face twists, and he looks away. 'No,' he says. 'I did not kill him.' He looks back at me and sighs. 'You want the truth. This is it. Father – the previous Father – died because he choked on his own vomit. He had overindulged in narcotics. The young Vessel with him also died, in much the same way.'

I think about those girls every year at the Harvest, and feel sick.

'He was corrupt, and venal,' Hand says. 'And his son was – is – the same. With the first Seed, I thought that the mother . . . but it became clear to me where the rot truly came from. But we would have changed all that, little Acolyte.'

'By killing him?'

'By *replacing* him.'

Hand's eyes catch the light from the lamp, and for a moment it looks like they are glowing. He grips my hands tighter.

'You would have rid us of Father,' he says. 'Then you would have done the same for the Seed. You would have made it appear as though the Seed killed Father, then killed himself in his anguish. We would have been rid of them both.'

I feel sick. 'Then who would have replaced them?' I say. But I don't need to ask. Not really.

'I would have,' the Hand of God says. 'I would have become Father. And you would have been my Hand.'

The world is slipping, slipping away from me. I hold on to the hands gripping mine.

'I would have made the Children anew,' whispers Hand. 'With you at my side. No more filth, no more perversion. Purity, and goodness. Perfection.'

'You still want this,' I say. 'You still want me to kill Father.'

'Yes,' says Hand. 'You're going to do it tonight.'

55

THEN

I follow the Recreant through a dark, narrow corridor into a brightly lit kitchen. It's small and cramped, with just enough space for a table, two chairs and a kitchen counter. Cups and crumbs are scattered across every surface. My feet stick to the floor.

'Do you, uh, want a coffee, or something? Tea? Water?' The Recreant looks around a bit helplessly. He's tall, with a belly that presses against the waist of too-small trousers. His hair needs cutting. He's got a thick beard, with the hairs over his top lip curling down almost into his mouth.

How can he be Father's son?

But he's not, I remind myself. Not really. He was made wrong.

The knife handle presses into my stomach.

'No, thank you,' I say.

'Right. Um . . . okay. Sorry. It's just, you've caught me a bit off guard.' The Recreant drags a hand through the tangle of dark hair on his head and laughs. 'Are you all right? You must have had quite a journey to get here.'

'Yes,' I say. He's leaning back against a kitchen cabinet.

Get behind him.

Knife across the throat.

He's said something.

'Sorry?'

'I said, how did you know about the Initiative? How did you contact them?' He's frowning, watching me. I concentrate.

'Phoenix Initiative, oh-seven-seven-two-nine-four-seven-six-one-eight-three.'

The look on his face is almost funny, but my code number seems to have worked because then he smiles.

'Did someone give you that number?'

'Yes,' I say. 'My sister.'

'Your sister? Oh, what am I doing, sit down, sit down.' He moves forward and pulls one of the chairs out as much as the available room allows. I feel the knife pressing into my leg and stomach.

'No, thank you. I'm all right standing,' I say.

'Okay. Fair enough. Fair enough.' He retreats to his former position, standing with arms folded against the cabinet. Father's name. How can I get behind him?

'So your sister gave you the number,' he prompts.

'Yes. I . . . she ran away. A while ago. But she left it for me.'

'She ran away too? What's her name? I might know her, know where she is.'

He might as well have slapped me across the face. Amy. He might know where Amy is.

'You know her?'

'Probably, or we can get in touch with her. The Initiative can.' He smiles.

The kitchen, the mess, even the Hand of God outside – it all recedes. I hear my voice coming to me like an echo of someone else's. 'Her name is Amy.'

The Recreant drop his arms, jerks upright. 'Your sister is *Amy*?' he says.

'Yes?'

'Jesus. Jesus.' He puts a hand to his head. 'Right. Well. I mean. Gosh. Sorry, it's just . . . she told me she had a sister. Amy, I mean. She never said anything about a brother.'

'Catherine,' I say.

'Yes – that's your other sister?'

'No,' I say. 'I am Catherine.'

He blinks, shakes his head a little. 'You – you're a – sorry, it's just – the hair, and—'

'He cut my hair,' the echo-voice says. I can't stop it. I'm just listening to it. 'He cut my hair and he gave me these clothes and he told me I wasn't a person anymore.'

'Who did?' says the Recreant. 'Who told you you weren't a person?'

I pull the knife out of my waistband. The Recreant's eyes widen. 'The Hand of God,' I say. 'He sent me here to kill you.'

56

NOW

I am arguing with Hand about ropes. He wants me to climb up the back of the Big House and break in through the skylight, as in his original plan.

'Absolutely not,' I say. 'I'm not climbing up any more fucking buildings.'

His mouth firms at my language, but I don't care. He needs me. I point at the entrance to the Big House on the rough plan of the building Hand has sketched on a piece of paper. 'I go in that way.'

'The entrance is guarded,' Hand says.

'Not if you call them away,' I say. 'You go up to them, tell them I've escaped and . . . I don't know, I'm armed and dangerous or whatever. You tell them to search the grounds with you. You stay with them, stay seen, and I sneak into the house while it's unguarded.'

Hand is staring at me. It's not his usual stare, of cold appraisal or false warmth. He looks – uncertain?

'This will work,' I say. He regards me a few moments more, then looks down and taps the sketch.

'There's a main staircase here, as soon as you enter,' he says. 'It should be quiet when you go in. Go up two floors, then in the east wing—' his finger slides to another point on the paper '—you will find Father's suite of rooms. He will likely be in the bedroom, here. I imagine you'll find him . . . unconscious.'

I look at the hastily sketched rooms. Neat little boxes for me to pass through. 'What's over here?' I ask, pointing to the other wing of that floor.

'It hardly matters.' He stands, starts to gather up the paper. I get up too, put my hand on it, stop him.

'It does. If I encounter someone, I might have to hide myself. I don't want to get boxed in, or run straight into a room full of . . . Guards, or Vessels, or something.'

Hand's eyes flick up, the rest of his body staying absolutely still.

'I am your Acolyte,' I say. 'I am doing your bidding. Father.'

His lips part, and he swallows.

'I want to do this right,' I say. 'Like it should have been done all those years ago. But I need to know everything.'

'Say it again,' he says.

'Father,' I say.

His eyes close, for a moment. Then he slides the paper closer to me.

'The west wing of the same floor is where Father's wife is located,' he says. I keep my eyes steady on his.

'And the next floor up?'

'The Vessels. But they're locked in. You won't need to go in there.'

'And above that?'

'The attics.'

I look down at the plan. 'You wanted me to go in through the attics. If the Vessels are locked into their floor, how was I supposed to get down to the next floor?'

'I would have given you the keys,' says Hand. Of course. He has keys for everywhere.

'Where are they?'

'Where are what?'

'The keys.'

'You won't need them.'

I put my hand over his. His skin is cool, and dry. 'I might need to get out through the attics. Just in case, if I get discovered, or the Guards come back in early.' He looks down at our hands. 'Please,' I say.

Keeping his right hand under mine, Hand leans forward, pressing me back against the desk. His face is so close that my nose touches his chin. I feel his breath on my eyes.

281

There's a sliding sound behind me, then a jangle of keys. Hand pushes the drawer on the far side of the desk shut, folds the keys into my free hand. He stays there, holding me against the desk with his body. I can feel him against my hip.

His thumb strokes my jaw. 'You're ready, Acolyte,' he says.

I look up at him. 'I'm ready, Father.'

57

THEN

The Recreant holds up his hands. 'Okay. Okay. Let's just . . . let's just calm down, all right?'

I shift my grip on the handle. Plastic crackles. 'He's outside.'

'Who's outside?'

'The Hand of God.'

The Recreant darts a look at the window, as though he'll see the Hand of God floating out there, eight floors up. His face behind the beard is utterly drained of colour.

'He sent me to kill you,' I whisper.

'Because I'm evil, right?' The Recreant looks at me, licks his lips. 'Because I was *made wrong*?'

I frown. He nods. 'I know, Catherine. I know all of it. What he's told you. I know it, because he told me often enough. When I was a kid, before I left, before I ran away. He locked me in the Atonement Room, beat me, soaked me with cold water and left me there . . . all because I was asking questions. Being difficult.'

'Being different,' that echo-voice says for me, and he nods again. He still looks scared, but he looks sad too, now.

'He did it to you, too, didn't he?'

'I've been there,' I say through numb lips. 'In that room.'

'They tell you you're wrong, and bad,' he says. 'And then they tell you you're special. You're special, and unique, and only they can see it.'

I collapse into a chair. The Recreant glances at the window again, then moves towards me, hands still raised.

'They did it to me, too, Catherine,' he says. 'Not the exact same as you, but close enough. It's what they do. It's how they make you believe their lies.'

'They?' I say.

'The Children. The Hand of God, the Brothers and Elders, all of them. Father. My father.' He gives a laugh that's almost a sob. 'My own father. You know the Hand of God killed my mother?'

I can't breathe.

'I left, Catherine. I ran. I got out. I couldn't be what they wanted me to be, so I ran away, and god help me, I left my mother behind. She "disappeared" after that. But I know what must have happened. He told me he'd do it. The Hand of God threatened me with it often enough. If I didn't toe the line . . .' The Recreant rubs a hand across his eyes. 'But I left anyway, and he killed her.'

He slides into the chair opposite me, lays his hands on the table between us. 'I had no idea what I was doing when I got out, Catherine. I wandered for ages, eventually got picked up by someone in a car – I'd never been in a car – they took me to the police, who took me to social services, and someone there got in touch with this group they'd heard about. This group that helps ex-cult members. They got me into hiding, helped me to get my head straight. I've been working with them since.'

I don't understand half the words he's using. I want to lay my head on the table and cry. Everything he's saying is so strange, so familiar.

I look up at him sharply. 'Can you read my mind?' I say.

He looks at me sadly. 'No, Catherine. And neither can any of them.'

I drop the knife with a clatter, put my head in my hands.

'It's okay – it's okay, it's hard at first, I know, but it's all going to be okay. Just breathe. In – and out. In – and out.'

I breathe along to his words, and feel the tightness in my chest dissolve a little.

'Catherine?'

I look up.

'The group that helped me – the Initiative – they helped your sister, too. She found us when she escaped. Do you want to know what happened?'

I nod, greedy for any news of her. The Recreant smooths the hair over his top lip. 'Well, she had been given the number by a friend of hers. A girl we were aware of, who was at risk of being drawn into the Children. What was her name—'

'Teneil,' I say thickly, thinking of a flapping, boneless arm. The man carrying her.

'That's right – Teneil. Her mother was an actor, really well known. They target people like that sometimes, people that can be useful to them. Rich and influential. Actors, politicians, wealthy and connected people. They fast-tracked her into the inner circle of the Children, but that meant her daughter, Teneil, wasn't indoctrinated as thoroughly as she usually would have been. She found us online, contacted us, let us know what was happening with her mother. But before we managed to get Teneil safely away, she disappeared. We assumed her mother had brought her to join the Children at Home. Once someone is in Home, we can't get to them. We've tried filing missing person's reports before, getting warrants and stuff, but it never goes anywhere. Anyway, months later, we get this phone call. A girl, saying that Teneil had made her memorise a number, explained how to use a phone, had told her to get in touch with us if she ever got out.'

'Amy,' I say. The Recreant nods.

'Amy,' he says. 'The Initiative picked her up, and I helped to get her story out. The reason she left.'

'Why did she leave me?' I say.

'She didn't leave you, Catherine,' he says, leaning forward. 'She was so worried about you. She talked about you all the time. But it wasn't safe for her there anymore.'

'Why? What was wrong?'

The Recreant hesitates, rubs the skin over his eyes. 'Catherine, when I was "the Seed", they wanted me to choose a wife from among the Daughters.'

'What has this got to do with—'

'Just let me explain. They did it at night,' he said, lacing his fingers together, then unlacing them, lacing them again. 'They brought these girls to me at night, two at a time – I was only about twelve or something – they were even younger – and they – they—'

He stands up abruptly, drags both hands through his hair. 'They presented these girls to me, Catherine. They got them to strip off, and they examined them in front of me for "flaws", and they made me watch it all. Then they left me alone with them, to talk to them. To choose them.'

I remember cool blue eyes, watching me. I remember Amy, shivering beside me. I remember the air on my skin.

'The Bad Night,' I say.

'It happened to you, didn't it?' He looks like he's about to cry.

'I was with Amy. It was after that night that she told me we were sisters.'

He nods, wipes his face. 'The Hand of God keeps this sort of book, a kind of list of all the births among the Children. Who their parents were. He wanted to keep track of the bloodlines, check that none of them got too close. So no Elders ended up with a Vessel that they'd fathered,' he says bitterly. 'So no Seeds ended up with a half-sibling. So that we all remained "Pure". The Elders who organised the "meetings" I had with the girls, they always had the book with them. The new Seed probably saw the records, noticed you had the same mother, told Amy.'

My mother is in that book. I think of the records, tucked into the Hand of God's bookcase. I was in there. Amy was in there. My mother, and my father. Numbers and a name.

'Amy was chosen,' he continues, sitting back down. 'After that night. The Seed chose her. I never chose any girls, I couldn't – but he chose her, and after that she was brought to him when he asked for her. Just to talk,' he says, holding his hands up. 'That's what Amy said. He just wanted to talk. But she knew what it was building to. She knew what it meant, what she'd be forced to do one day. And after everything with Teneil, she left.'

'So it wasn't my fault?' I say, and until this moment I hadn't realised that that is what I have always thought.

'No, Catherine. She stayed as long as she did because of you. To try to keep you safe. But in the end, she had to run. And she couldn't take you with her.'

The Recreant looks at the knife on the table. I follow his eyes down to it. I think about a blade flashing in the moonlight. I think about how it feels when I look into Sullied men's faces and feel the world slip away from me. When I know that there are demons under their skin. I think about how it never happens when I look at Hand. But then, it hasn't happened with the Recreant, either.

'I've done terrible things,' I say.

'No, Catherine.' I look up. There's no fear or disgust in his eyes. He just looks sad. 'You've been made to do terrible things.'

The Recreant moves his hand forward, across the table. He leaves it open and waiting.

'We can help you, Catherine,' he says. 'We can get you out. We can get you to Amy.'

58

Now

We go over and over the plan, until the sun is high in the sky and my eyelids are drooping.

'You need to sleep,' says Hand. He holds the study door open for me, and I look at the closed door to my tiny old box room as we step into the corridor.

'You still have my bed?' I say. Hand takes my shoulder and guides me to the stairs.

'No,' he says.

I've only ever been upstairs once before, when he took me up to the roof through the attic. The doors upstairs were all closed, so this is the first time I've ever seen where he sleeps.

I can't call it a bedroom, though it is. It's just too impersonal. There's nothing here. Just a bed with a grey blanket, and an empty side table. Not even a lamp. The floor is bare boards, the walls featureless.

Hand pulls the curtains closed, cutting out the sunlight. I sit on the bed, start to take off my boots. For a second, I think he's going to get into the bed with me, but he walks past, towards the door.

'Why did you never get anyone else?' I say. Hand pauses at the door. 'Why not just get another acolyte after me?'

It's the first time I've directly referenced running away. Hand steps back into the room, sits on the end of the bed.

'There was no one else suitable. No one else with your particular gift.'

I think about all the things I've ever wanted to ask him, all the answers I've never had. A scrap of conversation comes back to me. *Progeny. Lineage.*

'Where do you go?' I say. 'When you disappear. You used to leave me alone all the time as well when I was a kid. Where were you?'

'Doing the work,' says Hand. 'Eradicating the demons. Securing our future. Gathering those who are loyal to me.'

I have a dim flash of a gym hall-type room, a circle of people sitting in the centre. Standing as Hand and I enter. I think of him visiting these little outposts of the Children, up and down the country, drawing all those people into his web.

'That's why you left me alone for so long? This time?'

'It was a test,' Hand says. 'I have set you so many tests. You pass them, every time.'

I look over at him. The curtains let in a thin slit of daylight, but it doesn't reach his face. He's just a shadow. 'What do you mean, a test?'

'Just that. A test. I needed to see what you were capable of. As when you were a child, and you took up arms for me. First, against that boy who took what wasn't his. Then, against the demons we sought out.'

'So this was another test? You wanted to see what I'd do when I came Home?'

'Yes. Showing you the picture got you here. Then, I waited for you to show me you were ready. To show me you were truly willing to commit to us again, to leave behind the Outside world. Then, to show me you were ready to act against the corruption here. I knew when the time would come. I was not out doing the work among the Sullied last night, I was here, waiting for you to show yourself. And look what you've achieved.' The shadow spreads its hands. 'You made it almost to the very centre of the rot.'

I try to sort through what he's told me. Had he always known I would realise that he was never taking me to Amy and find her myself? Had he known the very day it would happen?

289

Or is he just reacting to events as they happen, and claiming foreknowledge?

Does it matter?

'Did you always know where I was?' I say. What I'm asking is: was my freedom ever real?

'You fell from my sight for a time,' Hand says. 'But among those loyal to me, there were some who knew I wanted to find you. Our influence has grown far beyond these borders. Word reached me of your location two years ago.'

I think about the pictures of me and Adi.

'Why did you wait so long? Why not come for me right away?'

Hand shifts his position on the bed. The creak of the bedsprings is startlingly loud.

'I would never have forced you Home,' he says. 'You had to choose freely to come with me. As you have always chosen freely. But you had been corrupted by the Outside world, and I had to wait for the right moment. Wait for the thing that would break through and show you that you needed to return.'

'The photograph of Amy's wedding,' I say. 'When was it taken?'

'A few months before I came to you. But this far after the wedding, there has been no sign of a new Seed. The Elders are dissatisfied. There has been talk of forcing a new marriage. With someone who will be able to produce a Seed.'

I think of Angela. *Father's wife is barren.* And what he'd told me in Dublin. *Amy is in some danger.*

'So . . .' I say slowly. 'You didn't want another marriage, the possibility of a new Seed.'

'No. I had, at first, considered that you might see the need to return if a new Seed was to be born from Amy, so I was waiting for that. But it became clear that wouldn't happen.'

'You thought I'd be more likely to return if Amy was pregnant?' I say.

'Yes.'

He was wrong. Amy was enough. Amy was always enough.

'But . . . don't you want to . . .' *kill the Seed*, I want to say.

'A new Seed – Amy's child – would be uncorrupted,' Hand says. 'I would claim it as mine. A new Seed would legitimise my position as Father. But it has to be from the right bloodline.'

'Amy's baby?' I say weakly. Had he been planning to take Amy as his wife? Take her child, and Father's, as his?

An image of pages and pages of neatly written numbers and names floats into my mind. The records. All those carefully detailed bloodlines. Curated for purity.

'Regrettably, it appears she cannot have children. I was hoping to avoid it, but . . . other arrangements will have to be made.' His fingers skate across the bedclothes, almost rest on my leg, then move away. 'When we are about our sacred business,' he says slowly, something distant in his voice as though he is talking to himself, 'nothing we do is a Transgression. If I am Pure, then my actions are Pure. Sometimes . . . sometimes I have to remind myself of that, when my duty becomes . . . burdensome.'

I shove away thoughts of what that might mean, exactly. I try to sort through everything he's told me so far. I've never had so many questions answered. I've run out of other things to ask. There's only that last thing.

Progeny. Lineage.

'Do you know who my parents are?' I ask.

Hand's silhouette nods.

'I – overheard – a conversation you had once,' I say. 'With an Elder. You suggested . . . you let him think that Father was my father. To protect me.'

'I did.'

I have to force the next words out. 'Was it true?'

'No. Father is not your father. I was simply fooling a credulous idiot so that I could, as you say, protect you.'

I think about the questions I could ask next. Who are my parents, then? Do I know them? Are they here? Who *are* they?

But he stands, and goes to the door, and I get under the covers, still clothed. Hand leaves, shutting the door quietly behind him. I think about the question I didn't ask him.

Is it you?

I must have slept because there was sunlight around the edge of the curtains and then, what felt like a moment later, everything was dark. But I can't remember it. Then there's food on the small table in the kitchen. I eat it, I suppose, because the plate is full then it's empty, but I couldn't say what it was, or how it tasted.

I watch Hand eating, watch the muscles in his face and throat move as he chews and swallows, and think about how we look nothing alike.

Outside, the sun has long set.

'What will happen to the Vessels?' I say. Hand lays his knife and fork neatly together on his plate.

'You won't need to go anywhere near them tonight,' he says.

'No, I mean, what will happen to them? When you are Father?' I say. His eyes don't meet mine.

'Father did not always have Vessels,' he says eventually. 'He was Pure, once. But he became corrupted. The Vessels are an indication of his corruption. His perversion. I had to monitor everything very carefully to ensure the rot didn't spread too far. To keep the rest of the Children as Pure as possible. Once he's gone, the poison in his blood will spread no further.'

'And what about Father's wife?' I say. 'What about Amy?'

He does look at me, then. His face is still, betraying nothing. 'Amy will be safe,' he says to me.

'And I will be your Hand,' I say.

'You will be my Hand,' he says. 'It's time to go.'

He's either our father, or he's not. Bloodlines. If Hand is our father, then any child of Amy's would already be connected to him. His bloodline. If he is not our father, then why would he want to raise another man's child as his own? Why not simply pick a wife and have a child of his own with her?

Perhaps he can't. He's unable, or unwilling?

Or he doesn't need to, because he already has two children. One will be his Hand, and one was supposed to bear the new Seed – to purify a polluted bloodline. But what will happen to Amy, now that she hasn't played her part in that plan?

As we walk to his car, I think about the Gate, and about the world outside. I think about Zoe's life, and how far away it is.

I think about how stories say that monsters need to be killed. I think about Father. I think about the men in the woods. I think about what those men wanted to do to me. I think about a knife, flashing in the moonlight. I think about how the world is better off without those men.

Hand picks up speed as he drives along the narrow road away from the Men's Quarters, past the Fruitfulness Hall, past the Worship Hall, and finally screeches the car to a stop in front of the Big House, gravel flying. He throws the door open and yells. The Guards move as soon as Hand barks at them, spreading out to search the grounds. You don't argue with the Hand of God.

I peek out from the footwell of the rear seats as he sends them off into the night, keeping one with him to search. As soon as they've disappeared into the gloom, I ease the car door open, slip out, and walk right into the Big House.

It's palatial. My boots squeak against the marble floors, echo from the high, arched ceiling. There's gold finishing and rich red curtains and polished surfaces everywhere. I think about the spindly chairs in the women's common room, and feel like spitting onto the perfect shiny floor.

But I have a job to do. The staircase rises before me, gently curving bannisters leading up then branching left and right. It's totally silent, even though it seems like every light in the place is on. The thick carpet muffles my footsteps as I climb to the second floor, and turn to the east wing.

Something prickles at the back of my neck. I turn, and almost shout aloud. My reflection, brooding in an enormous mirror. I thought it was a Guard, or a shadow.

I look away, towards the east wing. Through an arch, a corridor curves away. He's through there, somewhere. A spider, hunched in a corner of his web.

And Amy's here, somewhere. Just along that corridor on my left.

I pad along the carpet, follow the corridor round through the arch. It opens out to a sitting room, couches and chairs here and there, a fireplace. Windows with the curtains drawn tight.

I skirt the chairs, make for a door on the far side. I wonder what Hand is doing. He said he'd keep the Guards busy for an hour.

It occurs to me that perhaps this is all some kind of set-up. I'm his fall guy. He pins the murder of Father on me, and a troublesome loose end is tidied away. Perhaps that was always his plan.

I think all this, but dispassionately, like I'm idly pondering the plot of a book or movie I half care about. It doesn't matter. I reach the door.

I raise my hand to push it open, then I change my mind and knock.

I wait. There's a shuffling from inside after a moment, then the door cracks open.

'Yes?'

'Don't shout,' I say, and Amy's mouth drops open. She grabs my arm and yanks me inside, slamming the door behind me. Her hair is mussed, her cheek marked with creases from her pillow.

'Why are you still here?' she says in a furious whisper. The room is dark except for a pool of light at the bedside. The bedcovers have been thrown back hurriedly. The furnishings are rich and plush and yet, like Hand's room, utterly impersonal.

'You didn't give me a chance to talk properly earlier,' I say. Amy stands with her arms crossed, again in that red nightgown.

'You have to leave,' she says.

'Are you going to call the Guards again?' I say. She looks down.

'Listen. You won't understand, but that was for your own good. You can't be here.'

'I'm not a little kid anymore, Amy,' I say. 'I know what's going on.'

She raises her eyes, throws up her hands. 'You have no idea what's going on.'

'I came back for you,' I say. 'You got me out, all those years ago. The Phoenix Initiative, remember that? The message, the hairbrush? I found it. Because of you. You rescued me, Amy.' I step towards her, carefully, as though she might startle and flee. 'And now I'm here to rescue you.'

Amy stares at me. 'You don't need to rescue me, Catherine,' she says. 'I'm here to rescue someone else.'

59

THEN

'You know,' the Recreant says, looking carefully out from behind the curtain of the front window. 'I almost just shut you outside the door earlier. When you said you were from the Children.'

'Why didn't you?' I ask softly. We're in the darkened front room, empty except for a sagging couch and a fold-out table. He glances back at me, the orange light from the open-air corridor outside lighting up the wild strands of his hair.

'You said you were running away. And then you said Phoenix.' He laughs. 'Or tried to, anyway.' He looks back outside, up and down. 'I think it's clear.'

He lets the curtain fall and moves to the front door. He unhooks the chain holding the door closed, then opens it. He steps out, looks back at me. I stay in the shadows. I feel like I'm being torn in two.

He holds out a hand. 'Come on.'

I reach out, then drop my hand.

'Look, I know how you're feeling,' he says. 'I know, okay? I've been there. Everything you know is falling to pieces. Just . . . just hold on to the one thing you know, absolutely know in your heart to be true. What is that?'

I try to think. It's like bees buzzing around my skull. I think about knives and push-ups and trousers and dresses and the Hand of God's eyes and hands on me. I think about the woods. I think about blood. I think about looking up at the stars. I think about Amy.

'I have a sister,' I tell the Recreant. 'I have a sister, and her name is Amy. And I want to find her.'

He nods. 'Good. That's good, Catherine. Hold on to that. That will see you through everything.'

I follow him out of the door. He leads me away from the way I'd come in originally. 'There's another staircase over here,' he says, glancing behind him. He tucks his hands into his pockets, ducks his head. 'Lets us out on the other side of the building than where he's waiting for you. We can get away.'

'Where is Amy?' I say, trotting after him.

'I don't know. I mean, I can find out,' he says. 'We need to get in touch with the Initiative. But first we need to get out of here. Get to another safe house.'

'Safe house?' He opens a door and we're in another stinking stairwell, identical to the first.

'Yeah – we've got a few in various places. They're usually a bit nicer than this one. I was just lying low, after the press interviews. Little flats and houses and things. We have them in a couple of countries.'

I clatter down the stairs after him. 'How did you know I'd be here, anyway?' he asks, stopping suddenly and turning to me.

'I don't know. We visited a church, and there was a man there. Gavin. He gave the Hand of God your address.'

The Recreant's face twists, and he starts down the stairs again. 'I don't know a Gavin. Could be a fake name, I suppose.'

'He's a police,' I say. The Recreant stops so abruptly that I crash into the back of him.

'The police gave him this address?'

'He's a useful pet,' I say, backing up.

He digs a hand into his hair. 'Fuck,' he breathes. 'We suspected, but . . . fuck. This complicates things.'

'Can we still find Amy?' I say.

'We can still find Amy,' he says distantly. 'God almighty. That's why none of the allegations ever stick, I suppose. Children in the police.' He seems to snap back into focus. 'Right. We need to get you away from here, and hidden from that fucking bastard.'

We almost sprint down the rest of the stairs, pause to peer out the bottom door and check it's clear, before running across the car park to a little yellow car. The Recreant unlocks it, opens the door for me. I stop, look back over my shoulder to the building, where the Hand of God waits on the other side.

'Remember your truth, Catherine,' the Recreant says, and his gentle voice brings me back.

'I want to find my sister,' I say, and get in the car.

60

Now

'Who are you here to rescue?' I ask.

Amy purses her lips. 'I don't know if you remember her. Teneil.'

Teneil. An arm, boneless, flopping. A man carrying her.

'Amy,' I say. 'Amy. Teneil's dead. She died years ago.'

'She didn't.' Amy steps forward, eyes bright. 'I thought so too, for such a long time, but she didn't die, Catherine. She's been here, the whole time.'

'Where?'

'Here. In the Big House. It's why I came back, why I agreed to be Father's wife. To get into here. But I just – haven't been able to find her yet.' She strides past me, pushing her hair away from her face.

'How do you know she's here?' Amy's not back because she's lonely, or because she regretted leaving, or because I didn't find her. Weight I didn't know was there shrugs away from my shoulders. I feel suddenly, madly, like laughing aloud. It wasn't my fault. This, too, wasn't my fault.

Amy sits down heavily on the bed. 'I've been working with the Initiative,' she says. 'The last couple of years, when it seemed safer. I stopped hiding and started working with them. Helping the ones who get out. It's not just the Children. There's loads of weird groups all over. But the Children is one of the biggest. Certainly lately. They're huge, they're in everything . . . anyway, one day, this woman turns up. Girl, really.' Amy bites a thumbnail and talks around it, her voice slightly muffled. 'Social services put her on to us. She was a Vessel.'

'A Vessel escaped?' I say, sitting down next to her. She smells like soap.

'I know, right? She's so tough. She told us all kinds of things, but one thing she said was that there was a woman who was kept prisoner in the Big House. I mean, more of a prisoner than the rest of the Vessels. Didn't get taken out to Worship, didn't get to mix with the rest of the Vessels, but they saw her sometimes, in Father's room. She'd be there with the rest of them sometimes, but she was never allowed to talk, and she – she was chained . . .' Amy stops, looks away.

'But how do you know that it's Teneil?' I say gently.

Amy looks down at her hands. 'Description matched,' she said. 'Approximate age, skin colour, hair type, eye colour – who else could it be? She – the escaped girl – said that he called her his "little demon".'

'Fucking hell.'

'So I had to come back,' Amy says, still looking down at her hands. She makes fists. 'I had to. She told me how to escape. They hated her because she was friends with me. That's why they hated you, too. I wasn't supposed to be close to anyone except the Seed. That was why I pushed you away, when I saw how they treated her, when I realised what they were doing. But she didn't care, she made sure I got away. She saved me. So I couldn't leave her here. Not when I knew—'

'I know exactly what you mean,' I say. Our eyes meet, and we smile. The years peel away.

'I can help you,' I say.

'How?' Amy throws up her hands. 'I don't know where she is. I've been everywhere in this fucking house that I can. She's not up in the Vessels' rooms, I know that. Not on the ground floor, or even in the cellar. I've even managed to get all around his rooms, while he's passed out. She's not anywhere.'

I try to think. 'Why did you keep going to the pond?' I ask absently.

'The pond? There's a mobile in there,' she says.

'There's a what?'

'A mobile. It's in a waterproof bag. The Initiative sorted it, so that I can contact them when I've found Teneil and need a pick-up. I smuggled it in when I arrived, threw it out a window into the pond. I go out and stare at it every night, thinking about bailing out. But I know that I can't. Not until I know she's okay.'

'Maybe she's not in the house.'

'She's got to be here,' Amy says. 'Katie – the Vessel – was sure of it. Said she never saw her taken in or out. They can see quite a lot from those windows.'

'Yeah,' I say, thinking of Angela.

'Catherine?'

'Mm?'

'How did you know to find me by the pond? How did you get away from the Guards? Why are you dressed like a Warrior? And is that a *knife*?' She points to the knife Hand gave me, sheathed in its case at my belt.

'It's a long story,' I say. Amy looks at me, chews her lip. I reach out tentatively, and she lets me touch her hand. 'You can trust me,' I say. 'I'm your sister. I came back for you. And I'll tell you everything – I will. I know a really nice coffee shop. I'll take you there when we get out, and tell you the whole thing.'

Amy smiles, shakes her head. 'I'd like that.'

'But first, we need to find Teneil,' I say. 'Have you ever tried the attic?'

'The attic?' Amy frowns. 'There's not – I've never seen any way up into it. There's no door, or anything.'

'There might be a hatch,' I say. 'Shall we go see?' I take the keys out of my pocket, and jangle them. Amy raises an eyebrow.

'Who *are* you?' she says. I stand up.

'My name is Zoe,' I say. 'And we're going to rescue your friend.'

61

THEN

I catch sight of the Hand of God as the Recreant drives us away. Or his car, at least. It's parked right where it was when I got out, round the far side of the building, the front of it just dipping into the smear of orange light from the overhang of the doorway. Inside is all shadows.

The Recreant lets out a long breath as he turns out of the car park. His knuckles are white on the steering wheel.

'I'm a coward,' he says. 'I should . . . that man . . .'

His eyes are shining.

'I'm sorry about your mother,' I say.

'Thank you,' he says very quietly. The shine in the eye closest to me spills and trails down his cheek, disappears into his beard.

He doesn't talk for a while. We spin through empty streets, getting further and further away. I'm feeling light-headed. Every so often, I'm gripped with sickening fear, thinking of what will happen when the Hand of God finds out that I've gone. What will he think? Will he go up to the flat, get in, realise I'm not there? Realise that the Recreant is not there? What will he do then?

I shiver, thinking about how angry he will be at my betrayal. But then I remember my truth, and I hold on to it. I have a sister, and I want to find her. I have a sister, and I'm going to find her.

After a while, the Recreant starts talking again. He tells me to call him Sam. It's the name he took when he started a new life, he says. He'd never had a name before.

'You'll need a new one,' he says. 'We'll have to find one for you.'

He asks more about the meeting with Gavin. I show him the thing in my pocket, tell him that it's full of 'incriminating pictures'. He makes a disgusted face.

'It's probably kids or something fucking horrific like that,' he says. 'Those fuckers. Those filthy bastards.'

He pulls over, tells me to open the car door and drop the thing behind the front wheel. I do, and he reverses over it, then forward, then back over it again. I open the door to check. It's in pieces, twinkling against the dark road.

We drive on, long enough that I start to get sleepy. I hear the Recreant – Sam – talking. I look over blearily. He's got one of the glowing things balanced on his thigh, and there's a tinny little voice coming out of it. I can't follow what the disembodied voice is saying. I rest my head against the door, and watch the streetlights swoop by silently overhead. They all blur into a long streak of light, leading a trail through the darkness.

'Here we are, Catherine.'

I open the car door to a rush of cool air. We're in the country somewhere, and it's just light enough now to see trees and grass all around a little house. A woman waits at the door. There's roses twining around the bricks above her head. She smiles. She's wearing a bright blue scarf tucked tightly in around her face and neck.

'Hello, Catherine,' she says. 'I'm Leila. We're going to take care of you.'

I let her usher me inside, Sam following. It's warm, with a fire crackling in a grate. I sink into a large green chair, so soft that it's like a bed. My head is full of cotton. I feel something tickling my nose, and open my eyes to see Leila tucking a butter-yellow blanket around me.

'You just sleep there,' she says. 'We're going to sort everything out.'

When I next open my eyes, it's bright outside and the fire is low. My neck hurts from the strange angle I've been lying at.

I sit up, and the blanket puddles to the floor. There's voices behind me. I follow them past a long table and chairs, to a half-open door. Peering through, I see the back of Leila's scarf, and the unruly head of Sam opposite. There's something in front of Leila, like one of the handheld things the Sullied use, but it's bigger and propped up. She's tapping at little black squares in front of it.

'. . . leaving today, in eight hours,' she says. 'We can get her on that one.'

'We need to. She has to get out of the country. Who knows what he'll do when he figures out what she's done. And now that we know we can't trust the police until we root out the mole—'

'Yeah, no, absolutely,' Leila says. She taps a couple more times, then makes a satisfied sound. 'That's booked, then. I'm going to call our contact over there. She can meet her, get her set up in the safe house.'

'Great. Thanks, Leila.' Sam yawns, stretches, catches sight of me through the door. I jump, back away.

'It's okay,' he says. 'It's all right, you can come in.'

I hang back.

'Come and sit down, sweetheart. Are you hungry?' Leila pushes the thing she's been tapping on away from her. There's a picture of a large boat on it, and some writing.

I stay standing. 'When can I see Amy?'

Leila sighs, glances at Sam. 'What?' I say.

'It's difficult, Catherine. We might not be able to get Amy right away,' he says.

'But you said—'

'I know, I know. You will see her again, I promise. It's just that it's a bit hot right now. We all have to go dark.'

Leila stands up. 'Cool it with the spy craft, James Bond. She's no idea what you're saying. Catherine—' She places a hand on my shoulder, and I shrug it off. She lifts her palms and nods. 'Okay. Catherine, it's really important that you understand that you're in danger. And not just you – Sam, too. And, yes, Amy.'

'Why?'

'This person in the Children, this "Hand of God" – he wanted you to kill Sam. Because Sam has been trying to expose the Children, and what they do. The Hand of God will obviously stop at nothing. And now that you're out, you're a threat to him, too. So we have to hide Sam, and we have to hide you. And we have to keep hiding Amy, because he might try to threaten her to draw you out.'

I look from Leila to Sam, horrified. 'He wouldn't. The Hand of God would never . . . he loves me,' I say. He does, doesn't he? And I betrayed him. He'll be so angry.

I think about the kinds of things he does when he's angry, and I feel sick.

Sam looks down at the table. Leila shakes her head. 'I know it's hard to understand, but he doesn't love you, Catherine,' she says. 'If he loved you, he wouldn't have tried to make you kill someone. If you love someone, you don't put that kind of stain on their soul.'

I think about my soul. I think about all the men in the woods. I think about stains.

The next few hours are a blur. Sam disappears, after hugging me tight and telling me that he doesn't mind that I almost killed him. Leila makes me stand by a wall, holds her little handheld thing up at me, and does something that makes it flash. She makes me eat something, but it might as well be sawdust for all I taste. Someone arrives and hands Leila a package, and says that they've never done such a 'rush job'. Then I'm in another car, and I think I sleep again, and then I smell something salt, bright and sharp. I hear birds calling, harsh and loud.

'Have you ever seen the sea before?' asks Leila. I don't answer. I don't know what I've seen or haven't seen.

Leila leads me to a line of people standing near an enormous boat, so big that it would dwarf some buildings. The front of it yawns open, a great mouth swallowing car after car. Leila tells me to listen. She says I need to pay attention. She takes out the package from earlier, the 'rush job', and tells me to look inside. There's a little book. There's a picture in it, and it's me, with my buzzed head and bruised-looking eyes. There's a name. She tells me I don't have to keep that name, but I have to pretend it's mine for now. I'm to show this to the man at the head of the queue, and this as well – she presses a strip of paper into my hand. It's called a ticket. They'll ask for a ticket. Give them this. Get on the ferry – are you listening, Catherine? – and someone will meet me at the other end. They'll find me. I'm to hide, and tell no one who I really am. One day, when it's safe, they'll tell Amy where I am, and she'll come and find me. Am I listening?

I look at the birds, wheeling above.

The salt air stings my cheeks as I watch the land recede. Leila is there, waving, her headscarf a bright blue dot that I focus on until I can't see anything at all. The ghost sensation of her arms around me, hugging me fiercely, lingers.

I stay there, watching the water until it swallows the world around me.

I think about stains that won't come out. I think about how the water makes the whole world look clean, and how much I want to just lean forward and let myself drop into it.

I think about the black curtain in my mind, the one that swings down when I try to think of the details of what happens in the woods, or with the Warriors that night in the Pavilion. I think about that black curtain, and I draw it down over everything. Over the knife, and the woods, and the stains. Over the Hand of . . .

What am I doing? What have I done?

I need him. I need to go back to him.

I can apologise. He will forgive me.

He loves me, he loves me . . .

I'm bent over trying to breathe, when a hand grips my shoulder. I wheel and knock it away.

'All right, all right, sonny, calm down, it's okay. Bit seasick, are you? Where's your mum, eh?'

The woman looking at me is enormous, the biggest woman I've ever seen. Her chin is nestled into the roll of her neck, her face framed by thick black hair twisted into ropes. Her face folds into a smile.

'No mum,' I manage to say.

'Ah, travelling alone, are you? Bit scary first time, eh? Someone meeting you the other end, are they?'

I nod.

'That's good. We're almost there, look!' She points behind me, and I turn to see distant hills. The woman talks a bit more, and then she's gone.

I watch the hills get closer and closer, then the ship comes to a stop with a judder. I follow the tide of people flowing out onto the land. There's a long line, and every tall man with dark hair that I see is the Hand of God. I pull the black curtain down every time.

This new land is grey, grey stone underfoot, grey fences, grey skies. People stream away to cars and buses. I look around, my stomach twisting around itself. How am I supposed to know who is here for me? What if there's nobody? What if I'm all alone?

'Hello, love?' I turn, and there before me is a woman, smiling under a cloud of bright green hair. I feel like there's nothing left in the world that can surprise me.

'It is you, isn't it? Leila sent me. My name is Meg,' she says, in a strange voice that I almost don't understand. The sounds are all wrong.

'It is you?' she says, tucking her hands into the pockets of her shapeless purple coat. 'Leila said to look for a young wan with a shaved head, and there's not many of them . . .'

She says the name that's written in the little book with my picture in it, asks if it's mine. Over her shoulder, I see the friendly woman from earlier, bellowing at a child who is running past her, chasing another child. 'Stop it, Zoe!' I hear her shout distantly. 'Get away from your sister!'

Seabirds whirl in the new sky above me. Behind the noise of engines and people, I can hear the rush of the waves, washing everything away. I think about stains, and I think about truth. I think about how I can make a new truth.

'It's Zoe,' I say to the woman with the bizarre hair. 'My name is Zoe.'

62

Now

Amy gestures for me to be quiet, then eases her door open and peers through the crack.

'It's okay,' I say. 'The Guards aren't here.'

She looks at me strangely. 'How do you know?'

We walk through her set of rooms. 'The Hand of God led them away. He brought me here.'

'What do you mean, he brought you here?' We start up the stairs, towards the Vessels' floor.

'He let me in here,' I say. Amy stops, turns to me, then shakes her head sharply.

'No. I need to know this,' she says. We've reached a little half landing, and she drags me behind a curtain that conceals a recessed window. There's a wide, padded ledge and Amy pushes me down onto it. The curtain is so heavy that it cuts off almost all light, but the window overlooking the garden lets in the glow from the moon.

'You need to explain,' Amy says.

'We don't have a lot of time—'

'Explain quickly.'

I pull together my scattered thoughts. 'Okay. Right. Um . . . what do you know about me?'

Amy blinks. 'What do you mean, what do I know about you?'

'I mean, what do you know about what happened after you left?'

'I don't . . . I mean, I know that you escaped yourself, a bit later. The people at the Initiative told me when I rejoined them.

307

But there were no records of where you'd been hidden. They were worried about leaks around the time you escaped, so a bunch of information had been destroyed or hidden and they'd even disbanded for a while. And . . . well . . .' Amy chews a thumbnail. Her nails are all bitten right down. 'Some of the original members of the Initiative had gone missing. Completely missing. It's possible that they had been killed. After the first couple of disappearances, a few went into hiding themselves. No one knows what's happened to them.'

I know, with a cold certainty, that it was Hand. Hand happened to them. Perhaps that was how he found me, after all that time. Maybe one of them told him, before the end.

I think about the woman with the blue hijab, who had been so kind, and so quick to hide me. I think about the Recreant. Sam. He'd chosen the name Sam. Did Hand find him, kill him? Did Hand kill both of them? Hunt them down, torture them to reveal my location, and murder them?

Amy is looking at me strangely. I'm breathing like I've just sprinted up a set of stairs. I need to calm down.

'Okay.' I try to drag my thoughts together. 'So, after you left – I don't totally remember all the details, but the Hand of God sort of . . .' I don't know how to explain this, or how much to explain.

'Sort of what?' Amy whispers.

'Sort of . . . took me in.'

'What do you mean, took you in?'

'He took me away from the Sisters.'

'But . . .' Amy casts about. 'But you're – I mean, you're a girl. How did he—'

'It's complicated,' I say. 'But he took me to live with him. He was kind of training me.'

'Training you for what?' Amy says. She grips my shoulders and I almost yelp with the pain. 'Oh, Jesus, Catherine, what was he doing to you?'

'It's okay—'

'But what do you mean, training? Like, did he . . . did he want you as . . . a Vessel?' She looks ill.

'No! No.' I grab her hands. 'It wasn't like that. I didn't know it all at the time, but he wanted to get rid of Father. Get rid of the Seed. He wanted to replace them, to lead the Children himself.'

Amy stares. 'What?'

'I know. He wanted me to be him, I suppose. He wanted his own Hand of God. I was supposed to – look, it's crazy. He wanted me to kill them, make it look like the Seed had murdered Father then killed himself, so that no one would suspect the Hand of God had anything to do with it. In the absence of anyone else to take over, he'd be the next most powerful one. Except I don't think all the Elders liked him, really. He probably wanted to get rid of them, eventually, too.' I trail off as I realise Amy is looking at me in horror.

'He genuinely wanted you to kill people?' she says.

'I . . . yes.'

Amy pulls me to her then, clasps me so tightly that the breath is squeezed out of me. 'I'm so, so sorry,' she's saying. 'Oh god, Catherine, I'm so sorry. I left you . . . I left you with him. I didn't know . . . I had no idea . . .'

'It's okay,' I say into her shoulder. She pulls away, holds my face cupped in her hands.

'It's not okay,' she says. 'It's not. I never would have left if I'd thought – but I had no idea – I didn't know he even knew you existed – that fucking psychopath . . .'

I cup my hands around hers. Our foreheads touch. 'I got away,' I say. 'I got away, and the Initiative hid me in Ireland. I was happy there.' My voice catches. 'I was so happy, Amy, I was free and everything was okay – but of course I still missed you – and I wanted to find you, I did, but I didn't even know how to start, and they told me I had to wait, wait and then one day you'd come and find me—'

Amy pulls me to her in a hug again.

'—But then he turned up, the Hand of God, out of nowhere, and he told me you'd married Father, the new Father, and I had to come – I had to come and get you.'

'Why would the Hand of God tell you that?' asks Amy. She leans back against the window and wipes at her eyes with her sleeve.

'He wanted to try it all again,' I said. 'Getting rid of Father and everything. So he brought me back. But he kind of tricked me, and then he left me alone for ages – I don't really understand it all. I think maybe he wanted to go through the whole thing again – taking me away from the Sisters, training me, building up to his plan . . . but then I managed to find you, and I suppose that kind of forced his hand.'

Also, he thinks the Elders are plotting to get rid of you, I don't say. *But he doesn't want a different wife with a Seed on the way, he wants you . . . and a Seed from the 'right' bloodline . . .*

I push those thoughts away, again.

'So . . . he brought you here tonight and took away all the Guards so you can . . . kill . . . Father?' Amy says slowly.

'That's what he thinks.' I watch Amy's face, a cold pit in my stomach. Have I told her too much? Does she hate me, now that she knows some of the truth?

'But you're not a killer,' Amy says, and she smiles warmly, drawing me to her again. 'You're my sister.'

I let her hold me. 'Yes,' I say. 'Yes.'

'Amy?' I whisper as we move up the stairs. I don't need to whisper, but the opulence of the space around me seems to enforce a hushed voice.

'Mm?'

'What happened to you that night – when we were taken to see the Seed? After I got sent away, I mean.'

Amy glances back at me. 'Do you remember it much?'

'Sort of. Just bits.'

'Well, after the Elder took you out, they left me alone in the room with the Seed. That was when he chose me, though I didn't know it at the time.' We round the landing and move up towards the Vessels' floor. 'He just wanted to talk. All the times I was brought to him after that as well, that's all he ever wanted. Or he wanted someone to listen to him, I suppose. I think he was probably

310

pretty lonely. He wasn't allowed near any of the other kids, or anything. I think the only time he ever saw anyone his own age was when the Elders brought girls to him to consider.' Amy shakes her head. 'So that first night he kept trying to talk to me, but I was so scared and freaked out that I didn't respond to anything, until he mentioned that you and I were "blood sisters". I think he was desperate to say something, anything, that would get a reaction from me by that point. I was so shocked – the whole blood family thing was so taboo, remember?' I nod. 'I think I spoke to him a bit after that, and then it was morning and I was taken away.' She laughs without humour. 'Straight to work detail. The kitchens. I was so tired, and so weirded out by the whole experience, and then I saw you. Looking as knackered as I was, scrubbing away at that enormous pile of dishes, do you remember? And I suppose I just wanted to – I don't know. Have someone confirm what had actually happened, maybe? It was all so surreal. None of the adults acknowledged what had happened, obviously. But you had been there. So I left you that note.'

'I'm glad you did,' I say.

Amy catches me in a half hug, slinging her arm around my shoulder and pulling me to her, as we come to the top of the stairs. 'So am I.'

The Big House is like a palace inside, but once we get up to the Vessels' floor, the opulence fades away and it looks more familiar, like the other buildings I've been in here. When we creep through the darkened corridor, past locked rooms with numbers pinned to the doors, we find a door without a number on it, and one of the keys we try opens it. Inside, there's mops and brooms and boxes.

'It's just a cupboard,' hisses Amy. I pull a cord, and light floods the little space. I point up, and she follows my gaze to see a padlocked trapdoor set into the roof.

'Help me with this ladder,' I say, pulling one out from behind a mop bucket. Amy helps me to unfold the ladder and manoeuvre it under the hatch. 'I always thought he was so loyal,' she says.

'Hmm?'

'The Hand of God.' Amy pushes her hair away from her face. 'He's just – always there, you know? Always by Father's side in Worship. Skulking around in here.'

'He comes here?' I say, putting my weight on the bottom rung of the ladder to test it. 'This is a bit wobbly.'

'You hold it, I'll go up first. Yeah, he's here quite a lot. The Elders convene here, and then he meets with Father pretty regularly too. I just always thought he was totally committed to it all. To Father, and the Children.' She climbs up the first couple of steps. Her nightgown, trailing, catches her foot, and she shakes it away impatiently.

'I think he must have been, once,' I say. 'But he thinks they've, like, lost their way or something. Become corrupt.'

'He's not wrong,' says Amy. She reaches the top of the ladder and lifts her hands, balancing. I pass the keys up to her, and she begins trying keys on the padlock.

'Yeah. Amy . . .'

She looks down.

'He said – or implied, I suppose – that Father – the old one and the new one as well – was hurting . . . children. Kids, I mean. Young children.'

Amy's mouth sets in a firm line. 'The Vessels start young,' she says. 'And there's all sorts of abuse here. The whole thing is disgusting. Someone should set fire to this whole fucking place.' The key she's trying turns smoothly, and the padlock clicks open. She drops the padlock and keys down to me, pushes up on the trapdoor. It's heavy, and doesn't budge.

'You're his wife,' I say. Amy pauses, her hands flat against the hatch.

'Sometimes you have to do things – even if they're awful things, things you know will . . . will stain you . . . if you know it's for the right reason,' she says quietly. 'He makes my skin crawl. He always did. Even when he was this lonely little boy I was taken to see, there was something . . . off . . . about him. But I took precautions. I got the coil, so I knew there was no way I'd end up pregnant. And the girl that escaped told us that he's so strung out half the time that he can barely . . . do anything, anyway.

The Hand of God has to sober him up for when he needs to lead Worship, did you know that? I've seen him drag Father into the bathroom and throw him under a freezing shower in his dressing gown. And like that, he's so . . . pathetic. So human. But then other times . . .' She meets my eyes. 'I wouldn't mind if you did kill him,' she says.

She gets her shoulder under the hatch and heaves. The trapdoor falls up and back with a thump. Amy pulls herself up through the small space.

'Wait!' I say. I climb up the ladder, and emerge into a cold, empty attic space that looks much like the ones I dimly remember in the other buildings. But there's nothing here.

Amy is standing, head ducked so it doesn't hit the low rafters. I can just see her in the dull square of light from the skylight. She looks around hopelessly.

'There's nothing here. Catherine – Zoe, I mean – there's nothing here! This isn't it!'

I rub my hands together. It's freezing in here. 'I can't think where else—'

There's a clinking noise behind us, and we both whirl around. The attic stretches into shadow. The noise comes again, and Amy pushes past me.

'Teneil?' she says. I follow her, ducking under the rafters. Amy is stumbling about, then bends over a pile of rags in the corner. The rags are moving.

'Teneil, it's me, it's Amy,' Amy is saying. She's crying. 'It's me, it's me, I'm so sorry, Teneil, I'm so sorry . . .'

I look over her shoulder. She's peeling the rags away from a face that is all planes and angles. The eyes are hollow sockets, the hair cropped so close to the skull that it's almost bare in patches.

Amy is pawing the rags away, and the thing under them – can it really be Teneil? – makes a moaning sound and tries to pull them back. Amy holds up a fistful of chains. They're wrapped around Teneil's ankles.

'The keys, Catherine, the keys!' she says. I pull them out of my pocket and Amy frantically tries one after another in the heavy padlock.

I look at Teneil. Her pupils are pinpricks, tiny against the thick ring of her irises. I know the exact shade of green that her eyes are, like a still pond, but it's too dark in here to see it.

'Amy—'

'What?'

'I think she's drugged, or something.'

Amy glances up at her, then back down at the padlock. The latest key turns. 'Oh, thank god! Right, you get her under this arm. I'll get this one.'

I pull Teneil's arm over my shoulder. It's like holding the branch of a sapling. They must barely feed her. What must it be like for her, chained up here in the dark and the cold between enforced visits to Father?

'Teneil? Teneil, it's us, it's Amy and Catherine. Do you remember?' Amy pulls Teneil's other arm over her shoulder as Teneil protests weakly. Between the two of us, we get her up and to the trapdoor. Her feet drag, only stepping once for every four or five steps of ours. She weighs as much as a child.

Amy crouches down by the ladder, holding Teneil around the waist. 'Teneil, we're going down the ladder. We're going to leave. Do you understand? We're going to leave here. Forever.' Teneil stares at Amy, then smiles a big, druggy smile and clumsily pats Amy's face. One of her front teeth is missing.

Amy goes down the ladder, and we cajole and push and half carry Teneil down to the cupboard below. I knock over the mop bucket, then stumble out with Teneil's arm slung around my shoulder again.

'We have to go, we have to go,' I say. I don't know how long we've been, but it could have been an hour. Amy takes some of Teneil's barely-there weight, and we make for the stairs. The Big House is silent and empty.

'There's car keys on that ring,' says Amy, panting as we hit the landing and begin down the next set of stairs, Teneil's head lolling onto her shoulder.

'The Hand of God's car,' I say. 'It's parked outside. But I don't know how to drive.'

'I do,' says Amy.

The marble floor echoes as we hurry across it, dragging Teneil. Amy shifts Teneil's weight onto me and opens the entrance door a tiny crack.

'Are they out there?' I whisper, moving Teneil's arm to hook around my neck. It keeps dropping away.

'There's no one there,' Amy whispers back. 'Okay, I see the car. I'm going to go out and start it. You get Teneil out.' I nod, and she pushes the door open and runs, her red shoes crunching through the gravel, her nightgown flying out behind her. I scoop Teneil's legs up so that I'm cradling her like a baby. Her head nods against my chest.

This is the woman who saved both Amy and me, back when she was just a girl. She'd been smart enough and brave enough to make contact with the Initiative, and she had realised what was happening to Amy and had given her the means to save herself. And for her closeness to Amy, and her refusal to fit in, to be quiet and subservient, she's been punished, and punished, and punished. She's endured hell. What's happened to me barely registers, against what she must have gone through.

I cradle Teneil close to my body. It's like holding smoke. 'Thank you,' I whisper. She doesn't respond. Her breathing is thick and irregular. We need to get her to a hospital.

Hand wanted me to go in through the attics. Did he want me to find her? Or did he think I wouldn't notice her, wrapped in her rags and strung out in a dark corner?

Who knows. What he wants doesn't matter anymore.

It's getting light towards the east. Hand's kept his promise, though – none of the Guards are in sight.

Amy opens the back door of the car, and waves me over. I make it to the car just as she starts the engine with a rumble, shockingly loud in the pre-dawn silence. I tip Teneil as gently as possible onto the back seat. She curls up on her side and puts her thumb in her mouth.

I get into the passenger seat. I can see the Gate up ahead, closed. but unguarded. It barely takes a minute for the car to reach it.

Amy has already separated the car key from the rest of the bunch of keys. I get out with them. One of them is really long – surely that one opens the Gate—

'Here! Over here! I've found her!'

I turn, but something crashes into me and I fall back against the Gate, the keys tumbling out of my hand.

'I've got her! I've got her!' It's the older Guard from the hut yesterday, the one who kicked me. I struggle, try to reach the knife still hanging from my belt, but he's on top of me and one of my arms is twisted under my back and I can't move.

'Leave her!'

It's Hand.

The Guard is pulled off, and I see Hand, backlit by the lights from the car. 'Get up,' he says to me. He is furious. The Guard is looking at the car, his hand shielding his eyes to see through the glare.

Hand grabs me by my collar and hauls me upright. I pull away, and Hand staggers after me, and we lurch out of the beam of the car's headlights. His hand is a vice around my collar, and I can't get free.

'There's a woman driving that car,' I hear the Guard say, and then there is a screech of wheels and an almighty crash and Hand and I are pelted with sharp splinters of gravel.

Hand lets go of me and turns to the car. Amy has driven it into the Gate, which is bowed forward like someone punched in the stomach. The engine cuts out, and there's a high *tink-tink-tink* noise. Steam puffs out from under the buckled bonnet of Hand's car, half obscuring the face of the Guard, who lies bent over it, his legs hidden under the twist of metal. He fixes his eyes on me, opens his mouth. Then he seems to look past me, and blood bubbles from his lips.

There's a thud, and I see Amy ramming her shoulder against the inside of the driver's door. It shrieks open, and she bursts out, blood trickling down from a cut over her eye.

'Get away from my sister,' she says.

Hand pushes me away and lunges towards her, his hands outstretched and clawed.

I grab a fistful of his jacket, heave him back to me and sink my knife into his side. Right between the fifth and sixth ribs.

He makes a kind of dull 'unh' sound – horribly familiar – and wraps his hands around my throat. We fall, him on top of me, and the elbow of my hand still holding the knife jars against the ground and the blade sinks in deeper. He lets loose a high, breathy scream.

I shove him off me, roll away. Amy is standing by the car door, gesturing wildly. 'Leave him, Catherine!' she shouts. 'Let's go!'

I pull myself to my knees. Hand coughs behind me. It sounds wet.

'You – you—' he's saying.

I get to my feet.

'You. Bitch.'

I turn. He's small, there on the ground, his shirt already dark with blood. His face is a white smear in the gathering light. There's a line of blood leaking from his mouth.

'You *bitch*,' he spits.

I kneel down next to him.

'You have a filthy mouth,' I say. 'You know what we do to boys with filthy mouths?'

I scrape a handful of mud from the ground. Hand's eyes are wide and fixed on mine.

I prise open his mouth and shove the dirt in. He gags and chokes, but I push and pack it in until his mouth is a black clog. The hand not pressed against his wound flails at me, but I knock it away easily.

'We make them eat their words,' I say.

Amy has reversed the car, dragged the Guard to the side and is hauling on the broken Gate. It opens with a shriek of metal.

'Get in, Catherine!' she says. I go towards her, and the rising sun.

There's an impact against my back, and I fly forward, my chin biting down into the gravel. There's a pain in my shoulder blade. A sunburst.

'You're mine,' Hand says, and blood and mud drool into my ear. There's another sunburst, high up on my thigh this time. I try to turn over, but he's lying half on my back, and I can't get all the way round. His face glares skull-white under a black-caked chin and cheeks. He raises a hand in the air, the knife pointing down and dripping with our mixed blood.

317

I think about stains, and I think about being washed clean, and I wonder if I've done enough.

A red flash cuts through the air between our faces, and Hand grunts. Another red flash. A shoe, drawn back to kick again and again. There's a dry cracking noise and the pressure on my back lifts, but the sunbursts remain.

'Catherine? Catherine, get up. You have to get up.'

'I'm tired,' I say, or think. I thought it was morning? It's too dark to be morning.

'Get up! Get up, Catherine!' Amy's face appears in the gloom. I try to focus on it.

'Hand—'

'He's gone,' says Amy. Is she crying? 'He's gone. I stamped down – I think I broke something – he's not breathing. He's gone, he's gone.'

'It's all right,' I say. I try to pat her face, but my arm won't work.

'I killed him. And the Guard . . .' Amy presses a hand over her mouth.

'It's okay,' I say. 'It's okay. I've got stains, too.'

Amy looks to the side suddenly. 'Oh god,' she says. 'Oh god. I think I hear them – we have to go. Get up. Get up, Zoe.'

I'm lifted, dragged. The sunbursts expand to supernovas, eclipsing everything.

When they fade, I see Amy's pale face, mouth set. We're in the car. I look back, setting off a glow of pain that suffuses my whole body, and see Teneil, still lying on the back seat. But her eyes are open, the same still green pools that I remember, and they are looking at me steadily. I think about that green colour, and I think about bloodlines.

'It's all right, Zoe,' Amy is saying. 'I've got you. Everything's okay.' The car rumbles to life and pulls off with a jolt. I scream a little.

'Stay with me, Zoe, okay?'

The car roars, and the world blurs past outside the window. The sky is pink and yellow. There are no walls I can see, or even tree-tops. Just sky. Endless, beautiful sky. Clear and true.

'Stay with me, Zoe.' Amy is looking ahead, bent over the wheel. 'Stay with me.'

One – My name is Zoe
Two – I have found my sister
Three – Hand is gone forever
Four – We are going home.

ACKNOWLEDGEMENTS

Writing seems like it would be a solitary process, but the truth is, of course, that this book wouldn't exist without the love, support, and expert advice of a vast number of people, which I am eternally grateful for. I hope I've managed to include everyone to whom I owe a specific thanks here.

First of all, of course, to my mum and dad, who have always believed that I could do this, and who obligingly read (and copy-edited, and supplied research for) everything I wrote from about age four onwards – thank you, guys, and I promise I'll write something cheerful one day.

I was incredibly lucky to have a parade of teachers who were endlessly encouraging and supportive when I confidently informed them that I was going to be an author, and spent their precious time reading the stories I regularly presented them with (or at least graciously and convincingly pretended to). A particular thanks to Mrs Marzella, whose comment to my mother that she expected to be reading my books when she was on her pension has always stayed with me.

I also benefitted greatly from the support of staff and fellow students on the MLitt in Creative Writing course at Glasgow University. Undertaking the course while working full-time and having a baby was made immeasurably easier by how enjoyable and useful all the classes and tutorials were (and the fact that no one minded if Oisín attended a session or two, albeit while fast asleep). I'd like to make particular mention of Zoe Strachan and Colin Herd, whose incisive feedback on early drafts was invaluable.

Thanks are also due to the writers I met through the MLitt who offered feedback on various draft chapters in our ad hoc pub workshops: Sarah Smith, Valerie Brentjes, Claire Kennedy, John Boursnell, and Murray McKinstray.

I am very lucky to have a number of close friends and family members who generously read various drafts of the complete novel and offered their comments and ideas – to Kim Robinson, Dawn McKeown, Nikki Gibney, and Jean Dargan, I can't thank you enough for your time and energy! I am also indebted to Yvonne Bowman for her service as a Galwegian accuracy consultant.

The first draft of this book was completed while on a retreat at the heavenly Moniack Mhor Creative Writing Centre, which I was able to afford in part thanks to their generous School Teachers' Grant.

Robbie Guillory is simply the best of agents, and I am extremely glad that I signed up to the literary agency open day in the very last available slot (though I am sorry that you missed your chance to get a pint before the train). Robbie has had a profound influence on this book, and I am eternally grateful for his comments and suggestions during the redrafting process (including getting rid of the holograms – what was I thinking?).

I can't imagine having a better editor than Sara Helen Binney at Raven, who polished up my rough drafts and made them shine. I'm not sure if it's normal to cackle with delight while reading editorial comments, but if it isn't, then I don't want to know. Thank you so much for everything (even the spreadsheets).

I also owe a huge thank you to Madeleine Feeny for her incredible copy-editing (so many 'oh gods' to prune), to Sharona Selby for her pin-sharp proofreading, and to Paula Akpan, for her insight and expertise as an authenticity reader. Thanks are also due to Mike Butcher for his absolutely stunning cover.

Writing this book, especially while having a small child, was only made possible by the unwavering support of my husband Dave, whose kindness, strength, and compassion makes me love him more every day. For all the extra childcare, the housework, the dinners, the pep talks, the proofreading, the late nights and early mornings, for believing I could do it and convincing me, too – thank you, my love.

My companion through a lot of the writing process was my son Oisín, who accompanied me to classes, conferences, and libraries, and even stayed obligingly asleep during the writing of some chapters. This book wouldn't be the same without you, little man.

Finally, I couldn't have written a book about the love between sisters if it wasn't for my own sister, Jojo. The first story I remember writing was for her, and in a lot of ways, this one is, too.

A NOTE ON THE TYPE

The text of this book is set in Linotype Sabon, a typeface named after the type founder, Jacques Sabon. It was designed by Jan Tschichold and jointly developed by Linotype, Monotype and Stempel in response to a need for a typeface to be available in identical form for mechanical hot metal composition and hand composition using foundry type.

Tschichold based his design for Sabon roman on a font engraved by Garamond, and Sabon italic on a font by Granjon. It was first used in 1966 and has proved an enduring modern classic.